A COMANCHE WOMAN

"You gave up your stallion for me? Warrior was your pride and joy."

"It was the only way to free you."

She couldn't believe all this had taken place, and she hadn't even known about it. "What would have happened if you hadn't paid him what he asked?"

"I didn't want to find out."

"Oh." A tremble of fear went through her as she imagined Crouching Wolf being the one to take her as his wife. It wasn't a pretty thought. The knowledge that Hunt had sacrificed his most prized possession to save her thrilled her; yet she regretted that he'd had to give up so much for her. "I'm sorry."

"I'm not. I wanted you with me, so I could keep you safe. All that mattered was that Painted Horse believed you were my woman." His look was fiercely protective.

She felt the intensity of his regard and knew she had to ask. "Am I your woman, Hunt?" Her voice was soft and full of invitation.

Time stood still.

Was she his woman? Her question, so enticingly asked, sent a surge of excitement through Hunt. He stared at Glynna, thinking she had never looked more beautiful. Dressed as a Comanche maiden, she appeared innocent yet seductive, alluring yet elusive. He was hungry for her.

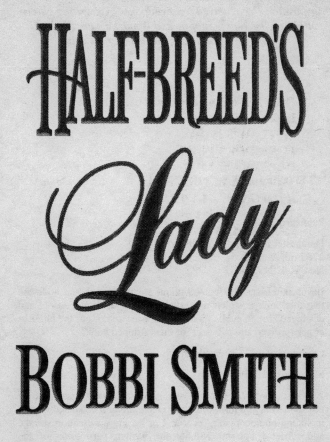

HALF-BREED'S

Lady

BOBBI SMITH

LEISURE BOOKS NEW YORK CITY

*This book is dedicated to Charles M. Schulz for the
inspiration I've received following Snoopy's writing career
through the years. Snoopy and Woodstock are the best!
Thank you, Mr. Schulz, for making me smile.*

A LEISURE BOOK®

October 1998

Published by

Dorchester Publishing Co., Inc.
276 Fifth Avenue
New York, NY 10001

Sketches by Harry Burman.

ISBN 0-8439-4436-6

The name "Leisure Books" and the stylized "L" with design are
trademarks of Dorchester Publishing Co., Inc.

Printed in the United States of America.

I want to thank the terrific people at Cowley Distributing in Jefferson City, Missouri, for all their help. John Cowley, Inez Killam, Uel Smith, Gerald Ratcliff, Jenny Ratcliff, Virginia Bruemmer, Jerry Cowley and Jeff Cowley—you're all wonderful! I'd also like to thank the "angels" who surround me at St. Joseph's PSR Program: Barb Blackburn and Laura Lucas, Kathy Bachista, Sherry Gibson, JoAnn Null, Shirley Peschke and Mark Recca. And two very special friends—Dee Stauffer and Ann Hinch.

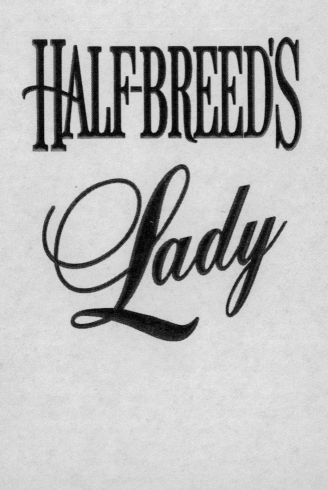

Prologue

"Hunt?"

Hunt McAllister was running an errand in town for his father when he heard someone—a female—call his name. Surprised, he stopped and glanced back to see Jenny Ross standing on the walkway beside her father's general store, motioning for him to come to her.

"You talking to me?" he asked, frowning slightly.

"I sure am," Jenny said softly, and she gave him a particularly inviting smile. Though she was only fourteen, it was obvious she understood the power of her femininity.

"What do you want, Jenny?" Hunt was cautious as he approached her. She was one of the prettiest girls in town. He'd noticed her around, and he was amazed that she'd spoken to him. He knew her father and brothers despised him because he was a half-breed.

"I was wondering if you could help me with something." Her gaze was hot upon him. He was only fifteen, but he was already tall, darkly handsome and whipcord lean. Her heartbeat quickened as he walked toward her.

"Aren't your brothers around?" Hunt knew how protective her brothers were of her and wondered why she hadn't asked one of them for help.

"I couldn't find them, and I was just hoping you would do it," she said, gazing up at him, looking helpless and fragile.

In spite of the warning voice in the back of his mind, Hunt found himself agreeing. "Sure, what do you need?"

"It's around back. . . ." She smiled brightly at him and started off down the narrow passage that led to the rear of the store.

Hunt followed along, his gaze on Jenny as she walked before him. Her hips were swaying ever so slightly in an age-old, enticing rhythm, and he felt a stirring within him that he knew he had to ignore. He was there to give her a hand—nothing more. When they reached the back of the building, Hunt discovered that the area was deserted.

"What was it you wanted me to do?"

"I want you to kiss me, Hunt McAllister," Jenny said boldly, moving to brazenly link her arms around his neck.

Hunt stiffened at her ploy. He put his hands at her waist to move her away from him.

"Jenny . . . this isn't a good idea." He had to extricate himself from her embrace immediately—there would be hell to pay if anyone found him touching her this way.

"You're wrong," she said, her eyes aglow. "This is a very good idea."

She moved even closer.

At the feel of Jenny pressed so intimately against him, Hunt went still. He looked down at her and saw the open invitation in her eyes.

"Hunt . . . please . . ."

He couldn't believe it. Jenny Ross wanted him to kiss her! A shudder racked him as he fought to maintain his usually strong self-control. He knew he should get away from her—for her sake and for his own—but she was in his arms, gazing up at him with such open adoration that he felt ten feet tall. He felt invincible.

Suddenly, the sweet scent of her and the softness of her body pressed close to his were just too enticing. Any thought of the ugly repercussions that might follow this encounter vanished. All that mattered was Jenny.

Unable to resist, Hunt wrapped his arms around her and crushed her to him. He kissed her hungrily. The need she'd created within him drove all logic from him.

Hunt's father had cautioned him to take care when dealing with whites. He'd warned Hunt that living in the white man's world wouldn't be easy, but Hunt thought that maybe, just maybe, things were changing—that maybe he could be accepted, that he could fit in. If Jenny liked him, maybe other people would like him, too.

Caught up in the wonder of Jenny's embrace, Hunt savored her nearness. When she whimpered and moved restlessly in his arms, desire began to burn hot within him. He deepened the kiss.

"Oh, Hunt . . ." she whispered.

It was then that the outraged shout erupted from behind them and shattered the intimacy of their encounter, changing Hunt's life forever.

"Get your hands off my sister!"

"John!" Jenny gasped and jumped guiltily away from Hunt at the sound of her brother's angry command.

"Damn right, 'John,' you little slut!" He snarled, charging forward to grab her by the forearm and drag her farther away from the half-breed. "I should beat you within an inch of your life!"

"Get your hands off her!" Hunt demanded, seeing the terror in Jenny's expression and wanting to protect her.

"The hell with you, breed! You think you can mess with our women and get away with it?" John shoved his sister harshly aside and turned on Hunt.

Hunt squared off, ready to fight John man to man, but he never got the chance. Her other two brothers, Chuck and Will, charged forward from where they'd been hiding and attacked him. Though Hunt was physically bigger than they were and put up a good fight, he was outnumbered. The three of them eventually overpowered him and knocked him to the ground, beating him severely.

"You don't touch our sister or any other white woman! Do you understand that, breed?" John snarled, emphasizing his words by kicking Hunt viciously in the side. Then he turned on his sister. "And you . . ."

"Leave Jenny alone," Hunt managed as he saw John advancing threateningly on her. He struggled to get to his feet, biting back a groan as agony sliced through him. He was certain John's kick had broken some ribs.

"You talkin' to me?" John glanced back at Hunt, fury evident in his features. He'd thought his last kick would have kept him down, but it looked like the stupid half-breed wanted more. "Grab him and hold him up!" he ordered his brothers.

Though Hunt tried to fight them off, the pain in his side was too savage. Chuck and Will grabbed him and held him suspended between them. They were laughing as Hunt continued to try to break free. Their grip was iron, though. They had no intention of letting him escape John's revenge.

"John! Stop it!" Jenny pleaded, rushing forward to try to save Hunt from their viciousness. "You're going to kill him! He didn't do anything wrong!"

"Shut up!" He shoved her away, knocking her to the ground this time. Infuriated by her attempt to defend the half-breed, he hit Hunt even harder.

Hunt went limp at the force of his blow.

"He's out, John," Will told him.

"Good, then he won't try to fight us anymore." He brutally continued to batter his unfeeling victim. When he'd taken his pleasure in beating him, he told his brothers, "Strip off his shirt and tie him to that tree."

"What are you going to do?" Tears stained Jenny's face as she ran forward to try to stop him again.

At her interference, John turned on her. His expression was cold and deadly. "I'm going to convince this boy never to go near another white woman."

"But Hunt didn't do anything wrong! I'm the one—"

"Don't ever say his name again! Do you hear me? And if anybody asks you about what happened today, you tell them that he attacked you! You understand me?"

"But that's not true!"

"You want everybody in town to know you're a slut?"

She gasped at his words. "John! All we did was—"

"We saw what you did!" His temper raged out of control, and he backhanded her, bloodying her lip. "You let a breed touch you!"

Jenny sobbed uncontrollably at being so brutalized by her own brother. "You hit me!"

"I'll do worse than that if you don't get the hell outta here! You just better pray that Papa don't find out the truth of what really went on here today!"

"But Hunt only—"

"I know what the bastard did!" John roared. "Now get outta my sight, whore! If anybody asks you what happened to your face, you tell them that McAllister hit you when he attacked you!"

"I won't! That's a lie!"

"You will." John pinned her with a cold glare. "Don't cross me, Jenny."

"That's right," Chuck put in, never daring to defy his older brother. "John's trying to protect your reputation. You think any white boy's going to want you after this?"

"Yeah," Will supported them. "It was the half-breed who dragged you back here and tried to rape you. He's the one who hit you and made your lip bleed. Just look at you. You're bruised and bleeding from his attack."

Jenny's eyes widened at her brothers' conspiracy of hate.

"Do what I say, Jenny," John told her. "Or I'll make sure your half-breed here never touches another woman—ever!"

Biting back a terrified cry, she ran, leaving Hunt bloodied, unconscious and powerless before their vengeful hatred.

"Tie him up," John repeated.

His brothers hurried to follow his order.

"I'm going to enjoy this." John smiled.

It was nearly half an hour later when they untied Hunt. He collapsed on the ground, his back bloodied from the whipping John had given him.

John stood over Hunt, feeling quite proud of himself. He was certain the half-breed would never forget the lesson they'd taught him today. He nudged him in the side with the toe of his boot.

"Remember today, breed. Don't ever forget it! Stay away from white women. They ain't for the likes of you."

Hunt didn't answer. He couldn't. He had been drifting in and out of consciousness and was only vaguely aware of what was happening to him.

The three brothers dragged him over to their buckboard and threw him in the back. They drove out of town and shoved him out, leaving him unconscious and bleeding in the brush alongside the road.

It was dusk when Hunt slowly regained consciousness. Pain racked every inch of his body, and he barely had enough strength to struggle to his feet. His back felt as if it were on fire, and agony seared his side. He swayed, staring around in confusion, momentarily disoriented. Once he recognized his surroundings, he knew he was a long way from home. Hunt started off across country, wanting to avoid the main road and the possibility of more trouble.

As Hunt slowly headed toward home and his father—his only safe haven, his only refuge—he thought of Jenny. He remembered how she'd tried to stop John from hitting him. The way John had treated her angered him. He hoped she was all right.

As his mind cleared, Hunt silently cursed himself for his weakness with Jenny. He'd been a fool not to remember his father's words of warning. He should never have let his guard down that way. He should never have kissed her. He should have remembered that he was different.

He would never forget again.

"McAllister!" The call came from the street outside Tom McAllister's house.

It was dark, and Tom was puzzled by all the shouting outside. He went out on the porch to see what was going on. He recognized Dale Ross standing in the street, rifle in hand, surrounded by his sons and some of the other townsfolk.

"Dale," Tom said cautiously by way of greeting, not sure exactly what the man wanted. "Is there trouble in town?"

"I'll say," Dale said with a growl, the threat in his tone obvious. "Where's your boy? I want him out here now!"

Tom knew a moment of panic. Hunt had not returned home that afternoon as expected, and he had begun to worry about him as the hours passed. Now he was even more concerned. "Hunt ain't here."

"So you say," Dale said challengingly. "Search the house, boys!"

"You just wait a damned minute!" Tom strode forward to block their way.

"Listen to me, McAllister! Your boy attacked my daughter today."

"Hunt wouldn't do that!" Tom exclaimed. He knew his son.

"Like hell! My boys caught him in the act. John, here, got there just in time to rescue Jenny! So save yourself trouble and send him out now!"

"I'm telling you, he isn't here. He never came home this afternoon." Tom began to wonder what had really happened that day. He seared John with a questioning look.

"Don't that tell you something? He done run off, because he knew I'd come after him once I found out what he'd done to my girl."

"How is Jenny? Is she with you?" Tom asked.

"No. She's home where she belongs. She ain't safe on the streets until I know your boy's learned his lesson!" Dale started forward.

Tom stood his ground. He did not get out of their

17

way, so Dale shoved him violently aside. Tom would have fought back to stop the other man's invasion of his home, but John and the others restrained him. Dale charged inside and searched the small house for some sign of the half-breed. He found nothing. Frustrated, he emerged even angrier than he'd been before.

"He ain't here! Where is he?"

"I told you. He didn't come home this afternoon. He left this morning, and I haven't seen him since. If your boys saw him with Jenny, I want to know what they saw and what they did to him!" He looked over at the oldest Ross boy. "Where is Hunt?" he demanded of John. "Where's my son?"

"I don't know," John answered.

Dale glared at Tom savagely. "We ain't seen him, 'cause if we had, he'd be dead. You tell your half-breed bastard that if I ever get my hands on him, I'm going to kill him. He can't do white women that way and live."

Tom was furious. He shook off the hold the others had on him and faced Dale. "My son wouldn't hurt your daughter."

"He hit her and tried to rape her. She done told me so herself, and my boys saw him tryin'!"

"That's a lie!"

"If it's a lie, why ain't your boy here?" Dale challenged. "He ain't here because he ran! That's why! Remember what I said, McAllister. He's a dead man if I ever get him in my sights."

With that, Dale turned and walked away. The rest followed him, echoing his sentiments.

Tom was shaken by the power of their hatred and

terrified for his son's safety. He didn't know what had really gone on that day, but something terrible must have happened to Hunt for him not to have returned home. Tom knew he had to find him and fast. Frantic with worry, he rushed back inside and strapped on his own sidearm. He was ready to search for his missing son.

Tom went to get his horse. As he was saddling up, he heard a strange thump, like something heavy falling, out behind the small barn. He drew his gun, expecting trouble, and went to investigate. He wouldn't put it past Dale Ross to have someone hiding out there, keeping watch for Hunt's return.

Tom didn't find the townspeople. Instead he found his son slumped weakly against the back of the barn. He knew immediately that his fears for the boy's safety had been real.

"My God, Hunt! What happened to you?" Tom asked in a hushed, strangled voice as he ran to his side. In the moonlight he could see how Hunt had been tortured, and fury filled him. Someone had done this to his boy! "Who did this to you?"

"Jenny Ross's brothers—" was all Hunt could manage before he collapsed into his father's arms.

Tom helped him up and half carried him inside the barn. He figured there still might be somebody out there watching the house, so it was best to keep Hunt hidden. Laying him down on some clean hay, he quickly set about doctoring him. He muttered angrily under his breath as he saw the extent of Hunt's injuries.

"What happened, Hunt? Dale Ross was here with his boys looking for you. He said Jenny claimed you

19

attacked her, and her brothers saw you do it."

Hunt looked up at him then, and Tom would never forget the look in his eyes—the pain and horror of what had happened and the tormented acceptance of a reality he couldn't deny or change.

"I didn't attack her." He told his father everything he could remember of what had happened that afternoon, of how she had lured him to a quiet spot and then demanded that he kiss her. "I had just started to kiss her when her brothers showed up. I'm sorry. I should have known better."

"There's nothing for you to be sorry for," Tom said gravely.

"I should have remembered what you'd told me. You warned me that I might run into trouble, but I didn't think. It was Jenny. . . ." He was silent for a moment, remembering how beautiful she was and how it had felt to hold her close. He remembered, too, how she'd asked him to kiss her. "But why did she lie to her father about what went on? I would never have hurt her. John must have been the one who hit her . . . or maybe her father did it."

Tom's jaw tightened as he realized what his son had faced alone that day. His innocence had been stripped from him. He had learned of man's hatred and woman's deceit. There would be no going back for him. "She must have lied to save herself. Her daddy probably would have beat her within an inch of her life if he'd found out she was with you willingly."

Pain showed in Hunt's expression at those words, and he realized the truth. His father had been right from the start. He should never have let himself think that things could be different. It was a mistake he would never make again. He closed his eyes, not wanting to see the tortured look on his father's face.

"Don't try to move. I'll be right back."

Tom returned to the house and came back a short time later with a bottle of whiskey. He held the potent liquor out to his son.

"Drink some of this. It'll help."

Hunt stared at the bottle, then shook his head. "No. It can't help. It can't change who I am." He'd seen the drunks around town, men who drowned themselves in liquor to hide from reality. He wouldn't become one of them.

His words were a knife in Tom's heart. "But it would ease your pain."

"I want to remember what this feels like. I want to remember everything that happened today." His expression was that of a man who had been to hell and had lived to tell about it.

"Well, I'm going to have one." Tom tilted the bottle to his lips and took a deep drink. "We've got to find a place to keep you safe until things quiet down."

Hunt gritted his teeth and pushed himself to a sitting position, fighting the agony that pounded through him. "I'm not staying. I'm leaving now—tonight. It's never going to quiet down. You know it as well as I do."

"No. You can't go. You're just a boy—"

Hunt cut him off. "I'm not a boy anymore. You warned me that it would be hard living in a white world, but until this afternoon I didn't understand what that meant."

"We'll keep you out of sight for a while. It'll pass."

21

"No. It won't."

Their gazes met and locked.

"Think about what you're doing. You didn't do anything wrong. You don't need to run. We'll work it out."

Hunt saw his father's anguish, but knew there was nothing the two of them could do. Jenny had sealed his fate when she'd lied to her father. "We can't change who I am."

"I'll go to the sheriff and tell him what really happened with Jenny."

"He won't care." Hunt's tone was flat.

Tom realized how close his son had come to being killed and knew Hunt was right. He'd been praying that his son could find a way to fit in with the townfolk, but their hatred for Indians was too fierce and too deeply ingrained to overcome. They would never let him forget that he was half Comanche.

Thoughts of Hunt's mother, his beloved Dawn Star, long dead these many years, haunted him. They had loved their son and had wanted the best for him, but it seemed he'd failed. His efforts to help Hunt live in the white world had almost gotten the boy killed.

Tom finally accepted that Hunt was right—Dale Ross would never give up seeking to punish him. Still, Tom didn't want to let him go. He loved him and wanted to keep him safe.

"You rest for a while. You're in no shape to be thinking about such things." He tried to delay Hunt's decision, not wanting to face it, not wanting to deal with it.

"No, Pa, I have to think about it. If they come back,

I won't have the chance to get away. I have to go, and I have to do it now, while there's time."

All hope drained from Tom's soul. He looked haggard as he thought of the life his son would lead alone—a man trapped between two worlds. He would have no peace, no rest. "I'll go with you."

"No. It would just make me look more guilty. They'd think we were both running, and they'd hunt us down."

Slowly Hunt managed to stand. No matter how severe his pain, he could not afford to show any weakness.

"Where will you go?" Tom was devastated. Both their lives were being destroyed by a woman's lies.

"I don't know. Someplace where people see me as a man and not as a half-breed."

Tom went to him, wanting to help, but the fierce, burning look of determination in Hunt's eyes kept him at arm's length. He saw for the first time a glimpse of the pride and fierceness of his Comanche ancestry in him. Hunt would have made an intimidating warrior. "I don't want you to go, son."

"I can't stay—not after this."

They stood in silence, staring at each other. Now, man to man, rather than father to son. They shared the pain of parting, knowing it was the only safe way for Hunt, yet agonizing over what their futures would be—alone.

"I'll need a gun." It was a statement.

Tom went back to the house and brought out his own gun and holster, a rifle and what his son would need to survive on his own. After Hunt had dressed, he took the sidearm and strapped it on.

23

"Here," Tom said, holding out a small leather pouch. "It isn't much. I wish I had more to give you, but it's yours." He handed him all the money he had.

"Thanks."

"Let me know where you are."

"I will."

When Hunt rode silently away and disappeared into the night, Tom watched him go. His heart was breaking, and he wondered if he would ever see his son again.

Hunt was cautious as he left home. Though his pain was great, he would not go easy on himself. There was no telling what Dale Ross might do if he caught up with him.

During the long hours of travel, Hunt thought about his future and what he was going to do. Though his mother had died when he was young, he remembered her people well. He decided to seek out his mother's tribe and live with them. He would learn their ways and be fully accepted by them.

He knew now that he would find no peace in the white man's world. His father's people would never accept him for the man he was.

To the whites, he would always be despised.

He would always be a half-breed.

Chapter One

Ten years later

Glynna Williams stared out the window of the stage-coach, studying the passing scenery with avid interest.

"I never realized Texas would be so beautiful," she told her Aunt Mimi. "I thought Colorado was glorious when I visited there last summer, but there's something about Texas. . . ." She frowned in concentration, as if trying to find the right words to describe what she was feeling. "It almost feels like I belong here. Does that make sense to you?"

"Absolutely. I haven't been to this part of the state before, but I did travel to San Antonio several years ago, and I enjoyed it very much."

"It's going to be wonderful to paint all this," Glynna went on excitedly. "I can hardly wait until we get to town, so I can start. I almost wish we could stop and take a look around. I'd love to make some preliminary sketches."

"Remember now, we have all the time in the world. That's why I planned our trip this way. If something appeals to you and you want to stay in one place for a while, we can do it. This trip is for you, and I want you to make good use of our time here and enjoy it. After all, you're the successful artist. I'm just your widowed aunt, along to play chaperon and keep you out of trouble," Mimi said with a grin.

"I'm glad you arrived at our house when you did last month. If you hadn't, I'm afraid I would have been disinherited by now and living on the streets." Glynna turned away from the window to smile at Mimi as she remembered the confrontation she'd had with her father, Mimi's older brother, back home in New York City.

"You were holding your own with him quite nicely, my dear," her aunt said. She had had run-ins with Charles often during their years growing up together, and she knew how stubborn he could be.

"It wasn't easy standing up to him that way," Glynna said.

Her father had been outraged when Glynna had told him that she wanted to go to Texas to paint. He'd wanted her to stay home and marry his handpicked choice for a son-in-law, Edmund Moore. The fight hadn't been pretty. Not that Glynna didn't want to marry Edmund. She loved him. He was certainly handsome and well educated. He was nearly perfect in all ways, in fact. It was just that she was excited about the success she was having with her paintings, and she wasn't ready to give it all up yet to get married. She'd explained that to Edmund when he'd proposed to her right before she and Aunt Mimi had left for Texas. He hadn't been happy about her evasiveness, but had told her he loved her and would wait for her until she was ready.

"Charles is a very forceful man. He likes to be in control at all times." Mimi remembered far too clearly how heated the exchange between father and headstrong daughter had been when she'd walked in on them that day. "You do him proud."

"He doesn't think so," Glynna said with some regret.

"If you were a son instead of a daughter, he'd be thrilled with your show of spirit."

"But I'm not a son. I'm his daughter, and you know what that means."

"Don't I, though," she sympathized, having fought the battle for her own independence all her life.

"I've always wanted to please Papa. I love him, I really do, but I'm just not ready to get married yet."

"And he obviously thinks you are."

"Of course he does! He thinks I'm an old maid! He told me so right before you got there!"

Mimi made a disgusted sound. "That man!"

"I'm only twenty-three!"

"I know, dear," she said soothingly. "Is that young Edmund fellow the one he thinks would make you a good husband?"

Glynna nodded. "I love Edmund. I've known him for several years. We get along very well, but right now my career is too important to me. Papa wants

27

me to stay home and get married, though. He wants me to be a perfect wife and mother, but I just can't— not now. Not yet."

Mimi reached out to pat her hand. "Don't let him make you feel guilty for following your heart. Don't give it another thought. You won, darling. You're here! In Texas!"

"I am here, but I have a feeling you're the one who really won the argument for me." She looked at her aunt adoringly. Mimi was quite unconventional, and Glynna had learned a lot from her over the years about how to stand up for herself.

"When I heard your father threaten to disinherit you if you went on this trip, well, I had heard enough. I had to draw the line somewhere, and that was it. Of all the obnoxious, domineering threats to make! I just wanted to level things out a bit," she said. A small, confident smile was playing about her lips as she gazed at Glynna.

"And you did a fine job." She was still in awe of her aunt's daring and quick wit in facing down her father. "It was a pure stroke of genius—not to mention kindness—to tell Papa that if he disinherited me for going west to paint, you would give me my inheritance from you early, so I could make the trip anyway. Did you see his expression?"

They laughed together at the memory.

"How could I have missed it? He's such an old fuddy-duddy sometimes, so stuck in his ways. It's up to us to show him that women aren't just supposed to stay in the bedroom and the kitchen anymore."

"Aunt Mimi!" Glynna was a bit embarrassed by her

outspokenness. Ladies didn't usually talk so openly about such things.

"I'm just speaking the truth. Instead of trying to hobble you with a husband, he should have been supporting you in your endeavors and cheering you on. He shouldn't be the biggest obstacle to your success. He should be your biggest fan!"

"I wish he was."

"Well, I certainly am. I'm so proud of you. Didn't one of your paintings of the Colorado mountains sell for several hundred dollars at the gallery?"

"Five hundred, to be exact," she told Mimi, still amazed at the amount the collector had paid for her work.

"That's fantastic! You're so talented."

"Thank you. I'm just thrilled that people actually like what I do."

"They more than *like* it. You're going to become a celebrity! Just wait and see—you're a woman artist of the West!"

"I'm so blessed to have you. You're the only one who really understands."

"I love you, Glynna. I want you to be happy." Her words were heartfelt.

"I am happy, Aunt Mimi. I'm in Texas!" She looked back out the window, her eyes aglow. "It doesn't get any more exciting than this!"

"Oh, I don't know. I think it will be very exciting when Glynna Williams's paintings of the untamed Texas landscape and its people are all that anyone's talking about in New York society. I'll have so much to brag about."

"That would be wonderful, wouldn't it? It would

certainly show Papa that I'm serious about my work."

"I think he found that out already the day we left. I don't think he really believed we'd make the trip."

Glynna grinned at her aunt conspiratorially and then turned her attention back out the window again as the stage rumbled on. There was so much to see. She couldn't afford to waste a minute. She might miss something!

Mimi gazed lovingly at Glynna. She had grown into an intelligent, beautiful young woman. She had a wonderful, promising future ahead of her, and Mimi wanted to make sure that she had every opportunity to take full advantage of it.

She hadn't enjoyed defying her brother that way during the confrontation, but she was certain it would ultimately be worth it. He had to understand that his daughter's painting wasn't a "hobby," as he'd called it. Glynna was making quite a name for herself as a Western artist. The oil paintings inspired by her trip to Colorado had sold very well. There was a growing demand for more of her work, especially the ones she'd done of the Indians she'd seen on her trip. They had proven, to everyone's surprise, to be among the most popular.

That was why Glynna had wanted to travel west again, and that was why Mimi had felt it necessary to stand up to Charles and force his hand. He'd backed down, but it hadn't been pleasant. Watching Glynna now as she studied the Texas landscape, Mimi knew it had been worth it. One day soon, she hoped Charles would realize just how talented Glynna really was.

"Aunt Mimi, if you've never been to this part of the state before, how did you know it was going to be so beautiful?"

"I've heard so many tales about how wonderful Texas is that I was certain any place we chose to go would be magnificent." Mimi turned her attention out her own window and gazed off into the distance. There had been more to her decision to choose this route than just chance, but she would explain that to Glynna later. Right now they were heading for the town of Dry Creek, and she couldn't have been more pleased.

"We should make Dry Creek by dark," Al Rollins, the stage driver, told Hank Sanders, the man riding shotgun with him.

"Good. I'm gonna enjoy having a drink or two at the saloon once we get there," Hank said with a tense smile as he kept a sharp eye out for trouble. This was the most dangerous part of the run into Dry Creek, and he had to stay alert. Renegades and outlaws were always a threat on this stretch of the road.

"You and me both," Al agreed, and he slapped the team's reins on their backs, urging them to a faster pace. The thought of relaxing in the bar and having a beer was a real incentive to make it into town on time.

Suddenly shots rang out, jarring the driver and his guard from their thoughts of the night to come. A bullet slammed into Hank's shoulder, and he collapsed on the driver's bench next to Al, bleeding severely.

Al desperately fought to get all he could out of his

horses. He cursed and swore at them as he whipped them harder and harder, hoping to outrun their attackers. Crouching low, he stayed in control of his nearly runaway team. But as more shots were fired and they closed in on him, he knew it was hopeless. He reined in and brought the stage to a halt. He almost made a grab for Hank's rifle, but stopped as four masked bandits galloped up before him with their guns aimed directly at his chest. He was trapped.

"Don't do nothing stupid," the leader of the gang told him. "Just throw down your guns and the strongbox, and do it fast!"

"Don't . . ." Hank moaned, lying half-unconscious next to Al.

But Al knew they had no choice. If they wanted to stay alive, he would have to do what the bandits said and give them what they wanted. He pulled the strongbox free of the driver's boot and shoved it out. It crashed heavily to the ground, and the outlaws hooted in excitement.

"You won't get away with this!" Al said threateningly.

The outlaws laughed as two of them hurried to dismount and loot the box, while the other two kept their guns trained on him. "We already have."

"Driver! What's happening?"

The sound of a woman's voice drew the outlaws' attention.

"Well, well, what do we have here?" one of the gunmen drawled as he stepped away from the now empty strongbox to open the stagecoach door. "Get out of there. Now! All of you!"

"Driver?"

"Do what he says, ma'am. They ain't foolin' with us," Al ordered, hoping the outlaws would go easy on his two female passengers. Unarmed as he was, there wasn't much he could do to save them, but he would have to try. Nobody was going to harm any women under his protection while he still had breath in his body.

Mimi was shocked as she stared out the stage doorway at the masked men who were obviously holding up the stage. In all her forty-eight years, she had never been in a life-threatening situation like this one before, and she wasn't quite sure of the protocol involved. The bandits' guns were pointed directly at her, so she assumed she should follow the driver's directions.

"Could you help me down, please?" she asked.

"Aunt Mimi! Just do what he says!" Glynna said nervously from behind her.

"But it's a long way down, dear, and I'm afraid I'll—" She was about to explain that she feared she'd fall without assistance, but she didn't get the chance to finish.

"Get the hell down out of there, woman! Or I'll give you something to be afraid of!" the outlaw said with a snarl. He was in no mood to deal with any prim and proper lady from back east, and her precise accent and expensive clothes pegged her as that. He had no idea what a woman like her was doing in a place like this, but he figured she just might be worth some money.

Mimi gave him her most genteel, offended look. "Really, sir, there's no reason to use profanity."

33

"Oooeee, looks like you're dealin' with a real live lady, there, Will," another robber taunted.

"Shut up, Chuck!" Will said, snarling. "Come on! Move it!" He motioned again for Mimi to get out of the stage.

As gracefully as she could, and with her head held high, Mimi descended. She had to half jump to make it, but she did so with aplomb. For a moment she was rather pleased with her execution of the descent, but then she looked up to find herself staring down the barrel of Will's six-gun.

"There's no reason for violence, young man. I've complied with your wishes."

"Well, beggin' your pardon all to hell and back, *ma'am*, but in case you haven't figured it out yet, this is a robbery," he said mockingly. "Give me all your money! Empty out your purse! Now!"

He gestured toward the small drawstring bag she was carrying, then looked inside the stage to see a younger woman standing in the doorway, watching him. She was a pretty young thing, but he was more interested in the strange wooden box she was clutching desperately in her arms, than in thinking about the fun he could have with her. There was no time for that now. They wanted money.

"What are you standing there looking at? Get down here, too!"

Glynna climbed down and hurried to stand with Mimi, who was handing over her purse.

"Gimme that box you got!" he demanded.

"No, it's my—" Glynna began.

Will fired a shot into the air to get her full attention, and he was glad to see her jump nervously at the threat.

"I done had about enough backtalk from her! I don't intend to take any from you. It won't pain me in the least to shoot the both of you! Now, give me the damned box!" He glared at her, the truth of his threat plain in the deadly look he was giving her.

For an instant, Glynna's gaze met his, and a shiver ran down her spine. His eyes were black and mirrored the viciousness Glynna knew must be in his soul. She knew better than to try to defy him, and reluctantly handed over her most treasured possession.

"What the hell is that?" the outlaw leader asked. He'd never seen anything like the small wooden box before.

"Damned if I know, Eli. Must be her family jewels, though, the way she was hanging on to it. Let's take a look-see. I think I got me some mighty fine loot here."

Will roughly unlocked the wooden case and threw back the lid. When he saw what was inside, he stared down at the contents in disgust. The only things in the box were paints and brushes.

"What the hell?" he complained, disappointed. He'd expected riches, not this.

"What is it?" The others were hoping there was a big haul in her treasure chest.

"There ain't nothing but a bunch of paints and brushes in here."

"Paints? What are you talkin' about?"

"You know—like them artists use."

They swore loudly, irritated that it hadn't been

something more valuable. Muttering a vile curse, Will flung the case away, not caring that the contents went flying or that the woman gasped in dismay at his action.

"What else we got?" one of the others demanded.

He rifled through Mimi's purse and started hooting over his luck as he pulled out her money.

"This your life savings, honey?" he asked Mimi. "Well, it ain't no more! It's ours now!"

He quickly pocketed the cash, gathered up Al's and Hank's discarded firearms, and got ready to ride. They were pleased with what they'd gotten for their efforts. The strongbox alone had held enough to keep them in whiskey and women for at least a month or two.

Another of the men dismounted and moved toward the team.

"What're you doing?" Al asked, tensing at his approach. After listening to them talk among themselves, he figured he was dealing with Eli Wilson and his gang. Nobody knew a whole lot about them, except that they were dangerous. He waited nervously to see what they would do next. Unarmed as he was, there wasn't anything he could do to stop them.

"We're gonna make sure you don't get word to the sheriff in Dry Creek," the man said as he drew his gun and smiled up at him evilly.

Al thought he was staring death in the eye. He glanced to where the two women were standing, pale and shaken, then looked back at the man he was certain was about to kill him. He girded himself for the worst, but instead of feeling the bite of hot lead, he was shocked when the outlaw simply unhooked the team of horses and turned them loose. The gunman fired into the air several times and watched in satisfaction as the terrified team took off at breakneck speed.

"That should slow you all down a bit."

The gang mounted up, ready to ride. They disappeared without looking back, leaving the victims of the robbery staring after them in outrage and horror.

"Ladies?" Al called out to them. "You all right?"

"Is it over? Are they really gone?" Glynna asked, still clutching her aunt's arm as she continued to gaze in the direction they'd ridden, as if expecting the outlaws to return at any minute and terrorize them some more.

"They're gone. They got what they wanted. We're just lucky we're still alive to talk about it."

"Who were they?" Mimi asked, still trying to come to grips with the notion that she'd just been held up in a stage robbery. She knew that in days to come she'd tell the story with a smile, but right now she was still too frightened to laugh about it.

"I'm thinkin' that was the Wilson gang. They're a mean bunch. I'd say we got off easy today—if you don't mind losing money."

"Money can be replaced. Our lives cannot," Mimi said, drawing a deep breath and gathering her courage once again. She patted Glynna's hand reassuringly. "Everything's going to be fine. We just had a taste of the real West, my dear. What do you think?"

Before Glynna could answer, Hank let out a low, tortured moan. Al immediately hurried to care for him.

"Can you ladies give me a hand?" Al asked. "He's

been shot, and I can't get him down all by myself."

"Of course we'll help!" Mimi answered. She and Glynna hurried to his aid.

It wasn't easy, but the three of them managed to lower the wounded guard to the ground. Al quickly started to doctor his friend's wound.

"Is there anything we can do?" Mimi asked.

Al was surprised by her offer, but warned her, "This ain't no job for a lady."

"Sir, there are times when being a lady is more of a hindrance than a help. This is one of those times. This gentleman was wounded while protecting us. We must do all we can to help him." She started to roll up her sleeves.

He couldn't argue with her logic, and if she was ready and willing to help, he was going to take her up on the offer. "You know anything about nursing?"

"A little. What do you need?"

"Clean bandages," he said, unfastening Hank's shirt so he could examine the wound. "It looks like the bullet passed clean through, but he's bleedin' pretty heavily. I need something I can bind him up good and tight with."

"Glynna, can you get to our bags? I have some petticoats in my trunk that we can tear up and use for bandages."

"I'll get them right away!"

Glynna hurried to retrieve the petticoats. She'd been watching her aunt in amazement. For all that she'd known her all her life, there was a lot about Aunt Mimi that she didn't know. Glynna made a mental note to ask her where she'd learned how to nurse, once they got into town and got settled. Unfastening the trunk from where it had been stored in the rear boot, Glynna pulled the heavy piece of luggage free and dragged it to where she could get into it. It wasn't easy, but she managed. Opening it, she rummaged through her aunt's belongings until she found the items she was looking for. She deftly tore one petticoat into strips and then rushed to where Mimi and the driver were nursing the injured guard.

"Here, Aunt Mimi."

"Thank you, dear. With any luck, Mr.—What is his name?" Mimi asked as she took the fine linen strips from her.

"Sanders," Al replied as he took the homemade bandages and began to apply pressure to the wound.

Mimi remained by the driver's side, offering what assistance she could, while Glynna looked on. Without proper medical supplies, they were limited as to how much they could do, but at least they stopped the bleeding, and that was an accomplishment.

"How's that feel?" Al asked Hank as he slowly came around.

"Hurts like hell," Hank said in a pain-filled voice. Then as his vision became more focused and he saw the two women standing nearby, he quickly added, "Sorry, ladies."

"I'm sure we've heard the word before, Mr. Sanders," Mimi told him with a gentle smile. "We're just glad you're alive."

"You're not the only one, ma'am," Hank said slowly, trying to smile, but failing miserably. The pain in his shoulder was unrelenting. "They got away?"

"Yep. They got everything in the strongbox, our guns and the ladies' money."

"Damn. Who were they?"

"I think the Wilson gang."

"And we're still alive to talk about it?" Hank was surprised.

"Yep. I think maybe the ladies here are the reason. They may be our guardian angels." Al looked up at Mimi and Glynna.

"We should take them with us on every run." Hank's words were slow. "Let's get on back to town. Maybe the sheriff can catch the outlaws."

"We can't. The gang turned the team loose."

Hank gave a weary shake of his head, but did not mutter the curse word he was thinking.

"You rest now. I'll see what I can do about rounding up the horses."

"It ain't goin' to be easy."

"I know." Al patted him supportively on his good shoulder, then stood up and walked over to Glynna and Mimi. "Looks like Hank's going to be fine. The bullet didn't seem to hit anything vital."

"Thank heaven."

"Amen to that," he agreed, relieved that his friend was going to survive. "It ain't a pretty wound, but it won't put him six feet under, either. He might wish he was for a couple of days, though."

"What are we going to do without the horses?" Glynna asked.

"I'm going to take a look around and see if I can find them. Even if I find only one, at least then I can ride into Dry Creek and get some help."

"Do you think anyone will be coming along?

40

Maybe someone who could help us?" Mimi looked up the road they'd just traveled, but saw no sign of civilization.

Al was trying to keep his worries about the other dangers in the area from the women. He knew they'd been through a lot already, but he realized there was no point in trying to protect them further. He had to tell them the truth. They'd been pretty levelheaded so far about everything; he just hoped they stayed that way. He didn't need any hysterical females to deal with. Things were tough enough as it was.

"There's not another stage due through here until tomorrow, so I don't look for any help that way. Even with us being late getting into town, I doubt they'll send anybody to check on us until morning."

"We're going to be stuck here that long?" Mimi asked.

"Maybe. Just depends on whether I can track down a horse or two."

"What would you like us to do while you're gone?"

"Just stay put and keep an eye on Hank. The big thing is getting him into town now, so the doc can take a look at him and make sure our handiwork was good enough."

"Of course, and Mr. . . . ."

"My name's Al, ladies. Shoulda told you that earlier. Just call me Al." He frowned then, thinking of them there alone and unprotected while he was gone. "I just wish I didn't have to leave you alone like this."

"You think there's a possibility we could be in more danger, even though we've already been robbed?" Glynna asked, startled at the thought. She wondered what else could possibly happen to them there in the seemingly uninhabited wilds of the Texas countryside.

Al looked a bit troubled, then told them his concern. "Renegades have been known to attack in this area. So take care. Stay close to the stage."

"Renegades?" Glynna's eyes widened at the possibility.

"It ain't likely, but stay close by just in case." He saw her reaction and thought she was scared.

Actually, though, Glynna wasn't frightened. She was thinking of what a magnificent painting it would make—fierce warriors charging over the hills on their powerful horses. She knew a painting like that would sell right away.

"We will, Al," Mimi assured him. "And we're not as defenseless as you think." She reached into the pocket of her gown and pulled out a small derringer.

"Aunt Mimi!" Glynna stared in shock at the weapon her aunt held with seemingly practiced ease. "You've had a gun with you all this time?"

"I learned early in life to expect the unexpected," Mimi told her. "It's just a shame the outlaw gang caught me so unawares."

"Well, you take care with that gun, ma'am." Al had thought her quite a woman before when she'd helped him with Hank, and now his high opinion of her rose still higher.

"Don't worry. I've taken lessons in marksmanship."

"I didn't even know you owned a gun, let alone that you could shoot one!" Glynna was completely taken aback by this revelation about her aunt.

Mimi smiled. "It's not much of a weapon, but it's better than being completely defenseless."

"Well, stay close around the stagecoach, and I'll do my best to get us going again."

"We will, Al. Good luck finding the horses."

"If anyone comes to help, have them fire two shots. I should be able to hear you, and I'll come straight back."

That settled, Al checked on Hank once more, then headed off to try to track down the missing team. He hoped he'd have some luck, but he knew it was a long shot. Still, it beat the heck out of sitting around just waiting for someone to show up.

"What do you want to do while we wait?" Glynna asked.

"I'll keep an eye on Mr. Sanders and make sure he's comfortable. Why don't you see about collecting your things?" She glanced over to where the outlaw had thrown her paint box. "I hope nothing was ruined."

Glynna had forgotten all about her paints in the excitement, but at her aunt's suggestion, she quickly went off to retrieve her possessions. She found the box and discovered that the outlaw had broken the catch in his eagerness to open it. It took a while, but eventually she collected all the paints and brushes.

After assuring herself that Hank was resting as comfortably as possible, Mimi took the time to wash up as best she could with the water from one of the canteens. She rejoined Glynna where she sat in the shade of the stage.

"I knew when we left New York that this trip was

going to be an adventure, but I never dreamed it would be this exciting," Glynna said.

"Can you imagine what your father would be saying right now, if he knew what we'd just been through? He'd never forgive me for subjecting you to such danger."

"He would be aghast." Glynna grinned widely at the thought. "But think of the inspiration I'll get from this. This is the real Wild West."

"Yes, it is," she agreed, patting her pocket with the derringer in it.

"Aunt Mimi, do you think it would be very dangerous if I just walked around a little and made some sketches? From the way the driver sounded, I think we're probably going to be here for a while."

"I think that's a wonderful idea. Do you want to take my gun with you?"

"I wouldn't know what to do with it. I promise I won't go far. I'll stay within shouting distance just in case you need me."

"Go on. I'll stay here and keep watch over the guard. But be careful. I think we've had enough real excitement for one day, don't you?"

"Absolutely," Glynna agreed. She got her sketchpad and a pencil and started off to capture on paper the essence of the landscape. Images were filling her mind, and she wanted to get them on paper so she could paint them later.

Mimi watched her go, and she smiled to herself. She let her thoughts drift as she settled in to wait. Charles had his hands full with Glynna, she thought. As Charles's younger sister by six years, Mimi knew she had led him a merry chase during their childhood with all her daring ways, but Glynna was proving to be twice the woman she was. Mimi was certain of it. If she could do anything to make Glynna's life easier than hers had been, she would do it.

Mimi had fought hard to achieve the independence she now enjoyed. Her life would have been very different if her husband James had lived, but he'd died in a tragic accident less than a year after their wedding, leaving her a very rich young widow. She had mourned James properly, but when her time of mourning was up, she'd forsaken the widow's life and had begun traveling and seeing the world.

Mimi had never experienced anything like this stage robbery before. It had been traumatic, but it had also been exciting. They'd just been robbed by real live Western outlaws!

Charles came into her thoughts again, and she wondered how to tell him about it. He had been adamant about the fact that he didn't want them going on this trip to the "uncivilized frontier," as he'd called it. When they'd had a moment alone, he'd told her that he would hold her personally responsible for Glynna's safety. Mimi smiled at the thought. Who would ever have dreamed that their stagecoach would be robbed, and in broad daylight? But no matter. They had survived the adventure unscathed. True, the outlaws had taken some of her money, but that had been only her pin money. She kept the bulk of her funds buried deeply in her trunk in a small hidden compartment. She and Glynna were in no way short of cash.

Mimi realized, though, that when the time came to tell Charles about the trip, she and Glynna were going to have to coordinate their versions of what had happened very carefully. What Charles didn't know couldn't hurt him, and they wanted to keep it that way.

Chapter Two

Glynna hadn't meant to forget the stage driver's warning to stay close, but as she roamed away from the road, sketchbook in hand, she became more and more entranced with the beauty of the wilderness surrounding her. She stopped several times to draw a particularly interesting scene, and soon any thought of possible danger was forgotten. Untamed though the area was, she sensed no threat, felt no fear. Her creativity was urging her on. This landscape was why she'd come to Texas.

Glynna wasn't sure how far she'd wandered from the stage when a vista unfolded before her that left her enthralled. Low-growing mesquites and cedars provided the perfect frame for the view of a distant mesa. It rose tall and powerful against the horizon, its colors vivid in the brilliance of the afternoon sun. There was a rather flat rock nearby, so she sat down there, never letting her gaze shift from the view that so captivated her.

She worked for some time, frowning in concentration as she tried to capture the essence of the wild beauty before her . . . the untamed land, carved by God's hand, untouched as yet by man's. She wished she had her easel and paints with her, but there was no time to go get them. She would have to paint the scene later in her studio from her sketches and from memory. There was no way she was going to forget this moment.

Glynna's concentration was such that she didn't hear the rustling in the brush nearby. She was too focused on her work, too lost in her creation to worry about what probably was nothing more than a jack-rabbit or a few birds. It was the man's shout that jarred her back to full awareness of where she was, and it was then that she glanced up and saw what looked like a bare-chested warrior, leaning low over his horse's neck, riding straight for her. The expression on his face was savage, and she was sure his intent was equally as frightening.

Jumping to her feet, Glynna stared at him, transfixed. He looked fierce, deadly; and then she remembered Al's warning that renegades might be in the area.

Frantic, she looked around, trying to decide which way to run, but in her panic she was lost. She realized that she'd been foolish to wander so far off, but the view of the mesa had been so exciting she'd paid little attention to anything else.

And now she was alone—about to be attacked by a renegade Indian!

The warrior shouted something at her again, and terror filled Glynna's very soul. He was riding toward her like the wind, closing on her with such lethal intensity that she was certain she was facing death. He was close enough now that she could see the sheen of sweat on his darkly tanned skin, and she knew she should run if she wanted to save herself.

Desperate to escape, Glynna felt her instincts take over. She began to flee from him, still holding on to her sketchbook and pencil. Brambles tore at her clothing and skin, but nothing stopped her headlong flight. She was running for her very life. The pounding of the horse's hooves shook the ground beneath her. It seemed she could almost feel the heat of the horse's breath on her back as the warrior closed in on her.

A strong arm snared Glynna around the waist. She was hauled roughly up against her attacker, crushed to his side as he continued to ride at top speed. She screamed as she twisted and turned, trying to free herself from the man's unyielding hold. His grip was iron, though, as he held her pinned against his rock-hard body.

"Let me go!" she cried as her sketchbook and pencil were lost in her struggles.

Horror filled her. Glynna had read accounts of what happened to women captured by Indians, and she was sure she knew what fate awaited her. She tried to throw herself from her captor's arms, but his hold on her was too fierce. There would be no escape. She continued to try to fight him, but he only tightened his viselike grip. She refused to surrender eas-

He was riding towards her like the wind.

ily, and battled on as best she could against his overpowering strength.

"You little fool! If you want to stay alive, stop fighting me!"

His harsh command stunned and silenced her. He spoke English? She went perfectly still. The breath was jarred from her as he handled his charging mount with a confident touch, turning the horse sharply and racing off in a different direction. She noted vaguely that he was a fine rider, and remembered being told that the Comanche were the best horsemen of all the tribes—but then she realized he was riding with a saddle. Confused, battered and bruised, she grabbed for the pommel and held on for dear life.

Hunt had grown furious as he'd fought to keep a protective hold on the woman he'd just rescued from the charging longhorn. It wasn't easy, especially since she'd been fighting him with all her strength. He was surprised a woman of her size would be so strong. She almost broke free once, but he managed to tighten his grip and keep her from getting herself killed.

Hunt had no idea what had she been doing sitting on a rock out in the middle of nowhere. He just knew she was lucky that he'd seen her, or she might have been dead by now. Longhorns were notoriously mean-tempered, and the stray bull he'd been trying to bring in since early that morning was no exception. It had charged him several times during the last few hours, and Hunt knew the female would have been an easy target for the animal's frustration and anger.

When Hunt was sure he was far enough out of the longhorn's path, he reined in. He glanced back and saw the bull standing some distance away, seemingly quiet for the moment.

"Let me go! Put me down!" Glynna demanded the minute they'd stopped. She twisted violently around, trying to get away from him.

"Oh, no. Not yet," he said in irritation, not completely trusting the wily bull. The animal had proven itself as cunning as it was mean-tempered. Hunt was more determined than ever to bring it in—which he still planned to do in spite of this interruption.

"Who are you? Why won't you let me go? What are you going to do with me?" Fear sounded in her voice. Even though she was trying to stay in control, her imagination was running wild.

He realized then that she hadn't seen the bull and had no idea of the danger she'd been in. He realized, too, that she was afraid of him. He hadn't meant to grab her up that way, but he'd had no choice. The bull had been ready to charge her, and sweeping her off her feet had been his only chance to get her out of harm's way.

"I just saved your life. Don't you realize you almost got yourself killed?" he demanded, loosening his hold on her a bit.

"You saved my life?" she countered in disbelief. As he relaxed his grip, she managed to turn around and get a look at this man who claimed to be her savior. "From what?"

Glynna stared at him in amazement. She'd thought he was an Indian warrior. Instead, she found herself gazing up into the most vivid blue eyes she'd ever seen. She realized then that this man was no renegade Comanche—he'd just looked like one for a moment when he'd come riding at her that way. Glynna had to admit to herself that he was handsome, in a rugged sort of way. His hair was black, and he wore it longer than most men did. His features were proud, his nose straight. His mouth was firm, and she wondered if he ever smiled. She'd never been this close to a man without his shirt on before. There wasn't an ounce of spare flesh on him. His shoulders were broad, and his chest was deep and strong. She was still amazed at how powerful he was. He'd held her, even as she'd kicked and screamed, with barely an effort.

As their gazes locked, Hunt got a good look at her, too, and he felt a jolt to the depths of his soul. This woman was beautiful. Her hair was long, dark and lustrous. She'd been wearing it restrained in a bun at the nape of her neck, but in her struggles with him it had come loose and now framed her face in a tumble of glossy curls. Her eyes were green and sparkled now with anger and intelligence. High color stained her cheeks. Her chin had a stubborn tilt to it that almost made him smile, but then he remembered that she'd almost ended up dead.

At the thought, Hunt instinctively tightened his arm around her again. He was sorry the minute he did it, though, for facing him as she was, her soft curves were pressed even more intimately against him. His expression darkened, becoming even more threatening. He didn't need this kind of trouble, and this woman did spell trouble for him. He wanted to get away from her as quickly as he could, but where she'd come from, he had no idea.

"I saved you from that bull," he answered, using his knees to turn his horse. When he did, she could see the longhorn standing a short distance away from them.

"He was charging me?" Her eyes widened at the sight of the bull and his lethal-looking horns. She trembled at the thought.

Hunt nodded. Tearing his gaze away from her, he demanded, "What are you doing out here all alone?"

"I'm not alone!" she replied indignantly. "The stagecoach is nearby . . . somewhere." She added the last a bit embarrassed, for she'd wandered so far away that she didn't know where she was.

"Stagecoaches don't just stop out here for no reason."

"We were robbed, and the outlaws ran the team off," she explained. "We were going to be stranded until help came or the driver could find the horses, so I came out here to sketch while the driver went to look for them."

"Do you have any idea how far you are from the road?"

She had the grace to look shamefaced. "Well . . . no . . . but—"

Hunt made a sound of disgust and said no more as he put his heels to his horse's flanks.

"Where are you taking me?" she demanded in a shaky voice, still not quite sure she could trust him.

"Back where you belong."

"But I need my sketchbook!" She couldn't just leave it behind. She'd worked too hard on her drawings. Her rendering of the mesa had been almost perfect.

"Forget it! It's too dangerous!"

"I won't leave without it! My drawings are my life!"

"You don't have much choice. If you try to go back and get it, you might not have a life," he told her, continuing on in the direction of the road, away from possible trouble.

Glynna knew escaping his commanding hold on her was impossible, so she declared defiantly, "I'll just come back for it later, then."

"If you want to risk getting yourself killed, go right ahead. I'll have no part of it."

He sounded angry, but she didn't care. She hadn't asked him to come riding up and grab her like some sort of knight in shining armor. She was about to tell him so when they emerged onto the road near the stagecoach.

"Glynna?"

Mimi had heard the sound of a horse nearing and had thought it was Al returning with the team. She was shocked at the sight of Glynna being carried back by a very handsome, shirtless man on horseback. Had the stranger been wearing armor, Mimi would have thought the scene straight out of a medieval fairy tale. The expression on the man's face, however, was anything but that of a hero rescuing a damsel in distress.

So her name was Glynna, Hunt thought, his expression grim as he saw the other woman standing by the stage. He rode up to the stranded vehicle and reined in. Loosening his hold on Glynna, he let her slide to the ground. He was surprised at how he regretted having to let her go, and he angrily forced the thought away.

Glynna knew she should thank him. She supposed he had saved her from possible harm, but somehow her pride and feelings had been hurt. She brushed herself off and then glared up at him. Before she could say a word, though, he wheeled his horse around and started to ride off.

"Sir?" Mimi was completely taken aback by what had just happened. She had no idea what had transpired between Glynna and this man.

Hunt looked back at her.

"Can you help us? We're rather stranded here until our driver finds our horses."

"I'll see what I can do." His tone was emotionless. And then he was gone.

Glynna turned to find her aunt staring at her. Even Hank was stirring and trying to prop himself up on an elbow to see what was going on.

"What happened to you? Who was that?" Mimi asked.

For the first time, Glynna realized how terrible she must look. Her dress was rumpled, and her hair had come loose from its sedate bun.

"I was just sitting there, sketching a wonderful view, and *he* came charging up out of nowhere and grabbed me!"

"Grabbed you?" Hank managed, immediately fearing the worst.

Mimi looked scandalized. "Did he harm you in any way?"

"No," she admitted in a low voice, looking from Mimi to Hank. She didn't want them to know how close she'd come to getting herself into real trouble, but she didn't want her rescuer to be accused of having done anything wrong, either—even though she thought he was as mean-tempered as the longhorn. "He didn't hurt me."

"If he didn't hurt you, then why do you look like that?" her aunt pressed. "Why did he grab you?"

"I look this way because I was trying to fight him off. For a minute I thought he was an Indian! You know how Al told us there might be renegades around here," she said, trying to explain. "I fought him the best I could, but then I realized he really had saved me."

"He saved you?" Mimi was growing ever more confused.

"There was a longhorn about to attack me, and I didn't even know it was there. I was too busy drawing."

"But surely a cow wouldn't hurt you. A buffalo, maybe, but a cow?" Her aunt was disbelieving.

"Yes, ma'am," Hank said weakly. "Them longhorns are meaner than a whole herd of buffalo. Smarter, too. Good thing he was out there to help you."

"Oh, dear." Mimi was aghast that her niece might have been killed. "Who was he?"

"I have no idea," Glynna answered, and she suddenly felt bereft that she didn't even know his name.

"He was probably a cowboy from one of the outfits nearby," Hank speculated. "Maybe he'll go find ol' Al and give us a hand." He sank back down, exhausted from the effort of talking. "It sure would feel good to get on into town."

"It certainly would," Mimi agreed.

"I lost my sketchbook and pencil," Glynna admitted. "I really want to go back for them."

"Absolutely not," Mimi insisted. "You're going to stay right here with me."

"But I'm sure I could find them again."

"We'll buy you new ones in town."

"If they even have them." She was sorry that she hadn't kept a tighter hold on them. She doubted there were any art supplies in a town the size of Dry Creek.

"That's the least of our worries. Let's see if we can get you cleaned up a bit."

It wasn't too much later that they heard the sound of horses again. They looked up to see the stranger riding back in. Al was with him, riding double, leading the stage's team.

"I found 'em, ladies. Thanks to Hunt here," Al announced as he dismounted. "I appreciate your help."

Hunt just nodded. He glanced over at Glynna. For an instant, their gazes met across the distance.

Glynna was almost spellbound by the intensity of his regard. She studied him for a moment as an artist would—his dark coloring, the line of his jaw, the powerful expanse of his chest and the width of his shoulders, the proud way he sat his horse. She understood now how she'd mistaken him for a warrior, for there definitely was an untamed air about him.

He didn't say anything, but urged his mount in her direction. Glynna stood unmoving, her breath catching in her throat as he drew closer.

"Here," he said simply, holding out her sketchbook and pencil to her.

"You found them!" Glynna was surprised by his gesture. She rushed to take them from him, smiling up at him for the first time. "Thank you!"

Hunt stared down at her. Her smile was mesmerizing. It was innocent and lovely, just as she was, and it jarred him. Suddenly he wanted to be away from there. He didn't say a word to her, but abruptly wheeled his horse around and rode off.

It seemed to Glynna that she'd barely said thank-you, and he was gone. Her smile faded as she turned back to her aunt, a bit puzzled by his quick disappearance. He had told her that it was too dangerous for her to go back for her sketchbook, and yet he had done it for her.

"Who was that young man?" Mimi asked Al.

"He said he was the son of one of the ranchers around these parts. Said his name was Hunt. Looked like a half-breed, but that don't matter to me none. I just appreciated his help," he explained as he worked to hitch the team securely to the stage.

Hunt. A half-breed. Pencil in hand, Glynna sat down and opened the sketchbook to a new page. In earnest, she began to draw.

"What are you doing?" Mimi asked, curious. She'd noticed the exchange between the two of them and wondered at it.

"I'm going to draw him," Glynna said simply as she sketched Hunt's face in bold lines on the blank sheet of drawing paper. If he was indeed a half-breed, it would explain her first impression of him. Inspired, she wanted to capture that part of him that was the warrior—the man who had ridden like the wind, at one with his horse. Glynna knew she would have to paint a portrait of him. Only using oils would she be able truly to show the man he was.

Hunt's mood was black as he headed back to where he'd last seen the longhorn. He found no sign of the ornery bull, and his mood grew even darker.

It had been one hell of a day, and it looked as though it was only going to get worse. He almost wished he'd never set out to round up strays in the first place, but it had needed to be done. Wiping the sweat from his brow, he tried to guess which way the stubborn, evil-tempered beast had run. He was determined not to let the bull get away. The animal had tried to gore him the day before when he'd almost managed to get a rope on it, and he was going to bring the longhorn in, even if it took him another week. And at the rate he was going, it just might.

Hunt's gaze swept over the horizon, and he saw the mesa Glynna had been so busy drawing when he'd first come upon her. He had no idea why he'd gone back to look for her sketchbook. The time he'd wasted could have been spent searching for the bull. But there had been something about her desperation that had touched him, and he'd wanted her to have it back.

Hunt hadn't meant to look at the pictures, but the sketchbook had been lying open when he'd found it. He had to admit that she was good. He'd never known anyone who had such talent. Suddenly he swore under his breath and pushed all thoughts of Glynna from his mind. It didn't matter how talented she was. He was never going to see her again, and that was exactly the way he wanted it.

Hunt spurred his mount on. He had work to do.

*   *   *

The rest of the trip into Dry Creek was difficult. Hank lay in the stagecoach, with Glynna and Mimi tending to him. They tried their best to make him comfortable, but every bump in the road brought a moan of pain from the injured guard.

It was after sundown when they finally rolled into town. Al stopped the stage before the sheriff's office, calling for help.

"What happened?" Sheriff Dunn asked as he came running out of his office.

"We were held up! I think it was the Wilson gang!" Al went on to tell him all that had happened. "They shot Hank! They got our strongbox and the ladies' money, too!"

Glynna opened the stage door and climbed down, then turned to help Mimi out.

"Hank's conscious, but the ride was hard on him. Is there a doctor in town?" Glynna asked the sheriff.

"Yes, ma'am."

Some of the men in the saloon came running over to see what was wrong.

"Go tell the doc we're coming, boys!" the sheriff ordered as he and Al carefully got Hank out of the stage. "You ladies can wait for me in my office, if you don't mind. I need to talk to you about the robbery. I'll be back just as soon as we get Hank down to the doc."

Glynna and Mimi watched as they transported the wounded man down the street to the doctor's office and carried him inside; then they went into the sheriff's office to wait.

"I hope Hank recovers," Glynna said worriedly.

"With any luck, he should be all right," Mimi reassured her.

They were pleased when the sheriff quickly returned. "I've already talked to Al about what happened, but I'd like to hear it from you, too."

"There were four of them," Mimi began. "And they were all wearing masks."

"So you didn't get a good look at any of them?"

"Not really, sir," Glynna answered.

"Al says he thought it might be the Wilson gang. Do you remember what they called each other?"

"One man—the one who was the leader—they called Eli. One was named Will and another Chuck," Glynna provided.

"And the fourth man?"

"They never said his name, as best as I can recall," Mimi told him.

Sheriff Dunn nodded thoughtfully. "Did they take all your money? I know they emptied out the stage's strongbox."

"No," Mimi answered proudly. "I learned long ago not to put all my money in my purse. They got only about twenty dollars. I keep the rest hidden."

"That's good. I didn't want you ladies to be without funds."

"Thank you for your concern, but we're fine."

"Other than losing the money, you weren't harmed in any way?"

"No, we were very fortunate. It could have been much worse, I'm sure," Mimi said, remembering how cold and vicious the outlaws had been.

"You're right about that. If it was Eli Wilson and

his gang who robbed you, you're lucky to be alive tonight."

"I knew coming to Texas was going to be an adventure, but I had no idea it would be this exciting," Glynna admitted, in awe of how coolly her aunt was handling all the events of the day.

"If we catch them, we'll try to get you your money back. Are you going to be in town for a while or are you just passing through?"

Glynna and Mimi glanced at each other. "I'm sure we'll be here at least another day. We'll be staying at the hotel if you need us for anything."

"Thank you for your help."

"I guess we'd better see about getting rooms at the hotel."

"Our one and only hotel in town is right down the street. I'll be glad to escort you there."

"Why, thank you, Sheriff Dunn. That's very kind of you."

They made their way to the hotel and registered, taking two rooms. The sheriff promised to have Al send their luggage over as soon as possible. Less than half an hour later, Al delivered their trunks to their rooms.

"How's Hank?"

"The doc says he's going to be just fine."

"That's wonderful."

"Yes, it is. I'm glad things turned out as well as they did for us today. It was pretty scary there for a while."

"We lost some money, but we're still alive . . . and so is Hank."

"Yes, ma'am. It's like you said—money can be re-

placed, but once we're dead . . . Well, you know what
I mean."

"Yes, Al, we do. Thank you for everything."

The hotel had a small dining room, and Glynna
and Mimi were pleased to find that they could still
get dinner that night. They ordered and enjoyed a
simple but hearty meal.

"I was wondering if you could tell me where Rev.
Paul Chandler's church is," Mimi asked the waitress
as they were finishing their meal.

"Yes, ma'am. His church is just two blocks over,
on the corner of First and Travis."

"Thank you. Do you know what time the services
are tomorrow morning?"

"Ten o'clock sharp," she answered.

"Thank you."

Glynna gave her a curious look. "You know someone here in Dry Creek?"

Mimi smiled. "Paul was a close friend of my husband James."

"You knew he was in Dry Creek all this time, and
you never told me?"

"I haven't seen him in years. I keep in touch with
his sister, Sally. She's a longtime friend of mine from
school days, and she's the one who told me that he
had established a church here."

"I don't suppose this preacher is the reason we
came to this part of Texas rather than going to San
Antonio, is he?"

"Why, Glynna, do you really think I'd do something like that? You wanted to come to Texas, and
we're in Texas. It just so happened that I knew where

64

Paul was, and I thought it would be enjoyable to see him while we were on our trip."

"Are you planning on attending services in the morning?"

"I'd like to, but you don't have to."

"Of course I'll go with you. I'm intrigued. It isn't often that you find an old friend from back east out in the wilds of Texas. I want to know more about him. What did you say his name was?"

"Paul Chandler, dear—Rev. Paul Chandler now."

"How long has he been preaching?"

"Almost twenty years, from what I understand, but I think he's been here in Dry Creek for only a few years."

"When was the last time you saw him?"

"Oh, it seems like it's been forever," she replied evasively, finding it hard to believe that it had actually been almost twenty-four years since she'd last seen Paul and that soon, very soon, she would be seeing him again. A twinge of regret touched her as she thought of how young she'd been then—and how vulnerable.

"Well, it will be fun to see how he reacts to seeing you after all these years."

"I'm sure he'll be surprised." Mimi didn't say any more.

"Were you good friends?"

"Oh, yes. He and James were very close, and we stayed in touch for some time after James died. I'm sure you'll like him."

They retired upstairs then and said good night before going to their own rooms.

As Mimi slipped into bed, her thoughts were on

the morning to come. Sally had told her how Paul had found religion and had begun preaching all those years ago. She wondered if he'd changed so very much. She wondered, too, how he would react to seeing her after all this time.

Mimi lay awake long into the night, bittersweet memories of a time long past haunting her.

Glynna found sleep hard to come by. She tossed and turned and finally decided to light her lamp and sit up for a while. Her sketchbook beckoned, and she opened it to stare down at the image she'd created of the man named Hunt. He stared back at her from the page—strong, proud, handsome, silent. He fascinated her.

She knew so little about him—only his name and that he was a rancher's son. She realized she would never see him again, and for some reason the thought troubled her. For though they might never meet again, she knew she would never forget him.

Chapter Three

The Church of the Saving Grace was definitely a frontier church. Small and rustic, it was bare of any ornate religious symbols. There was only a cross hanging on the front wall over the lectern.

Mimi and Glynna slipped inside and sat in one of the back pews just as the service was about to begin. The folks around them smiled in welcome, but most people kept their attention trained on the pulpit, waiting for the charismatic Rev. Chandler to appear and the service to begin.

"Your reverend must be good to get this many people to show up for church," Glynna whispered to her aunt.

"He's not 'my reverend,' " Mimi responded in a hushed voice as she looked around at the crowd of faithful gathered there, "but you're right. He must be."

Paul had always been charming and had always had a way with words. It looked as though he had finally put his God-given abilities to good use.

Mimi could only imagine how much he must have changed over the years. Memories of another time and another place came to her then as she sat in quiet reflection. It had been the year after James died. She had decided to travel, for the pain of remaining in New York surrounded by well-meaning family and friends had been too great. Everything there had reminded her of him, and she'd needed to escape. James's wealth had been considerable. As a rich widow, she could very well do as she pleased. Overprotective Charles had tried to convince her that, as a lady, she should stay right there in New York and assume her place in society as James's widow, but Mimi had wanted no part of society. She'd had no desire to grieve for the rest of her life. It was far better to keep busy and explore the world. She'd reasoned that, maybe, if she kept busy enough, the pain of her loss would ease. Her travels had eventually taken her to San Francisco. She'd known that Paul had taken up residence there, and she'd looked him up.

Images of the innocent she'd been haunted Mimi as she remembered those days. Paul had been so handsome, and she'd fallen madly in love with him. She hadn't meant to. She hadn't planned it. It had just happened.

Paul had not been capable of returning her love, though. He had seemed tormented by unknown demons, driven to drinking to excess and gambling. She had loved him enough to put up with his behavior, until the morning when she'd discovered that he'd left—just vanished, leaving her only a short note telling her that he was no good for her. . . .

"Good morning." The sound of Paul's deep, resonant voice drew Mimi back to the present . . . to this small, plain church in Dry Creek, Texas, and the tall, distinguished-looking man who had come before the congregation.

"Good morning," those gathered for worship returned.

Mimi found she couldn't look away from the sight of him standing at the pulpit. Paul had aged well. He was a bit heavier, not fat, but muscled. His dark hair was tinged with silver at the temples, but otherwise he looked much the same to her. He was as devastatingly handsome as ever with his dark eyes and classic features.

Her heart ached for a moment, and then she grew angry that she'd allowed herself to be so vulnerable. Mimi stiffened and lifted her head with pride. She was no longer the Mimi Randall who'd cried for days after Paul had disappeared. She was her own woman, and she was in charge of her own destiny. She had vowed that she would never allow anyone to have that much power over her again, and she'd kept that vow all these years. She'd come here deliberately to confront him and put to rest her memories of that time. She needed to know why he'd run from her, if he'd truly loved her as deeply as she believed he had.

"Heaven is all around us!" Paul announced in a powerful voice as he began his sermon. "You need only to open your eyes to the world we live in to see the glory of God."

Mimi listened, mesmerized, trying to find the man she'd loved all those years ago in the preacher speaking to his congregation. As she was gazing up at him, he looked her way, and she saw him frown and momentarily look just a bit disconcerted. He went on quickly, the pause almost imperceptible.

"Life is like a poker game—it's a gamble. You never know what the next day is going to bring, just as you don't know what cards you're going to be dealt in the next hand. Don't live for tomorrow—don't live for the cards that might come your way. Live for today. Play the cards you're holding now! You may not get another chance. Go for the best you can do with what you've got. That's what God expects from each and every one of us. That's the gift we can give to God—to live our lives to the fullest." Paul continued preaching, his years of practice serving him well as he struggled to collect his thoughts.

It was Mary Catherine. She was there. She was in his church!

Paul couldn't believe it was actually her, but there could be no mistake. She'd hardly changed in the time they'd been apart—her beautiful auburn hair, her green eyes, her mouth. . . . The woman who'd haunted his dreams for all these years was as lovely as ever.

Continuing his sermon, Paul glanced back toward Mimi again. This time he noticed a young woman sitting next to her. A shock went through him, for she was a youthful image of Mimi. He reasoned that the girl must be her daughter.

Paul was surprised to find that it bothered him to think that she had married—even though he had left her a note that had encouraged her to forget all about him and find true happiness in her life. With irritation, he realized that she must have taken his advice.

Annoyed by the direction of his thoughts, Paul forced himself to concentrate completely on his preaching. The past was over. He couldn't change anything, even if he'd wanted to. As he'd said in his opening statement, life was a gamble. You had to live for the day and play the cards you were dealt.

"Be a cardsharp in the poker game of life!" he exhorted his congregation. "The stakes are high—eternal salvation or eternal damnation! You make the wager . . . but just remember that the wages of sin are death! Following God's plan for you is a sure bet!"

"He's very good, Aunt Mimi," Glynna told Mimi when the last "Amen" had sounded, and everyone was leaving church. "Did he want to preach when you knew him?"

"No, dear. I think religion was probably the furthest thing from his mind back then," Mimi answered, as she stood up to file from the pew.

Paul had gone outside to greet his congregation as they left, and Mimi girded herself for the encounter to come. In an unconsciously nervous gesture, she smoothed her skirts, wanting to make sure that she looked her absolute best.

"You look wonderful," Glynna told her, sensing that her aunt was a bit tense about the upcoming reunion. "I take it you didn't write him to let him know we were coming?"

"No. I wasn't even certain that I would get the chance to see him while we were here. Sally had told me that sometimes he rides out on the range, preaching to the people who can't get to church. There was no way of knowing if he'd be here or not, or if he'd even want to see me, so I took a chance."

"You mean you gambled that he'd be here," Glynna quipped, using the theme from the sermon.

Mimi almost laughed out loud at her witticism. "You obviously were impressed with his gospel message this morning."

"I was," she answered thoughtfully, realizing how clever he'd been in tying real life to the sacred. "He's a gifted orator."

"Yes, he is. It seems he's finally found himself here in Dry Creek."

Though Paul's appearance hadn't greatly changed, it seemed inwardly he'd changed a lot. What had driven him to give up his drinking and gambling and turn to God? Mimi had no idea, and she found herself wondering if she'd changed that much, too.

Mimi pushed the thought from her, knowing it didn't matter one way or the other. They meant nothing to each other. She had come here only to satisfy her curiosity about what had happened to him.

"What was he like back then? Was he a gambler?" Glynna asked.

"Yes, he was."

"Was he good at it?"

"He was very good. He lost occasionally, but he

always had the sense to know when to fold before he lost too big."

"I think I'm going to enjoy meeting him, but this must be very strange for you, since you remember him so differently."

Mimi just smiled as they made their way out into the aisle and then left the building. It was going to be strange, but she was as ready as she'd ever be to put her last demon to rest. It was time to face Paul again and to tell herself that she definitely had been better off without him.

Paul had been talking to one of the elderly ladies in his flock when he felt Mary Catherine's presence and looked up. It staggered him to think that he could still be that aware of her nearness. It had always been that way for him, though. His gaze sought hers, and even with the crowd of churchgoers gathered around them, Paul was shaken by the power of the emotions she stirred within him.

"Mary Catherine." He said her name softly and managed a smile as he held out his hand to her.

Glynna glanced at her aunt in surprise. Everyone knew that Aunt Mimi's given name was Mary Catherine, but no one ever called her that. She'd been called Mimi ever since she was a child.

"Hello, Paul," Mimi replied as she took his hand. His touch, warm and strong, sent a shiver of awareness through her. She fought against it. "It's good to see you again."

"It's good to see you, too," he answered. "How did you know I was here?"

"Sally and I stay in touch. She wrote and told me several years ago that you were planning to settle in

73

Dry Creek and to build a church here. I was on a trip to Texas and decided to make Dry Creek one of my stops."

"I'm glad you did," he said. His gaze darkened as he gazed down at her. The years had enhanced, not lessened, her loveliness. She was still the most beautiful woman he'd ever known.

"I have someone here I want you to meet," Mimi said, drawing Glynna forward for the introduction. "This is Glynna, Charles's daughter."

"Oh . . ." He was surprised, and though it bothered him to admit it to himself, he was pleased that Glynna was not her daughter. "You looked so much alike, I had thought she was yours."

"Glynna, this is my old friend Paul Chandler," she went on quickly.

"It's a pleasure to meet you, Rev. Chandler," Glynna said politely. "You're a very good preacher. I enjoyed your sermon today."

"Thank you." He looked back at Mimi. "Are you two free for dinner tonight? I'd love to visit with you both and catch up on everything."

Mimi actually hesitated, but he didn't notice, for Glynna quickly accepted.

"We'd love to."

"Fine. Are you staying at the hotel?"

"Yes."

"There's a small restaurant just down the street from there. Why don't I come by for you around six o'clock?"

"We'll be waiting," Glynna answered.

"That will be lovely," Mimi added.

They moved off then, so he could finish greeting the rest of his congregation.

"I think he was glad to see you," Glynna said. "But why does he call you Mary Catherine? I've never heard anyone call you by your real name. Even Papa calls you Mimi."

"Paul always called me by my given name," she answered, remembering far too clearly the night when he'd first kissed her. He told her that Mimi sounded too childish for the woman that she was and that he was going to call her Mary Catherine.

"Dinner tonight should be interesting."

"Yes, I think it will be. But until then, what would you like to do?"

"It would be fun to ride out and sketch some more landscapes away from town, but there's not really enough time before dinner."

"We need to find someone who knows the area and can show us around. Maybe Paul can suggest someone for a guide."

"That would be wonderful. As vast as the countryside is, we'd probably get lost if we tried to ride out on our own."

"I have no doubt about it."

"How long do you want to stay here in Dry Creek?" Glynna made sure she sounded innocent as she asked. Since she had never seen her aunt react this way to any man before, she was certain that, even though Mimi denied it, she cared deeply for Paul Chandler. She smiled to herself, thinking how alone Aunt Mimi had been for so many years and how much fun it would be to play Cupid for her.

Mimi looked a bit surprised by her question. "We'll

stay as long as you want to, dear. This trip is for you. When you're ready to move on, we'll go."

"I think I'd like to stay here for at least a few more days."

• "Fine. That will give you plenty of time to work."

They returned to their rooms, Mimi to rest a little and Glynna to start painting.

Paul returned to his small house after he'd finished at the church, and he sat in his parlor in silence, staring off into the distance. Mary Catherine's appearance in town had stunned him. It had been so long. . . .

He had thought he was over her, but seeing her today had been pure torment for him. So often over the years, he'd regretted leaving her, but his life had been hell back then. She'd deserved better . . . and that had been precisely why he'd disappeared. He knew it had been a cruel thing to do, but at the time he'd believed it was the only way.

And now she was back.

The knock at her hotel room door startled Glynna as she stood before her easel, paintbrush in hand, concentrating on the image she was creating. Only at the interruption did she realize how much time had passed. It was after five! She had been so engrossed in her work that she'd forgotten everything else.

"I completely forgot the time!" she said as she opened the door to let her aunt in.

"You've been so quiet, I wondered what you were

up to. Mind if I take a look?" She was curious to see what Glynna was working on.

For some strange reason, Glynna felt shy about Mimi seeing the painting, but she did not try to stop her from crossing the room to study it.

"Glynna," Mimi said softly, in awe of what was being created on the canvas. "This is wonderful!"

As she stared at the rendering of the man named Hunt, her respect for her niece's talent grew even more. She was impressed. Somehow Glynna had managed to capture the raw excitement of the stranger who had saved her from possible harm. Her bold strokes had brought him to life right there on her canvas. It was a powerful picture, showing him riding fast, leaning low over his horse's neck. Her ability to create such beautiful, realistic scenes was definitely a gift.

"Your talent is amazing. I don't know how you do it," Mimi told Glynna.

Glynna was standing back, frowning as she studied her work. "Do you really think it looks like him?"

"Oh, yes, but when I saw him he didn't look quite that intense. Is that how he looked when he came riding at you to save you from the longhorn?"

Glynna nodded. "I was terrified. He looked so . . ." She paused, searching for the right word.

"Savage?" Mimi provided.

"That's what I thought it was at the time. Now that I know why he was charging at me at way, though, I know it wasn't a bloodthirsty look. It was more a look of fierce determination."

"Well, he looks all that and more in your painting. This is one of the best you've ever done."

"Thank you." She wiped her hands on her paint rag, knowing she had to quit for now. "It's almost time for dinner, isn't it?"

"Yes, Paul should be coming for us soon. That's why I thought I'd check in on you."

"I'll get cleaned up and be ready to go when he gets here."

Mimi started from the room.

"By the way, Aunt Mimi, you look very nice tonight," Glynna told her, noticing the gown she'd donned to wear to dinner. It was a deep emerald green, and the color was very good on her. Her aunt always paid careful attention to her appearance, but tonight she looked even lovelier than usual. That convinced Glynna that her aunt truly was interested in the reverend.

Paul arrived at the hotel on time to take them to dinner. He knocked on Mary Catherine's door and waited for her to answer. He wasn't sure why he was a little nervous, but he was.

"Good evening, Paul," Mimi said, as she opened the portal and stood before him.

He gazed down at her, thinking she'd never looked prettier. "You look lovely, Mary Catherine."

"Why, thank you," she said politely, as if his compliment was just ordinary conversation. Secretly, though, she was most pleased that he'd noticed.

"Are you ready to go?"

"Absolutely, all we have to do is get Glynna and we can be off."

Glynna was ready to go, and they engaged in small talk as he escorted them to the restaurant.

"So what in the world brought you to Dry Creek?" Paul asked after they'd settled in at a table.

"We almost didn't make it," Mimi said.

"Did something happen?"

"The stage we were on was robbed."

"You were on that stage!" He was shocked that they'd been in such danger. "I heard the talk about the robbery, and how there were two ladies from back east on it."

"That was us."

"Thank God you weren't hurt!"

"They did shoot Hank, but the sheriff told us that he's going to recover."

"Do they know who did it? Did the sheriff say?"

"Yes. They thought it was the Wilson gang, but they weren't sure."

"How much did they get away with?"

"They stole some money from Aunt Mimi, but mostly they were just after the strongbox," Glynna told him.

"You were very lucky." He looked over at Mary Catherine, and tension filled him at the thought of her in danger.

"We know. For a few minutes there, I was afraid I might not get to paint any of Texas," Glynna agreed.

"You're here to paint?" He looked back at her with real interest.

"Glynna is an artist, and a very fine one, too, if I do say so myself. She toured Colorado last year, and her paintings of the mountains sold very well at the gallery. Her work is very much in demand now back in New York, so she decided to come to Texas for more inspiration."

"I've never met an artist before. I'd love to see some of your paintings. How did you get started?"

"A stroke of luck—pun intended." Glynna laughed. "While I was in school, an art teacher told me I had potential and that I should work at my painting. My father allowed me to go to Paris to study at an institute there for six months, and when I came back home, I knew what I wanted to do."

"You're very lucky to have found out so early in life," Paul said. "Many people are middle-aged before they figure out what they're good at."

"I've been very blessed," Glynna admitted. "Just to be able to do what I love and get paid for it is amazing."

They laughed.

"So, you think Texas will inspire you?"

"It already has," she answered, her thoughts centering on Hunt.

"Considering how successful her paintings of Colorado have been, Glynna wants to concentrate on the West, and possibly even do some more Indian paintings, if at all possible. Those that her trip to Colorado inspired were excellent."

Paul looked a bit stricken at the thought. "I wouldn't wish too hard for any Indian encounters while you're here in Texas."

"Why?" they both asked.

"Because the only Indians around here are renegades off the reservation, and after meeting them, you might end up dead."

"Oh." Glynna paled at the thought, remembering her initial reaction to her encounter with Hunt. She had been terrified, and he had been civilized. She could just imagine what running into a real renegade would be like. The thought was chilling.

"I know our driver Al mentioned after the stage was robbed that we should be careful because there might be some renegades around. . . . Have there actually been raids here lately?"

"There has been one band of renegades causing some trouble in the area." He didn't want them to know any of the details of the attack on a ranch west of town. It had been deadly, and by the time help came, the Comanche had been long gone.

Glynna and Mimi shared a troubled look.

"But don't worry about that. As far as painting scenery goes, there are some beautiful vistas north of here. Tom McAllister's a friend of mine, and he's got a big spread out that way. He'd probably enjoy showing you around, if you planned to stay for a while."

"We'd appreciate any help you could give us," Glynna told him. "I was hoping I could make just such an outing. The scenery on the ride into town was wonderful."

"Have you made any plans for tomorrow? If not, we could ride out to the McAllister ranch in the morning and talk to old Tom."

"That would be wonderful. What time would you like to go?" She was excited by the prospect.

"It's over an hour's ride to his ranch house, so we should head out by eight or so."

"You don't have to work tomorrow?" Mimi asked.

"Sunday is my hardest workday, so I can take Monday off with no problem. My boss is lenient with me." Paul grinned.

Bobbi Smith

He looked so youthful and charming that Mimi's heart constricted. Had it really been so long ago that they had been happy together? How could so many years have passed so quickly?

After they'd eaten, he walked them back to the hotel and bade them good night.

Mimi was pleased that Paul was going to help them find a guide who could take them out into the countryside. She'd been disappointed that they hadn't had the chance to speak on a more personal level, but realized that she should have been prepared for that possibility, since Glynna was with them. She told herself that it didn't really matter, anyway. If he'd truly cared about her all those years ago, he wouldn't have abandoned her. Obviously, as far as any kind of relationship between them went, the past was just that—past.

And that was fine with her.

Chapter Four

It was well after midnight. Hunt lay in bed, staring up at the ceiling. He was tired, but sleep would not come. He had finally brought in the longhorn that had given him such trouble. The bull had been smart and fast, but his own patience and perseverance had won out. The animal was back with the herd where it belonged.

Hunt tossed and turned, seeking comfort and forgetfulness. His body was exhausted, yet his mind gave him no rest. *She* was constantly there in his thoughts . . . her beauty beckoning to him . . . her smile mesmerizing—and taunting, for he knew there could never be anything between them.

Closing his eyes, Hunt wished himself asleep. Fight it though he might, a vision of the woman still floated before him. *Glynna*. In his mind, she enticed him, and he struggled against the attraction.

As his thoughts grew jumbled, his guard slipped. He wondered how Glynna would feel in his arms—not fighting him, but welcoming him.

Sleep claimed him then. And with sleep came the dream. . . .

Glynna was there—in his embrace—her sweet curves pressed tightly against him. He reached for the pins that held her hair up and freed the dark mane from its confinement. She lifted her arms to link them around his neck, drawing him down to her.

"I want you to kiss me," she whispered.

He bent to her—as their lips met, it was ecstasy. He had never known a kiss so sweet—

Then, suddenly, hands were brutally upon him, tearing him from her, dragging him away.

He looked back and it was no longer Glynna, but Jenny, and she was laughing as her brothers beat him.

"Never touch a white woman again. Stay away from white women—"

Hunt sat up in bed, shaking from the power of the emotions the nightmare evoked in him. Sweat beaded his brow, and his breathing was harsh.

With a curse, he threw himself from his solitary bed and went to stand at the window. It was still dark out . . . as dark as his soul.

He turned away from the night view and left his room to seek out the bottle of whiskey his father kept downstairs for medicinal purposes. Without a thought, he opened it and took a drink straight from the bottle. It burned all the way down and he was glad. It would strengthen him, and it would kill the pain. He put the bottle away before he was tempted to drink more.

Raking a hand through his hair, Hunt stood in the middle of the dark parlor—alone. It had become a way of life for him—being alone. It had taken a while for him fully to understand that he did not fit in either world, white or Comanche. But he understood that now.

When Hunt had left his father after the terrible encounter with Jenny's brothers, he had sought out his mother's people. He had hoped to fit in there. But the time he'd spent in the Comanche village had shown him that he didn't fully belong there either. Not that he hadn't tried. He had studied hard under his uncle's tutelage. His mother's brother, Striking Snake, had taught him along with his own son, Painted Horse. Hunt had worked hard and had learned all the skills he'd needed to survive as one of the People—how to ride, hunt and track. He'd mastered the use of a bow and arrow, too. Yet, for all his accomplishments, he had still felt like an outsider.

His vision quest had revealed to him the truth of his torment. He had seen himself standing in a mist. His face had been divided—half had been white, the other half Comanche. He had been both white man and warrior. And he had been neither. He had been alone.

When Hunt had returned to the village from his quest, he had taken the Comanche name of Lone Hunter. He was destined to fit in neither world. On his shield, he had painted the face from his vision— the face of his torment.

The whiskey finally eased his tension, and Hunt

went back upstairs to his room. He knew he wouldn't sleep, though. The rest of the night would be long and empty. He would wait for dawn.

The following morning Paul came for Glynna and Mimi in a buckboard. They were waiting for him in the hotel lobby, dressed in suitable attire for venturing into the wilds. Glynna wore a split leather riding skirt, blouse and vest, while Mimi had donned a fashionable yet practical riding habit. They both wore boots and Stetsons.

"You dressed smart," he told them, pleased, as he took Glynna's art supplies from her and stowed them safely in back. He then helped them up to the driver's bench.

"I learned it was ridiculous to worry about fashion when I was in Colorado," Glynna told him. "Sometimes it pays to be practical."

"It can be pretty rough if you're out wandering around on foot," he said.

"I found that out when we were stuck on the road after the robbery."

"I stopped by the sheriff's office last night, and he said that there hasn't been any word on the gang. Looks like they got away clean."

"Did he say how Hank was doing?" Glynna asked, concerned.

"He's coming along just fine."

"That's good news."

He climbed up beside them, and they headed out of town for the McAllister spread.

Glynna found herself falling more and more in love with Texas. It was a harsh, rough land, yet in that harshness she found pure beauty. The colors, the textures and the wide-open spirit of the land were all there just waiting for her to capture them. Some people hunted with guns; she hunted with her paintbrush. She grew more and more excited with each passing mile.

"Tom McAllister's had a pretty rough year," Paul was telling them as they neared the ranch. "He's been sick, and his son came back about six months ago and stayed on to help him with the ranch."

"It must be a very rugged life, living out on a ranch," Mimi observed.

"It's not New York City, that's for sure," he commented. "A man's got to fight for everything. Nothing comes easy."

"How did you end up here in Dry Creek?" Mimi had to ask. "And how in the world did you end up preaching?"

He was silent, thoughtful for a moment; then he answered her. "It was the year after we last saw each other. I'd been gambling and drinking all night. Another gambler accused me of cheating and shot me point-blank over a hand of cards. I thought I was a dead man. I nearly was."

"I didn't know. . . ." Mimi went pale at the thought that he'd been gunned down.

"A preacher in town stayed with me while the doc worked on me, and between the two of them, they saved me in more ways than one."

"You took up preaching after that?" Glynna was curious.

"Not right away. I went back to my old ways for a while, but it didn't take me long to realize that gambling was wrong for me. I had to straighten out my life. I figured God had given me a second chance, and I owed it to him to do something with it."

"I would never have thought you would end up a minister," Mimi said quietly.

"I would never have thought it either. Life's strange sometimes. We never know what challenge is going to come our way."

"I know," Mimi agreed, and said nothing more.

She was very glad when the McAllister ranch came into view.

Hunt was working in the stable with the horses when he heard Gib, one of the hired hands, call out that someone was riding in. Visitors were a rare thing at the ranch, and he went outside to see who was coming.

"Looks like it might be that preacher man driving the buckboard, Hunt," Gib said. "And he's got two women with him."

Hunt was surprised that any women would be coming out to the ranch, but then he shrugged, thinking they were probably friends of the reverend's just along for the ride. Or at least he allowed himself to think that until the carriage drew close enough for him to get a look at its occupants. He scowled and muttered to himself under his breath when he recognized one of the women as Glynna.

"I'll go tell my father that we've got visitors," he said tersely, turning away from the sight of the incoming buckboard.

The memory of his dream taunted Hunt as he stalked away. He didn't know why Glynna was coming to the ranch. He wondered how she'd found out where he lived and what she wanted. Whatever her reason for coming, he planned to make himself scarce. He didn't want anything to do with her. She was walking trouble for him.

Hunt went inside to get his father.

"You say we got company coming?" Tom said, looking up from his desk, where he'd been doing some paperwork.

"Looks like Rev. Chandler is riding in," he told him.

"I wonder what brings Paul out this way. I hope nothing's wrong in town." Tom got up slowly and headed outside to greet his guests.

Hunt deliberately went in the opposite direction, out the back door, and returned to the stable. He'd let his father handle whatever it was they wanted.

"Afternoon, ladies, Paul," he said, smiling up at them as the buckboard drew to a stop before the house. "What brings you to these parts?"

"Thought you might be missing me, Tom," Paul returned with a chuckle as he jumped down and turned to help Glynna and Mimi descend.

"That I have been." He laughed. "I miss those Sunday sermons of yours . . . and a good card game, too."

Paul clapped the elderly man on the back. "I've got two friends here I'd like you to meet, Tom. Ladies, this is Tom McAllister, a very dear friend of mine. Tom, this is Mrs. Mary Catherine Randall and her niece, Miss Glynna Williams."

"Why, it's right nice to meet you," Tom said.

Bobbi Smith

"It's nice to meet you, too. We've heard a lot about you from Paul," Glynna told him.

Devilment twinkled in Tom's blue eyes. "You have, have you? I'm not sure that's such a good thing."

Mimi and Glynna laughed. They immediately both decided they liked him.

"If there was anything bad to know about you, Paul didn't tell us," Glynna confided.

"Well, good. I can rest easy then. Come on inside and relax a bit. That's a goodly drive out from town."

"Oh, but it was a beautiful drive," Glynna said, staring excitedly around at the ranch, trying to take it all in.

The house was a basic two-story building, not fancy in any way, with a simple porch across the front. There were several outbuildings, a large stable and corrals.

Tom glanced at Glynna in surprise. "Beautiful, heh? I would have taken you for a city girl."

"I am, but I can appreciate beauty when I see it."

He was pleased with her answer as he led the way indoors. He was moving slowly, as if every step pained him. "I'm curious, Paul. What brings you out here?"

"You don't think I came just to see you?"

"Old sinner that I am, it's a possibility, but I doubt you came this far with these lovely ladies just to save my soul," he joked.

"I'd drive for a week to save your soul, Tom, but I think you're in reasonably good shape with God," Paul returned good-naturedly.

"I hope so."

"Well, Tom, to tell you the truth, we have a celebrity of sorts with us here."

"Oh?" He glanced at him, curious.

"Glynna is an artist. She's making quite a name for herself back east painting pictures of the Wild West, and she's come to Texas to do us justice."

"Have a seat," Tom offered, gesturing them into the small parlor.

Glynna and Mimi settled on the sofa while Tom and Paul sat in the two chairs facing them.

"So you're an artist, are you, missy?"

"Yes, sir I'm trying."

"No 'sir.' I'm just Tom."

Glynna smiled sweetly at him.

"How'd you come to Dry Creek?"

Paul explained their trip to him. "So I was trying to think of a place where she could safely ride out into the countryside and do some painting, and I thought of the Rocking M. I was hoping you'd be agreeable."

"Of course. That'd be fine. We'd be honored." He smiled at Glynna. "I'll have to find somebody else to ride out with you, though. I'm not sitting my horse much these days."

"Have you been doing what the doc said?" Paul asked, concerned. He could tell that his friend's health was not good. He was a frail shadow of the robust man he used to be.

"He can't do anything for me. I'm just getting old, is all. It's a good thing my boy's back. He's been a big help to me."

"I heard the talk that he'd returned."

"I missed him. I'm glad he's here."

"So am I," Paul said seriously, knowing how much it meant to the old man to have his son, Hunt, home again. They'd had a rough life, and he was glad that things were working out for them now. "Is he here? We could introduce him to Mary Catherine and Glynna."

"He was a minute ago. I guess he went back out to the stable. Let me go see if I can find him. He'd be the one to take the ladies out, since I can't. I'll be right back." Tom left them for a moment as he went outside.

"He's such a nice man," Glynna said when he'd gone out of earshot.

"Tom's all right," he agreed. "His life hasn't been easy, but he's made the best of it."

"Is he married?"

"He was years ago, but his wife died. She was Comanche. A lot of people hated him for marrying an Indian."

"So his son's half-Indian?" Glynna asked, glancing at her aunt.

Mimi met her gaze, and they both wondered.

"Yes."

"What's his name?" Mimi asked.

They heard Tom come back inside, and he appeared in the doorway with Hunt by his side.

Glynna's eyes widened at the sight of him. He seemed to fill the whole doorway and almost dwarfed his father. Where Tom seemed old and bent, Hunt was tall and virile and exuded a sense of power. He looked different today, more civilized. He was fully clad, his shirt fitting him tightly across his broad chest. His blue-eyed gaze was sharp. He missed nothing, yet his expression revealed little of what he was really thinking.

"Hunt, you know Rev. Chandler, and these two ladies are friends of his from back east. This is Mrs. Randall and Miss Williams. Ladies, this is my son, Hunt McAllister."

Hunt was irritated. The last thing he'd wanted to do was see Glynna again. His dream the night before had been enough to drive him to drink, and he wanted to push all thoughts of her from his mind. He didn't want to see her again or be near her. She was beauty and innocence, and beauty and innocence had no place in his life. He'd tried to convince his father that he was busy in the stable and didn't have time for social visits, but his father had insisted that he come meet the two women.

"We've already met," Hunt said flatly.

Tom cast a quick, surprised glance at him. "You have? When?"

"Your son was kind enough to come to our rescue, Tom," Glynna spoke up, smiling at them. "Our stage had been robbed, and the outlaws had set our team loose. Hunt showed up and helped our driver find them."

"That was kind of you, Hunt," Paul told him.

"You never said anything to me about that," Tom said, looking at him with pride.

Hunt acted indifferent. "I was out hunting strays. I just happened upon the ladies where they were stranded out on the road and managed to find the team without too much trouble."

"We appreciated your help," Mimi put in. "Without

you, we might still be sitting there waiting for someone to show up."

"Hunt, Miss Williams is an artist. She paints pictures of the West, and Paul here was wondering if you'd have time to take her out around the ranch and let her do some painting."

"No."

He answered so quickly, the others were shocked. Tom frowned. "No?"

"I can't take any time off from working the stock." His tone was as curt as his expression was cold. "It's the busy time of the year around here. There's too much to be done."

"You can't spare a day or two?" Tom pressed.

"You can get one of the hired hands to do it. I haven't got the time." He started to turn away, then realized his father was angry with him. "Ladies." He nodded politely toward them. "Reverend."

With that, Hunt was gone.

"Well, I'm sorry about that," Tom apologized, confused by his son's abrupt departure. "I thought sure he'd have time enough to help you out a bit."

"That's all right, Tom. I was afraid we'd be imposing on you," Paul said, knowing the old man was embarrassed.

"You're not imposing on me. I'd be delighted to have you here. It's just Hunt. He's single-minded about some things, and he's been working the herd for several weeks now."

Glynna had been taken aback by Hunt's coldness. She'd known he wasn't friendly from the way he'd acted when they'd been with the stage. Today, however, he'd just dismissed them as if they didn't exist, and that annoyed her.

"I'm sorry if we bothered him," Glynna said tightly.

"Don't worry about Hunt. I'm sure one of the other boys would be glad to take you out. We've got room for both of you here at the main house, if you'd like to stay on for a while. I can arrange things for you with Maria, our cook. I'm sure she'd be happy to have some female company for a change."

Mimi and Glynna exchanged glances, and Mimi quickly asked before Glynna could say anything, "Are you sure we wouldn't be putting you out any?"

"No. It'd be a pleasure to have you. Paul, you can stay on, too, if you want," Tom invited, believing the women would feel more comfortable having him close by, since they knew him.

"It's up to you, ladies. Would you like to spend some time here at the Rocking M?" Paul asked. "We can ride back into town, get your things and come back out tomorrow."

"That would be wonderful," Mimi answered.

She had a feeling her niece would just as soon have packed up everything and left Dry Creek, judging from the tension she felt between her and Hunt, but she also knew Glynna was intrigued with the man. Why else had she been so intense while painting his picture? She wanted to throw the two together and see what happened.

"What about you, Paul?" Glynna spoke up.

"I can come along. It would give me a chance to minister to folks out this way, while you're painting." Paul was surprised that he found himself agreeing to stay at the ranch with them.

"That sounds just fine," Tom said, smiling. It would be good to have the reverend's company for a few days, and he certainly wouldn't complain about having two pretty women around the place. "I'll talk to the men and see who we can spare to take you out riding."

"We certainly appreciate all your help, Tom," Mimi said.

"My pleasure, believe me."

Their plans made, Tom invited them to stay on for the noon meal. Hunt did not come back to the house while they were there. They ate without him; then Paul, Mimi and Glynna headed back to town.

"Hunt McAllister is certainly an interesting man," Mimi said, curious to find out if Paul knew any more about him than he'd already told them.

"He's a hard one to figure," Paul said, "being a half-breed and all."

"He doesn't seem very friendly," Glynna put in.

"He isn't too fond of white folks."

"And I take it white folks aren't too fond of him?" Mimi asked.

"There's prejudice, that's for sure."

"I had the feeling he wasn't too fond of anybody," Glynna remarked. She had yet to see the man smile.

"Well, you don't have to worry about him. He won't be bothering you any." Paul wanted to put her mind at ease about Tom's son. "There was a bad incident back when he was just a boy, and ever since then he steers clear of doing much socializing."

"What happened?"

"I didn't know Tom or Hunt then. It happened in

another town. Tom's moved on since then and bought this ranch, but back there, some boys beat Hunt up for supposedly attacking their sister."

"Attacking their sister?" Glynna repeated, stunned. "Why would he do something like that?"

"I don't think he did, but I wasn't there and have only heard the talk about it. I think he was all of about fifteen, and some girl accused him of trying to rape her. Her brothers beat him pretty badly, and then her father came after him, wanting to kill him. He ran off. Tom told me he went to live with his mother's people for a few years, then drifted for quite a while before coming back here to help him."

"Hunt's lucky he got away from that girl's father," Mimi remarked.

"I know. They probably would have shot him or strung him up. Tom rarely talks about those times, but I know it scarred him and the boy. That's why it doesn't surprise me that Hunt mostly keeps to himself. I think he's happiest that way. As lonely as Tom was for all those years, I'm just glad Hunt came back to help his father now that he needs him."

"Well, it's no wonder that I mistook him for an Indian the other day when he rescued me from that longhorn," Glynna said thoughtfully.

"Hunt rescued you from a longhorn, too?" Paul looked at her in surprise.

She quickly explained their first encounter to him, how she'd wandered away from the stage to sketch. "Yes, Hunt wasn't wearing a shirt, and he came riding at me at top speed. It scared me to death. I didn't even know the bull was there. All I knew was that a man who looked like a warrior was about to grab me up and carry me off."

"It's a good thing he did."

"Yes, it was. I might not be here talking to you if he hadn't."

She fell silent then, thinking of the man who'd saved her from certain harm, and wondering how he could possibly have attacked a young girl when he'd been just a boy himself. For all that he had been cold and less than friendly to them, he had put himself at risk to save her life. That wasn't the action of a man who would harm a woman.

"I'm sure your judgment is right about him," she went on. "He may not like us very much, and judging from the way other whites have treated him, it's no wonder he keeps a distance."

"He's a quiet one, that's for sure," Paul said. "But he's taking care of Tom, and that's what's important to me."

"Tom's seriously ill?"

"I'm afraid so. I talked to the doc about him last time I saw him in town, and he said there's nothing much he can do for Tom. It's his heart."

"That's too bad. He seems like a wonderful man," Mimi said.

"He is a good man. I think you're going to enjoy getting to know him better."

"Maybe he'll let me paint a portrait of him as a way of thanking him for his hospitality."

Mimi looked at her, pleased. "That's a wonderful idea, darling."

"Good. I'll do it."

*　　*　　*

It was dusk before Hunt returned to the house. He was quiet as he sat down to have dinner with his father.

"They'll be back tomorrow, and they'll be staying for several days," Tom told him.

Hunt merely grunted, trying not to act as if he cared one way or the other.

"You know, you could have been a little more sociable while they were here today. Especially since you'd already met them."

"It didn't matter. Rev. Chandler brought them to see you, not me."

"You're my son. I expect you to be a little more mannerly to them while they're staying here with us."

"I'll see what I can do," he replied evasively, quickly trying to think of jobs he could do that would keep him away from the ranch house during the duration of their stay.

Tom was sad as he looked at his son. Hunt had grown into a fine young man, but all the troubles he'd had growing up had hurt him. Tom knew that except for himself, Hunt didn't trust anyone. He supposed that was only natural, considering the life he'd led. He only wished he could have made things better for him. He'd tried his best, but his best just hadn't been good enough. His boy had been hurt, and there had been nothing he could do to stop it.

"I'd appreciate it. Paul's a good friend. If he wants our help with this, it's the least we can do. I'll have Diego take the women out and show them around. I think they'll be safe enough with him."

"He'll do fine," Hunt said quickly. As long as he wasn't involved, he didn't care.

"You don't think he's too young?" Tom knew the youth was only thirteen.

"He knows the ranch. It'll make him feel important to be showing the ladies around."

"That settles it then. I'll tell him tonight so he can start thinking about the best places to take them. You got any ideas?"

Hunt wanted to say, "As far away from me as possible," but he didn't. "She'd probably like it out by the river. The view is good there. I'd warn Diego not to ride too far out."

"Don't worry. I'll tell him. The last thing the two of them need is more trouble. After being held up on the stage, guess they've had enough excitement. We don't need to take any chances that they might run into a band of renegades. It's been quiet since that last raid, but there's no telling when they might attack again."

They concentrated on their dinner then, the conversation turning to other things. Hunt was glad for the chance to talk about the herd and ranch business. He wanted the distraction. The thought that Glynna was going to be back the following day and would be staying under their roof left him restless. He was going to be glad when she'd gotten her look at the Texas countryside and headed off again to wherever she was going next. The farther away from him she was, the better.

That night before going to bed, Hunt had another shot of whiskey. He didn't want the dream to return.

Chapter Five

Paul found himself looking forward to spending the time out at Tom's. He didn't ask himself why. He just packed what he needed and was ready to go first thing the next morning. Paul told several of his congregation where he was going to be in case they needed him for anything, and then he loaded up the buckboard and headed off to pick up the women.

"Good morning, Glynna," Paul greeted her when he found her waiting for him in the small hotel lobby. "Is your aunt about ready to go?"

"She'll be down in a minute. She just had a few more things to pack."

Paul found himself smiling in spite of himself. One thing he remembered about Mary Catherine was that she always made an entrance. He supposed some things never changed.

"Are these your trunks?" There were two good-size

trunks near her, and he was surprised that she traveled with so much.

"Yes. Only one is for clothes, though," she told him with a smile. "The other is for all my supplies."

"I was wondering how many dresses you needed for the trip." He grinned back at her.

Paul hefted one trunk and carried it outside to load it on the buckboard. When he came back in, Mary Catherine was descending the stairs with the hotel owner, smiling at him as he carried her things for her.

Paul felt a twinge of some emotion as he watched Mary Catherine with the other man, and he tried to ignore it. She was as lovely as he remembered, but there was nothing left between them. He'd seen to that, and he had no right to hope otherwise.

Paul knew that since he'd first seen her during the service on Sunday, there had been moments when it had almost seemed as if they'd never been apart—that all the years hadn't passed. But every time he'd allowed his thoughts to drift that way, he'd brought himself up short. He did so now again, turning his full attention back to Glynna.

Paul found it odd at discovering that the younger woman had been watching him, smiling slightly. He wondered at her expression, but said nothing about it as he picked up the second trunk with her art supplies and took it outside with the other.

"Mr. Stone, thank you so much for all your help. We'll see you in a few days upon our return," Mimi told the hotel owner graciously.

"We'll be looking forward to seeing you again, Mrs. Randall. You, too, Miss Williams," he said as he walked outside with them to load the luggage he'd been carrying.

Glynna bade him good-bye, too, and climbed up to the driver's bench. Mimi joined her there, with help from Mr. Stone. She smiled warmly at him, thanking him again for his thoughtfulness.

Paul had tried to finish stowing everything quickly, so he could get around to the front of the buckboard to help them up, but the other man had beaten him to it. Paul frowned, irritated with himself for the way he was reacting to things this morning. He had long ago given up the temptations of the flesh—drinking, gambling, women. He and Mary Catherine were to-gether again only because Glynna had needed some-where to paint. Otherwise this reunion would never have taken place. They meant nothing to each other, and they had nothing in common anymore. She was a society lady. He was a frontier preacher.

Paul finally climbed up to the driver's bench and sat down next to Mary Catherine. The sweet scent of her perfume came to him, and he tightened his grip on the reins, causing the team to step nervously about. He slapped the reins impatiently on the horses' backs, ready to be gone.

"Have a safe trip," Jason Stone told them.

Glynna and Mimi both waved good-bye to him, while Paul just kept driving.

"Your rooms will be upstairs," Maria told Mimi and Glynna as she showed them through the house. "Señor Tom sleeps downstairs now since he does not feel well. It is hard for him to climb the steps. Señor

Hunt said he will sleep out in the bunkhouse while you are here."

"We never meant to put anyone out," Glynna protested.

"Señor Tom would have it no other way. He wanted to make sure you had enough privacy."

"That's very kind of him. We appreciate his thoughtfulness."

Maria smiled. "It will be nice to have you here. My Diego is going to take you out for your rides. He is excited about it."

"Diego is your son?" Glynna asked.

"Yes." She beamed, a very proud mother. "He will do a fine job for you."

"We don't doubt it for a minute."

"Reverend Paul." Maria looked at the minister as she started to lead the way up the stairs. "Señor Tom said we will fix a bed for you in the parlor."

"That will be fine," he said in agreement. "Where is Tom?"

"He's down at the corral with Hunt and the others."

"I'll have to go see what he's up to as soon as we're unloaded. Shall I help bring in some of the ladies' things?"

"Diego should be doing that," Maria said as she started upstairs with Mimi and Glynna.

"I'll find him and give him a hand." Paul went in search of the boy so they could get Glynna and Mimi settled in.

Glynna had already realized that the house was definitely a man's domain. The rooms downstairs were austere and utilitarian. She expected the bedrooms would be the same way, spartanly furnished with only the real necessities of life.

"This room is yours," Maria told Glynna, pointing across the hall. "And, Mrs. Randall, this is yours." She took Mimi into her room.

Glynna was surprised when she entered the bedroom and found herself staring at a vividly painted Comanche shield hanging on the wall opposite the foot of the bed. The colors were vibrant and the painting intriguing. She stood, spellbound, studying the man's face depicted on the shield. The face was painted half red and half white. Glynna crossed the room to look at it up close.

"That is Señor Hunt's from when he lived with his mother's people," Maria said from the doorway.

The sound of Maria's voice behind her startled Glynna, for she'd been caught up in trying to understand the meaning behind the image on the shield. "Did Hunt paint this himself?"

"Yes. It scares me," she said. "I do not like it."

"What scares you?" Mimi asked as she came to stand beside the cook in the doorway. When she saw the shield, she was as intrigued as Glynna and went into the room to get a closer look. "Fascinating."

The sound of male laughter outside drew Glynna's attention, and she found herself wondering if it was Hunt. After viewing his shield, she suddenly wanted to see him. She went to the window to try to see what was going on outside. She had a good view of the outbuildings, the stable and the corrals, and from her vantage point, she could see two men in the main corral holding the reins of a very big, very skittish black stallion. They were trying to keep the horse under control, while another cowboy got ready to swing up into the saddle. She watched in fascination as the man mounted the horse and the others let go of the reins.

The sleek, beautiful beast was still for a moment and then suddenly tore into action, rearing and bucking. It twisted violently, trying with all its might to dislodge the man from its back.

As the horse spun around, Glynna got a look at the rider and realized it was Hunt. She was mesmerized as she watched the way he managed to stay in the saddle. With sheer grit and determination, Hunt held on for dear life, in spite of the stallion's best efforts to throw him.

A small cry of alarm escaped her when the beast gave a powerful lunge and Hunt went flying. She couldn't see where Hunt had landed, but she was certain that he must have been seriously injured from the force of being thrown. She started to hurry from the room.

"What is it?" Mimi asked, seeing her expression.

"Is something wrong?" Maria wondered. The young woman was pale and looked almost frightened.

"Hunt was trying to break a horse down at the corral. He was thrown. He must be hurt."

"I don't think you have to worry about Señor Hunt," the cook tried to reassure her. "He is a very tough man, and he's the best horseman on the ranch."

"But I didn't see him get up." Glynna hurried on.

Mimi and Maria went along with her just in case she was right. Accidents did sometimes happen.

Paul and Diego were just carrying the trunks in the front door as the three women passed them on their way out.

"Something wrong?" Paul asked, seeing Glynna's stricken expression.

"I'm not sure." Glynna quickly told him what she'd seen. "They're down at the corral."

Paul put down the trunk he'd been carrying.

"I guess we'd better go, too," Mimi said.

"If Hunt is hurt, I need to be there," Paul said, following along with her.

Glynna reached the corral ahead of the others and smiled when she discovered that Maria had been right about Hunt. He had not been hurt. He was standing off to the side knocking the dust off himself, looking positively surly, as the other two cowboys chased down the stallion and got a firm hold on it again. Glynna didn't understand why she felt such great relief at the sight of him uninjured, but she did. She stood there quietly, watching the standoff between man and horse.

"You ready to give it another try, Hunt?" Gib called out, chuckling. "Or are you going to call it quits for the day?"

"No," Hunt said in a growl.

"That's what I thought," Gib said, smiling broadly at his boss's determination. It was a rare day when a horse got the best of Hunt McAllister. He knew his boss wouldn't give up until he'd tamed the wild stallion.

Hunt didn't say anything more. He just strode up to where they were holding the bronc still for him. He was unaware that they had an audience now. He was concentrating only on what he had to do—and that was ride the stallion.

Glynna watched Hunt as he moved toward the proud horse. She was mesmerized by the way he walked—he was so confident, so determined. There was a fierceness about him, but there was also a steadiness that tempered it. It was a rare combination. She was surprised when, instead of immediately mounting up in challenge to the balking mount, Hunt went to look the horse in the eye. He began to talk to the stallion in a low, quiet voice. She tried to hear what he was saying, but she was too far away to make out his words.

The horse was standing rigidly in the center of the corral, held in place by Gib and Wes. It strained at the hold the two men had on it and rolled its eyes in terror. The stallion was ready for the danger it sensed was about to come, but at the sound of Hunt's voice some of the wildness and fear seemed to ease from it. A great shudder ran through the magnificent beast. It stood quivering, waiting nervously for what was to happen next.

Hunt ran a hand down the horse's powerful neck. He spoke softly to it. Then in one smooth move, he was on the animal's back. He nodded to Gib and Wes, letting them know to release their hold on the reins.

Glynna had never seen anyone mount so effortlessly. It was almost as if Hunt had flown into the saddle. As she watched, the horse sidled nervously around the corral. It resisted Hunt's domination, fighting against the tug of the reins and the pressure from his knees. The stallion bucked several more times, but each time the fury of its action lessened. It twirled unexpectedly in a circle, wanting desperately to rid itself of the unwelcome weight of the man on its back. It wanted to be free once more, but when the rider could not be dislodged, the horse stopped and stood near the middle of the corral, trembling in exhaustion. When Hunt gently tugged on the reins, the stallion responded.

"Ooooee!" Gib chortled in amazement, although he knew he shouldn't have been in the least surprised. "You do have a way with horses!"

"Must be that gentle touch of his," Wes said, grinning in approval at his friend.

"Wonder if that 'gentle touch' of his works on women?"

"We'll have to ask some of the girls down at the saloon and find out!"

"Even if it does work on women, I doubt he'd let us watch him do that kind of riding!"

Both men laughed as they watched their boss bring the stallion under his control.

Glynna's gaze was riveted on Hunt, watching him move in rhythm with the horse. She had been the only one standing close enough to the rail fence to hear the ranch hands' remarks. She felt her cheeks grow warm at the mental image their words evoked—of Hunt talking softly to a woman—of Hunt's strong hands stroking and gentling a woman. She turned away to hide her embarrassment and started back up to the house.

"Looks like I was worried for nothing," she said as she passed the cook. "You were right, Maria. Hunt is a very fine horseman."

*Glynna's gaze was riveted on Hunt, watching
him move in rhythm with the horse*

"That's a magnificent stallion," Mimi remarked, moving closer to the corral to watch Hunt handle him. She was in awe of his riding talent. She'd done some riding herself back east and considered herself a competent horsewoman, but her ability was nothing compared to Hunt's. "Does he plan to sell it?"

"Oh, no, ma'am," Gib answered, suddenly realizing that the others were there, looking on. "Hunt's going to keep this one for himself. He's worked too danged hard to break him."

"I can see why. That is one fine piece of horseflesh," Paul put in.

"That he is," Tom said, coming to join them from where he'd been watching from the stable.

Hunt had been focusing completely on the stallion, but he glanced up now to see the group standing at the rail. He caught sight of Glynna, too, but she was walking away. His gaze followed her. He hadn't realized that she had returned to the ranch already, and he knew he'd have to stay away from the house—and her—for the next couple of days.

The stallion must have sensed the sudden tension within him, and it moved skittishly beneath him, reasserting its independence.

"Easy, boy," he soothed, forcing his attention back to the half-wild horse. There was a lot of work to be done before the stallion would be completely broken. "I'm going to call you Warrior. You're strong and brave, and I think you're probably going to keep fighting me as long as you can."

The stallion pranced nervously at his words, proving Hunt right. He smiled and, keeping a firm hand on the reins, urged the animal to a trot around the corral.

Glynna was feeling a bit foolish as she returned to the house. She should have realized that Hunt was too good a rider to be injured while breaking a horse, but when she'd seen him fall and hadn't seen him get up, it had worried her. She wondered why she'd cared so much or why she found him so fascinating. True, he had saved her life and he had brought her sketchbook back to her, but he had never really been friendly. In fact, he'd almost seemed angry when he'd done it, and his attitude toward her since then had not been kind.

Frustrated by her own train of thought, Glynna thanked Diego for having taken her things upstairs and then went up to her room. She opened the trunk holding her supplies and got out her sketchbook. Pencil in hand, she pulled a chair over to the window and sat down in the light to draw.

An image of Hunt, fighting to stay astride the big stallion as it fought to be free of his control, was burned into her mind. She began to draw, intent on showing the stallion's power and Hunt's firm resolve to master it.

"Glynna?"

Mimi's call from outside the bedroom door interrupted her concentration some time later.

"Come on in."

Mimi opened the door to find Glynna engrossed in her drawing.

112

"What's captured your imagination this time?" Mimi asked as she went to her.

"What do you think?" Glynna was frowning as she studied the image of the untamed horse and determined rider.

"This is wonderful," Mimi told her as she stared down at the picture. The work was still sketchy, but showed great promise. Glynna had definitely captured Hunt's serious expression and the power of the horse. "You caught the feel of it so perfectly."

"Is the stallion good enough? He's such a beautiful animal, I want to make sure I do him justice."

"Oh, yes. I'll go away and let you keep working. This may turn out to be one of your best drawings yet."

Glynna gave her a quick smile and went back to work.

Mimi let herself out of the room and closed the door quietly behind her.

"You'll be joining us for dinner tonight." It was a statement, for Tom would brook no argument from Hunt as they stood in the stable together.

"I've still got a lot of work I should be doing," Hunt countered. He didn't want to defy his father or hurt him, but he did not want to spend any more time than necessary with their visitors.

"Then get at it, because I expect you to be at dinner. It isn't often we have company, and Maria's making a special meal. We're eating at six." With that, he left his son.

Hunt was frustrated, but respectful of his father's wishes. He put his aggravation to good use, working

113

hard the rest of the day. As six o'clock neared, he cleaned up and changed clothes and headed up to the house to join the others for dinner. As he let himself in, he could hear the conversation coming from the dining room. Glynna was laughing about something that had just been said, and the sound of her laughter touched him. It was genuine and heartfelt, and he realized there had been little reason for laughter or happiness in his life. He paused and listened to the conversation.

"And you say your paintings are very successful?" Tom was asking Glynna.

"Yes. It was a surprise to me when they began to sell so well, and people began to ask for them in the gallery. I was painting what I loved. I hadn't thought about painting to sell at that point. My trip to Colorado had been for fun. I'd wanted to see the Rocky Mountains and to paint them, but for my own pleasure. I had no idea that my work would create this much interest."

"That's wonderful."

"I'm so proud of her," Mimi said, gazing at Glynna fondly. "It's taken a lot of bravery on her part to do this. Her father was not supportive of our trip."

"Charles wasn't?" Paul was surprised by this news. He knew Charles.

"No, my father thinks it's a ridiculous thing for me to waste my time painting. He wants me to get married."

"I didn't know you were engaged," Paul remarked.

"I'm not—not officially, anyway. Although Papa has already handpicked the man for the job," she said with a laugh, though the laughter didn't reach her eyes.

"Here's Hunt now," Tom said with pride as Hunt strode into the room.

"Evening," Hunt said as he sat down in the empty chair. He found himself sitting directly opposite Glynna.

"We're glad you could join us," Paul told him. He'd met Hunt only a few times, but he'd always admired him, especially for the way he'd returned home to take care of his father. "We've been wanting to talk to you."

"Oh?" Hunt glanced at him questioningly.

"The horse you were breaking today was beautiful," Mimi said, meeting his gaze straight-on and giving him a friendly smile.

"Warrior's spirited, all right."

"The name Warrior suits him," Tom added approvingly. "He's a fighter."

"We were watching you," Mimi went on. "You did a fine job breaking him. Where did you learn to ride so well?"

He tensed slightly at the question, but answered quietly, "My father taught me."

Tom knew Hunt was avoiding the full truth, so he added it, unashamedly. "Hunt was a good rider as a boy, but it wasn't until he spent time with his mother's people that he became an outstanding horseman. I've never seen anyone who can sit a horse the way he can."

"Paul was telling us that you'd lived with the Comanche for a while. What was it like?" Glynna gazed at Hunt, studying him in this civilized social setting.

She tried to find in him the man she'd mistaken for a warrior only a few days before. He had seemed as savage and untamed as the land then. Sitting across from her now, he was as powerful as ever, but the power in him tonight was leashed, tightly controlled.

"Why do you want to know?" Hunt asked, stiffening imperceptibly at her question. He rarely spoke of those times.

"I saw your shield on the wall in the bedroom, and the painting on it is fascinating. Did you make that yourself?"

"Yes." He realized then that Maria had given Glynna his room to sleep in.

"It's wonderful. You did a fine job. I did several Indian paintings after I visited Colorado, and everyone in New York loved them. I was hoping I could visit a Comanche village while I'm here."

"You don't want to find yourself in a Comanche village."

"Why not?" She was puzzled.

"My mother's people are all on the reservation now. The only Comanche running free are the renegades, and you don't want to be anywhere near them."

"Paul mentioned that the other night. Are they really that dangerous?" She looked at both men.

"They're deadly," Paul put in. "They have raided in the area, and they've spared the lives of none of their victims. It's been tragic."

"Why do they leave the reservation?" Glynna asked in all innocence. "From what I'd read back home, I thought the government was providing them with all they needed. They have land and clothes and food.

116

Why are some of them off the reservation raiding?"

For a moment, she thought Hunt looked almost sad, but whatever the expression had been, it was quickly masked.

"The Comanche have roamed this land for hundreds of years, living off the buffalo. Then the whites came, and all that changed. The whites settled on the land and slaughtered the herds. They forced my mother's people onto the reservation. The officials promised them that they would supply them with what they needed, but what they really need is their freedom."

"It must be terrible for them, knowing their old way of life is over," Mimi observed.

"Their spirits are broken. It's a sad time, and that's what makes the renegades all that much more dangerous. They're men who believe they have nothing left to lose."

Silence fell over the table at his last statement. Maria came bustling in with food right then. They were glad to be distracted from their somber thoughts of the dangers of such desperate men.

Paul said grace, and the meal was delightful. Conversation turned to general topics and then back to Glynna's work and their plans for the next day.

"Diego will be ready whenever you are," Tom told them. "Do you have any idea what time you'd like to start out in the morning?"

"Early is good. In fact, if it's not a problem, I'd love to be out in the countryside by dawn."

"I'll tell Maria to be sure that he's got the horses saddled about half an hour before daybreak."

"We'll be ready," Glynna promised.

"I think I'd better call it a night. I need to check on the stock one more time," Hunt said, pushing his chair back from the table to stand up.

"Hunt," Mimi ventured, "would you mind if I went out to the stables with you? I'd love to get a close-up look at Warrior."

"Not at all."

"Glynna, are you coming with us?" Mimi asked.

Not ready yet to go up to bed, she quickly agreed. "I think I'll join you," Tom said.

The four of them left the house, leaving Paul behind to settle into the makeshift bedroom Maria had created for him in the parlor.

Their conversation was mostly about horses as they visited the stables. Glynna remained quiet, just listening to her aunt and Hunt discuss his work with Warrior.

"Well, I'm getting tired, so I think I'd better call it a night. Good night, Hunt," Mimi said, having enjoyed their discussion.

"Good night, Mrs. Randall."

"Please call me Mimi; everybody does," she invited with real warmth. She found she liked this quiet, serious young man.

"Night, son," Tom said, leaving the stable with her.

"Glynna, are you coming?" Mimi asked.

"I'll be right along. I just want to talk to Hunt for a minute."

"All right, dear."

Mimi and Tom went on.

Hunt could have sworn under his breath. He'd been tense enough when she'd accompanied them to the stable, but at least his father and Mimi had been there, too. He started to brush down Warrior, just so he'd have something to do with his hands.

"Hunt," she said, then waited until he looked up at her. She sensed he was aggravated about something, but she wasn't sure what.

"What?"

"I realized over dinner that I never really thanked you for all you did for me that day at the stage. That was very brave of you, and I appreciated it, even though I acted ungrateful at the time." Glynna moved closer to him.

Hunt stiffened at her nearness.

Glynna stood on tiptoe and kissed him on the cheek. "Thank you, Hunt."

With that, she smiled gently at him and left him to his work.

Hunt stared after her, the heady, sweet scent of her perfume still filling his senses. A deep yearning stirred within him. He fought it down. He took to brushing the stallion again. But even as he worked at the horse's coat, his thoughts were on Glynna and the knowledge that she would be sleeping in his bed that night.

Paul had remained behind at the house to unpack what he'd need for the next day. He was planning to ride out with the women and Diego and help keep watch over them. He did not know why he was going along. He certainly could have ridden out to several of the neighboring ranches, but he found he didn't want to be away from Mary Catherine. She was back in his life for at least a little while, and he didn't want to waste a minute of the time they had together.

Paul tried to tell himself that he had ended their relationship years ago, but the shock of seeing her again had brought back all the feelings he'd had for her. He wondered how he'd ever left her, and, once he'd gone, how he'd ever managed to stay away. She had meant everything to him—and that was why he'd deserted her.

Paul felt restless and decided to go outside. He stood on the porch for a while, just enjoying the cool quiet of the evening, and then he walked off into the night, seeking peace. He'd been having trouble finding any since seeing Mary Catherine sitting in his church pew on Sunday. It seemed even his most fervent prayers were going unanswered.

Mimi and Tom had almost reached the porch when Mimi noticed Paul coming out of the shadows.

"It's a beautiful night," Paul said.

"That it is," Tom agreed. "But this old soul needs to get some rest. I'll see you two in the morning."

"You're going to get up and see us off?" Mimi was surprised. He seemed so tired and weak that she knew it would be a great effort for him to rise that early.

"I'm up before daylight every day. There's too much to do on a ranch to lie abed. Good night."

Mimi started to follow him inside, but the sound of Paul's soft call stopped her.

"Mary Catherine." Paul said her name in low tones, not wanting her to go indoors just yet. He was frustrated that he'd been with her and Glynna for several days now, and he still hadn't managed to have a moment of privacy with her. This was his chance.

Mimi glanced back at him.

"Will you walk with me? We haven't had much of a chance to talk since you've been here."

She hesitated, her emotions in turmoil. This was Paul, and he wanted to be alone with her to talk with her. When she'd originally thought of traveling to Dry Creek, she'd hoped this moment would come, but now that it was here, she wasn't sure she really wanted to be alone with him. The truth was, she still harbored such anger at him that she was almost tempted to hit him. She wouldn't. She was a lady, first and foremost. She wouldn't use violence on a man of God, though heaven knew she was tempted. She only hoped that maybe he would explain to her tonight why he'd left her so abruptly and so coldly after a night of sweet loving all those years ago. She needed and deserved an answer.

Mimi turned away from the house and walked back to Paul's side.

Chapter Six

"I thought I would never see you again," Paul told Mimi quietly as she came to him. He thought about holding out his hand to her, but hesitated.

"I wasn't sure I wanted to see you," she answered honestly, and together they began to walk a little farther from the house so they could have more privacy to talk.

The darkness of the night surrounded them, and Paul stopped and turned to gaze down at her. In the pale moonlight, she looked exactly as she had in their youth.

"I've missed you, Mary Catherine." His voice was strangled.

The words touched her, but Mimi hardened her heart against them. She looked up at Paul to find a strangely tormented look on his face. She wondered why he was agonizing, when he had been the one who'd deserted her. She had been the one left alone. His abandoning of her had changed her life forever. She didn't understand why he had gone. She had never understood it.

"Why did you go, Paul?" she said, finally asking the question that had haunted her.

"I had to," he said. Then he added, "I'm sorry."

He wanted to reach out and take her in his arms. He wanted to somehow find a way to erase the pain he saw mirrored in her eyes. It seemed he had done nothing but hurt her.

"It's too late for apologies, Paul."

"Then why did you come? Why are you here?"

"For Glynna. She wanted to come to Texas to paint, and once we'd made our plans, I remembered that your sister had told me you'd built a church in Dry Creek."

"Glynna's a lovely girl," he told her. He realized then that he'd been harboring a faint hope that Mimi had come to Dry Creek because she'd cared enough to seek him out. Obviously it had been a foolish, ridiculous hope. He forced the thought away, forced himself to deal with reality. "Charles and his wife have done a wonderful job with her."

"I guess you didn't know that Victoria died years ago. Charles raised Glynna by himself."

"I'm sorry about Victoria."

"We all were."

"Charles has obviously been a very good father."

"He did do a fine job. It's just a shame that he's pressuring her to marry Edmund Moore."

"Who is he?"

"A very nice, very rich young man. Charles wants

to groom him to take over the business, since he doesn't have a son of his own to inherit."

"This Edmund sounds eminently suitable."

"Oh, he is. Glynna seems to think that she loves him, but I'm not so sure of that. She's still so young, and she has so much living yet to do."

"She sounds very much like you at that age." He smiled, remembering.

"You have no idea," she replied.

Paul looked at her again. This was Mary Catherine, the woman who had tormented him for years—haunting his empty days and long, lonely nights. He had missed her, worried about her, longed to hold her again, and now she was here, with him.

"You never married again?" he asked, directing their conversation back to more personal matters. He wondered why she hadn't started a new life for herself.

"No."

Mimi looked up at Paul. After his betrayal, she had never seriously considered the question of marrying again. There had been many men ready and willing to take her to the altar, but her trust in men had been destroyed. Her brother Charles had been the only man she'd ever relied on after Paul.

She'd had no need for a husband. She'd had her freedom, and money enough to allow her to enjoy that freedom. She'd seen absolutely no need for a man to complicate her existence.

There had been a time in the days after Paul had gone when she would have given anything to have him back, loving her. She had lost James to an untimely death. She had thought she'd found happiness a second time with Paul, only to lose him, too. Those had been terrible, pain-filled years for her, yet she'd managed to survive and had become stronger because of her ordeal. Mimi lifted her chin in an unconscious gesture of pride in her own survival.

Paul saw her look and couldn't stop himself from reaching for her to take her in his arms. It seemed that all he had ever wanted to do was protect her, and in protecting her, he had hurt her more than he'd ever known. Paul wasn't sure what to expect. He wasn't sure if she would come to him willingly or reject him. He knew he deserved the latter, but he prayed it wouldn't happen.

Though Mimi would not admit that she'd deliberately sought Paul out, the truth was that she had. She had wanted and needed to see him one more time.

With infinite care, Paul drew her to him. He lowered his head to capture her lips in a kiss. The feel of her in his arms, at long last, sent a powerful emotion pounding through him. Paul shuddered and deepened the embrace, parting her lips to taste her sweetness.

Mimi had held herself aloof from involvements with men since their parting. She had allowed herself to enjoy male companionship, but she'd never given in to the need for a sensual relationship. Paul's kiss, however, even after all this time, had the power to sweep her away—to make her forget herself and lose herself in the absolute wonder of his love.

Love.

It was that word that tore Mimi from his arms.

Love!

125

He didn't know the meaning of the word. She had loved him, and he had walked away without a backward look, without a care for her or her well-being. He'd disappeared in the middle of the night, and he'd never tried to contact her again.

She'd been a fool to seek him out here. She'd been a fool to think that the pain was completely gone. She'd been a fool to think that seeing him again wouldn't matter. Anger drove all desire from her.

"Mary Catherine?" Paul was confused by her sudden withdrawal. He'd wanted her, needed her—and then . . .

"Good night, Paul," she said, in a voice devoid of any emotion. She disappeared into the house.

Heavy sadness filled Paul as he watched her go. In all the time they'd been apart, he'd never stopped loving her, but he had hurt her too badly, caused her too much pain. He had seen it in her eyes again tonight, and the thought was a knife in his heart.

Paul suddenly needed a drink. It was these feelings that had driven him to whiskey and gambling in the first place after James's death. Whiskey had helped him forget the reason for his pain. If only for a little while, he knew he could find forgetfulness in the depths of the bottle.

But Paul knew losing himself in drunkenness was no cure. The only thing that had saved him—the only thing that had given him the strength to go on living—had been his faith. It had been God's forgiveness that had pulled him from the depths of despair, and he grasped for that saving grace now. He needed strength far superior to his own mortal weakness to help him through these difficult times.

Paul wandered farther from the house. He needed privacy to pray for that strength. He had to face his own failings.

The memories came to him in a rushing torrent as he gazed up at the sky. It was a beautiful night, clear and star-studded, but he saw no beauty. In Paul's mind's eye, he was reliving the day nearly twenty-five years before when he'd been at a picnic at a friend's country house in New York.

All his friends had been there, including the recently married Mary Catherine and James. No one had known that he'd loved Mary Catherine. He had been too shy then to approach her or tell her of his feelings. He had worshiped her from afar. When she'd fallen in love and married James, it had been too late to win her for his own, and he'd been devastated. He'd borne the loss in silence, no one ever suspecting his true feelings for her.

At the picnic, he had challenged James to a horse race. He'd wanted to prove, at least in the race, that he was the better man. He'd known his horse was faster and more surefooted, but James had always liked to brag that he was the best. Paul had been determined to prove to Mary Catherine in a roundabout way that she'd married the wrong man.

It had been childish of him to goad James into the race. He knew that now, but somehow he'd been driven to do it. He realized later that Mary Catherine hadn't been aware of any of his feelings for her. He had been furious that she'd married another man, and yet he'd had no one to blame but himself, for he'd never told her that he loved her, had never shown her that he cared.

That afternoon, he and James had raced. As he'd known he would, Paul had quickly established a good lead and was certain to win. James, a man who took everything in life as a challenge and never took any defeat lightly, wasn't about to give up. He'd taken a shortcut over rough terrain, and just as they'd been racing for the finish line, James's horse lost its footing and fell.

James had been killed instantly, right before his wife's eyes.

Paul had won the race, and, in winning, he had lost his soul.

To this day, Paul had never forgotten the look on Mary Catherine's face when she'd run to her husband and dropped to her knees beside him. She had been crying uncontrollably and begging him to get up. Paul had reined in and rushed to help, as had their other friends, but it had been too late. James had broken his neck in the fall.

The memory of that terrible day was with Paul always. No one had heard him taunting James and challenging him to the race. Only he knew what had been said between them. Only he knew the guilt he felt for pushing his friend to race to his death.

Paul had been there for Mary Catherine. He loved her and wanted to ease her pain. But the knowledge that he'd been the cause of her pain never left him. He'd helped her all he could, but the look on her face when she'd finally realized that James was dead was burned into his consciousness.

Paul had taken to drinking heavily that very day. After the funeral, he could bear it no longer. He'd left

New York for the West and had taken up gambling and drinking.

Looking back, Paul realized he'd had a death wish. He hadn't cared if he'd lived or died. He traveled aimlessly for some time before settling in San Francisco. He had engaged in a decadent lifestyle there, trying every vice.

And then Mary Catherine had come to him.

It had been his dream to have her, to love her, to make her his own. But he had forfeited that dream the day James died.

When she had sought Paul out on one of the "grand tours" she'd taken after emerging from her year of mourning, their time together had been heaven—and hell.

He still loved her. There had never been any doubt about that. She meant everything to him, and the thought that she had come to him had been pure ecstasy. But he could not hide from the guilt that plagued him. He could not hide from the darkness that tormented his soul.

Mary Catherine had told him she loved him while they were together, yet he still had not told her of his true feelings or proposed to her once she'd come to his bed. He'd felt he was betraying James.

It had been in a fit of drunken despair that he'd left her in the middle of the night after having made love to her for rapturous hours on end. Their coming together had been ecstasy. It had been perfect. It had been his dream come true, holding her in his arms, loving her with all his heart, mind, body and soul. Yet when he'd awakened in a cold sweat from the horror of his recurring dream of James's death, he had known he had to leave her. He could not live a lie. He could not take her for his wife, though it was the one thing on earth that he wanted more than anything else.

And so he had done the hardest thing he'd ever had to do. He'd denied himself that which he wanted most—Mary Catherine's love. He'd left her as she lay sleeping. His note of explanation to her had been short and cold. He never made another effort to contact her. She was better off without him.

Images of what his life had been since they'd parted played in his mind as Paul found a quiet place to pray.

It was a long time later when he returned to the house and went to bed.

It was in the predawn darkness that Glynna and Mimi were roused from their sleep. Glynna had been sleeping lightly, for she was excited about the day to come. She was up, dressed and ready to go in a very short time. She was waiting out front with Diego when Mimi came downstairs.

"Are you ready to go now?" Diego asked. He had loaded all the painting supplies on their packhorse and he was ready to mount up if they were.

Mimi glanced back toward the house and wondered where Paul was. He'd said the day before that he would be riding with them, and she'd expected him to be outside ready to go, too.

"Is Paul coming?" she asked Diego.

"No, ma'am," he answered. "He rode out a little while ago. He said it was important that he use this time to visit the other ranches nearby."

Mimi quickly hid her shock at his words. She asked herself why she was surprised by Paul's leaving. She knew she should have expected as much from him. She busied herself with getting ready to ride out. "Then let's get going. The dawn's going to be here before we know it."

Glynna had sensed that her aunt was distressed by Paul's absence. She found it a bit strange, too, that he would say he was accompanying them and then decide against it at the last minute. She knew that her aunt and Paul had spent some time together the night before, and she wondered what had transpired between them.

Telling herself that it was none of her business, Glynna mounted her horse. As she did, she caught sight of Hunt standing in the stable door, looking their way. He looked so ruggedly handsome in his tight denim pants, light-colored shirt and boots that her breath caught in her throat. When he did not call out in greeting or acknowledge her in any way, her spirits sank. After their conversation the night before, she'd thought they were coming to be friends.

Determined not to let him think that she cared whether he noticed her or not, Glynna put all thoughts of Hunt from her mind and concentrated on the adventure ahead. She'd traveled for days and covered hundreds of miles just for this moment. She was bound and determined to take full advantage of her time painting. Nothing was going to stop her from having a wonderful adventure today—not even the thought that Hunt McAllister acted as if he didn't know she existed.

Glynna did not look back in Hunt's direction. She

did not see him watching her until they had gone from sight.

Dawn found her working at her easel on the bank of the river that crossed the Rocking M. The sky was a rainbow of color: vibrant aqua, streaked with varying shades of white, pink and gold. She was trying her best to recreate the beauty on her canvas, but there was little time. She had to work fast.

Silence surrounded her. The quiet seemed to stimulate her creativity. She let her imagination reign as she listened to the sound of the river's flow and the chirping of the birds as they welcomed the new day.

The sun was high in the sky and it was growing warm when Glynna finally stopped and stepped back to study the canvas. What she'd managed to capture was a good start, but she planned to work on it more back in her room later.

"How are you coming along?" Mimi called from where she sat resting in the shade.

"Fine. I'm ready to stop for now. I can finish it later," Glynna answered, cleaning her brushes. She was more than pleased with their excursion.

With Diego's help, they packed up their things again and headed back. As they rode in, they saw two strange horses tied to the hitching rail in front of the house.

"Looks like we have company," Diego told them.

As they dismounted, Tom appeared on the porch. Glynna and Mimi were surprised to see that the sheriff and one of the deputies from Dry Creek were with him.

"I told you they'd be back around noon," Tom said

to Sheriff Dunn. "How did it go, Glynna?"

"It was wonderful, Tom. Thank you." Carrying her paint box, she was already heading for the porch. "Hello, Sheriff Dunn. I hadn't expected to see you again. Is something wrong?"

"Miss Williams, Mrs. Randall," he said, nodding to them. "Deputy Spencer here has been talking to Hank and they've come up with an idea. It sounded good to me, so I thought we should ride out here and talk to you about it."

Glynna was puzzled. "Of course. You know Aunt Mimi and I will do whatever we can to help you catch that gang."

"I was hoping you'd say that," the sheriff said with a smile.

"Let's go on inside and sit for a while, so he can tell you what he's got in mind," Tom suggested. "Diego, you go ahead and take care of the horses and the rest of Miss Glynna's things."

"Yes, Señor Tom." Diego hurried to do as his boss had ordered while the rest of them went indoors.

"Miss Williams," the sheriff began.

"Please, call me Glynna."

"Glynna," he repeated with a smile, "Hank was telling Deputy Spencer that you're an artist. The two of them got to thinking. They were wondering if you could remember what the members of the gang looked like and maybe draw some pictures of them for us?"

Glynna frowned and glanced quickly at her aunt. "They were wearing masks, so we could see only their eyes. I remember a little, but—"

"If you could do sketches of them, it sure would

give us a better chance of catching them. We could make up wanted posters and get them out for people to see."

"I'll help you, Glynna," Mimi offered, hoping that between the two of them they could come up with fairly decent likenesses of the outlaws.

"Would just drawings of them with their masks on be good enough?"

"Whatever you can remember about them and get down on paper would be more than we have right now," Sheriff Dunn told her, his frustration obvious. "They're a slippery bunch—dangerous, too. I want to put them behind bars where they belong."

"How soon do you want the drawings?"

"How long would it take you to do them?"

"Half an hour, maybe?"

"That fast?" The deputy was impressed.

"Let me see what I can do. I'll have to get my sketchbook. I left it up in my room."

She went upstairs and returned to join them a short time later, sketchbook and pencil in hand. "I'd better sit at the table. It will be easier for me that way."

Mimi went with her, while the men waited expectantly in the other room. Glynna and Mimi hovered over the sketchbook as she tried to re-create the faces of the men who'd so terrified them that day. It took the better part of an hour, but at last she finished the final picture.

"You can come take a look now," Glynna called out.

They were beside her quickly, staring down at the four drawings she'd spread out on the table.

"This one was called Will," she told them as she pointed to the picture of the man who'd thrown her paint box away as if it had no value. She would never forget him. "Then there was Chuck and Eli. Eli seemed to be the leader. The other man stayed off to the side and kept a gun on everybody. He was the one who drove off the horses."

Sheriff Dunn, Deputy Spencer and Tom studied the drawings for a long minute.

"I don't recognize any of them right off," the sheriff said in disappointment. He looked up at Glynna. "I was hoping I'd recognize one of them right away."

"I understand. They're a mean bunch. It would be good if they were locked up."

"It would be very good."

"How is Hank, Deputy?" Mimi asked, thinking of the wounded guard.

"He's up and moving now."

"When you get back to town, please tell him 'hello' for us."

"I'll do that."

"Can I pay you for these pictures?" Sheriff Dunn asked.

"Heavens, no, Sheriff. I hope they help."

"I do, too."

The lawmen left then, taking the four drawings with them. They planned to put wanted posters up around Dry Creek, and they were going to have copies of them printed and sent to neighboring towns, too.

Tom, Glynna and Mimi enjoyed a light lunch together, and Glynna told their host all about her outing that morning. She showed him the painting she'd started.

"This is very good,". Tom said, impressed with her use of color. "Was it really that pretty this morning?"

"It was prettier," she admitted. "I plan to work on it some more this afternoon."

"You did a fine job. It's no wonder they're asking for your paintings back in New York City."

Glynna actually felt herself blushing at his praise.

"I was a little surprised when I got up this morning and found Paul all ready to ride out," Tom said, making conversation.

"We were, too," Glynna said.

"Last night, I know, he was planning on going with us. I don't know what caused him to change his mind," Mimi added.

"I guess he just had to move on."

"He does do that," Mimi said, keeping her anger out of her voice. She told herself she didn't care about Paul Chandler.

"Have you known the reverend for a long time?" Tom asked.

"Oh, yes, for more than twenty-five years. He was a friend of my husband's back in New York."

"Paul's a good man. The people around here truly appreciate him."

"It's good to know that he finally found his calling," Mimi said with a smile that seemed a little tight. She hoped Tom didn't notice.

"He wasn't the preacher type back in New York City?"

At that, Mimi had to laugh. "Oh, no. In his early days, he enjoyed his gambling and liquor."

Tom chuckled. "Well, ol' Paul hasn't given them up completely. That man can still play one mean hand of poker."

"Paul's beaten you, has he?"

"Quite a few times." He was grinning. "Once, he needed some more money for building the church, so he came into the saloon and challenged us to a pretty high-stakes poker game. We were thinking that he was only a preacher man and that he couldn't be any good at gambling. We learned our lesson real quick."

"How did he do, raising money for the church?" Glynna asked, laughing at the thought of the reverend winning handily at the gaming tables for a godly cause.

"As soon as he had the amount he needed, he quit the game."

"Paul always did cut and run," Mimi remarked.

"He may have cut his losses, but he didn't run this time," Tom said. "He got that church built in real good time, and the gambling men respected him for it, too. Most of them show up pretty regular for his services."

"He does give an interesting sermon," Glynna said.

"Heard him, did you?"

"Sunday morning, and he was very good. The church was full," Glynna replied.

"People appreciate a good preacher, somebody who knows what he's talking about. He's not just shouting at them and telling them that they're all going to Hell. He's speaking from experience. They respect him, because they know he understands what they're going through."

"Where's Hunt?" Mimi asked, directing the conversation away from talk of Paul. The way she was feeling right then, if Tom said another nice word about Paul, she just might scream. She was rather proud of the fact that she was managing to control her emotions so well.

"He and Gib are out checking on the herd today, but they should be back before too long."

Glynna was glad her aunt had asked. She had to admit that she'd been wondering where Hunt was, too. She'd looked for him as they'd returned, but had seen no sign of him out by the stables.

"Is he going to work with Warrior again tonight?" Mimi asked. She certainly wanted to be there to watch, if he was.

"I'm sure he will. He's determined to saddle-break that horse. Warrior's a stubborn one, though. He's giving Hunt a run for his money, that's for sure," Tom told them, smiling as he thought of how hard his son had been working with the stallion. "Most horses don't give Hunt this much trouble."

"It probably means that Warrior is the smartest horse he's ever broken."

"I believe you're right about that," he agreed. "That's why he wants him. That's why he's being so patient with him. He appreciates a good piece of horseflesh, and Warrior's the best we have on the ranch."

They went upstairs to rest for a while after eating lunch, but Glynna was too excited even to think about lying down. She wanted to keep working. While they'd been talking to Tom, she'd come up with the most wonderful idea for the painting she was going to give him, and she wanted to get started on it right away.

Dragging her easel and supplies with her, Glynna let herself quietly out of the house. She didn't want Tom to hear her and possibly follow her. This picture was going to be a surprise. A shady spot a short distance away gave Glynna the panoramic view of the ranch house and outbuildings she'd wanted, so she went to work. Her inspiration was to create a painting of the Rocking M, with Warrior in the corral, and in the center of the picture, like a painting within a painting, she was going to put a portrait of Tom.

It was going to be her most ambitious effort so far, but she thought she could do it. She certainly was going to try.

Chapter Seven

Hunt smiled to himself as he rode the powerful stallion around the corral. The headstrong mount had finally been curbed. He'd just spent several hours working with him again, and he was satisfied with the progress they'd made. He dismounted finally and led Warrior into the stable.

"Do you think he's fully broken now?" Mimi asked as she followed Hunt to watch him rub Warrior down.

"After today, yes," Hunt told her, giving her a slight smile. In spite of his intentions, he was coming to like this elegant woman from back east. She was pretty and intelligent, and she always talked to him as if she truly respected and valued his opinions.

"He's worth all the work you've put into him."

Hunt stroked Warrior's neck. "I know."

"If you ever want to sell him, I'll be first in line."

"No, I've waited too long to own a horse like this. I won't be selling him."

"If you change your mind, just let me know," she told him, smiling. She saw the pride in his expression as he cared for the horse, and knew he'd never part with the stallion. "I'll see you at dinner."

As she came out of the stable, Mimi caught sight of Glynna working at her easel a short distance away. She thought about going to speak to her, but knew she was concentrating and needed to work uninterrupted. There would be time later to see what she'd created this afternoon.

Hunt finished tending to Warrior and started out to the bunkhouse to get cleaned up and ready for dinner. It was near dusk, and he was tired. It had been a long day.

Hunt noticed Glynna in the distance at her easel. Though common sense told him to keep going, he found himself heading toward her. He told himself he was going over to speak to her because he hadn't seen any of her work except for the sketches that first day. He walked up from behind her and managed to get a look at her work without Glynna knowing he was there.

"You are good."

The sound of Hunt's voice so close behind her startled Glynna. She'd been concentrating and hadn't noticed him approaching.

"Oh—Thank you," she said, turning to him, her paintbrush still in hand. She was surprised to see him, and her smile of welcome was a bit tentative.

For some reason, Hunt definitely had the ability to unsettle her.

Hunt moved nearer and stood beside her, gazing down at the painting with open interest. Before him on the canvas was a panoramic view of the ranch, and it was impressive. What touched him the most, though, was the portrait of his father staring back at him from the center of the picture. Somehow, Glynna had managed to capture the true essence of his personality. There was a glimmer of good humor shining in his eyes, and the half smile that was only his curved his mouth. The portrait within the painting was a wonderful effect.

"I knew from your sketchbook that day at the stage that you had talent, but this is wonderful," he said in true appreciation. "I've never seen anything like this before."

"Thanks. Your father's a very special man, and I wanted to give him a present for letting Aunt Mimi and me stay with you."

"That's very kind of you." Hunt looked at her, and for the first time, he smiled.

His smile affected Glynna profoundly, and her heartbeat quickened. She stared up at him, amazed by the transformation of his features. He had gone from serious and almost threatening to gentle and good-natured in just that instant, and she found him completely and devastatingly appealing.

"You should do that more often," she said in an almost breathless voice.

"Do what?" His smile disappeared immediately, and he frowned, not understanding what she meant.

"Smile," she answered gently.

"Oh." He did not smile.

"Would you like to see what else I've been working on?"

He nodded, and she went to unwrap the canvas she'd put carefully aside. She'd brought along the picture of Hunt that she'd started, just in case she felt the inspiration to do more with it while she was outside.

"What do you think?" She held up the painting for him to see. "That's how you looked the first time I saw you."

Hunt was shocked. He was staring at a likeness of himself—bare to the waist, riding at top speed and leaning low over his horse's neck. Glynna was a far better artist than she realized. She was insightful. She had captured the warrior in him. The man in the image was not Hunt McAllister, but Lone Hunter.

"I am going to remember this trip for the rest of my life," she was saying as she awaited his reaction.

"Why?"

"Because I've had more adventures in the last few days than in all my twenty-three years."

She sounded so pleased by the thought that he was amazed. She could have been killed that day—if not by the longhorn, then by the outlaws who'd robbed the stage before he happened upon her, and she thought it was an adventure. He had never met a woman like Glynna before. And what was puzzling him even more was that she knew the truth about him, and she was not terrified of him or repulsed by his Comanche side.

Hunt dragged his gaze away from the painting to look at her. Though he didn't mean to, he found himself grinning at her again when he noticed a smudge of blue paint on her cheek. She'd obviously tried to wipe it off, but had only succeeded in smearing it.

"Why are you smiling again?" She was curious, wondering what he found funny.

"Here." He reached for a paint rag that was lying near the easel and moved to wipe away the paint on her cheek.

Glynna's breath caught in her throat at his gesture. There was something intimate about it.

The memory of Gib and Wes's conversation the other day in the corral about whether Hunt's touch was gentle enough to tame a woman came to her and left her tingling with sensual awareness of him. Hunt was standing so close. . . .

She lifted her gaze to his and was mesmerized by the tenderness she saw mirrored in the depths of his eyes as he concentrated on wiping off the offending paint.

Hunt was transfixed as he touched her. Glynna was smart, talented and beautiful. She was everything a man could want in a woman, and she was looking up at him with such invitation. . . .

For a fleeting instant, an image of Jenny crossed his mind, but it quickly vanished. This was Glynna, not Jenny. He was a man now, not a boy.

Unable to help himself, Hunt let the cloth slip from his hand, and he reached out and cupped her cheek. With infinite care, he bent to her, his lips seeking hers.

For an instant Hunt's kiss was tentative, precious, cherishing, as he hesitated, waiting for her reaction to his boldness.

And then Glynna responded, giving a soft whimper as she lifted her arms to encircle his neck. Her unspoken invitation fired Hunt's carefully controlled desire. He crushed her to him with a low growl of pure male sensuality.

Hunt forgot that it was still partially daylight outside. He forgot that he had vowed never to care for another white woman. He deepened the kiss, his mouth moving over hers hungrily as he held her enfolded in his embrace.

Glynna was swept away by the power of his need. She reveled in the intimacy of being in his arms. It thrilled her to know that beneath his harsh, seemingly unfeeling exterior, Hunt was a passionate man. The knowledge was heady, as was his heated caress. She trembled, enraptured by the hunger he displayed. She had never felt anything like the excitement that was coursing through her as Hunt held her close. She had no thought of Edmund at all.

It was Tom's call from the house that dinner was ready that shattered the beauty of the moment.

At the sound of his father's voice, cold, hard logic returned to Hunt. It drove him from Glynna's embrace. He moved away from her, needing to put distance between them. His breathing was strained as he fought to bring his raging desire under control.

Hunt stared down at her in the sweet shadow of dusk, seeing the high color in her cheeks and the glow in her eyes. He wanted to reach out to her and take her in his arms again. He wanted to hold her and touch her. He wanted to claim her for his own in all ways.

When he realized the direction of his thoughts, he

gave himself a fierce mental shake. He kept a tight rein on himself as he waited for his desire to cool.

As Hunt's passion ebbed, fury replaced it. He was angry with himself for his weakness in letting his guard down. He knew better than to touch Glynna. Caring for her would ultimately mean only trouble and pain.

Hunt tried to understand how he could have forgotten himself so completely. Hadn't he overheard her say at dinner that she was all but promised in marriage to a man back home? Slowly he realized that, somehow, Glynna had managed to get too close to him. Her paintings were testimony to the fact that she understood him too well. He took another step back, even farther away from her.

Watching Hunt, Glynna could see his harsh control slip back into place, and she shivered at the change in him. The man who had shown her such passion and desire had disappeared. It was almost as if he'd never existed. In his place stood the cold, unfeeling man she'd dealt with for the last few days. She found herself wondering if she'd imagined the passion of his kiss and his touch.

"I'm sorry. That shouldn't have happened," he said in a voice that reflected no emotion of any kind.

His words were like a slap in the face, and Glynna stiffened resentfully. "Why not?"

"Because you're a white woman and I'm Comanche."

"You're a man, Hunt McAllister."

He looked at her dispassionately, wanting to keep her away from him, not wanting her to know how her kiss had truly affected him. Didn't she realize he was protecting her, as well as himself? "To the rest of the world, I'm a half-breed. Now go on up to the house, before something happens that you'll regret."

"It already has!" she lashed back at him. She was sorry now that she'd kissed him, and sorry that she'd let herself think, for even a moment, that underneath his unfeeling exterior, he might be a different man.

She gathered up her things and walked away.

Her words had cut Hunt, but he told himself he felt nothing. He watched her disappear inside, then returned to the stable.

A short time later, after she'd washed up and come back downstairs for dinner, Glynna learned that Hunt wouldn't be joining them for dinner that night. She was actually glad. She felt like a fool, kissing him that way. She didn't know what had gotten into her. She loved Edmund, didn't she? She was all but engaged to him. What was she doing responding to Hunt that way, especially since she knew he didn't care one bit about her? Glynna turned her thoughts to anything and everything but Hunt McAllister.

"Do you have any idea where Diego is taking us tomorrow?" Glynna asked Tom as they were finishing the meal.

"I think up a little farther north. There's a good view of the canyon there. You'll enjoy it."

"You have a wonderful place here," Mimi told their host. "You must be very proud of what you've built up, and through your own hard-work."

"It's home," he said, contented finally after so many years of sadness. "Especially now that Hunt's back with me. It's good to have him here. Now that

147

I'm not feeling so well, I don't know what I would have done without him."

"Children are definitely a blessing," Mimi responded, smiling at Tom as she glanced at Glynna.

"It's a shame you never had any of your own," Tom remarked, looking at Mimi.

Mimi went slightly pale at his words. "Yes. My husband died before we had the opportunity to have a family, and I never wanted to marry again after losing him."

"She all but raised me after my mother died," Glynna said, smiling at her. She'd seen Mimi's sudden look of sadness and wanted to let her know how much she appreciated her. "She would have made a fine mother."

"Why, thank you, sweetheart. That's very kind."

"It's just the truth. Well, if you two will excuse me, I'm going on upstairs now," Glynna added, leaving her aunt and Tom to their conversation. "It's been a very long day, and I want to rest up for tomorrow."

"Of course, dear," Mimi said.

"Good night," Tom told her.

Glynna went to her room and locked herself in, then threw herself on the bed, disgusted. She had tried not to think about Hunt during dinner, but he'd dominated her thoughts all evening long. She didn't want to think about the man. He was arrogant and hateful, and if she never saw him again, that would be fine!

She was glad they would be leaving soon. The way she was feeling right now, their departure couldn't come soon enough to suit her. Angry with herself for feeling this way, Glynna got up and stalked to the window. She knew she had no one to blame but herself. She was the one who'd wanted to come to Texas. Well, here she was—in Texas. It was a beautiful night, but she didn't notice. She saw only the darkness.

Giving a strangled sigh, Glynna sank down in the chair and stared at the paintings she'd left propped against the wall. Hunt stared back at her from the canvas. He looked dangerous, and she realized that he really was a danger to her—he was a danger to her heart.

Glynna gave a shake of her head and told herself she should have remembered—Hunt was different from any man she'd ever known. He'd fascinated her from the first. Why else would she have drawn so many sketches of him? Why else had he haunted her thoughts? And then, when he'd kissed her. . . .

Glynna tried to tell herself that she was overreacting, but the memory of Hunt's embrace was emblazoned on her mind and her senses. His kiss had been perfect, everything she'd ever dreamed a lover's kiss should be—tender, passionate, exciting.

Edmund's kiss had never affected her this way, and Edmund was a perfect gentleman—sophisticated and suave. He treated her like a lady and would make the perfect society husband. He was wealthy and good-looking and—Glynna frowned. Though she was listing all of Edmund's good points, it occurred to her that she hadn't thought of him very often, and she hadn't missed him at all during her travels.

Again, the memory of being in Hunt's arms returned. She remembered the rapture of his touch and his kiss. It had been heavenly.

Glynna tried to look at her situation logically. She wanted to analyze the reason why she'd responded so wildly to Hunt. Was it his very untamed nature that drew her to him? Did she believe that she could tame him? Was he the ultimate challenge for a woman? Or did she truly believe that inside his cold exterior a passionate, warm man did exist and she wanted to prove it? What was there about Hunt that attracted her so strongly?

Certainly Hunt was handsome, but she'd known many good-looking men. None had affected her this way. Hunt was strong. Her mind drifted, and she remembered how wonderful it had felt to be crushed against his hard, muscled chest.

Glynna gave a disbelieving shake of her head at the direction of her thoughts. Trying to be rational wasn't helping at all.

Sighing again, she looked around the room, wondering what to do for the rest of the night. She was certain she wasn't going to be getting any sleep. With only one more day left to finish the painting for Tom, Glynna decided to work on that. She turned up all the lamps in the room and went to work.

It was in the wee hours of the morning when Glynna finally put her brushes aside, turned down the lamps and went to bed. But sleep still proved elusive—the heated memory of Hunt's kiss denied her any rest.

"What was so important you couldn't have dinner with us?" Tom demanded as he found his son working in the stable.

"I had a lot of work to catch up on, and I can always get something to eat later."

Tom looked irritated. "You know the women will be leaving soon."

"Good."

He was surprised by Hunt's reaction. "They haven't bothered you any. Why do you resent their being here so much?"

"I don't care if they're here or not." Hunt looked up at his father. "I just don't have time for socializing."

"You should make time. You can't spend your whole life with cattle and horses."

"Why not? They're a lot more agreeable than people."

Tom grunted in irritation over his son's jaded view of life. He understood where it had come from, but he knew if Hunt continued this way and made no effort to change, he was going to end up alone in the world, for his own health was not good. He wasn't going to be around too much longer.

"You're going to have to work things out for yourself one day, son. Not everybody's like the Rosses were. You've got a home here, and you do have friends on the ranch and in town. That's a lot more than some people can say."

Hunt continued to work. "I know. I just had a lot to get done tonight, so I thought I'd keep at it."

"Well, good night." Tom wasn't fooled, but he didn't press his son any further. Hunt was his own man now. He made his own decisions. He had ever since that night, when he was fifteen.

*　　*　　*

Mimi had retired shortly after Glynna had gone up to bed. She'd fallen asleep right away, but awakened early, long before she needed to be up to meet Diego. Paul . . . He'd been in her thoughts since the night before. He'd disappeared again, just as he had all those years ago. She had no idea if he would return in time to accompany them back to Dry Creek. She supposed that if he didn't show up by the time they got back from their painting excursion that day, they would have to make other arrangements for someone to accompany them into town. In a few days' time, they would be on the stage leaving Dry Creek forever.

Mimi knew the trip had been worth it. She'd learned what she needed to know. Paul might have changed outwardly—he'd given up drinking and gambling to excess—but in his heart he was still the same man. She'd never understood the demons that drove him, and she had come to believe now that she never would. At least now she knew that she hadn't failed their relationship in any way. The problem and weakness had been Paul's. She'd been guilty only of loving him. And he hadn't had the ability to love her back.

Having discovered that he hadn't married over the years since he'd left her, Mimi now believed that he wasn't capable of loving anyone or being totally committed to a relationship. The knowledge was a relief, and gave her some solace. The reason Paul had left her was still a mystery, and she accepted now that she would never know why he'd gone.

In truth, it didn't matter anymore. Though she had loved him, and still did to some extent, Mimi made the conscious decision never to let Paul Chandler cause her pain again. If she saw him once more before they left, that would be fine. And if he was gone from her life forever, so be it.

Mimi smiled in the darkness. Her burden was lightened. She felt freer than she had in ages.

Mimi's thoughts turned to Glynna. Her niece was having a grand adventure, and Mimi was fortunate to be with her. It was exciting to see everything through Glynna's artistic eyes. She was a brilliant, talented young woman, and Mimi was proud of her.

Though she was eager for a new day and a new adventure with Glynna, Mimi knew it was still far too early to think about getting up. She remained in bed, enjoying the quiet, at peace with her life.

Painted Horse sat at the campfire with the other braves who'd joined him in his raiding party. They had been gone from the reservation for weeks now and were enjoying their freedom, such as it was. They had found no buffalo to hunt. The animal that had fed their people for centuries no longer ran freely across the land in massive herds. The white hunters had nearly wiped it out of existence. So instead of hunting, Painted Horse and his warriors had taken to paying the white man back for his treacherous, lying ways. They had begun to raid the white man's homesteads, wanting to drive these new settlers from their ancestral lands.

Painted Horse closed his eyes as the peyote he'd been chewing began to take effect. The plant gave him visions that foretold the future and helped him to lead his braves safely on their raids.

The others gathered there watched closely as their leader swayed slightly, moved by the power and clarity of what he must be seeing in his vision.

It was hot. The sun was high overhead and the air was still. Before him, the canyon stretched for miles. There were no buffalo. The land was empty of all life.

He heard the sound of a horse coming and looked back to see a beautiful white woman on a magnificent black stallion. She was riding as swiftly as the wind. As she neared the canyon's rim she reined in, and the stallion reared.

"The hunter will come," she announced. "Do no harm to the prize he seeks. His vengeance would be swift and deadly."

She turned the horse and raced away.

He watched her until she had disappeared from sight and his vision faded.

Painted Horse awoke from his dream. He did not know who the hunter was and he didn't care.

"I will find a great prize tomorrow when the sun is high," he announced to the others.

They had been waiting to hear what he had seen. They all knew Painted Horse's visions were prophetic.

"Where, Painted Horse?"

"Near the canyon. We will find it there."

"What is it we seek?" Crouching Wolf asked. Some of the other braves followed Painted Horse without question; he did not.

"The finest stallion of all. We will find him soon."

The others were pleased. Horses were the best spoils of their raids.

They waited for the first light of day, then started for the canyon.

Mimi never did get back to sleep, and when Maria came to wake her, she was already dressed and ready to go. Glynna came downstairs shortly after. They hurried to eat the breakfast Maria had prepared for them while Diego loaded the packhorse. They rode out as the sky was lightening in the east, heading north for the canyon area.

Neither Glynna nor Mimi thought to look back at the ranch house as they rode away. They were both looking forward to the adventures of the day. They were excited about what was to come.

It was near midday. Painted Horse had ridden ahead of the others to scout the area and had come upon the small campsite. Moving quietly, he'd gotten close enough to see the white people there. He'd immediately recognized one of the two women as the beauty who'd ridden the stallion in his vision. His ability to foretell the future was powerful indeed!

The warning in his vision came to him:

The hunter will come. Do no harm to the prize he seeks. His vengeance would be swift and deadly.

Painted Horse considered the warning as he looked for the stallion. He saw only three riding horses and the packhorse tied there. He frowned. It was the stallion he wanted. The stallion was the prize he wanted to claim for his own in this raid!

He turned his attention back to the woman. She

was the same dark-haired beauty who had spoken in his dream. She would lead him to the stallion. Through her, he would get what he wanted.

He continued to watch as the woman, along with an older female and the boy who was with them, loaded boxes on the back of the packhorse. Obviously the boxes were of great value, for they handled them with care.

Painted Horse backed silently away. He was ready to meet the rest of his raiding party and attack.

Glynna's mood was quiet as she packed up the last of her painting supplies. She paused to take one final look at the canyon. The view was as majestic as Tom had said it would be. She had been painting continuously since they'd reached the lookout point that morning, and she was pleased with the results. As breathtaking as the scene was, though, she was sure that some New Yorkers would think it was her imagination, and not nature, that had provided the panorama.

It was not her painting, though, that caused her mood to be so thoughtful. It was knowing that the next day they would be returning to Dry Creek and would soon be catching a stage out of town. She would be leaving the Rocking M, and Hunt McAllister, forever.

Glynna had told herself repeatedly that she was being absolutely ridiculous. Even so, she wondered why she found herself almost constantly thinking of the man. Why couldn't she get Hunt out of her thoughts? She was only tormenting herself. Hunt had made it perfectly clear that he wanted nothing to do with her. She had no doubt whatsoever that he would be glad to see the last of her.

"Glynna? Are you ready to move on to another site?" Mimi called to her from where she stood by the packhorse.

Jarred from her thoughts, Glynna turned away from the beauty of the wilderness to join her aunt. "I'm coming."

It was as she looked in Mimi's direction that she saw the attackers—renegades riding straight for them.

Glynna had time to scream only once.

Chapter Eight

Diego heard Glynna's scream and knew she was in trouble. He turned from the packhorse, only to find a renegade charging straight at him. He grabbed for his gun. It was the last thing he would ever do. The Comanche had his rifle ready, and he shot the boy before he had time even to take aim.

"Diego!" Glynna cried.

Terror filled Glynna as she realized what was happening, but her need to go to Diego's aid overcame her fear. She started toward the fallen youth, but did not make it. The renegade swooped down upon her and grabbed her from behind, yanking her up onto his horse's back.

"Glynna!" Mimi had been hurrying to help Diego, too, when she saw the warrior grab Glynna. Her heart-rending scream sounded in the wilderness.

Glynna wasn't going to give in easily to her captor.

She erupted in fury. With all her might, she swung her paint box at him, catching him in the face. The sharp corner of the wooden box cut him near his eye. Bleeding heavily, he released her with a grunt of pain. She fell roughly to the ground and lost her hold on her box and all her supplies.

"Run, Glynna!" Mimi yelled to her.

Glynna frantically got back to her feet and started to run to where Mimi knelt over Diego.

Mimi had reached the boy and dropped to her knees beside him. She'd carefully turned him over, hoping to help him, but had quickly realized the bullet had found its mark. Diego was dead.

Tears streaked down Mimi's face as she looked up toward Glynna. Pure terror filled her as she saw yet another warrior charging up behind Glynna.

"Look out!" she shouted, terrified. She jumped up to try to save her niece from certain harm, drawing her derringer from her pocket. No one was going to hurt Glynna if she could help it!

Glynna had thrown her paint box aside and was racing at top speed toward her aunt and Diego. Before she could reach them, though, a second renegade closed in on her. He snared her and threw her, facedown, over his horse's back in front of him.

"Let me go!" she screamed, kicking and fighting.

The Comanche's grip was unyielding and painful. There was no chance to escape. The motion of the horse was brutal, knocking the wind from her, as the renegade galloped through their campsite.

"Glynna! No!"

Mimi saw the way the warrior was manhandling her niece and lost control. She had learned how to

159

shoot at a hunt club back home, but had never seriously considered the possibility of actually killing another human being until now. Swinging around, gun in hand, she was ready. As the warrior holding Glynna rode by, she fired at him. She was horrified when she missed, and he raced off out of sight. Furious, she threw the derringer aside and ran to get Diego's gun. She grabbed it up and fired, hitting another of the attackers squarely in the chest. He fell from his horse and lay unmoving.

At the sound of the gunshots, Crouching Wolf wheeled his horse around. He was angry at the way the younger woman had hit him and had managed to break free. He was still bleeding from the cut above his eye and wanted revenge. He had seen the older woman and had thought about taking her captive, but when she went for the other gun and shot Coyote Man, he knew it would be too difficult to disarm her. He rode at her from behind and shot her.

Mimi had just been taking aim at another of the raiding party, when suddenly the bullet slammed into her back. She cried out Glynna's name once more in heartbroken sorrow before collapsing, unconscious, to the ground.

Glynna heard the sound of the shots and then heard her aunt scream her name. She tried to lift her head to see what had happened, but her captor hit her, forcing her to remain still. She heard him shout something to the other warriors who were with him as they galloped away. The pounding pace was jarring, bruising her. Fear for her aunt's safety and terror for her own filled Glynna, and she began to cry.

In her hysteria, she thought of Hunt and the day he'd saved her from the longhorn. What an innocent she'd been to think that he had meant to harm her! These renegades were deadly savages. Hunt had proven himself a hero by rescuing her. These Comanche with their hideous war paint had killed Diego and done something terrible to Aunt Mimi. This time she was truly in danger. This time she was facing the real thing. Glynna hung on for dear life. She had no choice.

Two of the warriors went back to claim their dead companion's body.

When they'd secured him to one of the riding horses, they raced away from the carnage, crossing mile after mile of Texas terrain.

Hours passed before they stopped to rest. The warrior who'd taken her prisoner threw Glynna to the ground. She lay sprawled there, staring up at him in terror as he dismounted and walked toward her. The renegade was not a tall man, but he was powerfully built. His bare torso was heavy and hard with muscle. His face was painted with black war paint in a hideous pattern that gave him a ghoulish look. His hair was parted down the middle and worn in two braids. He was clad in only a breechclout and moccasins. He looked like something out of her worst nightmare, and she trembled at the thought of what he was going to do to her.

Refusing to show him her fear or cower before him, Glynna started to get to her feet. She wanted to face him bravely, but he shoved her back to the ground. He didn't say a word, but reached down to grab her hands. Glynna fought him, kicking and twisting, but he held her easily, and quickly tied her wrists in front of her. He pushed her back down then and went to talk with the others.

Glynna watched them carefully and tried to hear what they were saying, but they spoke the Comanche tongue, and she couldn't understand them. She was tempted to make a run for it, but there was nowhere to go. The land around them offered no shelter, no place where she could seek refuge. She was a captive. Glynna reasoned that if the warrior had wanted to kill her, he would have done it by now. So she remained where she was, waiting to see what was going to happen next.

The warriors tended to their dead friend, burying him beneath a pile of rocks. Then they all painted their faces black. That done, they were ready to ride again.

Her captor returned to Glynna and motioned for her to get up. He mounted his horse and pulled her up to sit in front of him.

Glynna tried to keep her mind blank. She told herself that if she didn't think about what was actually happening to her, she would be all right—for a while. Thoughts of Aunt Mimi and Diego came to her, and she prayed that they were alive.

The raiding party rode off again at top speed. They headed farther and farther away from the Rocking M, farther and farther away from any hope of rescue.

It was late, almost dinnertime, in fact. Tom was starting to wonder what had happened to Diego and the women. They had been due back several hours before. He was standing on the front porch, keeping watch, when Hunt approached.

"You look worried. Is something wrong?"

"I hope not," Tom told him. "I was just keeping a lookout for Diego. He should have been back with Mimi and Glynna by now."

Hunt frowned and looked out across the land. "Where did they ride to today?"

"Up by the canyon. We thought that would be the best place for Glynna to do some painting."

Hunt was frowning as he considered the lateness of the hour. "Think I'd better ride out and take a look around before it gets too dark?"

"Thanks, son. It couldn't hurt. The odds are there's nothing to worry about, but I'd feel a lot better knowing you were out there checking on them."

Hunt nodded and started back toward the stable. "I'll take Wes and Gib with me, too."

"I'll be waiting right here to hear from you."

Hunt told the other two hands what they had to do, and the three men were soon saddled up and ready to ride. Hunt saddled Warrior for the trip. The three men made sure they were armed before they rode from the ranch. They were hoping there wouldn't be any trouble, but they never rode out unprepared, just in case.

Tom watched them leave from the porch.

"Señor Tom? Where are they going?" Maria asked as she came to stand with him.

"I was getting a little worried about your boy, Maria. He was due back with the women from the canyon a while ago, and I haven't seen hide nor hair of them."

"You think something happened?" She was suddenly concerned.

"I hope not." His tone was edgy as he tried to smile at her.

"Dinner is ready if you want to go ahead and eat. I can save the rest for the others when they return."

"Save mine, too. I'll wait and eat with them. I want to hear about their adventures today."

"Yes, Señor Tom." Maria went back inside as Tom settled in on the porch. She hoped her son returned soon. She hoped they were just running late.

Hunt had no trouble finding their tracks from that morning. They followed the trail for over an hour, keeping watch for some sign of returning hoofprints. They grew more and more concerned with each passing mile, though, for there was no indication that the women had come back toward the ranch. It was near dusk when they stopped for a moment.

"Do you think we missed them?" Gib wondered. "Do you think we should head back and see if they're already there?"

Hunt was staring quietly off into the distance. "No. Something's wrong. Let's keep looking."

They traveled on, still following the trail. They had just come to the top of a small rise when they saw the carnage in the campsite below. They could see Diego lying unmoving on the ground, and a woman lying facedown nearby.

"Oh, God," Wes said in a strangled voice.

Hunt wasted no time on talk. He put his heels to Warrior's sides and raced toward the site. Horror filled him at the thought that Diego and the women had been massacred by renegades. He sawed back on his reins, bringing Warrior to an abrupt stop, dismounted and was running toward the bodies before either Wes or Gib could follow.

One look at Diego told Hunt all he needed to know. The boy was dead—had died instantly. He went on, dreading what he would discover next. He feared the other victim was Glynna, and he girded himself for what was to come. Only when he reached the woman's side did he realize it was Mimi who lay facedown in the dirt, a bullet wound in her back. Pain tore at Hunt. With infinite care, he knelt beside her and slowly, carefully took her in his arms and turned her over.

Hunt was shocked when she gave a soft groan. He had felt certain that she was dead. It was nothing short of a miracle that she was still alive.

"Wes! Gib! She's alive!" he shouted to the others, and they were beside him in an instant.

Mimi's eyes fluttered open. There was torment and agony in the depths of her gaze as she looked up at Hunt. It took nearly all her strength to lift one hand and clutch desperately at his arm.

"Hunt . . . renegades . . ." she whispered. Pain and panic were etched in her features as she fought to stay conscious. She had to tell him what had happened. She had to let him know about Glynna. "They took Glynna—"

The exertion exhausted her, and Mimi lost consciousness.

"She was shot in the back," Hunt told them. "She's still alive, but I don't know for how long."

"What do you want to do?"

Hunt carefully laid Mimi back down so he could examine the gunshot wound. "She needs to see a doctor. You've got to get her back to the ranch tonight. I don't know if she'll live until morning without help."

"What are you planning?" Gib knew his friend.

"The renegades took Glynna. I'm going after them, and I'm going to bring her back."

"She could already be dead, Hunt," Wes said, trying to talk sense into him. He saw the determination in Hunt's eyes and feared for his safety.

"If they'd wanted Glynna dead, they never would have taken her in the first place. They would have killed her here. I'm going after them."

Gib understood. "What do you need?"

"Nothing. You just take care of Mimi." He stood up.

"We'll get her back to the ranch as fast as we can," Gib promised.

Hunt started for his horse, and it was then that he saw Glynna's sketchbook and pencil lying in the dirt. He picked them up, holding them as if they were precious, then stowed them in his saddlebag. A terrible resolve filled him. He had to ride out now; there was little time left before dark.

"Hunt, wait," Wes called out.

He looked back toward them.

"Be careful," Gib said.

He raised one hand in farewell, then was gone, following the cold trail that led to the north and west.

Wes looked at Gib. "If anyone can find her, Hunt will."

They hurried back to where Mimi lay. Her wound

was serious. They dressed it as best they could, and they were glad she was unconscious. They could only imagine the pain she would have been in, had she been awake.

It was nearly dark when they were finally ready to start back to the ranch. They'd found the packhorse nearby and were using it to transport Diego's body. It would not be easy going for them, and they hoped the grievously wounded Mrs. Randall would survive the trip.

It was dark, and that told Tom everything he needed to know. He'd been hoping that Hunt would return quickly, having met the others on the trail on their way back in. It wasn't to be. Something had happened to Diego, Mimi and Glynna—something bad.

"No sign of them yet, Señor Tom?" Maria asked, trying desperately to control her fears about her son's fate.

"Not a thing, Maria. I don't like this. I don't like this at all."

"Neither do I," she said, sighing raggedly. "Maybe a horse got away from them and they had to ride double, and it's slowing them down."

"I hope that's it. If so, Hunt and the boys will find them and bring them right on back home where they belong."

He tried to sound positive for her sake, for he could tell the worry was taking its toll on her. He knew what it felt like to think your only son might be in serious trouble and not be able to help him, and he could sympathize.

Maria went back inside, wanting to keep busy. If she was doing something, she wouldn't have time to think.

"We're almost there," Gib said to Wes as he caught sight of the lights from the ranch house in the distance.

"How's she doing?"

"She's alive," was all he answered. He'd been holding Mimi in front of him for the duration of the trek, and praying the whole time that she'd make it until they got her back.

"That's about the best we could hope for. As soon as we get her inside, I'll ride for town and get the doc."

"Good. She's going to need him. I hate like hell to be the one to tell Maria about Diego. You know how she feels about the boy."

Both men fell silent as they faced what they knew was coming. It was going to be one of the hardest things they'd ever done—telling Maria that she'd lost her son. Both men would have gladly avoided it, if there had been any other way. They cared about Maria and would never have done anything to hurt her. She was a kind and gentle woman who deserved better than what life was handing her.

They heard the sound of shouts coming from the house, and they knew someone had spotted them. There was no quickening their pace, though, for fear of injuring the wounded woman even more. When at last they reined in, Tom and Maria were there, watching and waiting anxiously.

"What happened? Where are the others?" Tom demanded, coming toward them.

"My Diego? Where is he?" Maria was frantic as she followed him.

"And Glynna?"

Wes dismounted and immediately went to Maria, trying to block her from seeing Diego's body on the packhorse.

"Maria." His tone was agonized as he began to tell her what had happened.

She looked up at him. Understanding dawned in her expression as she saw his torment, and with the understanding came horror.

"*No!*" she cried. She pushed forcefully past him. She stopped suddenly when she saw the body of her son. "Oh, God—"

Maria let out another scream and ran to her dead child. Wes stayed with her to comfort her as best he could.

"Diego's dead?" Tom asked solemnly, looking up at Gib.

"Yes, and Mrs. Randall here was shot, too. Can you help me get her down?"

Tom hurried to his side. Gib carefully lowered Mimi into his arms.

"Did renegades do this?" Tom stared down at her. Her face was ashen, and she was barely breathing.

"Yeah . . ."

Gib dismounted and took Mimi back from Tom.

"Where's Hunt, and what about Glynna?" he asked as they started toward the house.

"Mrs. Randall was conscious when we found her. She told Hunt that renegades had taken her niece."

"So Hunt went after them," he said, already certain of what had happened.

"He rode straight out. He said he wouldn't be back until he found her."

"Hunt will find Glynna," Tom said solemnly. "Let's get Mrs. Randall inside. One of you had better ride for the doc right away."

Concerned about Maria, Tom glanced back to see Wes walking with her, his arm around her shoulders supporting her as they came to join them.

"I'll go for the doc," Wes offered.

Gib entered the house with Mimi and carried her straight into Tom's bedroom. With great care, he laid her, on her stomach, on the bed. Wes took Maria into the parlor, while Tom went to see to Mimi's injury.

"Give me your knife," he said to Gib.

Tom cut Mimi's blouse away so he could get a good look at the wound.

"Tell Wes to head out for the doctor now." There was urgency in his tone. "There's no time to waste."

Gib hurried out into the parlor where Wes was sitting beside Maria trying to comfort her.

"Wes. The boss says you need to ride to town right now. Get Dr. Peterson back here fast."

Wes stood up to go.

"Maria, I'll be back in a few minutes," Gib promised as he walked Wes outside.

He saw him off to town, then tended to Diego's body. He returned to the house to stay with Maria, while Tom did what little he could to help Mimi.

Nearly two hours passed as Tom kept vigil by the bedside, watching over Mimi and tending to her needs. It was late when they heard the sound of horses riding in. Gib ran outside to see if it was Wes returning or Hunt coming back with Glynna. He found it was Wes returning with Dr. Peterson.

"Hurry, Doc; she's not doing well," Gib called out as the doctor reined in.

The doctor dismounted and rushed inside.

"She's in here," Tom said as he entered the house.

Dr. Peterson hurried into the bedroom to find the wounded woman lying unconscious on the bed.

"Wes told me she'd been shot by renegades."

"They were attacked up by the canyon," he explained.

"They?"

"My cook's son, Diego, was killed, and there's another woman missing."

Dr. Peterson looked grim at the thought of a white woman taken captive by the Comanche. He quickly set to examining the injured woman. There was little doubt that he had to get the bullet out of her as fast as possible.

"I'm glad she's unconscious," he told Tom as he finished his examination. "I'm going to have to dig deep to get that bullet out."

"How bad is it?"

"She's very weak, and she's lost a lot of blood. I don't know if I can save her or not."

"What can I do?"

"Pray," was his solemn answer.

Tom nodded and left the room. He wondered where Paul was. The preacher had said that he would return to the ranch to escort the women back to town. He knew they were scheduled to leave the following morning, and yet there was no sign of him. They could have used his prayers. Glynna, Mimi and

Diego needed all the prayers they could get.

Tom found Maria sitting in a chair in the parlor, staring off distantly, her expression blank. Wes and Gib were sitting quietly with her.

"What did the doc say?" Wes asked quickly when he saw Tom.

"He's got to get the bullet out. He said we'd all better start praying. I was just wishing that Paul was here."

The two men nodded in silent agreement.

Maria looked up at him, her face tear-ravaged in her sorrow. "Señor Tom, what will I do? My boy, my Diego—he's dead."

Tom went to her. "I'm sorry, Maria."

She was too emotionally exhausted to respond. She could only rock back and forth, and cry her son's name.

"Do you want to go to your room and lie down for a while?" Tom suggested.

Maria nodded weakly, and Tom helped her up. He walked her to her room and stayed with her until she was resting quietly. Leaving Maria, he went upstairs to the rooms Glynna and Mimi had been using to see if he could find their home address. He found the name and address he needed in with Glynna's things, and he was just starting from the room when he glanced over at the two paintings she'd left propped up in the corner.

Tom found himself looking at his own image, and he was amazed by Glynna's talent. He looked at the other picture and stared in appreciation at the painting of Hunt. His son looked fierce and warriorlike. Tom smiled grimly to himself. Tonight, more than ever before, they needed Hunt to be that warrior. They needed his skills to find the ones who'd murdered Diego, shot Mimi and kidnapped Glynna. Staring at the image of Hunt, Tom knew his son could do it.

He left the room to find Wes and Gib. He was going to send one of them back to town, for they needed to send a wire to Glynna's father in New York City and let him know what had happened.

Gib agreed to make the trip this time, and Tom and Wes went outside to see him off. As he was about to leave, they heard another rider coming in.

"Do you think it's Hunt coming back with her already?" Wes wondered, hopefully scanning the dark countryside for some sign of the rider.

"It's only one horse. If it is Hunt, then it means something terrible has happened to Glynna," Tom said worriedly.

All three men were greatly relieved when they found it was Paul returning.

"Thank God, you're back!" Tom called out.

Paul was startled by his shout. While he'd been gone, he'd agonized over the time he had spent with Mary Catherine. He'd been sorry that he'd run from her again. He had made up his mind to come back to the ranch and tell her everything. He was going to be totally honest with her and tell her the complete truth of his feelings for her. Now, though, he sensed from Tom's welcome that something was very wrong.

"What's the matter?"

"We were hoping you'd get back tonight. There's been trouble . . . big trouble."

"What happened? Where are Mary Catherine and Glynna?" he asked as he reined in and dismounted in a rush. He hurried to stand before the three of them, looking from one to the other, wanting answers to his questions. At their awkward silence, his expression became strained with unspoken terror.

Finally, Tom spoke. "They were out by the canyon today, and renegades attacked them."

"No." The heartsick denial was strangled from him. He should have been with them. He never should have let them ride out with just the young boy to protect them. Guilt seared him. "Mary Catherine? Glynna?"

Tom quickly went on to tell him what had happened. "The boy Diego was killed. Mimi was shot—"

"Is she alive?" He was horror-struck

"Barely. The doc just got here from town. He's working on her now."

"What about Glynna?"

"She was taken captive. Hunt's gone after her."

"Dear Lord." Paul's thoughts were chaotic. Guilt over his own failure to protect the women assailed him. Pain over Diego's death stabbed at him. If he'd been with them, he might have been able to stop it. If he'd only been there, he might have been able to save the boy.

"I was just sending Gib into town to wire Glynna's father. His name is Charles and he's in New York City, right?"

"Yes. That's him. He'd want to know. He'll come as soon as he gets word."

Tom nodded to Gib to go into town and send the telegram.

"Where's Maria?" Paul asked, forcing his personal feelings aside, turning to the faith that had guided his life during the last twenty years. "I want to see her."

"Come on in. She was resting in her room, but I know she'll want to talk with you. Diego was all she had. He was her whole life."

Paul followed Tom to Maria's room in the back of the house. She was awake and got up to speak with Paul.

Tom left them alone, knowing they needed privacy. He returned to the parlor to wait for Dr. Peterson.

It was nearly half an hour later when the doctor emerged from the bedroom. His clothes were covered with blood, and his expression was serious.

Tom stood up as he came into the parlor. "How is she, Doc? Is she going to live?"

He shook his head wearily. "I don't know, Tom."

"Did you get the bullet out?"

Peterson nodded. "Yes, but it wasn't easy. She's one tough lady, or she would have been dead by now."

Paul had heard the doctor's voice, and he and Maria came out of her room to speak with him.

"Hello, Rev. Chandler," Peterson greeted him.

"How is she?"

"Alive, but only barely. We won't know for hours whether she's going to make it or not."

175

Paul stiffened at his statement, fearing the worst. "May I see her?"

"For a minute. She's unconscious."

Paul left them and walked quietly into the bedroom where Mimi lay on the bed. His heart constricted at the sight of her. She was deathly pale and unmoving. She lay on her stomach, her face turned toward him, her eyes closed and dark circles beneath them. The doctor had covered her with a blanket, and only the slight rise and fall of it gave any indication that she was alive. Paul dropped to his knees beside the bed. He wanted to touch her, to hold her, to tell her that he loved her.

"Mary Catherine . . . I love you," he said softly, knowing she couldn't hear him, but not caring. He had to say these things before it really was too late. "I'm sorry I ever left you. I'm sorry I hurt you."

He fell silent as he searched for a way to phrase what was in his heart. Tears burned his eyes as he gazed down at her. She looked so fragile, so helpless, so beautiful. He had lost her once, had deliberately thrown away her love. He could not lose her again— not now—not to death.

"Mary Catherine, listen to me. Don't leave me. I love you. Give me another chance, and I'll spend the rest of my life proving it to you."

There was no response from her. Paul did not move away, but stayed there beside her. He reached out and brushed a lock of hair from her ashen cheek. Her skin felt almost cold to his touch, and he began to shake.

Paul bowed his head and began to pray, fervently, harshly, demandingly. God answered all prayers. He knew God did! He wanted to make sure God heard this one and knew how important it was. He prayed for grace for Diego's soul and peace for Maria's torment. He prayed for Glynna's safe return. And he prayed that Mary Catherine would recover.

He did not ask for anything for himself.

With God's grace, if she lived, he would be given the opportunity to earn her love again.

Paul remained beside the bed for a long time. Then he returned to Maria to minister to her pain.

The night was long.

Chapter Nine

Until that night, Hunt had never fully appreciated all the lessons his uncle had taught him during the years he'd spent with his mother's people. Striking Snake had been a fierce taskmaster, and Hunt had learned much under his tutelage. He was glad now for the humiliation he'd suffered at his hands, learning the Comanche ways. His uncle's demands had forced him to be his best, to hone his skills.

His tracking ability was serving him well now. The night was cloudless and the moon was bright, so he was able to continue to trail the raiding party. Glynna's life was at stake. He could not stop until he found them.

Warrior was proving to be as fine a mount as Hunt had hoped. The stallion had not faltered. They rode on through the night, their pace slow but steady as they followed the signs that indicated the renegades' passage.

Hunt's thoughts were dark. Guilt haunted him. The responsibility for what had happened fell to him, and he knew it. His father had come to him first and had asked him to take the women out, and he had refused. His father had needed him, and he had let him down.

If he had been with Glynna and her aunt, things would have turned out differently. He would have known the renegades were near. He would have known how to fight them off when they'd attacked. He could have prevented this disaster.

Diego had been little more than a boy. Certainly, at thirteen, he'd been no match for warriors on a raid. His death proved that. And now Glynna was a captive and her aunt lay seriously wounded, possibly dying—and it was all because of him. He'd been afraid to be near Glynna. He'd been afraid of what he'd been feeling for her and had wanted to stay away from her.

Glynna . . . The memory of the night before, when he'd found her painting near the house, returned to him, and a muscle worked in his jaw as he struggled to control his emotions. Glynna was beautiful, and holding her and kissing her had been heavenly. He'd wanted her, yet he'd deliberately sent her from him. Even now, he knew it had been the right thing to do. There had been no point in allowing himself to love her. There could be no future for them together.

But Glynna was going to have a future. He was going to see to it. That was why he was following her, and that was why he was going to free her from her captor.

Hunt urged Warrior to a faster pace. He knew the raiding party would not rest, and he was many hours behind them.

Dawn was brightening the sky in the east, and still the raiding party rode on. Glynna was past exhaustion as she sat slumped before her captor on his mount. The miles they'd covered through the long night had seemed endless, yet they had not stopped to rest. She understood far better now why the white ranchers feared the Comanche so much. These warriors knew the land. The handled their horses far better than anyone she'd ever seen, with the exception of Hunt, and they were deadly and without conscience.

Thoughts of Aunt Mimi and Diego assailed Glynna, and she wondered how they were. She feared they had been seriously injured or maybe even killed, and she wondered if she would ever see them again. Her aunt was so special to her. Aunt Mimi had always been there for her, never missing her birthdays or holidays. Glynna's mother had died when she was an infant, and Aunt Mimi had been the one she'd turned to whenever she'd needed female advice or comfort. Thinking of home, she thought of her father and wondered, too, if she would ever see him again. Her heart ached with loneliness and despair.

Glynna remembered the tales about other white women who'd been taken captive and had survived. They had told of how they had suffered torture and abuse at the Indians' hands. Glynna hoped she was strong enough to survive.

She had come to Texas for adventure. She had wanted to see the land and the people. She had wanted to experience the Wild West and paint it, but she'd never wanted this. The stage robbery had been traumatic enough. Now she was a renegade's captive.

Thoughts of Hunt came to her then. In her mind's eye, she relived the moment when he'd swept her up in his arms to save her from the bull, when he'd returned with her sketchbook, and when he'd smiled the other night. His kiss had been the most wonderful thing she'd ever experienced. He had been so exciting, so warm and passionate . . . but then the man who had shown her such tenderness had vanished, and he'd turned cold and indifferent again. She wondered if he'd learned yet about what had happened to them that day. She wondered, too, if he'd care.

Dr. Peterson came out of the bedroom and went to seek out Tom and Paul in the parlor.

"Is she better?" Paul asked the minute he saw the physician.

"No. There's been no change," he answered. His expression was grim.

"What more can you do for her?" Paul pressed. He had been sitting by Mimi's side for most of the night and was growing more and more worried with each passing hour. She'd shown no signs of improvement.

"I've done everything I can. Now it's just a matter of waiting it out."

"How long?" Tom asked.

"There's no way of knowing. It could be hours, or it could be days. By all rights, with what she's been through, she should be dead by now. A lot of *men* couldn't have lived through what she just did."

"Mary Catherine's a very strong woman," Paul declared. "She'll make it."

"I hope you're right, Reverend," the doctor said, understanding his need to remain optimistic, even in the face of such devastating odds.

"I do, too," Tom put in.

"Gentlemen, I'm going to go back to town. There's nothing more I can do for her. It's in God's hands." He met Paul's gaze. "If you need me, just let me know."

"Thanks, Doc," Tom told him as he walked him from the house.

Paul stood in the middle of the parlor, searching for the strength he needed to get through the rest of the day. In just a few hours they would be burying Diego. Gib and Wes had built the coffin for the boy overnight.

"I guess we'd best get ready for the burial," Tom said as he came back inside. His expression was sad. His shoulders were bent with sorrow.

"I know. It's going to be a long day."

Paul lifted his gaze to look out the window. In the distance, he could see two of the ranch hands digging Diego's grave in the grove of trees that overlooked a small creek. It was a shady, peaceful place. Diego would find his final rest there.

The knock came at Charles Williams's study door, interrupting the serious conversation he'd been having with Edmund about business interests. He looked up in irritation as he called out, "What is it?"

"A telegram was just delivered for you, sir," the maid answered. "It's from Texas."

His scowl disappeared, and a smile lit up his face. "It must be from Glynna," he said to Edmund. Then he called out to the maid, "Come in, come in."

The gruffness of his tone disguised his pleasure at the thought that Glynna had taken time to wire him. They hadn't parted on good terms, and he'd been missing her. He couldn't wait for her to get back home, where she belonged.

The door opened and the diminutive maid hurried in to hand him the telegram.

"Thank you, Trudy."

"Yes, sir." She rushed from the room and closed the door on the way out.

"I'm glad she's contacted you, sir," Edmund began, though he was more than a little irritated that Glynna hadn't bothered to contact *him* in all the time she'd been gone. He planned to marry her just as soon as she returned from this crazy trip of hers. She was not only a beautiful young woman, but her family's wealth was equal to his own. Theirs would be a fine match. The thought of the Moore fortune coupled with the Williams estate was very impressive. "I've been missing her."

"So have I," Charles admitted as he tore open the envelope and started to read. "What the hell?" he roared, surging to his feet and knocking his chair over backward. "And Chandler's there, the son of a bitch!"

"What's wrong? Who's Chandler?" Edmund was shocked to see Charles go deathly pale.

"Good Lord, man!" He ignored Edmund's questions, looking down at him but not really seeing him. His expression was tortured. "I have to leave for Texas now! This morning! *Trudy*!" he bellowed, tossing the wire carelessly across his desk toward Edmund as he ran to open the study door.

"Charles, has something happened to Glynna?" Edmund demanded, startled by his mentor's reaction to whatever news was in the telegram.

Charles motioned for him to read the wire as he disappeared out into the hall.

Edmund couldn't imagine what news could have caused such a terrible reaction, and he snatched up the telegram and began to read.

Dear Mr. Williams,

Your daughter and sister were introduced to me by our mutual friend Rev. Paul Chandler. They came out to stay at my ranch so Glynna could do some painting.

Earlier today, your daughter and sister were attacked by renegade Comanche while they were on an outing. Mrs. Randall was shot and grievously wounded. Your daughter was taken captive by the raiding party. We are searching for her now and doing all we can to get her back.

You can reach me at the Rocking M ranch in Dry Creek, Texas.

Tom McAllister

Edmund stared down at the wire in disbelief, then dropped it back on the desk and followed Charles from the study. He found the older man rushing up the staircase.

"What are we going to do?" he asked.

"I'm going to Texas to take care of my sister and find my daughter!" Charles declared.

"I'm going with you," Edmund said quickly.

"There's little time to pack. I've already sent a man to the train station to check the schedules. Go home, get what you need and be back here in an hour."

"Yes, sir!"

Edmund hurried from the Williams mansion. He wondered how long it would take to get to Dry Creek, Texas. He wished he were there right now. He wished he'd married Glynna before she'd even thought of going out west again. He'd been a fool not to forbid her to go. She was, after all, going to marry him. Surely she wouldn't have dared to defy him the way she'd defied her father.

Worry ate at him. The Comanche had taken her! Anything could have happened to her by now! She could even be dead!

His emotions were strained. He hoped to God that they found her soon. He hoped when they reached Texas that they would find out she'd already been returned and was unharmed. The thought of his future bride being held by hostiles was disgusting to him.

It was late in the afternoon when the raiding party finally stopped. They'd found a secluded campsite near a small creek and were settling in for a rest.

Glynna had no idea what they were saying to each other, for they were speaking their native language, but she sensed all was not easy in the group. It was plain to her that the warrior who'd taken her captive was the leader, but there was another man who seemed almost threatening in the way he talked to him and gestured wildly in her direction. Glynna decided to be as quiet as she could, in hopes that they would ignore her and leave her alone.

Crouching Wolf was angry as he glared at Painted Horse. "I want the woman."

"She is my captive. You will not touch her," Painted Horse told him.

"She is only a white woman. What is she to you? I had her first!" He looked over to where the woman sat on the ground. He had never had a white woman, and he wanted this one.

"She escaped you, Crouching Wolf," Painted Horse taunted. "She is my woman now. She is the woman in my vision. I am to guard her and keep her from harm. She will bring me the greatest prize ever."

"The horse in your vision? I will give you a horse for her."

"The stallion in my vision was more magnificent than any you've ever seen. Somehow, through her, he will be mine. Only then will I give up the woman."

"I will give you five horses for her!" Crouching Wolf countered, thinking Painted Horse wanted more.

"No. She is mine."

Crouching Wolf was furious, but said no more. He would wait, and when the time was right he would take the white woman for his own. He walked away from his leader in disgust.

Painted Horse watched Crouching Wolf go and knew the matter was not ended. The other warrior was headstrong and violent, and he did not like being denied.

They still had another two days' ride to their main camp, a very small village hidden deep in the recesses of a canyon to the west. Painted Horse knew the site would not be safe forever, but it was as close to a haven as he could find for now. Certain that they were being followed, he realized they could only afford to rest for a little while before pushing on. They would feed and water their mounts, sleep for a short time, then ride on again.

He looked up in Crouching Wolf's direction and saw the warrior deep in conversation with some of the others. He did not trust Crouching Wolf; the sooner they reached their safe haven, the better he would like it.

Returning to his captive's side, he handed the woman a small piece of dried meat, then sat down near her.

"What are you going to do with me?" Glynna asked, trying not to sound too terrified, but knowing she failed miserably. She doubted he knew English, but she thought it was worth a try to find out.

Painted Horse ignored her question and did not look at her. She did not need to know anything of what was to come. It was better to keep her ignorant of his plans. If she was afraid of him, she would be easier to control.

Glynna tried to keep from trembling as she ate the

small portion of food he'd given her. She only hoped that someone had discovered what had happened to her and that they were searching for her even now.

Mimi regained consciousness slowly, as if swimming upward from a deep, black vortex. She groaned softly as she became aware of herself and her surroundings. She knew she was lying on her stomach on a bed, and that every inch of her body was screaming in pain. For a moment she had no idea who she was, where she was or how she'd even gotten there—and then her memories returned.

Her eyes flew open as she recalled the horror of Diego being killed in the Comanche attack. She remembered seeing Glynna running toward her. She also remembered grabbing up the gun and shooting one renegade, and then the memories ended in a blur of agony.

"Glynna," she called, frantic to know what had happened to her niece, if she was safe, but her throat was parched and the word was barely a whisper.

Tears filled her eyes and traced paths down her cheeks as she tried to garner enough strength to call out. Surely someone was near. Surely someone would help her. She had to find Glynna! She had to keep her safe!

"Glynna!" Again she tried to cry out her name, stirring a bit at the effort it took.

This time she managed a hoarse whisper, and Paul heard her.

Paul had been standing at the window looking out, waiting and hoping for a change for the better in Mimi's condition. He'd been staying by Mimi's bedside keeping watch over her since the doctor had left the day before.

As each hour had passed, he'd grown more and more fearful that she would not recover, that she would slip away from him before he had the chance to explain all that had happened and to tell her that he loved her.

"Mary Catherine!" Her name escaped him in a moment of complete joy. He was on his knees next to the bed in an instant, taking her hand, gazing into her eyes.

Mimi saw Paul and wondered vaguely why he was there with her. He'd left her without a word. Why had he come back? She managed a frown as she tried to think, but the pain was too great and she could remember only the terror of the attack and her fear for Glynna.

"Glynna?" she whispered.

Paul was leaning close so he could hear what she was saying.

"Don't worry about Glynna right now. Just concentrate on getting well," he said tenderly. He did not want to tell her the bad news that her niece was missing. She needed all her strength to win the battle to stay alive; he didn't want to say anything that would demoralize or hurt her.

Mimi would have none of it, though. She didn't care if she lived or died. Her only concern was for Glynna.

"No, tell me—how is she?" Her eyes closed as she finished speaking. The energy it had taken to just say those words had sapped her.

For a moment, Paul thought she had lost consciousness again. "Mary Catherine . . ." There was an edge of panic to his voice. The fear didn't leave him until he saw her eyelids flutter.

"Tell me," she insisted.

Mimi's gaze met Paul's, and he could not avoid telling her the truth.

"Glynna was taken captive by the renegades. Hunt's gone after them to bring her back."

"No!" A small, pitiful cry escaped her at the thought of the danger Glynna was facing. "Oh, God, no."

"I promise you, Mary Catherine, Hunt will find her."

A sob choked her. Glynna had been taken from her! She moaned, a heartbreaking, keening sound, and closed her eyes to the sight of Paul's worried expression.

Paul stared down at her, feeling completely helpless. It was his fault all this had happened. He should have been with them that day. He should never have let them go out with just Diego to protect them. He'd been a damned coward, leaving as he had on the pretense that he was paying calls to families in the area who didn't get to church. He had made the calls, but the truth was that he had been running from Mary Catherine again. He hadn't been able to deal with his feelings for her, and so he had tried to hide from them. Paul was filled with self-loathing.

"I'm sorry," he said tenderly as he reached out to brush a tear from her pale cheek. "I'm so sorry I wasn't there to help you."

Mimi didn't respond. Almost gratefully, she had slipped away into unconsciousness again, for in the blackness there was no pain—of the body or of the soul.

"She regained consciousness for a moment," Paul told Tom when he went to him where he was waiting in the parlor.

Tom smiled for the first time in days. "That's good news, Paul. Real good news."

"I know." He was relieved.

"Did she say anything?"

"She just asked about Glynna, then lost consciousness again."

Tom studied his friend for a moment and decided he had to ask. "How did you and Mimi come to know each other?"

Paul thought back over the years. "I loved her, and I let her get away from me. It was the biggest mistake of my life."

Tom knew the confession cost Paul a lot. "I figured she meant a lot to you."

"I never realized how important she was to me until now—until I'd almost lost her forever."

"Maybe God's giving you a second chance."

"I hope so. I intend to make good use of it." Paul looked up at his friend, his pain showing plainly in his features.

"You stay with her, Paul," Tom reassured him, going to pat him on the shoulder. "What's past is over. You can't change it. You've got the future to think about now. With Glynna missing, Mimi's going to need your strength."

Tom's kind words helped Paul, and he returned to Mimi's side and took up his vigil again.

*   *   *

Glynna had lost all track of time. Her life had become a blur of riding until she was ready to collapse, resting for a short time, and then riding again. Her captor was always near, so she never had a chance to escape. She could only endure.

It was on the fourth day after the raid when they began a descent into a deep canyon. The terrain was rough and the trek was made slowly and carefully. She was surprised when they reached the bottom of the canyon and discovered that a village was there, almost completely sheltered from view.

Some of the Comanche came out of their tepees to welcome the raiding party back. They stared at Glynna with open interest and called out to Painted Horse, asking him what he was going to do with her.

Glynna knew they were talking about her from their gestures, but she had no idea what they were saying. She tried to ignore them as she stared about the village. She realized how smart the renegades had been to select this site. It was practically impossible to see from above and would be easily defensible. Her despair deepened as she realized that she probably would never be rescued, for no one would be able to find her. She wanted to cry, but refused to give in to her despair. Not now. Not with all these people staring at her. Instead, she lifted her head high and stared right back.

Painted Horse was feeling quite proud of himself as he reined in before his own tepee. He slipped down from his horse's back and then pulled his captive down and motioned for her to go inside. He was glad when she quickly did as she was told. It made him look powerful to the others. The white woman was his to do with as he pleased—and he pleased to keep her safe until the stallion in his vision came to him.

Crouching Wolf was still angry and still determined to find a way to claim the white woman. He did not understand Painted Horse's need to keep her for himself when he was more than willing to pay a good price for her. His gaze narrowed as he watched the captive walk into the other warrior's tepee. The time would come when he would take her from him.

Painted Horse followed Glynna inside. He stared at her where she stood across the tepee from him. "What is your name?"

"You speak English?" Glynna was shocked.

"Yes. What is your name?"

"My name is Glynna."

"That is a strange name. I will call you Vision Woman."

She frowned, not understanding why he'd named her that, but she did not ask. "What is your name?"

"I am Painted Horse."

She stared back at him, angry and frightened. "What are you going to do with me?"

"You are mine. You will work." He held out a container for water. "Go to the stream and fill this."

"Untie my hands," she said, holding her wrists out toward him.

"Go," he ordered coldly, ignoring her request. He was not yet ready to trust her. Maybe in another day or two when she'd proven that she wouldn't try to flee, he would untie her.

Glynna took the water container from him and left

the tepee. She was aware of the others watching her, but she kept her head held high and did what Painted Horse had told her to do. He hadn't harmed her yet. She would cooperate, try to earn his trust, and maybe find a way to escape.

When Mimi awoke, it was daylight and Paul was asleep in the chair beside the bed. She lay perfectly still, fearful of the pain she knew would come if she tried to move. The memory of their earlier conversation haunted her. She wondered how long she'd been unconscious.

"Paul?" Her throat was dry, but she managed to say his name out loud.

Paul awoke immediately. Mimi had been unresponsive for another entire day, and he'd been growing more and more desperate with each passing hour. He'd begun to fear that she would never regain consciousness again.

"Thank God," he said, going to her.

"Water," she managed.

Tears filled his eyes. He offered up a silent prayer of thanks as he hurried to pour her a small glass of water from the pitcher on the nightstand. He returned to her side, and with great care he helped her take a drink. Just the simple act of drinking was exhausting for Mimi, but she managed.

"Glynna? Is there any news?"

Paul pulled his chair close by the bed so he could sit where she could see him more easily. "No. Not a word. Hunt left the day of the raid, and we've heard nothing since."

She nodded slightly. The pain of just that simple

movement overwhelmed her. Paul had always left her when she needed him the most, and she couldn't understand why he was staying with her now. "Why are you here?"

Paul was surprised by her question, but he understood it. "I couldn't leave you."

Mimi closed her eyes at his words. If only he had said that to her all those years ago . . .

Pain was throbbing through her, giving her no peace. She wondered vaguely if this was what it felt like to die. She opened her eyes to look straight at him. She might never get another chance to tell him—to say what needed to be said. She could feel her strength ebbing even as she tried to speak again. "You have to find Glynna. You have to save her. You can't let them hurt her—"

Paul saw the anguish in her expression. "Hunt's gone after them. If anyone can find her, Hunt will be the one."

"No, no, you don't understand," she protested, tensing as she struggled to tell him what he needed to know.

"What don't I understand, Mary Catherine?" he asked, leaning closer, sensing her desperation and worrying about it. They were all frantic over the fact that Glynna had been taken captive, but Hunt was the best person to do the tracking and searching for her.

"You don't understand. . . ." She paused to draw a ragged breath, and then she spoke again, the words torn from the depths of her soul. "Glynna's your daughter."

Chapter Ten

Paul could only stare at Mimi aghast for a long moment. He saw the pain in her eyes. He saw the heartbreak, too.

"My daughter?" His voice was choked with emotion. He couldn't fathom what she'd just revealed to him.

Glynna was his daughter?

"I don't understand," he went on in confusion. "Charles is her father—she's your niece."

Mimi saw his distress. With what little strength she had left, she told him the truth she'd kept hidden from nearly everyone for the last twenty-four years. "After you left me, I discovered I was going to have your baby."

Paul looked even more stricken.

"I was alone. I had no one to turn to. I couldn't find you. I didn't know where you'd gone."

He was shamed to the depths of his soul. She had needed him, and he had deserted her. "Mary Catherine, I—"

She weakly raised a hand to stop him. "Let me say this while I can," she managed. "I went home to Charles. He was the only person I could trust, the only person who loved me." A lone tear traced down her cheek as she remembered how her brother had protected and cared for her. "He had been about to travel overseas, so he arranged for me to accompany him and Victoria on the trip. We stayed away almost ten months. When we returned, it was announced that Victoria had given birth to a beautiful young girl and they'd named her Glynna. No one ever suspected. . . ." Her voice was fading with her strength.

Paul could only gaze down at her, his respect and love for her growing with every secret she revealed. She had suffered most grievously because of him.

"I can never repay Charles for his kindness to me. I could have been such an embarrassment to him."

"You had my baby."

"Our baby."

"Glynna doesn't know any of this?"

"No!" Mimi was horrified that he would even suspect such a thing. "I've always protected her. I've kept her shielded from any shame or taint on her name. To all the world, she is, and always will be, Charles Williams's daughter."

The thought that his own daughter bore another man's name hurt Paul deeply, but he knew he had no one to blame but himself. "It must have been terrible for you, having to give her up."

She still remembered every detail of the day when

she'd held her daughter for the first time, only to have the newborn whisked away from her and handed over to Victoria. "I could have stayed in Europe and raised her by myself, but I didn't want to do that to Glynna. I wanted her to have a real family. I wanted her to grow up surrounded by love. I didn't want her to be ashamed of her mother—of me—and Victoria was a wonderful mother to her." Again her tears fell.

"Mary Catherine," he began slowly, humbly, "you are so special. I don't know how to tell you what you've always meant to me—"

"Don't." She tried to silence him. Her tone was as harsh as she could make it.

"No." Paul had waited too long. He would not be silenced. "I've listened to you. Now you must listen to me."

She closed her eyes and drew a ragged breath.

"Look at me," he insisted, knowing this was painful for both of them. When she opened her eyes and her gaze met his, he began. "I was in love with you long before you married James." He saw the surprise in her regard, and rushed on. "What you don't know is why I left you that day in San Francisco. Didn't you ever wonder why I was gambling and drinking so much when you found me in California? I rarely drank back East. I led a quiet life there, loving you from afar. When you married James, my dreams for the future were shattered. I was furious and I was jealous, yet it didn't matter. There was nothing I could do—you loved him."

Mimi had been greatly weakened by the effort to tell him her truth. His fervor in revealing his story, however, gave her a new desire to fight the overwhelming pain of her wound and to hang on to consciousness and listen.

He continued, "The day James was killed at the picnic, I'd been drinking heavily. It was the first time I'd seen you since you'd married, and I was enraged at how happy the two of you were. I challenged James to the horse race, knowing my horse could easily beat his. I goaded him into it. I wanted to prove to you that I was the better man. I wanted to get your attention some way." He glanced away from her, the pain of that day returning full force. "I wanted you to look at me the way you looked at James. I wanted you to see me as a man, and not merely as a friend."

"Oh, Paul." She sighed, remembering.

"When the accident happened, I was already ahead of him, riding for the finish line. I could see you. You were standing up, waving. You looked so excited and happy. I told myself that I was going to remember that look on your face forever—and then suddenly you were screaming. Your expression was horrified, and you were running past me. You didn't even see me. I turned and looked back, and I realized then what had happened. I followed you, and you were holding James, but he was already dead. After the funeral, I left New York. I've never been back. I started drinking and gambling. I didn't care if I lived or died, and then you found me in San Francisco. *You came to me!* I thought you were a godsend. I had never known love could be so sweet. I loved you, Mary Catherine, more than life itself, but I couldn't stay with you, knowing I was responsible for James's death—knowing I'd killed the man you loved, and caused you all that pain. The guilt was overwhelming. What right did I have to enjoy your love? What right did I have to any happiness? James was dead, and it was my fault."

"No." She was shocked by his revelation.

"Each day we were together, my love for you grew, yet I knew I didn't deserve you. I couldn't face what I had done to you. I couldn't bear it, so I ran from you. That's why I left in the middle of the night. I knew I could never face you with the truth. And now, to discover that I abandoned you when you needed me most—when you were pregnant with my child . . ." He shook his head in abject misery.

"Paul." Mimi's heart ached for him. She had never guessed he'd carried such torment with him all these years. "Paul, you're wrong—so wrong about all of this."

"No," he denied. "I should never have forced James into that race."

"You didn't force him or goad him into it. James wanted to race you. He'd been talking about your horse for weeks and bragging about how he wanted the chance to prove it wasn't as fast as you thought it was. The very morning of the picnic, he told me that if he got the opportunity, he was going to race you."

Paul was stunned. "I thought I—"

"No," Mimi said gently. "It was a terrible accident. It was not your fault. You had nothing to do with it. Nothing at all. James raced you because he wanted to."

All the years of believing himself responsible for

200

James's death had taken their toll on Paul. He sat there, his thoughts in chaos, trying to make sense of his life. "But I hurt you."

"Paul." Mimi said his name in a soft whisper. "I never held you responsible for his death—never. I loved you. You're the father of my child."

He looked up from the depths of his despair. Mary Catherine had just said that she'd loved him. Was it possible that she still did? Was there any way he could make up to her all the sorrow he'd caused in her life? "I love you, Mary Catherine. I always have and I always will."

She managed a faint smile at his declaration, but her thoughts were on Glynna. "Find our daughter, Paul. Please—find her."

Paul leaned forward and pressed a kiss to her cheek. In the midst of their tragedy, a light had shone upon him. He was torn, not knowing the best thing to do—whether he should stay there and keep watch over Mary Catherine until he knew she was going to fully recover, or whether he should get as many men together as possible and go after the renegades who'd taken Glynna.

Glynna was his daughter.

The truth was mind-boggling. His first impression of her had been right. Glynna was Mary Catherine's child. And she was his, too.

A fierce desire filled Paul, unlike anything he'd ever known before. The renegades had tried to destroy everything that was important in his life. They'd tried to kill Mary Catherine and had taken Glynna hostage. His thoughts right then were not those of a man of God. His thoughts were those of a man who wanted justice. Grim determination filled him. He was going to see the renegades pay for their murderous ways.

Glynna was trying to stay out of everyone's way. The less anyone noticed her, the better. She was hoping that when the time came and she finally got the chance to run away, she'd be able to sneak off and get a head start without anyone missing her right away. So far, though, she'd had little luck escaping Painted Horse's watchful eye. It seemed he was everywhere, always watching, always alert to her movements.

Painted Horse kept her busy doing menial tasks. She was going down to the stream again now, to fetch more water for him. She didn't mind the work, but as the daylight hours passed and night drew near, a different fear overtook her. They had ridden so hard and so fast on the trail that she hadn't had time to think of anything but keeping up. Now it was growing dark, and Glynna found herself dreading the night to come. She would be sleeping in Painted Horse's tepee, and for the first time she would be alone with him.

Terror seized her soul. The night loomed threateningly before her. She had no weapon and no way to defend herself if he did attempt to attack her.

Glynna swallowed tightly. All her life she had dreamed of a wedding night filled with love and romance. She'd dreamed of a handsome man sweeping her off her feet and carrying her away. She had saved herself for that moment, wanting to give herself freely in the bonds of marriage to her husband. Now her dreams were about to be destroyed.

Glynna prayed for the strength to endure whatever fate was to befall her. She prayed desperately for rescue, for someone to save her from what she was sure was the horror to come at Painted Horse's hands.

Glynna thought of Edmund and tried to imagine him coming to her rescue. Somehow she found it impossible to picture him fighting off the renegades to save her honor. He was a gentleman. He was kind and thoughtful, but there was no way he could rescue her from this.

Hunt seared her thoughts just then, and she knew if anyone could save her it would be he. He was strong and fierce, and the type of man who would let nothing stop him from getting what he wanted. She wondered vaguely if he wanted her, and the memory of his kiss and embrace returned, sending a shaft of heat through her. She had never known such an irresistible attraction to a man before. She wondered if that was what love really was.

Love—Hunt?

The very idea shocked her. Did she love Hunt? How could she, when she barely knew him? Not that she wouldn't have liked to know him better, but it was obvious that he would let no one close to him except his father.

Glynna sighed, pushing the thought from her. What did it matter? By morning she would have to face a new reality. That reality frightened her, so she lingered on the banks of the stream as long as she could. She dreaded returning to the tepee.

Finally, knowing she could stay there no longer, Glynna filled the water container and started back to where Painted Horse waited for her. As she passed by a clump of bushes, she was lost so deep in thought that she was completely unprepared for Crouching Wolf's sudden appearance before her. He blocked her path, and she looked up at him, startled.

Crouching Wolf was a big man, a very mean-looking man. The wound where she'd hit him with the paint box was an ugly, red slash above his eye, and his black-eyed gaze glittered dangerously as he glared down at her. His mouth had a cruel twist to it that sent a shiver down Glynna's spine.

"It is good that you fear me, Vision Woman," Crouching Wolf told her in English.

"I'm not afraid of you!" She tried to be brave, hoping he wouldn't dare hurt her since they were so close to the village. She suddenly wondered if Painted Horse was near enough to see them together.

"You should be." His smile was cold. "You are mine, you know."

"No, I'm not!" she countered.

"In the raid, you were mine first. When I take you from Painted Horse, there will be no escape for you. No one does what you did to me and gets away with it." His words were a very real threat.

"I'm just sorry I didn't hit you harder!" She was angry at his intimidation.

"You will never get another chance. I will teach you how to be a good woman. You will learn many lessons at my hands." He was concentrating on her so completely that he didn't notice Painted Horse coming up behind him.

"Vision Woman will never be yours, Crouching

Wolf," Painted Horse announced loudly, drawing the attention of the others nearby. "She is mine, and mine alone."

"By all rights, she should be my captive!" Crouching Wolf snarled.

"Do not push me. The woman is lost to you," Painted Horse responded. He had been right to be suspicious of Crouching Wolf, and he was glad that he'd kept a careful watch over Glynna.

A murmur went through the the group listening to their conversation. They thought Painted Horse might fight Crouching Wolf for daring to try to claim what was rightfully his—the white woman.

"You have been my friend for many years. I do not want to fight you over the woman, but know when I tell you this that it is so. She belongs only to me."

"You are a fool, Painted Horse! Coyote Man is dead because of your vision and this woman! You say because of her, you will claim a fine horse, but I have offered you many horses and you have refused them."

"It is my right to accept or refuse offers." Painted Horse stared at the other warrior in disgust. "I am tired of your arguing. It is ended here, now. Do not speak to me of this again."

Crouching Wolf was furious. Painted Horse had humiliated him before everyone, but the time would come when he would get even. He stalked away, all the while planning what he would do next.

Painted Horse turned to look for Glynna, wanting to make sure she was unhurt. He did not see her.

"Where is Vision Woman?" he demanded.

No one knew where she'd gone.

"We must find her!"

Painted Horse immediately went for his mount. Eagle Claw and Tall Grass ran with him. They began to search for the missing captive. Even though darkness claimed the land, it did not take Painted Horse long to find her tracks. Trailing her, within minutes he found her running along the edge of the stream.

Glynna had thought she could get away. She had thought the fight between the two men would keep them busy for a while, and she would have the time she needed to escape. But when she heard the sound of the horse coming up behind her after only a few short moments of freedom, she knew she'd been wrong.

Glynna feared it was Crouching Wolf coming after her. She ran harder, but it was no use. Painted Horse urged his horse forward and circled before her, blocking her from going any farther. She stopped and looked up at him, trembling from terror and exhaustion. She expected him to be angry with her for running. She was surprised when he drew near enough for her to see that the look on his face was almost one of relief.

"We will return to the village," he ordered.

Glynna expected him to pick her up and carry her back with him. Painted Horse made no effort to carry her back, though. He stayed on his mount and waited for her to walk past him; then he herded her quietly along.

With as much dignity as she could muster, she headed back the way she'd come. She felt as if she were walking to her doom. It was the longest walk of her life. She had almost been free!

Again she faced the horror of the night to come. There was no way out. She was Painted Horse's captive.

When they reached the village again, Painted Horse ordered her to the tepee while he went to see to his horse. He was worried about Crouching Wolf, but knew there was little he could do until the man revealed himself. He started back to the tepee, pondering what to do to keep Vision Woman safe. Crouching Wolf wanted her, and it was up to him to protect her until the hunter came.

Painted Horse's mood was black when he returned to find Glynna huddled on the opposite side of the tepee. He could see the terror in her eyes. Irritated, he lay down on his blankets and looked over at her again.

"Come here," he commanded.

"I will sleep here."

"You will sleep with me."

Still, she made no effort to get up and do as he'd told her. Painted Horse was tired and angry. He got up and went to her, and, reaching down, he took her by the arm and pulled her to her feet. She resisted as he brought her to his blankets. He lay down and drew her down with him.

Glynna was holding herself rigidly, trying not to shake with fear. She was terrified of what was to come. When he started to untie her wrists, she wondered if she was strong enough to hit him. If she could knock him unconscious, she might be able to escape again. Desperation filled her.

Painted Horse saw the pure terror in her eyes. He understood it, but he didn't like it. He gave her no chance to break free, but quickly retied the rope around only one of her wrists and then tied the other end around one of his own.

"Now sleep," he said, then stretched himself out on the blankets.

Bound together as they were, Painted Horse would know if she tried to get away during the night. He closed his eyes. He needed rest.

Hunt reached the edge of the canyon at sundown. He knew it was the perfect place for the raiding party to seek shelter, for it was protected and easily defensible. The trail that led down into the depths was rocky, making tracking more difficult, but he had no choice. Glynna was near. He had to find her.

Moving slowly and cautiously over the rough terrain, Hunt continued on. He would not stop his pursuit until he had freed her. The moon was bright again, so he made steady progress.

It took some time, but Hunt finally located the village several hours before dawn. From his hidden vantage point, he studied the layout and tried to estimate the number of warriors there. He considered riding straight in, but decided to wait for daybreak. He would make sure of what he was up against before venturing forth.

Hunt's instincts were telling him that Glynna was there, but the warrior in him warned him to use caution. He tended to Warrior, not wanting the horse to stir and alert anyone to his presence; then he returned to his hiding place to await the dawn.

* * *

Glynna lay confused and unmoving next to Painted Horse. She feared that the simplest shift in her position might waken him and result in unimaginable horrors at his hands. She wondered why he had not ravished her immediately. Being forced to wait this way was only making it all the more excruciating.

Glynna closed her eyes. She tried to picture herself back in New York City. It was impossible. The sounds and smells of the Indian village were too foreign to allow that fantasy. Her thoughts drifted to Aunt Mimi, and worry consumed her. She feared her aunt and Diego were dead, and she prayed they were not. Glynna wondered if her father and Edmund had been notified of what had happened and if they would come west to help look for her. She wondered, too, if she'd ever be found.

Though she didn't want to think about him, Hunt slipped into her thoughts again. He had saved her from the longhorn, and she was certain he could save her from the renegades. Thoughts of his smile, his kiss and his embrace returned, and she clung to them in the darkness of the night. Hunt alone offered her hope in the midst of her despair.

Glynna realized that Hunt didn't care about her. He'd made that quite clear to her, but surely he wouldn't leave her here, a helpless capture of the raiding party. Memories of their conversation over dinner returned, and she recalled how Hunt had told her that she didn't want to end up in a Comanche camp, that it would be too dangerous. He had been right.

Thoughts of how innocent she'd been then made

209

Glynna grimace. Had it really been only a few days before? She had been so caught up in the joy of her work—in painting beautiful scenes and interesting people, that she hadn't accepted the reality of what the Wild West really was.

Her work . . . Glynna grasped at the thought of her paintings as a distraction from the terror surrounding her. She focused on what she'd originally wanted to see in a Comanche camp and realized she'd been given an opportunity. She didn't have any of her art supplies with her, but she could study her surroundings and hoard the images. Someday, and she hoped it would be soon, she would be back at her easel working. Thoughts of the paintings she would do as soon as she was rescued helped her through the long, empty hours of darkness.

As the sky lightened and the village came awake, Hunt was watching. He could see the women moving about the campsite, stirring the fires, and the men slowly emerging from the tepees, but there was no sign of Glynna. His tension grew. He began to anticipate the worst. He worried that he would have to fight his way in to find her. He worried that she might not be there at all, that he might have missed a clue to her location on the trail in.

Hunt was planning his next course of action when a warrior came out of his dwelling on the far side of the camp. The renegade looked around himself and seemed quite contented with the new day.

Still hidden at his vantage point, Hunt smiled to himself. The man below was his cousin, Painted Horse.

Unwilling to wait any longer, Hunt stripped off his shirt and mounted his horse. He kept his pace slow as he started down the trail. He might not find Glynna in the village, but Painted Horse might know where she was. Hunt controlled his eagerness to hurry. He did not want to appear threatening in any way as he rode in. He heard the shout go out that he was coming, and Hunt could see the warriors grabbing up their weapons.

Painted Horse heard the other warriors' warning calls and ran to see who was entering their village. As the rider came into view, he could only stare in disbelief. It was his cousin, Lone Hunter, approaching, and he was riding the most magnificent stallion he'd ever seen—it was the stallion from his vision.

Painted Horse remembered the words of his vision—the *prize the hunter seeks*—and he understood it now. Lone Hunter had come for the woman named Glynna. He smiled.

"Do not harm him. He is one of us," he called out as he waited for his cousin to come to him.

The others in the village relaxed then, but they remained wary of the man who rode alone into their midst. He was a stranger to them. They could tell he was not fully Comanche, but he did not look fully white, either.

Hunt was aware that all eyes were upon him, yet he kept his gaze focused on his cousin across the camp. He kept his pace steady and slow, and did not stop until he'd reined in before Painted Horse.

"It is good to see you, Lone Hunter," Painted Horse said.

211

*Lone Hunter had come for the woman named
Glynna.*

"It is good to see you, too," Hunt answered, swinging down to greet him. It troubled him that his cousin was off the reservation, for he knew the dangers that faced him as a renegade. "How is Striking Snake?"

"My father is well, as is my mother."

"Good." He looked around the village, searching for some sign that Glynna was there, but saw nothing that indicated she was.

"You have traveled far?" Painted Horse asked.

"I have been tracking you for days." Hunt grew serious.

Painted Horse nodded in understanding. "A vision told me you would come."

"Your last raid was on my father's land."

Painted Horse was surprised, but did not show it.

Hunt went on. "Do you have the woman?" He met his cousin's gaze directly, not wanting to waste any more time. If Glynna was there, he wanted her.

"Yes."

"You have taken what is mine."

"She is your woman?"

"She is mine. I want her."

At his statement, a smile curved Painted Horse's mouth. "If, as you say, she is yours," he said slowly as he looked past Hunt to where Warrior stood, "then there will be a bride-price to pay to claim her."

Chapter Eleven

Hunt almost managed to hide his shock at Painted Horse's words. "A bride-price?"

"If she is to be your woman, then you will take her as your wife, but the cost to claim her will be high." Painted Horse wanted to make sure that Lone Hunter had come not for the other whites, but truly on his own. Only when he was certain of his motive would he return the prize to the hunter, as his vision had revealed.

"How high?"

"Your stallion is the finest I have ever seen." He went to the horse and ran his hands over Warrior, examining him closely. "I will accept this horse as your bride-price. Then you will have Vision Woman as your wife."

Hunt stared at his cousin, trying to understand his ploy. Painted Horse hated the white men who had driven the Comanche from their ancestral lands, and he wanted revenge against them. If Hunt married Glynna, he would prove to Painted Horse that she was his woman, that he wasn't there for any other reason, that no one else had sent him in search of her.

If he married Glynna, she would be ruined in the white world. . . .

The terrible realization haunted Hunt, but he knew there was no other way to save her. Protected as she was in the village, he could not rescue her or help her to escape. The odds were too great against them. The most important thing was to keep her safe, and this was the only way to do it.

Marry Glynna . . .

Hunt rationalized that the marriage would be valid only in the eyes of the Comanche. He would make sure that no whites ever found out what happened while they were together. It would be too damaging to Glynna's reputation if anyone learned that she had been his Comanche bride.

Marry Glynna . . .

Hunt looked at Warrior, then at his cousin. He knew what he had to do. "It is done."

Only then did Painted Horse allow himself to smile. He picked up Warrior's reins and swung up into the saddle. "I have made a fine bargain."

"No. I have," Hunt countered.

"You will stay with us for a time." It was a statement.

"I will."

"The prize you sought is there." He pointed to his

tepee. "She is yours, Lone Hunter. No harm has come to her."

With that, he put his heels to Warrior's sides and raced from the camp. Hunt watched him go, then turned toward the tepee. Relief surged through him. Glynna was here. He had found her.

He had also just married her.

Hunt drew a deep breath and went to check on her. He was sure she was frightened, and he wanted to reassure her as quickly as he could that everything would be all right. She had been through hell these last days, and it was time to put her fears to rest.

Hunt made his way to the tepee and stood in the doorway. The sun was at his back as he looked inside to see Glynna lying asleep on a blanket. His heart thudded almost painfully in his chest at the sight of her. She was resting peacefully and seemed to be fine, but he couldn't be sure she was all right until he'd talked with her.

"Glynna?" he called, just loudly enough to rouse her. He did not want to startle her. He was certain she'd had enough shocks in the last few days.

Though she had been exhausted from staying awake all night, Glynna had not managed to fall asleep until Painted Horse had left her alone that morning. He had retied her wrists together before going, but she had been too tired to fight him or to care. Almost the moment she'd lain down again, she'd been asleep. The dreams had come then, wild, disconnected visions of renegades and longhorns, of Aunt Mimi and Diego, of her father and Edmund and of Hunt snatching her up to safety.

The sound of Hunt saying her name dragged

Glynna back from the abyss of her fitful slumber. Confused, she lifted her head to see the figure of a tall, broad-shouldered man standing in the doorway across from her. He was silhouetted by the sun, and she couldn't make out his features. For a moment she thought it might be Hunt—that at last he had come for her—but the memory of her dreams convinced her she was imagining things. It couldn't really be Hunt.

Then he said her name again.

"Glynna."

And she knew it was he. This wasn't a dream! Hunt was the man standing before her! He had come to save her.

"Hunt! You came."

Hunt saw her anguished look and immediately went to her. Kneeling beside her, he wanted to reach out to her, but he held himself back. She looked frail and terrified. Her hair was wild about her; her eyes were wide with disbelief. His every instinct told him to take her in his arms and never let her go, to clasp her to his heart and shield her with his strength, but he didn't want to do anything that would further upset her. It took all of his considerable self-control to deny himself and wait for her response.

"Are you all right?" he asked gently.

"I am now," Glynna said. She lifted her tear-filled gaze to his.

"Were you hurt in any way?" He studied her carefully, taking in every detail, looking for any sign that she'd suffered abuse.

"No," she whispered.

She couldn't believe he was really there. But he

217

was. Her tears began to fall. She no longer needed to be brave. She could give in to the emotions she'd been fighting so hard to keep at bay. Instinctively, in one swift move, she went to him. A great sigh escaped her as his arms enfolded her, giving her safe haven.

"You did come for me. I prayed that you would," she said softly as she clung to him, reveling in his strength. "You rescued me from the longhorn, and I knew you would rescue me from the renegades—I knew you wouldn't leave me with them."

Glynna's words of trust stormed the defenses of Hunt's heart. Hunt looked down at her, and warmth and tenderness filled the long-frozen void within him. He could no more have let her go than he could have stopped breathing.

"You're safe now," Hunt promised in a husky voice.

"I know," she said simply.

He worked at the rope on her wrists, freeing her, then shifted them both to sit on the blankets. He drew her across his lap, cradling her to him. He had ridden for days on end and had gone without sleep, desperate to find her. And now Glynna was there with him, and she was unharmed. This moment, holding her this way, made every treacherous mile worthwhile.

"Thank you," Glynna said, rubbing her wrists. She rested back against his chest, and in that instant she knew her days of horror were over. In Hunt's arms, she was protected from all danger. Peace filled her.

A great sense of relief swept over Hunt, and with that relief came joy. The joy surprised him. This woman in his arms had somehow managed to touch him as no one else ever had. He realized then that, against all logic and his better judgment, he had come to care about Glynna. He should have been tormented by the reality of his feelings, but, in truth, acknowledging the way he felt about her left him strangely tranquil.

Hunt knew he should put Glynna from him and concentrate on getting her back home as quickly as possible to ease the others' worries. But they were there, alone together, and it felt so right to hold her this way. Slowly, tenderly, he bent to her.

Glynna felt Hunt stir and looked up at him. She saw his intent mirrored in his eyes. A thrill of anticipation shivered through her. She did not resist, but welcomed him like a flower opening to the sun.

Hunt's lips met hers in a soft kiss, and all the world vanished except for the two of them. Desire stirred deep within Hunt, but he denied his baser needs. This moment was too fragile and too beautiful. It was innocence and trust and bliss.

When the kiss ended, neither spoke. There was no need. Their kiss had said it all. Hunt held Glynna quietly, secure in the knowledge that she was with him.

The powerful sound of Hunt's heartbeat was calming to Glynna as she rested against his chest. She started to close her eyes to savor the moment—she was safe; Hunt was there. Then, suddenly, the horrifying memory of the raid returned, and along with it her fears for Aunt Mimi and Diego.

"Hunt, what about Aunt Mimi? Is she all right? And Diego?" She sat up straight, searching his expression for the answers she needed. He looked very serious, and she feared the worst.

"When we reached the site of the ambush, we found that your aunt had been shot, but she was still alive."

"Thank God. And the boy?" she pressed.

"I'm sorry, Glynna. He was killed." Hunt hated telling her the truth, but there was no point in lying to her.

She gasped in heartbreak. "But he was so young."

Hunt drew her close again, wanting to soothe her, but there was nothing he could say or do that would change what had happened. He could only hold her and wait for her pain to ease.

"I'm all right," Glynna said, straightening up as she forced herself to be strong. Though she was completely exhausted, her sadness over Diego's fate and her concern for Aunt Mimi would give her no rest. She had to return to the Rocking M as quickly as possible. In her mind, she could still hear the sound of gunshots and Aunt Mimi's cry.

"Are you sure?"

"Yes. Let's go back. Can we leave right away? I have to make sure Aunt Mimi's all right."

"We'll go soon," he told her. "For now, you need to rest and get some strength back."

"But I have to go to her. She might need me. It's all my fault that this happened—that Diego's dead and Aunt Mimi's wounded. It was my idea to come here to Texas." She was frantic and miserable.

"If anyone is to blame, it's me. I should have been the one riding out with you while you were painting.

I shouldn't have trusted your safety and your aunt's to Diego."

She was shocked by his words. She couldn't imagine how he could even think that way. "This wasn't your fault. There was no way you could have known that the renegades were near."

His expression was grave as his gaze locked with hers. "You could have been killed."

She saw the agonized look in his eyes. "Hunt, you came after me. You followed our trail for days. You're here now. You rescued me."

Glynna reached up to draw him down to her for a kiss.

"Thank you," she whispered against his lips.

At her gentle gesture, a dam broke within him. His mouth claimed hers in a hungry, devouring exchange. His desire sparked an answering fire within Glynna. She pressed herself even more tightly to him, returning his passion with abandon.

Hunt's lips never left hers as he slipped an arm beneath her knees and lifted her so they lay together upon the blankets. Her every sweet curve was molded to the lean, hard length of his body.

Glynna had never lain so intimately with a man before. His hard-muscled body intrigued her even as his nearness aroused her. She ran a hand over the width of his chest and heard him draw a sharp breath at her action. She knew nothing of seduction or enticement, but she was learning. When his mouth left hers and he pressed a hot kiss to her throat, she gasped at the sensations his caress evoked.

The sensual sound forced Hunt back to reality. He

went still and rested against Glynna, curbing his need, reining in his runaway desire. He was angry at his own lack of control.

Had he saved her from Painted Horse only to take advantage of her himself?

After a moment, Hunt shifted completely away from Glynna and sat up. He glanced down at her to see her cheeks flushed and her expression questioning as she looked up at him. His gaze drifted lower, to the swell of her breasts taut against her blouse. His breathing grew ragged. He wanted to unbutton the offending garment and bare the beauty of her to his gaze and to his touch, but he didn't. He would control his need to caress her. He would control his hunger for her. Even though she was his wife . . .

"Hunt?" She was mystified as to why he'd stopped kissing her and moved away from her.

"When we leave the village, the trip is going to be long and hard. You need to rest."

She almost told him that what she needed was for him to kiss her again. She reached out and put a hand on his arm, and she felt him tense at her touch. "How soon will we be leaving? This afternoon?"

"No. We won't start back for another day or two."

"Why? I want to get out of here now," she told him, eager to be away from her captors.

"I understand, but I told Painted Horse that I would stay on for a few days."

It suddenly occurred to her that Hunt had managed to ride into the middle of the renegade camp without firing a shot, and that he had come to claim her without so much as a fight. "Do you know these renegades?"

"Painted Horse is my cousin."

Her surprise was real. "Did you know it was he when you were tracking us?"

"No. I didn't find out until just before I rode in this morning. I saw him come out of this tepee."

"And they didn't try to kill you when they saw you?"

"No. They knew I was one of them."

His words sent a shiver of awareness through her. Bare-chested as he was, he did look the warrior as he sat beside her. He was proud and powerful.

Intimidating though his presence was, she had never been so glad to see anyone in her whole life. Hunt had come for her, just as she had hoped he would.

Hunt glanced down at her to find her gaze upon him. "Do you want to rest now?"

"Yes." She had to admit she was exhausted.

"Then sleep."

"Painted Horse won't be back?" She looked nervously toward the entrance to the dwelling.

"Don't worry. Painted Horse will not bother you again."

"He did not harm me, but the one called Crouching Wolf is dangerous. He feels that I should be his." She went on to explain what had happened the day of the raid.

Hunt's expression darkened. Crouching Wolf—he would remember and keep watch. "I'll stay with you. No one will ever hurt you again."

Glynna believed him. She slipped her hand into his and found his warm, strong grip reassuring. Her eyes closed. She could rest now. Hunt was there. She fell asleep quickly, and rested easily. Her nightmares were gone.

Hunt remained at her side for a long time. He watched over her quietly, and he took the time to study her as she slept. She looked almost fragile as she rested, but he knew there was nothing fragile about her. Glynna was an extraordinarily strong woman to have survived what she'd been through.

And she was his bride, too, though he hadn't found the right moment to tell her yet.

Hunt was certain that Reverend Paul would have something to say about the Comanche way of taking a bride. A slight smile curved his lips. If Glynna had been a Comanche maiden, she would have been given the chance to reject his offered stallion and so reject him, but she was a captive. She was Painted Horse's property, and the warrior could do whatever he wanted with her. So now she was his bride.

It was a long time later when Hunt finally went outside to seek out his cousin. Many years had passed since they'd last talked, and Hunt wanted to renew their friendship.

Across the camp, Crouching Wolf sat with Tall Grass, watching Hunt as he came out of Painted Horse's tepee.

"Who is the stranger in the village?" Tall Grass asked him.

"He is Lone Hunter, cousin to Painted Horse."

"You know him?"

"He lived with us for some time before we were sent to the reservation." He remembered the other

man well. Even though he had been half-white, Lone
Hunter had mastered all the Comanche skills with
seeming ease and had bested most of the other boys
in camp. Crouching Wolf had resented him even
then.

"Why has he come here?"

"I do not know, but it is strange that Painted Horse
has left him alone with Vision Woman."

Tall Grass cared little about the woman, but he
understood why Crouching Wolf did. He had captured her first in the raid, even though she'd managed to escape him. "You know she is his, and he can
do what he wants with her. He has spoken often of
the horse in his vision and how he would claim it
through Vision Woman."

Crouching Wolf only grunted in response.

"Did you see Lone Hunter's stallion?"

The question irritated him. "No. I was not here
when he rode in."

"It is the finest I have ever seen."

Crouching Wolf tensed at this news. Was Lone
Hunter to take the white woman as his? "Where is
Painted Horse now?"

"He is with the horses, tending to Lone Hunter's
fine stallion."

Crouching Wolf left without saying another word.

It was near dusk when Glynna awoke. She was surprised that she'd slept so deeply and for so long. Hunt
entered her thoughts immediately, and she wondered if she had dreamed him or if he was really
there. It was then that she realized her hands were
untied, and she knew the truth. A sweet smile curved

her lips at the thought of him. He was there.

Glynna rose and smoothed out her clothing as best she could. She was dirty and unkempt, but there was little she could do about it until they got home. She ventured forth from the dwelling. Hunt would be nearby, she had no doubt.

Hunt was sitting with Painted Horse by the campfire, and he caught sight of Glynna the moment she came outside. He stood up and went straight to her.

Painted Horse watched him go to the woman. He knew his cousin well, for they had spent several years together as youths. He had never seen Lone Hunter so concerned about a female before, but his actions proved the truth of his claim—she was his woman.

Still, Painted Horse had to admit that he was surprised by his cousin's feelings for Vision Woman. Lone Hunter had sworn never to care for a white woman, yet now he had taken one as his bride. Painted Horse did not ponder the question too long, though. His vision had been a good thing. He now owned a fine stallion because of her. He was most pleased.

Glynna saw Hunt coming toward her, and she was relieved.

"You slept well?"

"Yes, thank you." She felt nervous standing so openly among the people who, up until that morning, had treated her as a captive. Now they were staring at her, watching her with Hunt.

"Come with me for a moment. I have something I want to give to you."

Hunt's words distracted her, and when he held out his hand to her, she took it. They walked to the pen where the horses were kept a short distance away. His saddle and saddlebags were there.

"Here." He opened his saddlebags and took out her sketchbook and pencil. "I found them near the canyon and brought them along with me. I knew you would want them."

"Oh, Hunt, thank you!" She looked up with obvious delight. "Thinking about my work is the only thing that has kept me sane since I was taken in the raid. I kept picturing in my mind all the sketches I wanted to make."

Glynna looked so happy and lighthearted that it was all Hunt could do not to kiss her right then and there. Instead he lifted one hand to her cheek, his caress light. She did not move away from his touch, but thrilled at it, standing spellbound before him.

Only the sounds of some young girls' giggles broke the enchantment that held them bound. Glynna glanced their way, and they ran off shrieking with laughter.

"We must be entertaining," she said, not understanding what the children thought was funny.

Hunt knew word was spreading around the village that he had taken her as his bride and that tonight was their wedding night. He wasn't about to explain that to Glynna, though. He was not going to say a word about her bride-price. He would keep her safe and take her home where she belonged as soon as possible.

At least, that had been his plan until she'd looked at him that way.

Suddenly all he wanted to do was kiss her. Something about having her near, smiling at him, made

Bobbi Smith

him forget that he was there to rescue her. He reminded himself that he shouldn't put her in any compromising situations, but then he told himself that he had married her, so he couldn't compromise her. It was logical—and it was crazy. He couldn't help himself.

"Maybe they knew that I wanted to kiss you, so they ran away so we'd be alone." His voice was deep and hypnotic.

Around them, all was quiet. The shadows of the coming night had lengthened, and they were alone. Glynna went to him and, looping her arms around his neck, drew him down to her.

"Maybe they knew I wanted to kiss you, too," she said softly against his lips.

Her mouth sought his, sweetly, softly. But Hunt wanted more. His lips slanted across hers in a passionate exchange that demanded a response from her. *Sweet* and *soft* were not what he was feeling right then. The kiss was a searing brand that ignited a fire of desire within him. He shuddered at the force of his emotion as his arms closed around her.

Glynna was swept away by the heated urgency of his embrace. A new, exquisite sensation was born within her, filling her with the driving need to be even closer to him. She knew this was Hunt. She remembered distantly the kisses they'd shared back on the ranch and how he'd sent her from him. But he was here with her now, and he wanted her. There was no denying the attraction between them.

At her eager response, Hunt was in danger of losing all self control. Glynna was everything he'd ever wanted in a woman, and she was in his arms, kissing him. She was his bride. The thought stopped him. He did not want to deny himself, but he did. As the kiss ended, he released her. It was one of the most difficult things he'd ever done.

"We'd better go back," he told her.

"I don't ever want to go back," she said.

"We'll leave soon, I promise."

"All right."

They started back, their path taking them along the creek.

The water looked inviting, and she quickly asked Hunt, "Do you think you could keep watch for me so I could take a bath? I feel so dirty in these clothes, and now that you're here . . ."

"I'll stand guard for you," he told her. "And I'll ask Painted Horse if you could have a change of clothes."

Glynna smiled at him, enjoying the idea of being clean again.

They made their way slowly toward the campfire. Hunt went to speak to Painted Horse, and his cousin sent one of the village women to get Glynna a traditional Comanche dress. She quickly brought it to them.

"Thank you," Glynna told her.

The woman didn't respond, but only looked up at Hunt and smiled knowingly before hurrying away.

Glynna felt the sting of jealousy when she noticed the look the other woman gave Hunt. The emotion surprised her.

"It should be protected enough for you here," Hunt said as he led her to the edge of the creek where there were some low-growing trees and brush to shield her from view.

"I'll hurry," she promised.

Glynna sat down on the bank and took off her boots, then stood and began to remove her split riding skirt. She glanced back toward Hunt only once to find him standing with his back to her, staring off in the distance. Hurrying, she shed the rest of her clothing and rushed into the chilly waters.

Hunt could hear Glynna splashing behind him as she entered the stream. He was tempted to turn to try to catch a glimpse of her, but he fought down the urge with an effort. He was standing guard for her. He would not betray her trust.

Glynna hurriedly scrubbed herself clean, then washed her hair in the cold, rushing water. She rose in wet splendor from the stream. She used her old undergarments to dry herself and quickly donned the Comanche dress.

The dress was made of soft buckskin and was nearly ankle-length. It was sewn at the sides with buckskin thongs and was decorated with beads and fringe. It was comfortable, but she felt strange wearing it.

"I'm decent now, Hunt, you can turn around," she told him as she gathered up her dirty clothes to wash them quickly.

Hunt had been gritting his teeth as he waited for her to finish bathing and get dressed again. The images his mind had conjured up of her unclad in the water had been far too tempting. He had had no idea, however, that she would look this beautiful in the traditional dress of his mother's people. He turned toward her and found himself momentarily speechless. He could only stare at the lovely picture she made.

Glynna's hair was unbound and hanging about her shoulders in a sleek, dark mane. The dress clung to her every curve, hinting at but not revealing the womanly figure beneath.

"You look beautiful," he said slowly, his gaze raking over her. Primitive emotions churned within him. He was thinking that for his own peace, he should bathe in the cold water, too.

She smiled at him. "I'm just going to wash out these clothes, and then I'll be ready to go back."

He said nothing, but watched her as she bent to the task. When she was finished, he helped her spread the garments out on bushes to dry. They went back to join the others at the campfire and eat the evening meal.

Crouching Wolf had seen Lone Hunter take the woman away from the village. He had circled around them, staying at a distance to see what he was going to do with her. Since he'd left Tall Grass, he had heard the talk that Painted Horse had given Vision Woman to his cousin for the bride-price of his stallion. There were no words to describe his outrage.

Moving quietly, Crouching Wolf found a hiding place across the creek upstream. From there, he watched the white woman and Lone Hunter together.

Vision Woman was beautiful, and he burned to have her. When she had finished bathing and they

231

had left the stream to return to the village, Crouching Wolf crept down to where her clothing was laid out on the bushes and took one of her garments for his own.

Chapter Twelve

Glynna had been sitting quietly at Hunt's side while they ate by the campfire. Painted Horse had joined them, and the two men were speaking in the Comanche tongue. She had no idea what they were talking about, but every now and then she would look up to find Painted Horse's gaze upon her. It left her wondering if they were discussing her, and, if they were, what they were saying.

With Hunt there to protect her, Glynna knew she had little to fear. He would keep her safe. It was only when she caught sight of Crouching Wolf watching her from the shadows across the campsite that she grew restless and a little nervous.

"I think I'll go back to the tepee now," she told Hunt. The faster she got away from the evil warrior, the better.

Hunt had been deep in discussion with Painted

Horse, and he glanced up at her as she stood to go. He was surprised to see how strained her expression was. He frowned. "What's wrong?"

"Nothing. I just want to rest, that's all." She thought about telling him the truth, but didn't want to cause trouble. Crouching Wolf hadn't done anything. It was just knowing he was there, watching her, that made her uneasy. She would be fine once she was in the dwelling, away from him.

"All right."

"Where will you be tonight?" she asked.

Painted Horse heard her question and smiled broadly at Hunt. Glynna noticed his smile and was puzzled by it.

"It'll be best if I stay with you," Hunt answered, hoping his cousin didn't make any remarks right then. When the time was right, he would tell Glynna about their "marriage." Until then, he really didn't want to bring it up.

She nodded, relieved that he was going to be close by. She hurried away.

"Vision Woman was worried that you would not spend the night with her?" Painted Horse asked, once Glynna had disappeared inside the tepee.

"White ways are different from our ways," he answered. "But she is my bride. I have paid for her."

"The stallion is strong and smart. He is a pleasure to ride," he said with a grin.

"The woman is beautiful and smart," Hunt countered, smiling, but not going any further in the comparison.

Painted Horse laughed. "Enjoy your wedding night, Lone Hunter. Your bride is waiting for you. I think, by morning, we will both be satisfied with our rides."

Hunt said nothing else, but stood up, still smiling, and followed after Glynna. Several of the others around the campfire made comments about the night to come that drew laughter from those gathered round.

From where he stood looking on, Crouching Wolf could only listen and grow more and more angry. It was true. Painted Horse had given Vision Woman to Lone Hunter for the bride-price of the stallion. Frustrated, but not about to give up, he knew he would seek his revenge on Lone Hunter, now, too. The other warrior was taking what should have rightfully been his.

Hunt was glad to enter the tepee and escape the knowing laughter that followed him. Glynna looked up quickly as he came inside.

"I didn't know you would be coming so soon," she said, suddenly a bit nervous.

She knew Hunt was there to protect her, but she hadn't even considered their sleeping arrangements for the night. Although, after all the nights she'd spent on the trail with the raiding party, having Hunt near was nothing to be afraid of. It was a blessing. The truth was, though, that she wasn't nervous because she was afraid of him. She was nervous because of her own feelings for him.

"I had to come. Painted Horse expected it of me," Hunt answered, trying to find a way to broach the subject of their married state.

"He wanted you to guard me?" she asked, fearing that the other warrior might know something about Crouching Wolf's intentions and be worried.

"No—not exactly."

"I don't understand." She was puzzled. "Is something wrong? I heard them laughing when you came in."

"No. There's nothing wrong. They were just having fun, taunting me."

"Why would they do that?" She sensed there was something important she didn't know.

"Well, the reason the children were laughing earlier, and the reason they were laughing at me now, is because they think this is our wedding night."

Glynna stared at him in shock. "They what?"

"They think this is our wedding night." Hunt hurried to explain. "They believe we're married."

"We're married?" she repeated, knowing she sounded like a dullard, but unable to help herself.

"Yes," he said. "To get you back from Painted Horse, I had to marry you in the Comanche way. I had to convince him that you were my woman. I had to prove to him that I had followed you here because I wanted you for myself, and the only way he would believe me was if I took you for my bride."

Glynna was staring at him, trying to understand everything he'd just told her. "And exactly how did we come to be married if there was no ceremony?"

"Oh, there was a ceremony—of sorts. Earlier, when I first reached the village, I had to pay him a bride-price to claim you."

"You paid a bride-price for me? You bought me from him?"

"No, I married you by paying what Painted Horse asked for you."

"How much did he want from you? What was my 'bride-price'?"

"Warrior," Hunt answered.

Glynna was astounded. She knew how much he cared for that horse and all the hours he'd spent training it. Hunt had paid a very high price for her. "You gave up your stallion for me? Warrior was your pride and joy."

"It was the only way to free you."

She couldn't believe all that had taken place, and she hadn't even known about it. "What would have happened if you hadn't paid him what he asked?"

"I didn't want to find out."

"Oh." A tremble of fear went through her as she imagined Crouching Wolf being the one to take her as his wife. It wasn't a pretty thought. The knowledge that Hunt had sacrificed his most prized possession to save her thrilled her; yet she regretted that he'd had to give up so much. "I'm sorry."

"I'm not. I wanted you with me, so I could keep you safe. All that mattered was that Painted Horse believed you were my woman." His look was fiercely protective.

She felt the intensity of his regard and knew she had to ask. "Am I your woman, Hunt?" Her voice was soft and full of invitation.

Time stood still.

Was she his woman? Her question, so enticingly asked, sent a surge of excitement through Hunt. He stared at Glynna, thinking she had never looked more beautiful. Dressed as a Comanche maiden, she appeared innocent yet seductive, alluring yet elusive. He was hungry for her, but he was determined not to act upon his desire. He wanted her desperately. The need within him was powerful, but he wouldn't let it rule him. The decision as to what happened next between them would have to be hers.

"You are my bride," he answered simply.

Glynna had been holding her breath, waiting for his reply. At his answer, she knew she loved him and wanted to be with him. What she felt for Hunt was not the simple affection and respect she felt for Edmund and had mistaken for love. What she felt for Hunt was powerful and overwhelming. She couldn't bear to think that there might be a day when they would have to part. She wanted to be in his arms for the rest of her life. Glynna smiled seductively at him as she walked slowly toward him.

"If I am your bride, then you are my husband," she said, lifting her gaze to his.

Hunt saw the full and open invitation in her eyes. He said no more, but just enjoyed watching her come toward him, the fringe on the dress swaying in a sensual invitation. He reached behind him to close the flap over the tepee's doorway.

In the semi-darkness Glynna had no trouble finding her way into Hunt's embrace. She wrapped her arms around him and held him close, lifting her lips to his for a flaming kiss.

At her offering, Hunt forgot any thought of caution or stopping. This was their wedding night. They were man and wife.

He lifted her up into his arms and carried her to the waiting blankets. He had longed for this moment ever since he'd first seen her, and, finally, she would be his.

Kiss followed heated kiss as he laid her on the blankets and followed her down, covering her body with his own. Glynna gloried in the hot weight of him upon her. She had never known such intimacy or such delight.

His lips left hers to explore the sweetness of her throat. The path they forged was searing and exciting.

At the thrill of his lips' caress, Glynna arched against Hunt in an instinctive invitation he could not resist. When Hunt sought the sweet weight of her breast in a bold touch, she gasped at the pleasure his hand created within her. The feelings he was arousing within her were wild and reckless. She wanted to know more, needed to know more. She began to caress him, sculpting the muscles of his back and shoulders with her hands, tracing paths of fire over him as she moved against him in a natural, age-old rhythm.

Hunt groaned. He knew she was an innocent, but in her naivete, she was more exciting than the most practiced lover. Unable to tolerate the barrier of their clothing between them any longer, he moved away from Glynna for a moment to help her shed the dress.

"Hunt?" She didn't understand why he had stopped kissing her, and she gazed up at him in breathless, confused bewilderment.

He didn't speak but simply reached for her. She offered no resistance as he lifted the hem of the dress and pulled over her head. He tossed the garment aside and took the time to gaze down at her as she lay back. Her beauty was bared to him for the first time. The fire that was burning within him was nearly uncontrollable. Glynna was perfection, from her high, firm breasts to the gentle swell of her hips and long, shapely legs. He ached to be one with her. He needed to be one with her.

The night air was cool upon her as Glynna lay back on the blankets. She was trembling, but it wasn't from the temperature. She was trembling from the look in Hunt's eyes as he gazed down at her. It was smoldering and raw, revealing his barely leashed desire.

"Hunt," she said softly as she lifted her arms to him to welcome him back.

Hunt went to her, holding her close as he kissed her. Only Glynna existed in his world. He sought only to pleasure her, seeking out her most sensitive areas with knowing caresses and rousing her to greater and greater heights of excitement. When his lips sought her breasts, Glynna gasped in surprise at the intimate touch. His mouth was hot and demanding upon her silken skin. She clutched him to her as the spiraling ache deep in the womanly heart of her grew almost intolerable.

Hunt could no longer bear to be separate from her. He moved away again just long enough to shed his own clothing.

Glynna watched as he undressed, and she was mesmerized as she stared at him unclad for the first time. He was the essence of raw male beauty. His shoulders and chest were wide and ridged with heavy muscles. His waist was lean, his legs long and straight. The proof of his masculinity intrigued her, even as she felt some embarrassment, for she had never seen a naked man before. Still, she thought him strong and powerful and beautiful. He was her warrior. He was her love. He was her husband.

A distant warning came to Hunt, telling him to stop now while there was still time, to save himself from the pain he would ultimately have to face in returning her to the white world and giving her up, but he ignored it. Glynna was gazing up at him, wanting him, needing him, just as he wanted and needed her. He threw all caution aside. He would live for the moment—this moment with Glynna. It would be worth it. He would celebrate what they had, here and now. He would love her while he could. He would face the pain later.

Hunt didn't say a word, but went to her, fitting himself to her velvet softness. He began to kiss and caress her again, rousing her to new heights, teasing her with promises of the ecstasy he knew could be theirs. When he moved between her thighs and sought the heart of her, she stiffened, frightened and unsure of what was to come.

"Easy, love," he told her. "It will hurt for only a moment."

She answered him with a fiery kiss, inviting him to teach her the ways of love.

Hunt could wait no longer. Slowly he pressed forward, entering her, sheathing himself in her. He claimed the proof of her innocence and made her his in all ways.

The ecstasy of being one with Glynna was more exquisite than he could ever have believed. He lay quietly, holding her close, their bodies joined, waiting for her to adjust to the newness of their union. When he felt the tension ease from her, he captured her lips in an urgent kiss and began to caress her again. He started to move, gently at first to teach her the rhythm, then more quickly as he was caught up in the searing intensity of their mating.

Glynna had been surprised by the pain she'd experienced when Hunt had made her his, but as he began to move within her, the pain lessened and then disappeared. It was replaced by a growing, aching need only he could satisfy. She found herself meeting him in his thrusting pace and reveling in his response to her movements. A feeling unlike anything she'd ever felt before began to fill her, taking her higher and higher, coiling ever tighter in its intensity. She wrapped her arms around Hunt, and when he reached down to lift her hips to his to guide her, she gave a moan of pure pleasure. Delight coursed through her. Caught up in the glory of their joining, she rode with him to ecstasy and beyond, crying out as he took her for the first time to the heights of pure rapture.

Hunt had never known loving could bring such ecstasy. They reached the peak of love's perfection together and then drifted on the aftermath, locked tightly in each other's arms, their bodies still one.

"I love you," Glynna whispered.

Hunt answered her with a cherishing kiss. It was long minutes later before he finally moved away from her. He kept her by his side, though, her head on his shoulder, her hand splayed on his chest, one

leg resting across his thigh. She was a part of him.
He never wanted to let her go.

Glynna was so overcome by the glory of what had
passed between them that she lay against him in a
haze of sensual bliss. She did not know what chain
of events had led her to become this man's wife and
to have her wedding night in a renegade Comanche
dwelling deep in the heart of Texas, but she was
there, and she was happy. Living in New York as she
did, she would never have guessed that her life would
lead her here, but she was thrilled.

A vague thought of Edmund intruded, but it did
not distress her. She could not imagine sharing with
Edmund what she and Hunt had just experienced.
What she felt for Edmund was friendship and nothing more. She knew that now. What she felt for Hunt
was pure love and physical attraction. He was devastatingly handsome, and she was certain he was a
wonderful lover. She let her eyes drift shut as she
relaxed in his embrace. This was Hunt. She loved
him.

Hunt lay staring off into the darkness. Making love
to Glynna had been as magnificent as he'd imagined
it would be. The feel of her nestled at his side sleeping filled him with intense emotion. He had made
love to her. He knew it might ultimately prove to
have been a disastrous decision for him, but he
didn't care. Loving Glynna had been glorious. She
had been responsive and eager and perfect. He wondered what he'd ever done to deserve her. At the
thought that they might have a future together, he

stopped. Neither of them knew what the future held. But for at least for this short period, he could claim her as his, and love her.

And he did.

Throughout the long hours of the night, Hunt took her again and again, unable to resist the sweetness of her passion, the joy of her rapture, the pleasure he found deep within her body.

Glynna lost all thoughts of shyness as she learned more of how to please Hunt. She was his equal, evoking exciting responses from him as she explored the secrets of his need, arousing him, teasing him, and ultimately slaking his desire, until shortly before dawn they both collapsed in ecstasy's aftermath, sated and well loved.

They slept on into the daylight hours, securely wrapped in each other's arms. Safe in their refuge, they had no cares, no worries. They had only each other. The tepee was their own private heaven.

Glynna awoke first. It was morning, and the village was stirring around them. She savored the warmth of Hunt's nearness and the memories they'd created through the night. She had known from his first kiss that day at the ranch that what she felt for him was powerful, but she'd had no idea that loving him would be so completely overwhelming. He had taken her innocence; yet, in doing so, he had given her a gift far more precious—he had given her his love.

A soft smile curved her lips as she watched Hunt sleep beside her. Her gaze lovingly traced his features. He was boldly handsome in a rugged way. His skin was bronzed from the sun; his features were strong and proud. While he slept, she saw a vulner-ability about him that she had never seen before. He was a cautious man, a guarded man. She wanted to plumb the depths of his heart and soul. She wanted to know everything about him. She loved him. He was her husband.

Glynna managed to slip away from Hunt's side without disturbing him. She put the dress back on, and then quickly retrieved her sketchbook and pencil. Settling in across the tepee, she began to draw Hunt. It was a labor of love, capturing the gentleness he revealed only while sleeping. With great care, she worked at the drawing, losing herself in the pure joy of it.

Hunt came awake slowly. He immediately realized that Glynna was no longer pressed against him, and he rolled to his side, wanting to draw her back to him. Instead of finding her slumbering peacefully beside him, he saw her sitting across the tepee, frowning in concentration as she worked on the sketch she was making.

Glynna sensed that he was stirring. She looked up and smiled to see that he was finally awake. "Good morning."

"Yes, it is," Hunt agreed in a warm, sensuous voice. "What are you drawing?"

"You."

He held a hand out to her. "Let me see the picture."

Glynna went to show him. He studied the likeness of himself.

"Do I look like this when I'm asleep?"

"Yes. You look very handsome, but I think I like

245

you awake better." She leaned over him and kissed him sweetly.

"I know I like being awake better."

"You must have been tired, to sleep so long," she said, a small smile playing about her lips. She put her sketchbook and pencil aside.

"Not anymore," he said, his voice turning husky with emotion as he reached for her. "But you're welcome to try to wear me out again, if you want."

She gave a throaty laugh and surrendered to his demanding caresses. Her last logical thought before she was swept away by his storming of her senses was that one day she would have to capture this part of him on the canvas—the lover, whose touch was ecstasy and whose kiss was heaven.

It was some time later when they finally dressed and left the tepee. The other warriors in the village gave Hunt knowing looks of approval, while the women thought Vision Woman was quite lucky.

Crouching Wolf barely stayed in control as he watched Lone Hunter and Vision Woman together.

Tall Grass was with him, and asked, "Why is this woman so important to you? There are many women in the village who would take you as a husband."

He shot Tall Grass a hate-filled look, but did not answer. No woman had ever escaped him before. No woman had ever hit him and gotten away with it.

Tall Grass left him to sulk alone. After he'd gone, Crouching Wolf reached up and touched the wound she'd inflicted on him. This woman needed to be taught a lesson.

Crouching Wolf was pleased when his chance to

find her alone came sooner than he'd thought. He saw Lone Hunter ride off with Painted Horse. Vision Woman retrieved the clothes she'd left near the stream and returned to the tepee by herself. Glancing around, he found that there was no one near, and he smiled at his good fortune. He would wait no longer. The need within him was strong.

Glynna had come back to the tepee to await Hunt's return. He had gone out for a ride with Painted Horse, for his cousin had wanted to put Warrior to the test. She took up her sketchbook and was about to go out to the campfire and start some new sketches when she looked up and saw Crouching Wolf coming through the doorway of the dwelling.

"What do you want?" she asked, backing up a step, not trusting him.

Crouching Wolf stood staring at her, enjoying the fear he saw in her expression. He wanted her to be afraid of him. He wanted her to beg him for mercy. He didn't approach her, but waited like a sly predator to see what she would do.

"I'll scream if you come any closer! Lone Hunter will kill you if you touch me!" she threatened.

In one blindingly fast move, he crossed the tepee and threw her to the ground. Her sketchbook fell from her grip. Glynna managed to cry out once before he brutally covered her mouth with his hand. With his other hand, he grabbed the neck of the buckskin dress and ripped it downward.

"You will learn not to fight me, Vision Woman, or you will die like the other woman did at your campsite!" He snarled as he groped at her. His touch was rough, his fingers bruising and pinching her tender flesh.

In abject horror, Glynna realized that Crouching Wolf had been the one who'd shot Aunt Mimi! How she hated him! She screamed her outrage, but his hand over her mouth stifled most of the sound. She twisted and bucked, trying to dislodge him, but his weight upon her was oppressive. Desperate to get away from his filthy pawing, Glynna managed to free one hand, and in one swift move she clawed at his face, tearing at him again where she'd struck him with the paint box.

Her attack was painful and infuriated Crouching Wolf. He slapped her viciously. The force of his blow bruised her cheek, but she got the chance to cry out for help again. There was no one near enough to hear her and come to her aid, though.

Hunt and Painted Horse hadn't ridden far when a strange feeling overtook Hunt. He reined in and looked over at his cousin.

"Is something wrong?" Painted Horse asked. He had thought they would be going for a longer ride, and he wondered why they'd stopped so soon.

"I need to go back. Something's wrong."

"What could be wrong?"

"I'm not sure. Did you see Crouching Wolf anywhere around when we rode out?"

"No, I haven't seen him since early morning."

He nodded tightly. "Neither have I, and that's what's bothering me."

He wheeled the horse Painted Horse had given him around and rode for the village.

*   *   *

Crouching Wolf liked some spirit in his women, but he was growing tired of Vision Woman's fighting. He was glad that no one had heard her scream. He didn't want to be interrupted. He pinned her to the ground and ripped at the dress again. He was hot for her, and he wanted to take her quickly and brutally, so she would remember it forever.

Crouching Wolf was reaching down to free himself from his loincloth when, suddenly, harsh hands grabbed him from behind, and he was thrown bodily from her. He looked up to see Lone Hunter standing over him.

Chapter Thirteen

Crouching Wolf smiled cunningly at Lone Hunter's outraged expression, but even though he was smiling, all the passion had drained from him. Still, he did not show any discomfort.

"We did not know you would be back so soon, Lone Hunter," he told him snidely in the Comanche tongue. "If Vision Woman and I had known, we would have gone someplace more private."

"Hunt!" Glynna ran to him, clutching her dress together to cover herself. "Thank God, you came back!"

Hunt glanced down at her. He could see the bruises on her face and the marks on the pale flesh revealed by the torn dress. He put an arm around Glynna as he turned his deadly glare back to her attacker.

"Do you always treat women so harshly, Crouching Wolf?" He deliberately spoke in English, so

Glynna could understand what was being said.

"Every woman enjoys a strong man," he answered in English, leering evilly at her. "Vision Woman said you were not man enough for her. She wanted me to show her the true way of a man and a woman. She invited me into the tepee. She spread her legs for me."

"That's not true!" Glynna exclaimed, looking up at Hunt, her eyes wide with horror at the other man's lies.

Hunt carefully put her from him and went to stand over Crouching Wolf. "You have not changed in all these years. You were a bad liar as a boy, and you are one now. A woman doesn't scream if she wants a man to take her."

"She was screaming her pleasure," he said quickly.

Hunt smiled at him. It was a deadly smile. "Get up. We will fight."

Crouching Wolf got to his feet, his gaze lingering on Glynna where she huddled on the opposite side of the tepee. "When I have killed Lone Hunter, I will come back for you. Be ready."

Hunt directed him outside. He turned back to Glynna. "Stay here." It was an order. He wanted her safe.

Her gaze met Hunt's. She saw the fury and the determination in his eyes, and then he was gone.

Glynna felt dirty and defiled from Crouching Wolf's assault. Holding the dress together in front, she got up to follow Hunt. Though he had told her to stay in the tepee, there was no way she would let him fight for her alone.

Hunt and Crouching Wolf found Painted Horse

251

riding up to the tepee when they went outside.

"Painted Horse! Tie our wrists," Hunt told him as he dismounted before them.

"You plan to fight? What happened?"

"He attacked Glynna," he answered grimly.

"Vision Woman wanted me. She came to me and begged me to take her," Crouching Wolf argued arrogantly.

Painted Horse knew the truth and ignored his lies. "You will fight in the clearing."

They made their way to the small, flat clearing nearby. The villagers saw what was happening and crowded around to watch. It wasn't often that there were such conflicts between the warriors.

Using a leather thong, Painted Horse bound their left wrists tightly together. He then handed each man a knife. There were no rules to this fight.

"To the death!" Crouching Wolf shouted as he lunged at Lone Hunter.

Hunt proved too quick for him. He dodged his attack and jerked his arm with all his might, wanting his opponent to lose his footing.

Crouching Wolf was agile and he was prepared. He stayed on his feet and circled his adversary, looking for a weakness he could exploit. He had always used deceit in his confrontations. He rarely could overpower other warriors, but he prided himself on being cunning and sly. He expected to defeat Lone Hunter; he would just have to be quick and dirty to do it. This was the moment when he was going to use his wiles to triumph over brawn. He slashed out at Lone Hunter, desperately wanting to draw first blood.

*"To the death!" Crouching Wolf shouted as he
lunged at Lone Hunter.*

Hunt avoided Crouching Wolf's attack. He kept moving, staying out of his reach, as he plotted his own strategy. When he saw the opportunity, he lunged. His move was swift and sure. He caught his enemy by surprise and his knife found Crouching Wolf's unprotected side.

The other man let out a grunt of pain and jerked back out of range, blood dripping from his wound.

They continued to circle each other. Cold, deadly rage was fueling Hunt's need for victory. The memory of how he'd found Crouching Wolf trying to hurt Glynna enraged him. He had almost succeeded. Hunt hated to think what would have happened if he'd returned just a few minutes later. The thought of Glynna being so abused sent him charging at Crouching Wolf. He cut him on the upper torso this time. He saw the stricken look on his enemy's face and smiled at him tauntingly.

"To the death, Crouching Wolf? Who's death? Yours?"

Crouching Wolf was irate. Lone Hunter had drawn blood twice, and he had yet even to nick him! He was going to win! He was going to kill Lone Hunter one way or another! And after he had spit on him, he was going back into the tepee to finish what he had started with Vision Woman. In a violent move, he threw himself to the ground and kicked out, knocking Lone Hunter's feet from beneath him and sending him sprawling. He launched himself on his opponent, going for the kill, but managed only to cut his upper arm.

Howls erupted around them from those looking on. They knew what a dirty fighter Crouching Wolf was and hoped Lone Hunter could defend himself against his trickery.

The pain from the wound to his arm only inspired Hunt to fight even harder. He blocked the attack, and they grappled in the dirt. They strained together, rolling back and forth, each fighting for supremacy. Sweat and blood covered them.

Glynna had quickly pulled on her own blouse over the ruined dress to cover herself before rushing from the dwelling. She hurried to the clearing to watch the battle, all the while praying fervently that Hunt would not be injured.

As Hunt was battling Crouching Wolf, he caught sight of Glynna standing there, a stricken look on her face. Wanting to end the fight as quickly as possible, he threw the other warrior off of him. It was a powerful move that sent the other man sprawling. Hunt kicked out and knocked Crouching Wolf's knife from his hand. He then tackled him and pressed his own knife at his enemy's throat.

Blood lust filled Hunt. This man had tried to rape Glynna. He had laid his hands upon her and hurt her. He wanted him to suffer for his savagery. He was tempted to kill him. His rage was so great that he was shaking with the power of it. If their situations had been reversed, Hunt knew Crouching Wolf would have slit his throat without hesitation.

Hunt loomed above his enemy now, staring down at him as Crouching Wolf thrashed about and tried to break free of his unyielding grip. He saw the fear in his eyes and felt him trembling. He smiled at him, enjoying his defeat.

"I have the power of life and death over you right

now, Crouching Wolf." He tightened his grip on him and nicked his throat with his knife to emphasize his words.

A hush fell over the onlookers as they waited to see what Lone Hunter would do.

Crouching Wolf said nothing. He was bleeding and defeated. He stared up at Lone Hunter, waiting for his next move. Humiliation was worse than death, and he almost prayed that his enemy would end it here and now.

Hunt held up his knife and the blade gleamed in the sunlight.

"I will spare your life, if you will leave this village and never come back," he told him in a harsh voice. "If I ever see you near my wife again, I'll kill you without question."

Then in one quick move, he severed the thong that had bound their wrists together. He stood up and stepped away from him. He watched and waited as Crouching Wolf got up and slowly slunk away, a defeated man.

Those who had watched the fight laughed at Crouching Wolf and made fun of him. They did not stop shouting at him until he had mounted his horse and ridden away for the last time. No one noticed when Tall Grass followed after him a few moments later; they were too busy watching as Vision Woman ran to her husband.

"Hunt!" Glynna flew into his arms, thrilled that he'd won. "Were you hurt?"

"It's not bad," he answered, ignoring the pain of his wound to hold her close. He cherished her nearness. The memory of finding Crouching Wolf assaulting her tormented him. She was all that mattered to him. "What about you?"

Hunt took Glynna by the shoulders and held her back from him so he could look at her. His expression was dark and troubled as he stared down at her. She had been taken captive in the raid because he hadn't been there to protect her. He felt the same guilt again now.

"As long as you're all right, I'm fine," she told him with a soft smile. She gazed up at him, all the love she felt for him shining in her eyes.

"It was a fine fight," Painted Horse said as he came to join them. "Crouching Wolf was lucky you spared his life. I would not have been so generous, had I been you."

"I hope I don't have cause to regret letting him go."

Painted Horse looked off in the direction the fallen warrior had ridden. He nodded slowly. "He is always a dangerous man, but especially when he is angry. Use caution. When you ride for your home, remember he could be near."

Hunt nodded.

The others gathered around to congratulate him and tell him what a good fight it was. He accepted their compliments, but kept a tight arm around Glynna's waist. He never wanted to let her out of his sight again.

"You're still bleeding. We should clean your wound," she said as the crowd around them moved away.

She led him down to the stream to wash the filth from him, so she could doctor the cut. He sat quietly on the bank while she ministered to him, washing away the gore and cleansing the wound. He noticed that her hands were trembling and he reached out to take one of them in his.

"Why are you shaking?" Hunt asked, his voice low and gentle.

Glynna stopped what she was doing and looked up at him. "You could have been killed."

"But I wasn't."

"Thank God. I was so afraid for you. Crouching Wolf is vicious."

Hunt cupped her cheek and leaned forward to kiss her softly. "I will protect you always."

His words sent a thrill through her. She kissed him back hungrily, letting him know without words exactly how much he meant to her, but in the back of her mind the question lingered: Who would protect him?

Charles and Edmund arrived in Dry Creek early in the afternoon. Their trip from New York had been exhausting, but they were past being concerned about being tired. Nothing mattered except that they were finally in Dry Creek. Now all they had to do was find someone who could help them find the McAllister ranch, wherever that was. The stage driver directed them to the stable in town, and there they found a man willing to rent them a carriage and take them out to Tom's place.

"You any relation to the two women who were attacked by the renegades?" Ken Wagner, the stable owner, asked as he hitched up the team to their carriage. They'd just told him they were from back east, and he knew the women had been, too.

"You know about it?" Charles asked quickly, wondering if there had been any new news.

"It's been the talk of the town since it happened. Hunt McAllister is the one who went after the raiding party. He's a half-breed, and he's good at tracking. As slippery as those renegades are, though, I don't know if even Hunt can find them. They're fast and they're deadly."

Charles grew even more tense at this news. He had been nearly frantic with worry about Glynna and Mimi. "What else have you heard?"

"Have they found Glynna?" Edmund added worriedly.

"I haven't heard anything yet. The doc went out to take care of the woman who was wounded, but no one knew if she was going to make it or not."

"Let's hurry," Charles insisted.

He thought of the letter he'd received and how Tom McAllister had mentioned that Paul Chandler was in the area. He thought about asking for him, but decided against it. The last thing he wanted to do at that moment was see Paul. He would think about looking him up later, once he had Glynna back and he was certain Mimi was well.

Ken rode along on his own mount with Charles and Edmund as they left town on the last leg of their desperate journey to the Rocking M.

"There she is. There's the Rocking M ranch house," Ken told them as it came into view.

"Good." Charles didn't say any more. He didn't care what the place looked like. He wanted only to get there, so he could find out what had happened.

Edmund stared at the ranch house and outbuildings in barely disguised disgust. He wondered what in the world he was doing in Texas. He knew for certain, after having made the trek out here in record time by rail and stage, that he was definitely a city man. He wanted nothing more to do with the primitive life that was led in the West. He preferred New York City. Now *that* was civilization. Once he and Glynna were married, he was going to make sure she never went on another of these ridiculous excursions again.

Tom heard Gib call out that there was company coming, and he hurried from the house to see who it could be. Even at a distance, he recognized Ken from the stable in town right away. He turned back inside for a moment to let Paul know.

"Paul! I think Glynna's father must be here. Ken's riding in with two strangers."

Paul had been at Mimi's side constantly. She'd been coherent for that short period of time when she'd revealed the truth about Glynna to him, but then she'd developed a fever. Mimi had been rarely conscious ever since.

Tom had sent word to the doctor about the change in her condition, and he'd come out to check on her again. He'd instructed Paul to bathe her with cool cloths to bring the fever down and to try to get her to drink all the liquids he could. Other than that, there had been little more any of them could do but wait and pray.

And Paul had been praying fervently and continually for God to grant him another chance with Mary

Catherine. He wanted one more opportunity to prove his love to her.

At Tom's call, Paul put his Bible aside. He checked on Mary Catherine to make sure she was resting comfortably; then he went to join his friend on the porch.

"That's Charles, all right," he told Tom as he came to stand at his side. "And that must be Edmund with him."

"That's the man Glynna's supposed to marry when she goes back home?"

"Yes."

"I'm glad they're here. I just wish we had some better news for them about Glynna."

"I wish we did, too. At least Mary Catherine's alive, and now that they're here, maybe she'll start to improve."

As the carriage with Ken riding escort neared, Paul could see Charles more clearly and was amazed at how little his friend had changed over the years. He studied Edmund, too, and felt an instant distrust of the man. He appeared arrogant and self-centered. Paul hoped it was just a bad first impression.

Paul and Tom called out a greeting to Ken, and then Paul left the porch and went forward to meet the carriage as it pulled to a stop. He was uncertain how Charles would react to seeing him again, especially now that he knew about Glynna. He owed Charles a debt he could never repay—this man had raised his daughter as his own. He was humbled by the thought of the help Charles had given Mary Catherine in her time of need and by the love he'd shown for her and her daughter.

Charles recognized Paul right away, and a rage unlike anything he'd ever felt before filled him. For twenty some-odd years, he'd controlled his hatred for this man, but now, with all the tragedy around them, it exploded. Paul was the man who'd nearly destroyed his sister! If Charles had had a weapon right then, he just might have been tempted to use it. Fury roiled within him. As soon as Ken stopped the carriage, Charles climbed down. He had one thing on his mind as he turned to face the other man.

Paul saw that Charles's expression was grim, but he attributed that to the trauma they were facing.

"Charles, I'm glad you came."

Paul walked toward him, wanting to fill him in on everything that had happened. Later, when they had some time alone together, he would talk to him about the past, but this wasn't the moment. Right now he was certain all Charles wanted were answers.

"Chandler, you no-good son of a bitch!" Charles raged.

Without thought, his control gone, he hit Paul full force. The power of the blow knocked the other man to the ground and left him sprawled flat on his back in the dirt.

Paul was dazed by the attack, but realized he should have expected it. Blood seeped from the cut in his mouth. He shook his head to clear it and rubbed his jaw. He was lucky it hadn't been broken.

"I guess I deserved that," he said slowly.

"You're damned right, you deserved that—and more! It's all because of you that this has happened to Mimi and Glynna! I know now that they came to this godforsaken place because you were here! If I'd known you were going to be here before they'd left, I would have locked them in the house and thrown away the key! I would never have let them out of my sight!" He glared at Paul in complete disgust.

"I understand," he said simply, offering no defense or excuse.

"Why Mimi felt she needed to see you again is beyond me!" Charles went on. "All you ever meant to her was heartache!"

"I know," Paul agreed solemnly.

"You don't know anything!" he retorted, near violence again. "Mimi would have been better off shooting you on sight than trying to talk to you again! Hell! If I had a gun right now, I'd do it myself!"

"And I wouldn't try to stop you."

Paul's calmness in the face of his fury put Charles off. He glared at him.

"But Charles, before you say any more, Mary Catherine's here and she's alive."

"Thank heaven!"

"She's inside. I've been staying with her ever since we found her after the raid."

Charles's gaze turned cold, and Paul could feel the hatred in it. "I'm here now. I'll take care of Mimi, just as I always have. You stay the hell away from her."

He turned his back on Paul and started toward the house, where Tom waited on the porch.

"I can't stay away from her, Charles. Mary Catherine's told me everything. I'm never leaving her again," Paul called after him.

At his words, Charles stopped dead in his tracks.

Aware that Edmund was sitting there, listening to all that was being said, he turned and looked at Paul, his face ashen, his eyes glowing with fierce, painful emotion.

"Don't say another word," he ground out.

Paul got to his feet and went to him. "Come inside. Maybe your being here will help her and give her more strength to fight."

Charles slowly got a grip on his anger. He held himself stiffly as he followed Paul to the porch.

Edmund was shocked as he slowly climbed down from the carriage. The usually calm, imperturbable Charles had just lost his temper and hit another man! It was incredible! He had never seen him so angry before. Edmund remembered that he had displayed a momentary flash of anger back in New York when they'd first received the telegram and it had mentioned Paul Chandler, but Charles hadn't said another word about him again on the whole trip. Now that they were face-to-face with him, though, the first thing he'd done was hit him! He wondered what had happened in the past to create such animosity between them and drive the usually controlled Charles to physical violence.

"Edmund!" Charles called to him.

He hurried to join them on the porch and was introduced to Paul and Tom. Ken tied up his horse and followed them.

"Has there been any word of Glynna?" Edmund asked quickly.

"Nothing yet," Tom answered. "Hunt will find her."

"Hunt's your son?" Charles asked.

"That's right."

"But they said in town that he was a half-breed," Edmund said disdainfully.

"He is." Tom turned a steely glare on the newcomer, and the discussion ended there.

Ken asked whether they needed him for anything else and then excused himself and headed back to town.

Tom led the way indoors.

"Mary Catherine's in here," Paul said quietly as he directed Charles toward her room.

"Edmund, you wait in the parlor," Charles told the younger man. "I'm going to see to my sister."

"Yes, sir."

Edmund was glad for the reprieve. The last thing he wanted to do was hover over someone's deathbed. As tense as he was, though, he didn't bother to sit down, but began to pace the room. He'd met Glynna's aunt briefly on several occasions, but had never been particularly fond of her. He'd liked her even less after the confrontation with Charles, when she'd forced him to allow Glynna to go on this trip to Texas. Her influence over Glynna was going to change, once they were married. He would see to it. No wife of his was going to be so aggressive. It wasn't an attractive trait in a lady.

Tom followed him into the parlor and eyed Edmund suspiciously from across the room. He'd known from the moment Edmund got out of the carriage that he didn't like him, and he wondered what Glynna saw in the man. He wondered why she'd want to tie herself down to a fellow like him. Glynna was an intelligent, talented woman. He had expected her to have better taste in men.

*   *   *

Charles entered the semidarkened room quietly to find his sister lying in bed, her eyes closed. She looked deathly ill. Her face was flushed from the fever that was ravaging her. Her eyes had dark circles beneath them. There was a gaunt look about her.

"How long has she been this way?"

"For two days now. Before that, she was weak from the wound, but recovering. Then the fever came."

Charles went to the bedside and gently brushed a lock of hair from Mimi's cheek. His heart constricted in his chest. His darling little sister . . . She looked so frail that he was truly terrified she might not survive. And Glynna . . . The fear that had haunted him for the entire trip reared its ugly head. Where was Glynna? Where was his precious daughter?

"Mimi, it's me, Charles. I'm here now. I'll take care of you." He looked back at Paul. "Leave me alone with her. I don't want you in here with us."

"No." Paul stood firm. "I'm not leaving her, and when she recovers, we're going to be married."

"Don't you think it's a little late for that?" Charles snapped.

"It's never too late to love," Paul said, not flinching in the face of Charles's intimidation. "I've loved her all my life. I'm not going to lose her again."

"You didn't lose her! You threw her away! Just like you threw away Glynna!"

"I had no idea about Glynna. Do you really think,

if I had known, that I would have been so low as to desert Mary Catherine when she was going to have my child?"

"That's exactly what I think."

"Well, you're wrong, and I'm going to spend the rest of my life proving it to Mary Catherine—and you, and anyone else who doubts me."

"It's going to take a lifetime and more to convince me."

"I would never have left her alone to raise my daughter."

"Glynna is my daughter, not yours! You lost any right to claim her as your own when you walked out on her mother."

They glared at each other across the room. Neither man said any more.

Charles sat down in the chair beside the bed, while Paul went to stare out the window.

They kept their vigil together, waiting, hoping, praying . . .

Across the hall, Tom decided to play the host, though he didn't particularly want to make Edmund feel all that welcome.

"Would you like something to drink? A glass of water do all right?"

"Yes. Water would be fine." Edmund would have taken anything to get the old man out of the room. Tom kept staring at him, and it made him uncomfortable.

Once Tom had gone to get him the water, Edmund began to pace again. It was then that he heard Paul's and Charles's voices raised in anger. Curious, he went to stand in the doorway of the parlor to listen.

Edmund heard their every word.

Chapter Fourteen

Edmund couldn't move. All color drained from his face as he stood there, listening in horror to the truth of Glynna's parentage. He was aghast. Glynna was illegitimate! The woman he planned to marry was a bastard!

Immediately, Edmund understood why he hadn't liked her aunt. The woman was a slut!

And Charles . . . It boggled the mind to think that such an upstanding, successful businessman would be a party to such a deception.

The thought of returning to New York City right then and there appealed to Edmund. He wanted nothing to do with such deceit and lying. He almost made the decision to leave, but the thought of the Williams fortune held him there.

Edmund's lip curled in disgust as he digested what he'd just learned. He tried to be logical about it and think things through. This new revelation was certainly going to test his acting abilities. He had no doubt about that. It had been difficult enough for him to keep up the pretense that Glynna's safety was all that mattered to him, when, in truth, he'd been wondering if he would ever be able to lay a hand on her once she was returned to them from her time as a captive of the Comanche. He could well imagine what was happening to her while she was with the renegades, and it turned his stomach.

The woman Edmund wanted to take for his wife and bear his children had to be a delicate flower who was beyond reproach. Much was at stake here. The Moore family name was the most important thing. There could be no scandal attached to it.

Frowning, Edmund considered his options. He now knew for a fact that Glynna was a bastard. She was also being held by savages, who were doing God knew what to her. In spite of himself, he shuddered at the images his imagination conjured up. He wasn't sure what he was going to do. Charles's holdings were impressive, but Edmund was wealthy in his own right. He didn't need the money, but marrying Glynna would have made him wealthier. He wondered if the money would be worth it. He cursed under his breath and went to sit on the sofa.

A happier thought occurred to him then as he tried to relax and ponder this state. With any luck, Glynna might never be found. He smiled at the thought. That scenario would solve all his problems.

If Glynna was never returned to them, he could play the devastated intended and then, after a reasonable length of time, get on with his life. He wondered how long he would have to wait for Glynna before announcing that he believed she was lost to him forever. He didn't want to appear too eager to end their association. Certainly his ties with Charles were beneficial, but the way he was feeling right now, tomorrow wouldn't have been soon enough.

The hours dragged by as Charles sat beside Mimi. He spoke to her almost constantly, urging her to recover and come home with him, exhorting her to pull herself out of the depths of unconsciousness and talk to him. She didn't stir or show any sign that she knew he was there.

"Has she come around at all in the last two days?"

"Once yesterday for a few minutes, but she was mostly incoherent and asking for Glynna."

Charles had been feeling helpless in the face of his sister's suffering, and at the mention of his daughter, he felt even more lost. For the first time in his life, all his money and influence meant nothing. He could not buy Mimi's health back, and there was no one he could use his influence on to help find Glynna.

"I hate this," he said in anguish. "There should be something I can do, some way to help."

"All we can do is sit here and wait, and hope that Hunt has found her."

Charles looked at Paul, his expression one of torment. "Who is this Hunt? I know he's Tom's son, but is he any good? Is there anyone else we can hire to go after her? A posse? Or maybe the Rangers would help? What about the cavalry? Wouldn't they be able to find her quicker? They're out chasing renegades all the time, aren't they?"

"Hunt started tracking them within twelve hours of the raid. There's no one else I trust more than Hunt to see this through."

"But can he do it?"

Paul looked at him seriously. "Yes. I'd trust him with my life."

"But would you trust him with your daughter?" Charles demanded hotly.

Their gazes locked. It was a moment of truth.

"Yes," he answered. "Hunt's faster and more effective than anyone else. He can go places where the army could never go. Trust me in this. Hunt's the best."

"But what if he can't find her? What if he comes back empty-handed?"

Paul looked pained. He knew it was a very real possibility that Glynna might already be dead. He didn't want to say anything, but it was something they had to face. "We'll deal with that then. Right now, for all we know, Hunt's already found her, and they're on their way back home."

"I'd like to think that."

"So would I."

They settled in again, in silence.

Glynna had retired early that night, exhausted by the events of the day. Hunt lingered by the campfire with Painted Horse. He planned to stay in the village for one more day, and then start back to the Rocking M. The going would be long and hard, and he wanted to make sure Glynna was well rested and over her ordeal with Crouching Wolf before heading out. When they had returned to the tepee earlier, Glynna had changed back into her regular clothes. She'd discovered that one of her more personal items was missing, but thought one of the other women had taken it. As she'd been changing, Hunt had seen the extent of the marks the other man had left upon her body. The urge to kill Crouching Wolf had been strong then, and he had been glad the other warrior was gone from the village.

"You will stay another day?"

"Yes, but we must leave the following morning."

"You will walk back to your father's ranch?" Painted Horse asked with a half grin.

"My cousin is a very generous man. I am sure he has two mounts that he would be glad to give me for the trip." Hunt grinned back at him.

"I can find two horses, but they will not be as fine as Warrior."

"No twenty horses are as fine as Warrior. I'm going to miss him."

"But you have your bride."

Glynna filled his thoughts then, and he smiled warmly. "Yes, I have my bride. She is worth ten Warriors. I made the best bargain."

"My vision was true. She was the prize you sought."

"She is my prize," he agreed, getting up. "And she is waiting for me now."

"Good night, Lone Hunter."

"It's going to be," he said, and flashed Painted Horse one last smile before he started off toward the tepee where his wife awaited him.

Wife. The thought that Glynna was his wife still had the power to amaze him. He knew he was play-

273

ing a treacherous game with himself, but he would face the consequences later. Right now, there was only Glynna, and she wanted him.

Hunt slipped almost silently into the dwelling and drew the door covering back down behind him.

"You're back," Glynna said softly as she heard him come inside.

"I was trying to be quiet so I wouldn't disturb you if you were asleep."

"I couldn't fall asleep until I knew you were here with me."

Glynna had been waiting for him, needing him. She shifted positions, bracing herself on one elbow. As she did, the blanket fell away from her shoulder to reveal one perfect, round breast.

Hunt's throat went dry as he stared at the beauty of her. "I don't think you're going to get much sleep now that I'm here," he managed, his gaze hot upon her.

Glynna gave a throaty laugh. "I was hoping you'd feel that way. I really wasn't very tired."

He went to her, mesmerized. She was lovely, and she was all his. They were here, together, in a world they had created—a world in which only they existed. There was no yesterday or tomorrow. There was only this moment in time and the glory of their love.

Hunt stripped away his clothing and joined her on the blankets. He had been worried that Crouching Wolf's abuse might have terrorized her. He had feared that she would not welcome him to her bed again. His fears had been unfounded. Glynna responded fully and ardently to his touch. With the greatest of care, he sought out each bruise on her pale skin and pressed a soft kiss to it.

"I'm sorry Crouching Wolf hurt you," Hunt whispered against her breasts.

"It doesn't matter anymore. You're here now."

Being in Hunt's arms was Glynna's heaven. She had never felt so safe as she did when she was with him. He was strong, yet gentle with her, and the combination was pure ecstasy.

When Hunt moved over her, they came together in a blaze of desire. There was no shyness between them. There was only love. Their kisses fueled the fire of their passion. Excitement seared them. They strained together, each touch inflaming their senses until the firestorm of their need consumed them.

In the aftermath of their love, they lay together, their limbs still entwined, their bodies still joined in love's embrace. They were at peace.

Glynna marveled at the power Hunt had over her. He had only to touch her, and she was his. She could not deny him, and she did not want to. If they could have spent the rest of their lives right there in that tepee, she would have been thrilled. In their safe haven, there was no future and no past, no danger, no hate, no fear. There was only Hunt and the endless pleasure of his love.

Glynna looked up at him, and saw that his eyes were closed and he appeared to be asleep. Unable to resist, she pressed her lips to his chest, and she was rewarded when he moved powerfully against her.

"You aren't asleep?" she asked with a knowing smile, pleased that she had such a strong effect on him.

"No, I was just resting to regain my strength."

"Have you regained it yet?" Glynna let her hands drift down his back to his hips.

At her teasing, Hunt rolled over, bringing her beneath him. "What do you think?"

His hips were firmly nestled against hers, giving proof that he needed no further inspiration.

They made love sweetly then, savoring each kiss and caress. The heat and burning excitement of their first union was replaced by tenderness and a slow-building desire that was equally fulfilling in its own way.

When, at last, their need for one another was temporarily sated, they slept. They were at peace with the beauty and glory that was theirs in their refuge of love.

"Charles?"

The sound of Mimi's voice dragged Charles from sleep, and he jerked awake to find his sister staring at him, sanity in her eyes.

"Mimi! Thank heaven!"

Paul had been dozing in a chair by the window, and he awoke to the sound of Charles's delighted words. "Mary Catherine?"

"Paul?" she said in a strained voice as she tried to look for him.

"He's right here, Mimi," Charles assured her.

She sighed in relief as Paul came closer so she could see him.

"I'm here, darling." He took her hand.

"Charles—how long?"

"I got here yesterday. I was so worried. I didn't

know if you were going to recover or not. How do you feel?"

Mimi managed a pained, small laugh. "Terrible. I'm so weak."

"You've been running a fever," Paul explained as he put a hand to her forehead. "But you're cool now. The fever's broken."

"Charles, I'm glad you're here."

"I had to come. I had to make sure you were all right."

She nodded slowly. "What about Glynna? Has there been any word about her yet?"

"Nothing," Paul told her.

Her deep, abiding fear returned. "I hope she's still alive. . . . But they were so deadly, so vicious." She closed her eyes at the memory of the raid. When she opened them again, her expression was haunted. "I don't know if she could live through that."

Charles fought down the terror that threatened at the thought of Glynna tortured by the Comanche. "She's a strong girl. Glynna will be fine. You'll see."

"I hope you're right, Charles. She's all we've got." Tears fell as she agonized over her daughter's fate. She closed her eyes and slept.

Charles and Paul regarded each other solemnly.

"She's going to be all right," Paul said in relief.

"Now if we just knew something about Glynna."

The rest of the night passed quietly.

Mimi awoke in the morning. She felt weak and terribly sore, but was simply glad to be alive.

"Didn't you go to bed last night?" she asked, startling Charles, who was again asleep in the chair beside the bed.

He sat bolt upright to find her smiling at him. "You're better!"

"Much, and I think I'd like something to eat," she announced. "But first could you help me sit up?"

"Are you sure you want to?" He knew how serious her wound was and worried that moving around might aggravate it.

"I have to. I just can't lie here anymore."

"I'll help you," Paul said from his chair at the foot of the bed. He got up and immediately went to her.

Charles faced off with him. "I told you when I got here, Chandler, that I was going to be taking care of Mimi from now on. I don't need your help."

"Charles," Mimi said gently. When he looked at her, she said, "But I do need his help."

Fury filled him. He wanted to lecture her about what a fool she was being, but this wasn't the time. He stepped aside and watched as Paul carefully put his arms around her and lifted her so she was in a sitting position. He quickly plumped the pillows and put them behind her.

"How do you feel?" Charles asked worriedly, seeing how pale she'd gone at the movement.

"It hurts, but I'm glad to be sitting up."

"I'll see about getting you some food," Paul said. "Tom and Maria will be thrilled to know you're improving."

"Oh, poor Maria," Mimi said sadly. "Diego's dead. How is she doing?"

"She'll never understand why God took her only

son from her, and there was nothing we could say to make things any better."

"Diego died trying to protect us. I want to talk to her so I can tell her about it—let her know how brave he was."

"I'll tell her."

A short time later, Maria came to Mimi. Charles and Paul left the two women alone.

"Maria, Diego was a hero."

"My son?" She looked at Mimi hopefully, wanting to believe that he'd been special.

"Oh, yes. He was trying to save us when they shot him. He was going for his gun, but there were too many in the raiding party. We didn't stand a chance against them. But he didn't try to run or hide. He stayed there and tried to fight them off."

Maria began to cry, and Mimi embraced her.

"He was a wonderful boy. I'll miss him."

"I miss him every day. I don't know how I will keep going without him."

"I understand," Mimi said, and she did, for her own child was in her thoughts constantly. She would know no peace until her daughter was back where she belonged.

When Maria left, Tom and Edmund came in to speak with her. Mimi grew tired quickly. After eating a light breakfast, she fell asleep again. As the day aged, her periods of wakefulness grew longer and longer, and her strength began to return.

"Tomorrow I'm getting out of bed," Mimi declared as she nestled down to sleep for the night.

"Oh, no, you're not," Charles told her. He wanted

to make sure she was nearly healed before she started moving around too much.

Mimi gave him her usual impatient look, and he laughed out loud.

"Why are you laughing?" she demanded indignantly. She wondered why he thought she was funny, when she was being very serious.

"I'm laughing because I'm happy. There was a time when I thought I'd never see you give me that look again!"

Her expression softened as she realized how Charles must have suffered worrying about her on the long trek to Texas. "I'm sorry I caused you so much pain."

"Nonsense. You're getting better. That's all that matters—that and Glynna coming home."

"She'll come back to us. I know she will."

"I hope you're right." He bent to kiss her forehead as she got ready to go to sleep.

"I know I am. Now you get some sleep."

"You, too. You look like you could use some."

"I could. Good night. I'll see you first thing in the morning."

"Good night."

Charles retired upstairs to the room Tom had given him. When he'd gone, Paul went in to check on Mimi. This would be the first night he wasn't by her side, and it worried him to leave her alone. He was glad that Tom had offered him the parlor to sleep in. That way, if she did awake and need anything, he'd be close enough to hear her call out.

"I just wanted to make sure you were still feeling all right."

"I'm going to be fine—really." She gave him a slight smile.

He bent down to her and kissed her tenderly. "You mean the world to me, Mary Catherine. God's giving me another chance with you, and I'm going to spend the rest of my life proving to you how much I love you."

She met him in the kiss.

"Mary Catherine?"

There was a question in his tone as he said her name, and she lifted her gaze to his.

"Mary Catherine, I want us to be married as soon as possible."

"Married?" She stared at him in surprise.

"Yes. I want you with me forever. Knowing you could have been killed showed me just what a fool I've been. I need you. I love you, and I don't want to face the rest of my life without you. I'll make you happy, I promise."

"I can't even think about my own happiness or the rest of my life until I know Glynna's safe."

"I know, but say you'll marry me. We'll face this terror together, and we'll worry about the rest later, once Glynna's back home with us."

"Paul, I—"

"Please, Mary Catherine. Will you do me the honor of becoming my bride?"

Her heart ached. She had longed for this moment for what seemed like eternity. Paul loved her and wanted to marry her. "Yes, Paul. I'll marry you."

Paul carefully embraced her and kissed her once more. "You'll never be sorry."

"I know." She smiled up at him. "I love you, Paul."

"I love you."

He stayed with her until she grew sleepy, then left her to rest. Paul was thrilled that she'd accepted his proposal, but he knew true joy would elude them both until Glynna returned. The thought of a future without her was bleak.

Glynna lay in her husband's arms, thinking of the day to come. "How early will we be leaving?"

"Just after dawn," Hunt told her.

"I'm glad. It's time. I need to get back and make sure Aunt Mimi is all right. How long will it take us to reach the ranch?"

"Probably five days."

"It didn't take us five days to get here."

"But I don't think you want to ride back at the same pace Painted Horse rode before, do you?"

She remembered the endless miles and how the raiding party had seldom stopped. Only when the horses had been ready to drop had there been any rest. "No. I don't ever want to ride like that again."

"Painted Horse is giving us two mounts. I told him we would be ready to leave early."

"Do you think we'll have any trouble with Crouching Wolf on the way?"

"I don't know. I hope not, but we'll just have to keep careful watch and make sure we don't give him any opportunity to surprise us in any way."

"Hunt, there's something important I've been meaning to ask you."

"What?" He wondered why she sounded so hesitant.

"I was wondering . . . would you teach me how to

shoot a gun? Aunt Mimi knows how, but I never learned."

He frowned. "If you're going to be a fast draw, I'd rather you stick to drawing with your pencils. The sketches you did of the village today were very good."

"Thanks, but please don't tease me about this. I'm serious about wanting to learn how to handle a gun. If I'm going to stay in Texas, I need to learn how to shoot so I can defend myself. Will you teach me?"

He didn't like it, but he knew she had a point. "All right."

"Thank you. You won't be sorry."

"If I teach you how to use a gun, you have to promise me something."

"Anything."

"You won't ever use it on me," he teased.

"I can't use it to steal your heart?"

"You don't have to steal my heart. I've already given it to you."

His statement so delighted her that she kissed him, and all thoughts of guns were forgotten. The rest of the night was lost in a haze of passion.

Glynna fell asleep in the early morning hours, but Hunt did not. He lay awake, waiting to face the new day. He was finally being forced to confront what he knew was to come. They would be returning to the ranch. They would be returning to the white man's world. This time of peace he'd found with Glynna here in the village would be over soon. He was going to have to give her up.

The power of the pain that came with that realization surprised Hunt. He had known when he'd allowed himself to enjoy the time they had together that it wouldn't be easy for them to part. But he'd never thought it would hurt this badly.

A burning ache grew in his chest. He wanted to hold Glynna to his heart and never let her go. He wanted to stay in the haven of this village and love her. But he knew it could never be. He had to take her home. He had to let everyone know that she was alive and well. He had to save her reputation, and for that reason he would deny that they had been married. He would deny that he'd ever made her his—though the times they'd made love had been the most exquisite moments of his life. He would force himself to give up the woman who had touched him as no other had ever done. He loved her, and because he loved her he would let her go. And he had to prepare himself, because it would be the most difficult thing he would ever do in his life.

Hunt looked over at Glynna where she slept beside him. His desire for her stirred within him, and he could not deny himself another taste of her love, there in their sensual refuge from reality.

Turning to her, Hunt pressed his lips to her throat. Glynna awoke with a sleepy smile and reached down to draw him up to her.

"I was dreaming of you," she whispered without opening her eyes.

"Was it a good dream?"

"A very good dream."

They made love again.

For Hunt, it was a bittersweet union. The end was so near, and yet he couldn't accept it—not yet . . . not yet.

He took her swiftly, powerfully, trying to fight off the demons that haunted him. This was Glynna and she was his now—for this moment. As long as he held her, nothing else mattered.

He was glad for the cover of darkness, for she could not see the tears in his eyes.

Dawn came far too soon for Hunt.

Chapter Fifteen

"I'm sitting in a chair today whether you two like it or not," Mimi declared, giving Charles and Paul a defiant look. She had bathed and changed into a new gown and wrapper. She felt like a new woman, and she wasn't about to be denied.

"We're only looking out for you. We don't want you to hurt yourself by overdoing."

"The only thing I've overdone is the time I've spent in bed. The way I feel right now, if I get back in a bed in the next month, it will be too soon!"

"Let me help you," Charles offered.

"No. I'm going to do it myself."

She was headstrong and independent, but today, Paul wasn't going to stand for any of it.

"You can be independent some other day," he declared as he scooped her up in his arms and carried her to a chair in the parlor. "There. Now enjoy the day sitting up."

Mimi had the grace to look appreciative. "I could have made it on my own, you know, but thank you."

"You're welcome," he told her, exchanging satisfied looks with Charles.

Paul quickly wrapped a blanket across her lap and tucked it beneath her legs.

"You're making me feel like a little old lady," she said.

"You don't look like one," Paul assured her.

"Thank you again." She did smile then.

Edmund came in once she was settled. They made small talk. He tried to be solicitous, but found it difficult. If Aunt Mimi hadn't agreed to accompany Glynna on the trip, none of this would have happened, and he wouldn't be stuck out in the middle of Texas right now.

The day passed quietly. It was late in the afternoon when Mimi finally had some time alone with Charles. Paul and Edmund had gone down to the barn with Tom to take a look at the horses.

"I'm glad we've finally got a minute to ourselves. There's something we need to talk about."

He gave her a curious look.

She looked him straight in the eye. "I told Paul everything. I told him the truth about Glynna."

"I know."

"You do?" She was shocked that he hadn't said anything to her before now.

"When I first arrived, Paul came out to meet me. I

couldn't help myself. I hit him. We exchanged words, and later, when we were alone, he told me that you'd told him the truth."

She could see the pain in Charles's expression, but said nothing as he continued to speak.

"What I don't understand, Mimi, is why? We've protected her all these years. Why did you tell Paul now?"

She looked tormented as she thought back to that day. It was all a feverish blur to her. "My only excuse is that I thought I was dying, and I wanted him to know before I died. He is her father, and he deserves to know the truth."

"I'm her father!" Charles countered, hurt.

"Yes, you are." She reached out and took his hand. "You've been a perfect father to Glynna, but I wanted Paul to know and to understand."

"I should have locked you in your rooms in New York and never let you out! When Glynna returns and we go back home, I think I may do just that!"

"Be nice," she scolded him. "I'm going to marry Paul."

"You're what?"

"Paul proposed and I accepted."

"That's ridiculous. He's playing you for a fool again."

"No, he's not. I still love him. I suppose I always have."

"How can you still love him after he deserted you that way? He left you pregnant and all alone!"

"I remember. But I also remember that it took two for me to get in that condition. I was a willing participant. I loved him. We were happy together, and Glynna is the result of our love."

"What are you going to tell her?"

"I don't know. That's why I wanted to talk to you. I want your opinion. I don't think I should tell her the truth. She loves you. She's your daughter. I think we should leave it at that."

"I agree, but what about Paul?" No matter what his sister's feelings, he didn't trust the man. He didn't trust him at all.

"Can you go get him? Tell him we need to talk?"

Charles went in search of Paul, not at all eager for the coming conversation. He found him in the stable, and they returned to the house together.

"Is something wrong?" Paul asked when the three of them were together.

"Charles and I were discussing what we should do about Glynna. We wanted your opinion." She looked up at him, seeing the question in his eyes. "We believe the best thing to do is not to tell Glynna the truth. We think she'll be much better off if we continue to live the lie we created all those years ago. Charles is the only father she's ever known, and she's always believed Victoria was her mother. She's happy this way. I don't want to ruin her life, trying to justify my own."

Paul was quiet for a moment. His silence troubled Mimi and Charles. They feared he would go against them, and they didn't know how Glynna would react to hearing his revelations.

Paul was tormented. He had just discovered that he had a daughter! Glynna was a wonderful, beautiful girl. He wanted to embrace her fully, to let her know that he was her father, and to spend the rest of his life making up for his absence in her life and her mother's. But Paul was man enough to know that his motives were completely selfish. In wanting to tell her the truth, he only wanted to be more important in her life. He wasn't thinking of how the news would affect her.

"You're both right," he said slowly. In agreeing, he knew he was giving up the greatest gift he'd ever been given—a child. But the self-sacrifice was worth it. Most of all, he wanted Glynna's happiness.

"Thank you," they both said at the same time.

Paul lifted his troubled gaze to look at them. His expression was strained as he thought of Glynna. "Let's just hope we get the chance not to tell her."

"I would like that," Charles agreed.

"The sooner the better," Mimi said. Then, turning her gaze toward the window, she asked, "I wonder where she is. I wonder if Hunt's found her yet."

Hunt's mood was dark as he said good-bye to Painted Horse that morning. He feared that if his cousin continued his dangerous raiding off the reservation he would never see him again. Their parting was solemn. He looked back only once to find Painted Horse watching him go.

Hunt set a steady, ground-eating pace as he and Glynna headed for the Rocking M. They rode for several hours without speaking.

"You're awfully quiet." Glynna finally broke the silence between them.

"I've been thinking about Painted Horse—and worrying."

"He's chosen his path."

While Painted Horse had not harmed her in any way, his raiding party had killed Diego, and Crouching Wolf had shot Aunt Mimi. She'd never felt comfortable in the village, but with Hunt by her side, she'd felt safe. Had she been a true white captive, the experience would have been completely terrifying.

"I know raiding is not the answer for them, but I'm not sure there is an answer. The Comanche way of life is over. The white men are everywhere, and they're not going to stop coming."

"You make it sound as if you're not one of them," she remarked. "You and your father own a ranch. You've settled here."

He cast her a sidelong glance, realizing again just how innocent she was about the way of things. "I'm not accepted in the white world."

"You could be."

"Maybe things are simple back in New York City, but out here they're not. I learned that lesson when I was young, and it's one I'm not going to forget."

"What happened?"

"Let's just say, when I was fifteen I was made to understand that I wasn't as good as whites. They didn't want me around, so they ran me out of town."

"Why?"

He hesitated to tell Glynna about Jenny and her brothers. It was an ugly, sordid tale. He had learned a lot from it, though. After a moment's thought, he decided to go ahead and tell her, for maybe then she would understand.

"I was accused of attacking a white girl named Jenny Ross. I did kiss her, and her brothers caught us. They decided that I'd tried to ruin her, and they beat me up pretty bad."

"How bad was it?"

"I was unconscious. When I finally came to, I struggled home, packed up and left. Her father had been there looking for me. He wanted to kill me. Luckily, I got away."

"How awful! Why didn't that girl just tell them what really happened?"

"You've got to understand. She tried to tell them, but they didn't want to hear."

"Well, she obviously didn't try very hard."

"Glynna, I'm a half-breed. The truth didn't matter to them. All that mattered was that my mother was Comanche."

"Well, they were wrong. You're a human being. That kind of prejudice must have been terrible for your parents," she sympathized, trying to imagine being so hated . . . so ostracized. How horrible to be immediately judged as unworthy because of one's parentage, and how unfair!

"My mother died when I was young. My father had to live with it, though. That's why I was hesitant to come here to the ranch and help him. I didn't want to cause him trouble."

"But Paul said you have friends in town."

He shrugged. "A few."

"That's more than some white men can say."

He was quiet. He didn't respond.

"Tell me about your mother. What was she like?"

"We didn't live in town when she was alive, so my memories of those times are happy enough. Honestly, though, I don't remember too much about her."

"And your father never married again?"

"No. He didn't want anyone else."

"He must have loved her very much."

"He did."

"We do have that in common," Glynna told him. "My mother died when I was still a baby. My father never remarried, either. Aunt Mimi is the closest thing to a real mother I've ever had."

"You were fortunate to have her. I like her."

"You do?" She was surprised. She had never heard him admit to liking anyone before.

"She's honest and intelligent, and she knows a good horse when she sees one." He grinned.

"She is a very special person. I don't know what I'd do without her. She was widowed long ago, but her husband left her a lot of money. She's used it to travel and have wonderful adventures. She's the one who planned this trip for us."

"I'm glad she did," Hunt said.

"So am I."

Hunt glanced over at Glynna and thought she looked beautiful. She was riding with a natural, easy grace. He would never have guessed that she was New York City born and bred.

At the thought of Glynna's life back east, Hunt tensed. With each mile they covered, they were coming closer and closer to the end of their time together. She was promised to another man. Though she had told him that she loved him when they were making love, Hunt knew Glynna didn't belong to him. No matter how much he wanted her, it could never be. He pushed the thought away. They still had four more days together.

"I just hope Aunt Mimi's all right," she went on. "Not knowing about her condition is awful. I've tried not to think about it, but I heard her scream during the raid and I haven't been able to forget it."

"Wes and Gib were taking her straight back to the house when I left them. I'm sure they got the doc out to the ranch right away."

"Aunt Mimi had an ulterior motive for coming to Dry Creek, you know," she told him, changing the topic to distract herself from her worries.

"She did? What was it?"

"She knew Paul Chandler from years ago, and she wanted to see him again."

"Paul's a good man. She could do worse."

"I like him, too." Glynna gazed at the wilderness surrounding them. "It will be good to get back."

"Very good."

They didn't stop until late in the afternoon, when they found a small stream to camp by. Once the horses were bedded down, Glynna sought Hunt out.

"All right, Mr. McAllister, it's time."

"Time for what?" He could not imagine what she wanted.

"My first lesson. I want to learn everything there is to know about shooting a six-gun."

"You're sure about this?"

"I'm positive."

Hunt drew his gun, and they went to sit at their campsite. He showed her how to load it and the proper way to hold it.

"Just remember, this is a dangerous, deadly weapon."

"That's exactly why I want to know how to use it."

"Let's see how good you are, then."

He took her a distance away from the horses and pointed out a small rock some distance away.

"Take your time, aim carefully and see if you can hit that rock."

Glynna did everything Hunt had told her to do, including squeezing the trigger slowly, but the gun jerked violently in her hand, and her shot missed badly.

"This isn't as easy as it looks."

"There's nothing easy about it."

"It's heavy, too. No wonder Aunt Mimi carries only a derringer."

"Do you want to try again?"

"Yes." She was determined.

It took almost half an hour before she finally came close to hitting her target. It was starting to get dark when they stopped for the night. They ate a small meal from the supplies Painted Horse had given them, and then Glynna bedded down for the night.

"I'm going to take a look around," Hunt told her. "Stay here. I'll be back."

He took his rifle with him and went to scout the area. He wanted to make sure there was no sign of Crouching Wolf and that all was going to be quiet for the night.

Glynna lay quietly, waiting for his return, staring up at the star-studded sky. It was a beautiful night. If she hadn't been haunted by her concern for Aunt Mimi, she realized this could be considered her honeymoon. She smiled at the thought. In all her wildest fantasies about being married, she'd never considered spending her honeymoon sleeping out under the stars. She'd always fancied herself going to Europe on a grand tour, staying at the finest hotels. This was as far as she could get from that fantasy, yet she had no regrets whatsoever. She loved Hunt.

Glynna saw Hunt returning then, and knew that one night here with him under the stars was worth a lifetime of luxury. She smiled at him.

"You took long enough," she said as he stretched out beside her.

"I just wanted to make sure it was quiet out there."

"And it was?"

He nodded as he took her in his arms. "There's not a soul around. It's just the two of us."

"I like the sound of that." She kissed him invitingly.

They made love with quiet joy, treasuring each kiss and touch. When their passions were spent, they rested together.

"This Comanche marriage was a good idea," Glynna murmured just before she drifted off, at peace in his embrace.

Her words stabbed at Hunt's heart as he held her. Even after their talk today about his past, she still did not understand the ugly truth they would be dealing with once they returned—he was a half-breed and she was a white woman. Their love could never be.

Hunt looked down at her as she slept so trustingly against him. He did love her—more than life itself, and for that very reason, he would not condemn her to a hate-filled existence. He was going to have to let her go, and he was going to have to do it soon. He closed his eyes against the thought. He sought sleep, but it proved elusive.

Glynna awoke at dawn to find Hunt gone from her side. She sat up quickly, worried that something had happened during the night. As she got up, she heard the sound of water splashing and made her way down to the stream to find Hunt bathing. He looked up at her, surprised to find that she'd awakened so soon. She had been sleeping soundly when he'd left her.

"I thought I'd take advantage of the stream while I could."

Glynna just smiled at him, enjoying the view. The water was deep enough to swirl about his waist, but the power of his chest and shoulders was bared to her, and he was sleekly dripping with water.

"Would you like some company?" she asked, starting immediately to undress.

Hunt grinned. He remembered how hard it had been for him to keep his back turned when she'd bathed at the renegade village, and the thought of actually bathing with her excited him.

"I'd love some company." He waited there for her to join him, wanting to enjoy watching her come to him.

When she'd shed her clothes, Glynna stood before him looking much like a goddess in the golden glow of the dawn's first light. She was lovely, and by the time she'd entered the stream and made her way to him, he was ready for her.

He waited there for her to join him.

"Do you want to bathe first?"

"First?" she asked innocently. "I thought that was all we were going to do."

Hunt gave a throaty chuckle as he lifted Glynna and brought her against him, fitting her legs around his hips. Glynna gave him a sensual smile as she pressed herself tightly to him. She linked her arms about his neck and kissed him.

"I've always enjoyed taking a bath, but I think I may like bathing even more after today," she said.

Hunt gave a low growl of hunger as he returned her kiss. Without altering his stance, he filled her with the proof of his desire, and she gave a purr of delight at the intimacy. All thoughts of bathing were lost as they surrendered to the love that overwhelmed them.

When at last the storm of their excitement had passed, they did bathe. It was well past sunup when they left the water to prepare for the new day. They ate a small breakfast and were soon on their way.

As Hunt rode out, he wished there was some way to stay there in the wilderness with Glynna forever.

Crouching Wolf sat at his campfire, deep in thought. The knife wounds Lone Hunter had inflicted on him were painful, but not as painful as the humiliation he'd suffered. He was well enough to seek his revenge, and he planned to do just that.

"They left the village yesterday?" he asked Tall Grass.

"Early. They are heading back toward the place where we took her."

Crouching Wolf nodded. "We will find them today."

His eyes were ablaze with fury and hatred as he looked over at his friend, and Tall Grass knew that he would have no peace until he'd found them.

"Does anyone know where you went?" Crouching Wolf asked him.

"I told no one that I was coming after you."

"Good. We will raid together."

The two renegades were deadly and determined as they sought Hunt and Glynna's trail.

"Something's been troubling me, and I was wondering . . ." Glynna said thoughtfully as they continued on their trip home much later that afternoon.

"Wondering about what?"

"What my name really is." At his confused frown, she went on, smiling, lighthearted, "Well, am I going to be Mrs. Hunt McAllister when we get back or Mrs. Lone Hunter?"

Hunt's grip on his reins tightened and his expression darkened. He didn't want to talk about this. He didn't even want to think about it for another day, yet she was looking at him expectantly, waiting for his answer. He struggled to find the strength to say what needed to be said. There could be no delaying. It had to be now.

Glynna saw the change in him—the way he tensed as he rode, how his expression turned stony, losing all warmth and emotion, and she wondered why.

"What's wrong?" she asked, reining in.

Hunt stopped beside her to face her. "There's

something I've been meaning to tell you about this 'marriage.'"

"What?" She was completely at a loss.

It was time. Hunt could avoid this moment no longer. He glanced over at Glynna, the look in his eyes devoid of emotion.

"The only reason I married you was to save you from the renegades."

"I don't understand."

"Painted Horse would give you to me only if I took you as my bride. It was the only way to free you, so I gave him Warrior as the bride-price, and he gave you to me. Now that we're away from the village, you no longer have to consider yourself my wife, and, in fact, once we're back at the ranch, it would be best if you didn't tell anyone at all about what happened."

"But we're married!" Glynna was shocked.

"Aren't you promised to someone back in New York?"

She paled at the mention of Edmund. "Didn't what we've shared mean anything to you?"

"What happened between us was not important. What's important is that you're free and you're safe."

"Why have you changed this way?"

"I haven't changed. I did what I had to do to get you out of danger."

"Oh, so making love to me was getting me out of danger? Making love to me was 'doing what you had to do'? I didn't realize I was such a chore!"

"I'm sorry. Things shouldn't have gone as far as they did between us, but I can't change that now. You said yourself that Crouching Wolf and Painted Horse had had words over you. To save you, I had to

301

do it the Comanche way. I had to pay the bride-price."

"And I know all about your bride-price!" she countered, anger, hurt and embarrassment stinging her. She'd thought he loved her, but now as she thought back over their days and nights together, she realized he'd never told her that he did.

"Glynna—"

"Oh, no," she said, fuming. "I promise you, Hunt McAllister, that as soon as we get back to civilization, I will get you another damned horse to replace Warrior! I wouldn't want you to feel that you'd paid too high a price for my freedom, and I'll also see to it that my father pays you a reward! I wouldn't want you to think that your precious time had been wasted coming after me. I know how much work you have to do at the ranch."

Glynna felt sick. She wanted to get away from Hunt. She needed to get away from him. She had thought that they'd shared something special, but she'd been wrong—so wrong.

Glynna was wheeling her horse around, ready to ride off and leave Hunt behind, when shots rang out around them.

Chapter Sixteen

Hunt had time to glance back only once and see Crouching Wolf taking aim at them again. He immediately urged his horse toward Glynna and quickly swept her from her mount, protecting her with his body, just as shots exploded around them.

Hunt silently cursed his own stupidity for having let his guard down as he dove for cover behind some nearby rocks, still holding her in his grasp. He should have been watching. He should have anticipated that Crouching Wolf would try to cause trouble for them.

"Stay down! It's Crouching Wolf!" Hunt ordered as he shoved her behind him.

"Give me a gun! I'll help you!" Glynna told him. She wasn't sure she could hit much, but she could try.

Bobbi Smith

"All I've got is my sidearm. I didn't have time to get my rifle."

"Can we get back to the horses?"

"No. They ran off." Hunt shifted his position a bit to see if he could get a good shot at Crouching Wolf.

Crouching Wolf and Tall Grass were watching, and both fired at him the moment he showed himself.

Hunt quickly ducked back down, swearing viciously as he realized his enemy wasn't alone. He would save the few bullets he had until he was certain he could hit them.

"There's someone else with him?" Glynna asked.

"Yeah. It looks like there's two of them."

He fell silent for a moment trying to figure out a way to escape, but without their horses, they were pinned down with only one gun. Things didn't look good.

Hunt's mood was fierce and his mind was racing as he tried to anticipate their attackers' next moves. There was little time. Another barrage came at them, and he returned two shots selectively, but with no luck. He didn't hit either man, and the firing continued.

"What are we going to do?" Glynna asked, knowing the seriousness of their situation.

"The only thing we can do—wait it out and hope Crouching Wolf tries something stupid." Even as Hunt spoke, though, he doubted it would happen. He was outnumbered and outgunned. Somehow, he had to keep Glynna safe. He could not let Crouching Wolf have her. There had to be something he could do. The only other weapon he had was his knife, but it

304

was better than leaving her unprotected. "Here." He handed her his knife. "Take this. Use it if you have to."

The look she gave him spoke volumes, but he had no time to say any more. Crouching Wolf and Tall Grass attacked then, riding at them full speed, their guns blazing. Hunt fired, trying to drive them back. One bullet found its mark. Tall Grass was killed as he charged them. But just as Crouching Wolf came at him, Hunt's ammunition ran out.

Hunt stood before Glynna and faced his enemy without fear. Crouching Wolf was sitting on his horse, smiling a feral smile, his rifle trained on Hunt's chest.

"Lone Hunter, it would seem that you could not defeat me, after all," he said with a sneer.

"I defeated you, Crouching Wolf, and I did not need to come at you from ambush to do it."

The renegade's smile didn't waver. "It does not matter how one wins a battle. It matters only that the battle is won." He looked over at Glynna. "As it was meant to be from the beginning, you will now be mine. It is time."

"No, Crouching Wolf!" came a shout from the distance.

Crouching Wolf panicked when he turned to see Painted Horse and a band of his warriors surrounding them.

"Painted Horse!"

"That's right! I did not trust you, and I was right. Your time of lies and deceit are over."

"No!"

Crouching Wolf turned back, ready to fire at Hunt,

but Painted Horse fired first. The evil warrior pitched forward, thrown from his horse by the force of the shot, and lay dead on the rocky ground.

Glynna cried out, and Hunt quickly took her in his arms and held her close.

Painted Horse rode in on Warrior, his men following. They were leading Hunt's and Glynna's horses.

"You are unhurt, Lone Hunter?" Painted Horse asked.

"We are fine, but only because of you. You saved us, my cousin. I thank you."

"I did not trust Crouching Wolf, and I was right. You will make the rest of your trip home safely now. No other will bother you. Here are your horses."

Glynna looked up at Painted Horse. He had frightened her for days, yet he had just saved their lives. Painted Horse was nothing like Crouching Wolf and Tall Grass. She knew she owed him a debt of gratitude. She left Hunt's arms and stepped away, looking up at the Comanche leader. "Thank you, Painted Horse."

He looked down at her and nodded. "It is good that Vision Woman is safe."

"Very good," Hunt agreed, knowing that without his cousin's help, he would have been dead.

Painted Horse directed his men to take the bodies of the two men with them, and then they rode off, disappearing as they'd come, leaving Hunt and Glynna alone.

Glynna couldn't believe that it had all happened so fast. She and Hunt had been arguing, and then suddenly they'd been fighting for their very lives. Now it was over as quickly as it had begun, and she was at a loss. Hunt had saved her again, but she knew now it wasn't because he loved and cared about her. It was only because he wanted to get her back home.

Hunt holstered his gun and turned to Glynna, wanting to make sure she hadn't been injured in some way. "Are you all right?"

"I'm fine," she answered, her tone cold. "What about you?"

The iciness of her voice let him know that their words before the attack had not been forgotten. "I'm fine, too. Glynna—" He wanted to say more, to try to ease the harshness of his earlier explanation, but she gave him no chance.

Glynna went on, not waiting for him to say any more, "We were very lucky Painted Horse showed up when he did. Now we can concentrate on getting back the ranch. That's all I care about right now. I want to make sure Aunt Mimi is alive and well, and then I want to go home."

Hunt didn't say any more, but brought her horse to her. She handed him his knife back and did not wait for any help from him. In fact, she didn't want any. She had had enough of his help. She mounted quickly. The closer she got to the Rocking M that day, the better.

Swinging up into his saddle, Hunt followed after her. She set a quick pace, and he knew it was going to be a long, hard ride for the rest of the day.

Hunt glanced back in the direction Painted Horse had ridden and despair filled him. His cousin was a good man with a good heart, but Hunt knew he would never find peace again in this world. Things had changed too much. The life he'd led had been destroyed, and there would be no future for him, if he could not accept that. He hoped Painted Horse would find a way to change, so he could live. He did not want to think about what would happen to him if he continued to raid.

Night came too soon for Glynna. The last thing she wanted to do was think about bedding down that night. If she could have had her way, she would have kept riding nonstop until they'd reached the ranch. When Hunt announced to her that they had reached the place where they would camp for the night, she reluctantly stopped. He tended to the horses, while she set about spreading out her own blankets and getting ready for the long hours to come.

Memories of the last several nights taunted her. She thought of how they had made love before the campfire and how they had come together so gloriously in the stream. She had believed Hunt loved her then, and she had given herself to him freely and without reservation. She had been wrong, though, very wrong.

Hunt didn't love her. He never had, and he never would.

They ate in relative silence, and as soon as she could, she turned in for the night. Lying huddled and alone under her blanket, Glynna sought sleep. Only in sleep would she find the quietude she so desperately needed.

But sleep did not come easily for Glynna as memories of the day's happenings played relentlessly in her mind. Turbulent thoughts of Hunt's cruel revelation and Crouching Wolf's surprise ambush would not be dismissed. Finally, late that night, she did drift off, but it was a troubled sleep that offered little solace or rest.

Hunt lay across the campfire from Glynna, his mood as dark as the moonless night. He had done it. He had convinced Glynna that their marriage was nonexistent and that what had happened between them had been a mistake, that he didn't love her. It hadn't been easy for him, but he was glad it was over.

Even as he told himself that he was glad that it was finished between them, though, Hunt knew it would never be over for him. When the attack came, he had been so desperately afraid that some harm would come to Glynna. He hadn't even thought about his own mortality; he had cared only about what was going to happen to her.

He loved her desperately. Yet their love could never be. He had known it from the start, and now he had to accept it. It was over. He would never know the joy of holding her or loving her again.

Hunt closed his eyes against the pain.

He would survive.

He had no choice.

It was hot. There was little breeze stirring, and Mimi was seeking what comfort she could, sitting out on the porch. She was feeling much stronger and was glad, but even feeling physically better didn't ease the pain of her worries about Glynna. Where was she? Was she alive?

"Mimi, I don't know how much longer I can stand this," Charles said as he came out of the house.

Mimi glanced up at her brother as he paced restlessly on the porch, and suddenly realized how much his concern for Glynna was taking its toll on him. He looked haggard and exhausted. Even his usually sharp-eyed gaze was dulled by the pain of his anxiety about his daughter's safety.

"I know," she said sympathetically. "Every day I get up believing that we'll hear something, and every day it's the same. Nothing. Where is she, Charles? Where can she be? Is she safe?" Tears threatened as she finally voiced her own terror.

"I wish to God I knew. If I did, I'd go after her myself. I know Tom and Paul told us that Hunt was the best man for the job, but it's been almost two weeks and we haven't heard a word. What if something's happened to Hunt? How long do we just sit here and wait for an answer that may never come?"

"I don't know. I was thinking the same thing. Do we stay here and wait until she returns?"

"If she returns," Charles said.

"Charles!" Mimi protested. "You can't allow yourself to think that way! You have to have hope! We have to believe Glynna's coming home to us!"

"But we've both read the accounts of white captives. Sometimes they're not found for years. Sometimes they're never found at all." Charles wearily rubbed a hand over his eyes, struggling to stay in control. He'd been strong for so long, but all the empty days and nights were wearing on him.

"Glynna will come home. If there's any way for her to come back to us, she will. She has to." Mimi tried to be firm in her conviction. She wanted to bolster Charles's spirits. Even though her own mood was as low as his, she wouldn't completely give in to it.

"You're right," he agreed, forcing himself not to think of the worst possible outcome. "But maybe it is time I contacted the cavalry or the Rangers. Surely there's someone, somewhere out here, who can help us. Lord knows, I've got money enough to hire more men to go after her. I'd give up my entire fortune if it meant getting Glynna back, but I don't think money has anything to do with this."

They shared a knowing look. It was so hard to sit by and wait; they were both used to taking charge and making things happen.

"Wherever she is, I know Glynna's thinking of us. We may not be able to talk to her, but she knows we love her."

"I hope so. She's been my whole life. All I ever wanted was for her to be happy."

Mimi looked up at her brother, open adoration for him shining in her eyes. "You know, Charles, you've always been my hero."

He was astonished by her statement. "I have?"

"Oh, yes. You are a wonderful man. You have always been there for me whenever I've needed you, and I love you more than I can ever tell you."

He smiled gently at her. "I love you, too, Mimi."

"I bet you didn't know it, but even when we were little, I thought you were wonderful," she said, grinning as she remembered their childhood.

"Even when you were causing me trouble?" It seemed he had always been saving her from one misadventure or another, trying to keep her out of trouble with their parents.

"But you always helped me. You were always there

for me. Always." She said the last with loving emphasis. "Just as you are now."

Charles leaned down and pressed a tender kiss to her cheek. "We'll find her. You just wait and see."

"I know," she said, believing him.

Mimi lifted her gaze past Charles and frowned. It looked as if someone was riding in, but she couldn't be sure.

"Charles . . ."

"What?" He saw the direction of her gaze and turned to take a look. "Someone's coming!"

She grabbed his arm. "Can you see who it is? Can you tell if it's someone from town or maybe—"

Mimi got to her feet. They both left the porch as they strained to see if they could identify the riders. She didn't recognize the horses, and, for a moment, she thought it wasn't Hunt. He would have been riding Warrior, and she would have known that stallion immediately, even at this distance.

"Oh, God, Charles. It's her," Mimi whispered as the riders finally drew close enough, and she could see that the one out in front was Glynna.

Mimi started to run. She was barely strong enough to walk a few steps, but the sight of her beloved daughter returning banished all weakness from her. She held her arms wide as her tears flowed unchecked.

Charles was right by her side, his gaze on Glynna. She was alive! She had come back to them! His heart was pounding, and he had never known such ecstasy. "Thank you, God," he prayed as his daughter raced toward them at top speed.

* * *

Glynna had thought the miles and days would never end. What had kept her going was the driving need to see her Aunt Mimi again. She knew every minute of the pounding ride would be worth it if she got back and found that her aunt was all right.

Hunt had told her that morning when they'd broken camp that they would reach the Rocking M that afternoon. She hadn't truly believed him until they'd crossed a creek some miles back and he'd told her they were now on Rocking M land. Until they'd come over the last hill and seen the ranch house, though, she'd feared it would never happen. And then when she saw Aunt Mimi and her father running toward her, her heart had filled with joy unlike anything she'd ever felt before.

"Aunt Mimi! Papa!" she cried as she charged toward them as fast as her weary mount would go. She didn't rein in until the very last minute, and then all but threw herself from the horse's back. She was sobbing uncontrollably as she ran into their waiting arms. "Oh! Aunt Mimi! Papa!"

"You're back!" was all they could say as they enfolded her in a strong, loving embrace.

They stood, crying, wrapped in each other's arms. There was peace in their world.

Tom, Paul and Edmund had been down at the stables when they heard the shouts from Mimi and Charles. Wes and Gib followed them as they ran for the house. The scene they came upon thrilled them.

Edmund hurried forward, acting eager to see Glynna, but in his thoughts he was less than grateful to the fate that had returned her to him. "Glynna! Thank God, you're here, and you're all right!"

313

Glynna looked up from where she stood in her father's and aunt's arms and managed to smile at Edmund. She had thought that her father might be there, but she hadn't even considered that Edmund might have traveled to Texas, too. "Edmund . . ."

Edmund opened his arms to her, and she had no choice. She went to him.

Mimi and Charles looked on. Charles's expression was satisfied at Edmund's display, but Mimi was frowning slightly as she watched them together.

"I'm so glad you're back," Edmund told her. "We've been going crazy waiting to hear some word about you."

"I'm glad I'm back, too," Glynna said tearfully, still being held close in his arms. She found his embrace comforting, but it was nothing like being held in Hunt's arms. Even as the realization came to her, she pushed it away. Edmund was to be her future, not Hunt.

Hunt had ridden in behind her, and was still mounted, looking on at the happy reunion. When Glynna went into the other man's arms, a fierce emotion stabbed him. He fought it down. He had no claim to Glynna. She was back where she was supposed to be with her family and the man she was promised to. He wasn't needed there. He had just started to ride toward the stable when his father came to him.

"I knew you could do it, son," Tom told him, beaming up at him, pride showing in his eyes.

Hunt nodded and, knowing he couldn't get away now, dismounted to stand with his father. "The raiders had taken her up north. They were camped in a secluded canyon, but I managed to find them."

"How'd you get her away from them?"

"I made a trade—Warrior for Glynna."

Tom knew how much the stallion had meant to his boy. He clapped him on the back. "I'm proud of you."

Hunt gave him a tight smile. "Is Mimi all right?"

"It was a bad gunshot wound, but she's getting better. Glynna's coming home will do more for her recovery than all the doctoring in the world."

"Good."

"That's her father, Charles, there with Mimi and Paul, and the other man is Edmund Moore, the man she's supposed to marry when she goes back to New York."

Charles looked up then to see Tom standing with the man who'd rescued his daughter and brought her home. He went straight to Hunt and held out his hand. "You must be Tom's son, Hunt."

"Yes, sir," Hunt responded, looking Charles in the eye as he shook his hand.

"I'm Charles Williams, Glynna's father. I can never thank you enough for what you've done for Glynna— and for Mimi and me." His words were completely sincere.

"I'm just glad everything turned out all right."

"Glynna's back with us. That's all that matters. Thank you, Hunt."

Hunt glanced Glynna's way to find her gaze upon him, even as she stood in the circle of Edmund's arms. Hunt's expression remained impassive. He displayed none of the emotion raging within him. He looked calmly back at Charles. "We were very lucky."

"We were all lucky—lucky that you were here so you could go after her so quickly. If it hadn't been for you, we might never have gotten Glynna back."

"Charles is right, Hunt," Mimi said as she came to speak with him.

Paul was at her side, his arm around her waist.

She went on, "Without your help, Glynna might have been lost to us forever. You saved her." Mimi's gaze met his as she drew him down to her so she could kiss his cheek. "Thank you for bringing her back to me."

Her heartfelt thanks touched Hunt deeply. "I'm glad she's back where she belongs, and I'm glad it's over now. Glynna's safe."

"Yes, she is."

They turned to look at Glynna as she stood with Edmund, his arm possessively around her shoulders.

Edmund was looking at Hunt, and he knew he should thank the man, too. He guided Glynna over to her rescuer.

"Thank you for bringing Glynna back safely," Edmund said, offering Hunt his hand, but still keeping one arm around her. "She means the world to me."

"I can understand why. She's a wonderful woman." Hunt shook hands with him, his gaze upon Glynna as he spoke. "You're a very lucky man."

"I know," Edmund replied, looking proudly down at her as if he owned her.

Glynna wanted to hit them both for talking about her as if she wasn't even there. Somehow she managed a benign smile, when all she wanted to do was glare at them for their arrogance. You're *a very lucky man*. . . . Inwardly she was seething at Hunt's cavalier words. She would have stormed off, but a display of temper right then would have raised too many questions—questions she didn't want to answer.

Wes and Gib came up to them then, to welcome them back.

"I think this calls for a celebration. What do you say?" Tom suggested.

"Absolutely!" all agreed.

"Let's go up to the house!"

The last thing Hunt felt like doing was spending any more time around Glynna and Edmund. It had taken all his considerable willpower not to hit Edmund for just having his hands on her. Hunt told himself that he had no right to feel that way. He had sacrificed that when he'd told her there was no future for them. She was free to do whatever she wanted to do and be with whoever she wanted to be with. He was out of her life forever. That was how he'd wanted it. But all the logic in the world didn't change the anger he felt at the thought of her with the other man.

Hunt told himself they were back on the Rocking M, and that was all that was important. He was certain Glynna didn't want to be around him either, but there was no way to avoid the festivities to come.

"I'm going to the bunkhouse and get cleaned up first," Hunt told Tom as the others headed for the house. "I'll join you shortly."

"All right, son. We'll be waiting for you."

Hunt took his horse and Glynna's and led them toward the corral. He would take as much time as he could getting cleaned up. That way he'd have to spend less time watching Glynna and Edmund.

"We'll help you with the horses, Hunt," Wes and Gib offered.

"Thanks."

Glynna glanced toward Hunt as he walked away with the two hired hands. A great sadness welled up in her as she watched him go. Even surrounded by friends as he was, Hunt was still a solitary man.

"Glynna?" Edmund saw the direction of her gaze and wondered what she was thinking. He'd noticed a look of near longing on her face and didn't like that at all. He wondered what had gone on between the two of them while they'd been alone out in the wild.

"Yes, Edmund?"

"You must be very grateful to Hunt for rescuing you."

"I am. I don't know what would have happened to me if he hadn't shown up when he did. I'm sure he saved my life."

"It's wonderful that he got there in time to help you."

"Yes, it was."

Something about the way she said it bothered Edmund deeply.

"Well, it's over now," he declared. "You're back with us, safe and sound. Just as soon as we can make the arrangements, we'll head home to New York City. Then we'll be back where we belong."

Glynna didn't say anything more as he led her toward the house. She knew she should have been thrilled at the idea of returning home, of leaving this wild, untamed land, but she felt nothing. She felt only empty.

They reached the house and went inside. Maria

came out of the kitchen to welcome her, and Glynna went immediately to her to embrace her.

"I'm so sorry about Diego," she told her.

"Thank you." Maria began to cry, both with happiness that Glynna had been rescued and sadness for her lost son.

"He was very brave that day. He tried to save us." Glynna held Maria close, feeling her pain, knowing how much she'd lost.

"Your aunt told me. I am glad that you are back here with us now. We were all worried about you and praying for you."

"Thank you."

They spoke a moment longer, Maria telling her about the funeral and where Diego had been buried. "But tonight we celebrate your return, and that is a happy time for us," Maria said, smiling in spite of her tears. "Would you like to bathe and change clothes? Your room is as you left it. We knew you would be back."

"Thank you, Maria. I would love to freshen up."

"Then you go on upstairs. I will bring the tub and water to you."

Glynna excused herself from the others and went upstairs to get cleaned up. Mimi would have gone with her, for she wanted to talk to her, but she was too exhausted from all the excitement outside.

Everyone settled in, and for the first time everyone relaxed together.

"It's really over, Tom, thanks to your son," Charles said, relief sweeping through him as he accepted the tumbler of whiskey Tom handed him.

"I knew he could do it. I'm just glad they got back

here as quickly as they did." Tom poured a drink for Paul and Edmund, too. Mimi had declined any liquor.

"Here's to Hunt," Paul said, lifting his glass, and the others followed suit.

They'd just finished taking their first drink when Hunt entered the house, followed by Wes and Gib.

"We were just toasting you," Charles said as he smiled at Hunt.

"Here, have a drink with us." Tom handed glasses to Hunt and the hands.

Mimi beckoned Hunt to come sit with her, and he went to her side gladly.

"I'm glad you're doing so well," he told her, and he meant it.

"So am I, but that's not important. What's important is what you did. How can I ever thank you for bringing Glynna home to me?" She touched his arm with heartfelt gratitude.

"You don't have to thank me. I'm just glad things turned out the way they did."

"Hunt," she said, lowering her voice, her concern for Glynna very real. "I haven't had the chance to talk with Glynna about this privately yet, but I wanted to know . . . was she harmed in any way by the renegades? Is she really all right?"

His expression was serious as he answered her in all honesty. "None of the renegades touched her. She was scared, and she'd been a little roughed-up when I found her, but otherwise she was fine."

"That's right, Aunt Mimi," Glynna announced as she appeared in the parlor doorway. "I am fine. Hunt got me away from the renegades before any harm could come to me."

Glynna had rushed through her bath and changed into a pretty day gown before hurrying back downstairs to join them. As she heard her aunt's question, she was glad to have the discussion over with as quickly as possible, for she could just imagine what everyone had been thinking.

They all looked up at the sound of her voice. Hunt stood up and moved away from Mimi as Glynna crossed the room toward her aunt.

Mimi felt like crying in happiness as Glynna came to her, looking for all the world as if nothing terrible had happened to her. Glynna was really here with her. Her baby was safe.

"Oh, darling, I am so glad that you're back!"

Mimi glanced over at Paul and saw him watching Glynna intently. His expression said it all. He loved her, and that was what she'd wanted. They would never reveal the truth, but would keep the precious secret in their hearts for the rest of their days. They would love Glynna, yet they would allow her her innocence.

Glynna sat down beside Mimi and swept her into a loving embrace. Remembering her wound, she took care not to hurt her in any way.

"I missed you so much, and I worried about you constantly," Glynna said, at last finding some peace in her aunt's arms. "You will never know how much it meant to me to see you standing there waiting for me as we rode up. Hunt had told me that you'd been seriously wounded, but we didn't know if you had lived or died."

Mimi lifted a hand to caress her cheek. "Well, don't you worry about me any longer. I'm fine now that you're here. All I care about is you, darling. You're safe—at last."

"Oh, Aunt Mimi! I thought I'd never see you again." Glynna hugged her once more, enraptured by the unconditional love her aunt gave her.

Paul came to stand by them. His heart was aching at the scene being played out. He marveled at how beautiful they both were and how blessed he and Charles were to have them.

"Mary Catherine and I have some news for you," Paul said, drawing a curious look from Glynna.

"You do?" She glanced up at him and then over at Aunt Mimi expectantly.

"Yes, sweetheart," Mimi said. "Paul and I are going to be married."

"That's wonderful!" she said, smiling brightly, delighted with the news. "I thought there was something going on between you, but I wasn't sure."

"I love Paul very much."

"And I love Mary Catherine."

"And I love weddings!" Glynna exclaimed. "I can't wait! This will be so exciting."

"Well, if you love weddings so much," Edmund said as he got up and crossed the room to stand before her, "then maybe it's time we spoke of ours."

Chapter Seventeen

"I want you to marry me, Glynna," Edmund went on. "Reverend Chandler can perform the ceremony for us, and we can return to New York City, a happily wedded couple."

Edmund stood before her, gazing down at her with what he hoped was a loving expression, as he waited for her answer. He expected Glynna to jump at his proposal. He felt he was being quite the gentleman by formally proposing this way.

Though Edmund did not know what had happened to her during the time she'd been an Indian captive, he could well imagine. He found Hunt's claim that she had not been harmed by the renegades impossible to believe. Not only that, but she'd traveled back to the ranch with Hunt, unchaperoned for all those days—and nights. If her reputation hadn't been ruined before her escape from the raiding party, it was now. So the most loyal thing he could do would be to marry her as quickly as possible to prevent any taint upon her family's name and upon her. He was feeling quite proud of the sacrifice he was making, but he believed the Williams fortune would make it worth his while.

A hush had fallen over the room at Edmund's proposal, and Glynna was completely taken aback. Of all the things she'd thought she'd have to deal with upon returning to civilization, a proposal from Edmund wasn't even a consideration. But here she was, faced with an ardent offer of marriage that left her at a loss. She believed Edmund loved her, and she knew he would make a good husband, for he was educated and wealthy and smart. But there was no way Glynna could even think about marrying anyone right now—not after Hunt. She had to have time to think things through, to understand herself and her own feelings. She couldn't—no, she *wouldn't* marry Edmund just because it was convenient.

"Edmund, you are so sweet," she said, quickly searching for the right words so she wouldn't humiliate him in front of everyone.

"I love you, Glynna, and I want you to be mine. Your mishap made me realize how much you really mean to me. I want you to be my wife, the sooner the better." He knew he was being rather ardent, but he wanted to sound convincing.

Hunt was standing alone when Edmund proposed. His only display of emotion at the other man's declaration of love for Glynna was to grip his glass until his knuckles were white. Beyond that he showed no outward sign that it had affected him in any way.

She meant nothing to him, and he meant nothing to her.

The memory of Glynna professing her love for him slipped into his thoughts. He tried to ignore it, but with the memory of her words came a vision of her naked in his arms, her body accepting his. He took a deep drink of his whiskey and hoped that no one noticed that his hand was not steady as he did. His gaze remained fixed on Glynna as he waited for her to accept Edmund's proposal.

From across the room, Mimi had accidentally glanced at Hunt when Edmund proposed to Glynna. She had long suspected that he felt something for Glynna, and, though he was trying his best not to show any reaction to the other man's offer of marriage, Mimi knew it had upset him. She could see it in the way his hand was shaking when he took a deep drink of whiskey. She sensed there was much more to Glynna and Hunt's relationship than either of them were letting on, and she wondered why they were trying so hard to act as if they truly didn't care about one another. When she got the chance, she planned to ask Glynna about Hunt and find out what her true feelings were for the man. He certainly was intriguing, and most handsome. Glynna could do far worse, and for some reason, in her thoughts, Edmund was on Mimi's list of "worse."

Glynna knew everyone was watching her. They were all waiting for her to answer Edmund, and she knew they all expected her to say yes. She could feel Hunt's gaze upon her, and that made her furious. How could he stand by and watch her marry another man? Hadn't he cared about her at all? The thought that he hadn't infuriated her. She knew he expected her to marry Edmund and live happily ever after. Well, he was wrong! She didn't love Edmund, and she would not marry someone she didn't love. She couldn't blurt that out now, though. She had to stall Edmund until she could talk to him privately and explain the truth of her feelings.

"Edmund, you are so wonderful to propose this way, but after all the excitement of just being reunited with you and Aunt Mimi and Papa, well, I need some time to rest and compose myself. Would it be all right if we spoke of our future plans tomorrow, when I'm feeling more myself?"

"Of course, darling," Edmund quickly replied, though he was seething inwardly. How dare she not accept him instantly? He had offered her a way to save herself and her reputation, and she dared to put him off! "I shouldn't have been so bold, but I've been so concerned about you that I wanted to make sure you never were lost to me again."

Glynna smiled at Edmund, but the smile didn't reach her eyes.

"Yes, my girl has been through hell these last weeks. All I want to do is make her life as easy as possible for her," Charles said, giving her a reassuring look.

She had never loved her father more than she did in that moment.

The conversation turned away from talk of weddings and back to the renegades. Hunt explained to everyone what had happened and how he'd traded Warrior for Glynna. He carefully left out any mention that the trade was really a bride-price, so no one was the wiser as to what had actually happened.

Or at least he thought no one was the wiser, but Tom's gaze sharpened as he listened to his son's telling of the exchange. He had seen the way Glynna and Hunt acted around each other, and he wondered now if the trade had really been a bride-price. He knew of such practices, having paid one himself for Hunt's mother when they had married. When the time was right, Tom knew he would have to ask his son the truth about what had gone on in the village and the truth about what had really happened between him and Glynna.

"Should you let the cavalry know where the renegade camp is so they can go after them?" Charles asked Hunt.

"Even if I did, by the time they got there the renegades would be long gone. They never stay in one place too long for just that reason."

Charles was disappointed that justice wouldn't be served and that the raiding couldn't be stopped.

"I understand your frustration," Hunt went on. "But know that the warrior who killed Diego and shot Mimi is dead. He won't be hurting anyone else."

"Good," Charles said, a little relieved at that news.

They spoke awhile longer, then ate the dinner that Maria had prepared for them.

Edmund was dancing attendance on Glynna throughout the evening, and Glynna was quietly ready to scream. She wanted the peace of being with her aunt and father. She didn't want to have Edmund constantly by her side. Having Hunt there, too, only made things more difficult for her. It broke her heart to think that he could watch Edmund with her and not feel something. But it was obvious that everything he'd told her on the ride home had been true. She meant nothing to him.

It was dark when Glynna finally pleaded exhaustion and excused herself for the night. She went up to her room and quickly undressed and got into bed. Weariness filled her, along with a sense of relief that she hadn't known since before the raid, but as she lay there, she found herself staring at Hunt's Comanche shield where it was hanging on the wall. As she studied the harsh face, rendered so starkly in the two colors, she realized that Hunt really was two different men. He was Lone Hunter, the brave warrior, who'd cared for her and who had rescued her from Crouching Wolf, and he was Hunt McAllister, a man who did not allow himself to feel any emotions. The knowledge gave her no solace.

Edmund and his proposal jarred her thoughts then, and Glynna realized that the prospect of spending the rest of her life married to him terrified her. She did not love Edmund and could not live a lie. The next day, she was going to have to find a way to be honest with him. She couldn't put him off. He deserved better than that from her. After all, he had cared enough to travel all the way to Texas with her father to see about her safety. Guilt plagued her, but Glynna knew she would have been even more guilt-ridden if she'd agreed to marry him feeling as she did. She would have been doing Edmund no favors, saddling him with a wife who loved another man.

At last, exhaustion won out. But as Glynna fell asleep, she found herself staring at her own painting of Hunt, which leaned against the wall. In the picture, he was riding toward her to rescue her. Glynna knew that he would never rescue her again. From now on, she would have to save herself.

Now that Glynna was back, sleeping arrangements were more crowded at the house, so Edmund was forced to join Paul, Hunt, Wes and Gib in the bunkhouse. He was less than thrilled with the arrangement, but knew he could not argue. With any luck, they would be returning to town soon and could get private rooms at the hotel there. At least, he hoped so. He had had about all of the Rocking M's hospitality he wanted for one lifetime. The sooner he got Glynna away from the ranch and Hunt McAllister, the better. There was something about the man that he didn't like, something about the way he'd caught him looking at Glynna that bothered him.

Edmund wanted Glynna all to himself, and to achieve that, he had to get her back to New York. Once she was home, he was certain she would behave normally. Her trips to these less than civilized places were going to stop. He would see to it just as soon as they were wed. She could paint as a hobby, but as his wife she wouldn't have time for such foolishness. She would have time only to cater to him and his needs. That was what a wife was for. She was a decoration and a hostess. Glynna would do well as both.

"It's good to know Glynna's back with us tonight," Paul said as he bunked down in the same room with Edmund.

"This will be the first good night's sleep I've gotten

since we found out she was missing," Edmund responded.

"We can all use some rest, especially Glynna."

"Let's hope she gets enough, so she'll be ready to accept my proposal tomorrow. I would enjoy having you marry us before we return to New York."

"I think you surprised her tonight."

"She shouldn't have been surprised. We spoke of marrying before she left on this trip, but she was too caught up in her painting to think about settling down. After this misadventure, I think she'll see the importance of assuming her proper role in society. She could have gotten herself killed, and for what? Just to paint a few pictures? It's ridiculous. She should concentrate on what's important—being my wife and Charles's daughter." Knowing the ugly truth as he did, Edmund was tempted to add a derogatory comment about her parentage, but he didn't.

"Everything will work out. It always does. Sometimes it might take a little longer than we'd like. Mary Catherine and I certainly had our difficulties, but if you're meant to be together, you will be."

"We are," Edmund said confidently, never doubting that Glynna would marry him.

Hunt was lying in his bunk in the other bedroom. He hadn't intended to listen to Edmund and Paul's conversation, but there was no way for him to avoid overhearing them.

Edmund's arrogance irritated Hunt. He hadn't liked the man from the moment he'd seen Glynna go into his arms, and the more he got to know about him, the less respect he had for him. Hunt knew it was none of his business what Glynna did with her life, but he hoped she didn't marry Edmund. She deserved someone who would treat her better, someone who would respect her creativity. He knew how much her artwork meant to her, and it was a shame to think that Edmund expected her to forfeit all her dreams just to please him.

Hunt rolled over and tried to push thoughts of Glynna and Edmund from his mind.

"Papa, I need to talk to you." Glynna went to Charles right after they'd finished eating breakfast. What she needed to ask him was important, and she didn't want to wait any longer.

"Of course, darling. Is something wrong?"

"No. What could be wrong? I'm back with you and Aunt Mimi."

He smiled. "I couldn't agree with you more, and as soon as Mimi's strong enough, we're going home."

"Before we go, there's something I want you to do."

"Anything."

"I would like to buy Hunt another horse. He gave the renegades the best stallion he'd ever owned to buy my freedom, and I feel I owe him at least that much."

"I'm glad you suggested it. I had already planned to pay him a reward for finding you, but we'll do both. How's that?"

"Thank you, Papa. It will mean a lot to me."

Charles hugged her. "We'll see about getting Hunt that horse, and then we'll go home. I'm really looking forward to being back in the city again."

"You have to admit, Texas is beautiful, though."

"It is, and the people here are some of the kindest I've ever met. We'll have to come back again sometime."

She nodded, but didn't say anything. Once she left Texas, she doubted she would ever return. The memories would be too painful, and she knew there was nothing here for her.

Edmund was growing irritated with Glynna. It was already midafternoon, and he had yet to find the opportunity to be alone with her. He had expected her to be eagerly waiting for the chance to speak with him that morning, but when he'd come up to the main house, he'd discovered that she'd already had breakfast and was outside in the small grove of trees at her easel, painting. Mimi was with her, ensconced in a chair beside her, watching her paint. Her aunt's presence allowed them no moment of privacy to discuss their plans for the future.

Now, as the day passed, Edmund knew it would probably be evening, after dinner, before he finally got to see Glynna alone. He hoped he wasn't too angry with her when the time finally came. He wanted to play the suitor, not lose his temper and berate her for the way she'd ignored him all day.

"You haven't spoken with Edmund yet, have you?" Mimi asked as Glynna continued to work on her painting of Tom and the Rocking M.

"No, not yet," she replied, her tone evasive.

"You don't seem too excited about the prospect. Aren't you eager to talk with him about getting married?" She wanted to know Glynna's true feelings for the man. She certainly didn't want her marrying someone she didn't love.

Glynna paused, paintbrush in hand, to look at her aunt. "I'm not sure," she said, frowning. "I know I should be. Edmund and I had talked about getting married back in New York before we left for Texas, but it was always something I planned to do in the future—not right now, not today or tomorrow."

"Do you love Edmund?" Mimi asked.

"At first I thought I did, but now I'm not really sure."

"Now?" If Hunt was the man Glynna loved, Mimi wanted her to realize it before it was too late.

"Now—after seeing how magnificent Texas is . . . after this chance to focus on my painting—I really don't think I can give it up." She thought about telling Aunt Mimi everything, but decided against it. It was best that no one knew what had happened between her and Hunt. Hunt certainly didn't care about her, so there was really nothing to discuss. No matter what her feelings were for him, he did not love her. There would never be anything between them.

"You really think Edmund would force you to stop painting?"

"He was not at all excited about my making this trip. In fact, he agreed with Papa. He thought I should stay home. He thought my painting was just a pastime. He doesn't take what I do seriously."

"That's not good. You need someone who's supportive of you." Mimi was frowning. Charles was difficult to deal with, but she knew ways to manipulate him. This Edmund, on the other hand, was proving to be a whole new problem. "Well, no one said the two of you have to get married right away."

"I know. It's just that I feel so guilty. He loves me and cares so much. Aunt Mimi, he traveled all the way out here with Papa because he was worried about me."

"If those are his true feelings, then it's far better that you be honest with him. Just explain everything to Edmund the way you just explained it to me. You're not ready to get married yet. You realize what a big commitment it is, and you don't feel you're capable of giving that much of yourself to anyone just yet. Surely, if he loves you, he'll understand."

"I hope he does, but I'm not so sure."

"Then he may not be the man for you."

"That's true."

"The important thing is that you talk to Edmund. He may surprise you. He seems like an intelligent man. If he truly loves you, he'll want to wait for you."

Glynna smiled slightly at the thought that things might go easily with Edmund. "I don't want to hurt him. I just don't want to rush into anything right now."

"Everything will turn out, you'll see."

Hunt had spent the day deliberately avoiding any place where Glynna might be. He stayed at the stables and even rode out with Wes and Gib for a few hours to get away from the house. There was no escaping dinner, however. His father expected him to be there, and so he was going, like it or not.

Hunt fully expected to be caught up in the middle

of a celebration of Glynna's upcoming nuptials with Edmund. He was rather surprised when the conversation over dinner was about everything but weddings. He wondered what had happened, but wasn't about to bring the topic up. He'd given up the right to have any say in her life. She did not belong to him.

"Hunt," Charles began, "Glynna and I were talking this afternoon, and we both agreed that we owe you more than we can ever say. We'd like to buy you another stallion to replace the one you gave up to save Glynna. Money is no object. It's the least we can do to repay you."

"You don't owe me anything," Hunt said quickly, stiffening as he remembered Glynna's words on the trail. "I didn't go after Glynna for a reward. It's reward enough for me to know she's back."

"Well, no matter what you say, Hunt, we're buying you a new stallion," Glynna said, her tone brooking no argument. "I know how much Warrior meant to you, and I insist."

"There's no need."

"There's every need," she countered, a spark of determination in her eyes as she met his gaze across the table.

Mimi noticed the unspoken tension between the two of them, and smiled to herself.

"We'll want to take a look around in the next day or two for your stallion, Hunt. We're planning to start back home by the end of the week," Charles told him.

Hunt only nodded in response as his thoughts dwelled on the reality to come. Glynna would be leaving soon. He would never see her again.

Bobbi Smith

*   *   *

The meal ended, and Mimi, Paul, Charles and Tom all went into the parlor to relax for a while. Hunt went back to the bunkhouse, and Edmund cornered Glynna.

Glynna had dreaded this moment all day, and she knew there was no way to avoid what was to come. She was going to have to tell Edmund that she didn't want to marry him—not now, and maybe not ever.

"Glynna? Would you take a walk with me?" Edmund invited.

"Of course. We need to talk."

"I agree."

Edmund took her arm as he led her from the house. He wanted to have privacy to discuss their future. He even thought it was time to kiss her. Maybe then she'd realize just how serious he was about this marriage.

The moon was out and the stars were bright in the black velvet sky. It was a beautiful night. A heavenly night. A night made for love.

When they were a good distance away from the house, Edmund stopped walking and took Glynna in his arms. He felt a slight resistance in her as he drew her near, and he wondered at it.

"Darling, I have missed you so much," he said in a husky voice as his mouth covered hers in a passionate kiss.

Glynna accepted his embrace, though it felt strange to be in another man's arms. His kiss was hot and demanding as he tried to stir an answering desire in her, but she felt no passion, no ecstasy, only a slight wave of revulsion as her heart told her, *He's not Hunt.*

Guilt overwhelmed Glynna. For all that her intentions had been good when she'd come outside with Edmund, she was finally facing the truth. She did not love him, and she could not marry him. Her father and Edmund might wish it were otherwise, but she could not change the way she felt. She could not marry Edmund, having known the beauty of Hunt's love.

Glynna pushed against Edmund's chest. When he broke off the kiss, she stepped back from him.

"I'm sorry, Edmund. . . . I just can't."

"I don't understand," he said, trying to read her expression in the moonlight.

"This isn't fair—none of this."

"Fair? What are you talking about? I brought you out here because I love you, Glynna. I want to marry you." Edmund thought he sounded besotted enough to convince her.

"I'm sorry, Edmund, but this just isn't going to work."

"What isn't?"

"I can't marry you."

"Why not? Is there something that I've done?"

"Oh, no, nothing like that. It's not you; it's me. It wouldn't be right for me to marry you feeling the way I feel."

"And how do you feel, Glynna?" There was an edge to his voice.

"I don't love you, Edmund." She had to be honest with him.

"What?" he demanded harshly. "When we were in New York, you said—"

"I know, but I was wrong. I thought what I was feeling for you was love, but it was really only friendship. I love someone else."

Her words were like a slap, and his expression turned ugly. "Who is it?" he asked in anger, taking her by the shoulders and giving her a fierce shake. "That damned half-breed? It's McAllister, isn't it?"

"Let me go!" She twisted free of his punishing grip. "You have no right to treat me this way!"

"Oh, that's where you're wrong, you little slut! What did you do? Did you give yourself to the whole tribe and McAllister, too, just to get yourself free?"

Glynna's eyes widened in shock at Edmund's vulgarity. "You're wrong!"

"I knew something terrible had happened to you, after being taken by the filthy Indians and then rescued by one," he said in disgust. "I don't know why I thought I could save you by marrying you, but you're right; we shouldn't get married. I don't want you to be my wife anymore."

She tried to be conciliatory. "Edmund, I didn't mean to hurt you. You'll find the right woman one day."

He laughed as he glared at her with open hatred. "Oh, yes, my dear, I'm sure I will, and she won't be you. I'd had my doubts when I found out the truth about you, but I thought it was important to stay in your father's good graces. Well, sometimes the price is too high. I don't need Charles's name or his fortune, Glynna. It isn't worth it to me to marry a bastard, just to claim them. The Moore name and money are enough for me."

"What are you talking about?"

His look turned positively savage as he answered, "Go ask your Aunt Mimi! Or should I say, 'go ask your mother'? She can tell you what you need to know."

"My mother's dead. She died when I was just a baby." Glynna was staring at him, aghast.

"Or so they told you. You should think again, my dear. Your aunt and your mother are one and the same," Edmund said, wanting to devastate her, wanting to inflict pure, raw pain on her.

"You're lying." All color drained from Glynna's face, and she went cold inside. She could tell Edmund was enjoying saying these things to her, and any warmth she'd felt for him was destroyed.

"It would be better for you if I were lying, but I'm not, Glynna dear. While you were missing, I accidentally overheard a conversation concerning you, between your—um—adoptive father and your real father. It seems the good reverend got your aunt pregnant all those years ago and then deserted her. Paul is your real father, and Mimi is your mother, not your aunt. So not only has your reputation been destroyed, but you were a bastard to begin with! I'm very fortunate to have found all this out before I married you. The taint and dishonor would have left my ancestors turning over in their graves. Good-bye, Glynna. With any luck, I won't have to see you again."

Chapter Eighteen

Glynna was in shock as she stood in the darkness, watching Edmund walk away. She was a bastard? A sense of utter disbelief filled her as she tried to comprehend exactly what Edmund had just revealed to her—Mimi was her mother and Paul, her father.

A sob caught in her throat. Could it be true? Was she illegitimate?

She thought of her father—Charles, the man who'd raised her and loved her all her life. There had never been a hint that he was not what he claimed to be. He had always been there for her. And Aunt Mimi—*Aunt* Mimi?

Her life suddenly seemed a nightmare of confusion and fear. Had the people she'd loved most in life deceived her so completely?

Tears burned in Glynna's eyes as she drew a ragged breath. There was only one way to find out the truth. She looked up at the ranch house and knew she had to confront them now. She had to know if Edmund was telling the truth. Girding herself, Glynna walked slowly back to the house. She knew the next few minutes were going to affect the rest of her life.

Under other circumstances, the brightly lighted house would have been a welcoming beacon in the night to Glynna, but not now. Her mood was nearly frantic as she entered and sought out her father, Paul and Aunt Mimi in the parlor, where they were still talking to Tom. She went to stand in the parlor doorway, and Mimi noticed her right away.

"Glynna, darling, are you all right? You look a bit pale." She rose to go to her, worried that something was wrong. "Did you have words with Edmund?"

Glynna stiffened visibly as Mimi reached out to take her arm. "Don't."

Mimi stopped, her hand dropping away. She was stunned by the unexpected rejection. "Glynna?"

Charles looked up at them. "What is it?"

"I need to talk with you, Papa," she said, the last word strangled from her. "And Aunt Mimi and Paul, too."

Tom could tell that something terrible had happened and that the family needed some time alone. He quickly excused himself. "I think I'll go check on the horses one last time. Good night, everyone."

When he'd gone, Glynna went farther into the room to confront them. She wasn't sure where to start or even how to start. How did she ask the man she'd believed was her father for twenty-three years if he was really her uncle? She supposed there was no better way than to be straightforward.

"Honey, what's bothering you?" Charles asked, approaching her.

Mimi had already returned to sit on the sofa next to Paul. She was tense with anticipation of what was to come. They were both looking up at Glynna, wondering if there was any way she could have learned the truth. They'd been so careful to keep the secret, yet the strained look on her face gave testimony to the power of her emotions.

"I just told Edmund that I didn't want to marry him," she began.

They all breathed a momentary sigh of relief, thinking that was her news and that it had been difficult for her to refuse his suit, but then she went on.

"Edmund was less than pleased with me." Glynna gave a slightly hysterical laugh at her own description of his mood. "He said it was probably for the best, because I was a bastard—"

Mimi gasped at her statement.

"And he didn't want the slight on his family's name. He said he'd wanted the Williams fortune, but he realized that marrying me would have been too high a price to pay." She looked straight at Mimi and Paul. Her expression was haunted. "Was Edmund telling the truth? Are you really my mother and father?"

Charles looked devastated, but he remained silent, allowing Mimi to do what she felt was best. He looked on, waiting for his sister to make her decision about all their futures.

Mimi stood up and went to her daughter. She looked Glynna straight in the eye as she answered her. "Yes. I am your mother, and Paul is your father."

"Oh, God." Glynna could hardly believe what had just been confirmed for her. It was true! All of it! "My whole life has been a lie!"

Mimi tried to hug her, but Glynna stepped back. "No. Not yet. I need to think. I have to understand." She looked wildly from Mimi to Paul to Charles.

Charles opened his arms to her and she flew into his embrace. He held her cradled against him as she cried.

"I'm sorry you had to find out this way, sweetheart," Charles said softly. "We never wanted you to be hurt. That's why we did what we did."

"But Papa—" Glynna stopped, wondering what she should be calling him.

"I am your father. You are my daughter," he said fiercely, seeing her confusion. "That will never change."

"I love you."

"And we love you," Charles said with unfailing devotion. "When Mimi came to me and Victoria all those years ago and told us of her circumstances, there was no way we were going to abandon her and her child. We're family, Glynna. We're there for each other in the good times and in the hard times." He gently touched her cheek as she gazed up at him.

"How did you manage the deception for all these years? How did you fool everyone?"

"Victoria and I were leaving for Europe on business, and Mimi came with us. We stayed away almost a full year, and when we returned we were proud to show off our new daughter. No one was the wiser, and we couldn't have been happier with the perfect gift God had given us—you."

She buried her face against his shoulder for a moment as she fought for control.

"Don't ever think that it was easy for Mimi to give you to Victoria." He glanced to where Mimi sat with Paul, holding his hand tightly, her face ashen, her expression guilt-ridden. "I'm sure it was the most terrible day of her life when she had to hand you over to another woman and forsake her claim to you for what she thought was forever."

"It's true, Glynna," Mimi said in a soft voice. "I thought about staying in Europe and raising you by myself, but I wanted more for you than that. I wanted you to be surrounded by a loving family. I wanted the best for you. That's why I gave you to Charles. That's why I've stayed in the background all this time, loving you and supporting you, but never able to tell you the truth about my love for you."

Glynna turned away from Charles and stood motionless for a moment. Then all doubts were thrown aside as she began to cry in earnest. She went to her mother. Mimi had never known such a flood tide of love as she wrapped her daughter in her arms. If she'd had her way she would never have let her go.

"I'm so sorry if I caused you any pain. That was the last thing I ever wanted to do," Mimi whispered.

Paul had stayed in the background, allowing Mimi and Charles to deal with Glynna's discovery, but he knew it was now time that he stepped forward and told her his part in the deception.

"Glynna, I've already told your mother how sorry I am for all the trouble I've caused, but I want you to know that I never intended to hurt anyone. I didn't know of Mary Catherine's condition when I left her in San Francisco. If I had, I would never have deserted her the way I did. I was a coward and a fool, and I plan to spend the rest of my life making it up to your mother and you—if you'll let me."

"Oh, Paul . . ." Glynna paused, confused, unsure whether to call him her father or not.

"Please, call me Paul. If you ever feel you want to call me your father, I'd be honored, but we both know Charles is the man who's earned that distinction. He's loved you and raised you from the day you were born."

Glynna went to Paul, and he held her close. Paul cherished the feeling of freedom that came from the truth being known.

"What are we going to do?" Glynna asked tearfully.

"We're going to be a family, that's what we're going to do," Charles said.

"But Edmund will tell everyone." Glynna realized that life as she'd always known it was over.

"Let him," Mimi said defiantly. "We have each other."

"We'll deal with Edmund later," Charles said, already planning several different ways to keep him silent. Charles was not without influence, and he knew very well how much the young man loved money. Pressure could be brought to bear whenever he needed it.

Glynna was still troubled. Her whole life—her whole existence—had been a lie. Everything about her had been false. All the while her adored "Aunt"

Mimi had really been her mother. It was almost too much to take in at one time.

"I think I need to be alone for a little while, if you don't mind."

"Of course not, darling. I know this has been a terrible shock for you. If there's anything you need from us, just let us know," Mimi said, watching her daughter carefully, feeling her confusion and pain and sense of betrayal.

Glynna didn't say any more, but sought the solitude of her bedroom. Her thoughts were deeply troubled as she tried to face what her life had become in the space of a few short minutes.

Paul stood in the middle of the parlor, his fists clenched. "I think I have to have a few words with Edmund."

"I'll do it," Charles said, starting for the door.

"No, Charles. You've been defending Glynna's honor for twenty-three years. Now it's my turn," Paul said.

"Paul, do you think this is a good idea?" Mimi touched his arm to stop him. She recognized the barely controlled fury in him.

"I think it's a very good idea." He kissed her quickly. "I need to have a few words with the man who just insulted our daughter. I'll be back."

Edmund had never been so disgusted in all his life. He stormed into the bunkhouse and all but threw himself on the bed. He lay there, staring up at the bottom of the top bunk, wondering what he was going to do next. With a vile curse, he got back up and dragged out his suitcase. He had had enough. He was getting the hell away from the Rocking M and going into town—now, tonight.

Hunt was in the other bedroom and heard him moving around. He walked to the doorway to see him angrily throwing clothes in his suitcase.

"Going somewhere?" he asked. He was curious as to why the other man would be leaving so quickly and so late in the evening.

"I'm leaving," Edmund answered curtly.

Wes and Gib came into the bunkhouse just then, and Edmund looked up.

"I'll pay fifty dollars if one of you will take me into town tonight."

They both looked at him as if he were crazy. "Tonight?"

"That's what I said. Are you both deaf?" His tone was condescending.

"No, we were just wondering what your rush is."

"It's time I head home, the sooner the better."

"I'll say." Paul's voice erupted from behind Wes and Gib. "Gentlemen, if you'll excuse me, I need a few moments of privacy with Edmund."

"Sure, Reverend Paul."

Wes and Gib left the bunkhouse, and Hunt disappeared back into his room as Paul faced Edmund.

Paul stalked forward. "You dirty, low-life son of a bitch!" And with that he hauled off and hit Edmund.

The younger man dropped to the floor, felled by his powerful blow. He stared up at Paul and saw pure hatred in his gaze.

"You called my daughter a bastard! I'll tell you who

the bastard is around here! It's you, you son of a bitch!"

"At least now Glynna knows who she really is!" Edmund threw back at him, furious.

"It's a good thing I don't have a gun on me right now, Edmund. As angry as I am with you, I just might forget my vows as a man of the cloth and pay you back for some of the pain you've caused tonight," he said, seething.

"You might talk big, but basically you've always been a coward, haven't you, Chandler?"

His last taunt broke Paul's self-control. In a rage, he threw himself at Edmund. He knocked the younger man to the ground, and they rolled together, pummeling each other. Paul's fury was savage as he finally pinned Edmund to the floor. He dealt him blow after vicious blow, wanting to punish him for his cruelty to Glynna.

Hunt had been trying to mind his own business in the other room, but when the shouting started and then the fighting, he came charging out to see what had happened. He found Paul on top of Edmund, beating him severely. Grabbing Paul by the shoulders, he pulled him off of the battered man.

"What's going on? What are you doing?" Hunt demanded, holding Paul back when the older man would have attacked Edmund again.

"I'm giving him a small taste of what he really deserves!" Paul said with a snarl, trying to break free of Hunt's restraining hold.

Edmund slowly got back to his feet. His mouth was bleeding and one eye was swelling shut already.

"To hell with you, Chandler, and your bastard daughter!"

"Get out of my sight before I forget that I'm a man of the cloth and do something I might regret!"

"Don't worry. I'm leaving now!" Edmund all but staggered over to grab the last of his things and slam his suitcase shut. He left the bunkhouse, yelling for Wes and Gib.

Left alone with Hunt, Paul finally relaxed. As Hunt felt the fury drain out of him, he released him and stepped back.

"Why is he leaving? I thought he and Glynna were going to get married," Hunt said.

"No, she was smart enough to turn him down. He's an arrogant ass, and she's much better off without him!" Paul's fury was unabated, but he knew there was nothing more he could do to Edmund.

"So she didn't accept his proposal?" A glimmer of hope glowed within Hunt, but he told himself it didn't matter. Still, none of Paul's explanation explained the fight.

"No, thank God. She deserves much better than Edmund."

"What did he mean, 'your bastard daughter'?" Hunt asked.

Paul sighed and realized there was no time like the present for the truth. "It's a long story—about twenty-four years long."

The two men sat down at the small table there in the bunkhouse, and Paul told Hunt everything, from the misunderstanding over James's death to his discovery just a few days ago that he was Glynna's real father.

"Evidently, the night I found out, Edmund overheard the conversation, and when Glynna told him she didn't want to marry him, he told her what he knew."

Hunt was stricken as he thought of how the news must have stunned her. "How is she?"

"I'm not sure. She was upset, but she seemed calm enough when she went upstairs. She said she needed some time alone, and I don't blame her."

"What about Mimi and Charles?"

"They'll be all right. They never wanted to hurt her this way. All they ever wanted to do was protect her."

Hunt nodded. He could well understand how devastated Glynna must have been when she'd learned that nothing she'd believed was real. Her father was not her father and her aunt was not her aunt. Hunt had an overwhelming desire to go to her and comfort her, but he denied it. He had nothing to offer her.

"Glynna will be all right," Hunt reassured him. "She's a strong woman."

"I hope you're right."

"You all love her. None of this was done to hurt her. You were just trying to protect her. She'll understand eventually that Mimi and Charles had her best interests at heart."

"We do love her, and you can't imagine how wonderful it is for me to discover that I have a daughter after all these years of being alone. I can't wait until Mary Catherine and I are married. Then we can be a real family, if Glynna will let us."

"It may take a while, but she'll come around."

Paul gave Hunt a tight smile, hoping he was right. "I just hate to think that my being reunited with

Mary Catherine has ruined her relationship with Glynna. I'd never wanted to cause trouble between them or do anything that would endanger their feelings for each other."

"You haven't. You did the right thing. You let the woman you love know how you feel about her. Mimi's happy, isn't she?"

"Yes," he answered thoughtfully.

"Together, you'll find a way to prove to Glynna that everything will be all right."

"Well, we'd better be calling it a night. Thanks for your help with Edmund."

"I helped you?" Hunt was smiling broadly. "If I'd known then what you just told me, I might have held him down for you, instead of pulling you off of him."

Paul smiled back at him. "Good night, Hunt."

The two men bedded down, realizing that both Wes and Gib had accompanied Edmund back into Dry Creek.

Hunt lay awake thinking of all that had happened that night and thinking of Glynna. He could well imagine how torn she must feel. A part of him ached to be with her, to hold her close and calm her fears, to comfort her, but he couldn't do it. He had nothing to offer her. He couldn't give her what she needed.

After an hour or two of sleeplessness, he rose and dressed and went outside. He stood by the corral, staring up at the heavens, trying to understand the confusion of his feelings. The woman he loved was sleeping in his bed, and yet he could not go to her and tell her that he loved her. She had been hurt enough by the revelations she'd learned that day. The last thing she needed was for him to profess to love her. She could have no life with him. She would be far better off returning to New York City with Charles, Mimi and Paul, and concentrating on her painting. That brought her happiness. He would only bring her sorrow and pain.

"Something bothering you, son?"

Tom's voice startled Hunt. Hunt prided himself on always being alert to his surroundings; he knew if his father could sneak up on him undetected, he was in a bad way.

"You could say that."

"You want to talk about it?" Tom came to stand beside him at the fence.

Silence answered him.

"That little girl is important to you, isn't she?" he asked perceptively.

"Why do you ask?"

"I know what Warrior meant to you, and I know what a bride-price is. I had to pay one for your mother." He managed not to smile as Hunt glanced over at him. "What really went on in that renegade village?"

"The leader of the raiding party was Striking Snake's son, Painted Horse."

"Your cousin." Tom was surprised at this news, but it helped explain a lot.

"When I reached their village, I told him I had come after Glynna because she was my woman. That's when he set the bride-price, and I paid it to get her back."

"But do you love her?"

Hunt sighed deeply. "I didn't mean to."

"But you do."

"Yes." It was the first time he'd admitted it to any-one.

"Then why aren't you with Glynna right now?"

"She didn't know about Painted Horse's demand before I gave them Warrior. Then once I'd told her about it, she cooperated so we could get home. But a bride-price means nothing in the white world. I can't hold her to a Comanche pledge."

"You can build on that pledge," Tom suggested, wanting Hunt to think about what he would be losing if he let Glynna get away. "She turned Edmund down tonight. That should tell you something about the woman."

"That tells me she's too smart to marry Edmund."

"Hunt, if you care about her, go to her—now, tonight."

"I know she's had a rough night, with what Edmund told her and all."

"What happened?"

"You didn't hear? Somehow Edmund found out that Charles isn't her real father. Mimi is really her mother and Paul's her father. Charles raised her for Mimi, so she'd have a good home life."

"I'll be damned," Tom said sadly, now understanding what the others had been talking about. "That little girl needs you more than ever now, Hunt."

"But I can't give her what she really needs. I have nothing to offer her." He finally revealed what was in the depths of his heart.

"If what Glynna wanted and needed was a simple, uncomplicated, boring life in New York City, she would have married Edmund. Look at your mother and me. We loved each other in spite of our differences. Nothing else mattered except that we loved each other and wanted to be together. But we had to be strong for each other. Are you strong enough to love Glynna, Hunt? It won't be easy—you know that—but if you really, truly love her, you have to take the chance. You can't stand back and let her go."

Hunt stood in silence, staring off into the night, his father's words searing his soul as he faced his own future.

Tom left him to his thoughts.

A short time later, Tom heard a rider leaving the ranch, and he looked out the window to see Hunt riding off. He went to bed, knowing his son had to have some time to think things through.

Wes and Gib escorted Edmund to the hotel in Dry Creek and were glad to accept the money he'd promised them. They were not sorry to be rid of him. He'd been in a bad mood on the ride in to town. Not that they didn't blame him for being surly. Reverend Paul had certainly taught him a lesson. They'd been surprised to learn that the man of the cloth had been so handy with his fists. Neither man knew what had brought on the fight, but they figured they'd find out the details once they got back to the ranch.

With the easiest twenty-five dollars they'd ever earned in their pockets, the two cowboys decided to stop by the saloon and have a beer or two before returning to the Rocking M.

"Hey, Wes! Gib! What are you two boys doing in town this time of night?" asked Joe, the barkeep, when they walked into the Diamond Straight Saloon.

"We had an errand to run and thought we'd come visit with you for a while before heading home."

"Good to see you. Come have a beer," Joe said, quickly filling two mugs for them.

They tossed money across the bar to him and grabbed up their drinks. As they chugged some of the beer down, Wes looked around the saloon. It was fairly crowded for a weeknight.

"Looks like business is good," Wes told Joe.

"Can't complain. Things have been steady. What's happened out at the Rocking M? How's the wounded lady doing? Did you ever get word back from Hunt?"

"It's over," Gib said. "Thank God."

"What do you mean, 'it's over'?"

"Hunt just got back with the girl. He found her and saved her from the renegades."

Joe whistled, impressed. "I always knew he was damned good at tracking, but this just beats all. Is she all right?"

"She's fine. Ol' Hunt had to give up his best horse to get her back, but she was worth the trade."

"And the injured woman? Is she better?"

"She's coming along real well. In fact, now that Hunt brought Glynna back, they've been talking about heading to New York City just as soon as she's strong enough to travel."

"I bet Tom's proud of him."

"I'll say. Hunt McAllister proved himself to be the best. We were lucky he was here so he could take out after them so soon. If they'd gotten too much of a head start, they might never have seen Glynna again."

Bobbi Smith

"Excuse me, friend, but did you say Hunt McAllister?" One of the men who'd been drinking at a table nearby stood up and approached Gib and Wes.

"Yep, we work for him and his father out at the Rocking M. Why?"

"I used to know a McAllister by that name. Is he a breed?"

Gib tensed at the way the man sneered the term *breed*. "Hunt's part Indian."

"I bet it's the same man, then. It's been years, but it's good to know that he's doing well. He and his pa got a ranch near here, you said. The Rocking M?"

"That's right. Hunt just rescued a captive from a raiding party. He brought her back in the other day."

The stranger nodded. "He saved a girl?"

"That's right. Brought her back in one piece, all safe and sound."

"Well, don't that beat all. That sounds just like the Hunt we knew. Thanks."

The man returned to the table where his companions sat.

Wes and Gib didn't pay any more attention to them. They were too busy enjoying their beer and catching up on the latest talk from around town.

Later, when Wes and Gib had gone, the stranger approached the barkeep. "My brothers and me were wondering if you could tell us where the McAllister ranch is. We're old friends of Hunt's, and we wanted to drop in and see him."

"Sure," Joe answered, and he gave them directions to the Rocking M. "I'm sure Hunt and Tom will be glad to see you."

"We hope so. Thanks."

The Ross brothers walked out of the Diamond Straight feeling proud of themselves. They had one thing on their hate-filled minds—revenge long denied.

"Sometimes things just fall right into our laps," John said, hardly able to contain his excitement. "We found Hunt McAllister, and we weren't even trying anymore."

"It took some years, but it'll be worth the wait," Chuck added.

"Won't it though. I can't wait to see the expression on his face when Hunt finally realizes who we are." Will gave a chilling laugh.

"Looks like he didn't take our message to heart. From what we overheard, it sounds like he's still messing with white women."

"This time we'll just have to solve the problem permanently."

As they were heading down the street, John suddenly stopped. "Look at this!" he said in a low voice, not wanting anyone else to hear him.

There, posted on the front of one of the buildings, was a wanted poster with their likenesses drawn on it. They were pictured with their masks on, but still the resemblance was uncanny.

"I didn't know they had wanted posters out for us. We'd better tell Eli when we get back to camp."

"I'd say we're damned lucky nobody noticed us tonight."

"Speaking of Eli, John, what are we going to tell him about the bank here in Dry Creek?"

"I ain't worried about the bank. I want to find McAllister. He got away from Pa that night we caught him with Jenny, but we ain't going to let him get away again. We'll let Eli know about the bank later. Right now, let's ride for the Rocking M. We'll take a look around and see if we can find a way to catch Hunt alone."

Chapter Nineteen

Mimi could not sleep. No matter how many times she told herself it was good that the truth had finally been revealed to Glynna, she knew the revelation had hurt her terribly. Somehow she had to make it up to her.

Too restless to stay in bed, Mimi rose at first light. After donning her wrapper, she left her room quietly and, without disturbing anyone, made her way upstairs to Glynna's bedroom. She needed to see her daughter. She needed to be alone with her for just a little while. She knocked softly on the door.

"Yes?" Glynna answered.

"It's me. Can I come in?" she whispered.

The door opened for her. Glynna stood before her in her dressing gown, looking as weary as Mimi felt. Mimi stepped into the room and waited until she'd closed the door before she spoke.

"You didn't sleep?"

"Not well. What about you?"

"Hardly at all. I've been too worried about you."

"There's nothing to worry about. I'm fine."

"I'd like to talk, if you don't mind."

Glynna went to sit on the bed, and Mimi sat beside her. They had often had such "girl talks" before, but this time was different—now they were truly mother and daughter.

"Edmund left last night," Mimi informed her.

"He did?" She was surprised and a bit relieved. She really hadn't wanted to see him again after his cruelty the night before.

Mimi half smiled. "I don't know exactly what went on, but Paul went down to the bunkhouse to have a few words with him. The next thing Charles and I knew, Tom was telling us that Wes and Gib had escorted him in to Dry Creek. According to Tom, Edmund looked like he and Paul had done more than just talk."

"I never wanted to hurt him, but I just couldn't go through with the wedding, knowing I didn't love him."

"As difficult as it was, it was a very wise thing for you to do. You're a smart young woman." She patted her hand.

"I'm not feeling very smart right now."

"Sometimes things happen in life over which we have no control. Then we just have to deal with everything the best we can. If you didn't love Edmund as you should, then you were absolutely right not to marry him."

"Thank you." Glynna sighed raggedly. She'd been

brave enough to end her relationship with Edmund, but she didn't feel any better. Her heart and spirit were still heavy.

"I love you very much, dear. I want you to know that."

"I do."

"Do you? I hope so. I've loved you since the first day I learned I was going to have you. Everything I did in the past, I did because I thought it would be best for you. I never meant for you to be hurt in any way. I was just selfish enough to want to be a part of your life because you meant so much to me. Glynna—" She stopped until Glynna looked up at her. Her gaze met Glynna's and she told her, "I'm sorry if I've caused you pain."

"I know," Glynna answered. She had always known that Mimi was a gentle, loving spirit.

Mimi hugged her then, knowing they would work their way through the bitterness. "There is one more important thing I have to say to you. All those years ago, when I woke up alone that morning in San Francisco, if I'd known where Paul had gone, I would have traveled to the ends of the earth to find him. I would never have let him get away from me. Our lives would have been very different right now if we'd just been honest with each other and stayed together. But I lost him, Glynna, and I've spent the last twenty-four years wondering what might have been. I don't want that to happen to you."

"I don't understand."

"Oh, I think you do," she said, knowing what was really in Glynna's heart. "You love Hunt, don't you?"

361

Glynna was shocked at Mimi's perceptiveness. "Well, I—"

"If you love Hunt, then you should go to him right now, tell him that you love him and never let him go!"

"But I can't! There's nothing I can do. He doesn't love me."

"How do you know that?"

Glynna told her about what had happened between them, about the bride-price and their Comanche marriage.

"So you're already married to him," Mimi said thoughtfully, a small smile curving her lips.

"By Comanche law only, and Hunt told me that that didn't matter once we were back in civilization. He told me that he only went along with the marriage to rescue me from the renegades, and now that we're back home, he doesn't want anything to do with me."

"That's not true, no matter what he says. I saw the way he reacted when Edmund proposed to you."

"What did he do?" Glynna had thought he didn't care. "He didn't say anything."

"No, he didn't say a word, but he was very tense."

"Hunt says I have no idea what being a half-breed means in white society. But I love him. All that's important is our love for each other."

"Maybe he's using that as an excuse because he cares too much for you. Maybe he's afraid, because he loves you and he doesn't want you to be hurt."

Glynna was thoughtful. "Remember the story Paul told us about him when he was young? Hunt told me more about it when we were alone together. Evidently he was almost killed by the girl's brothers, and they told him to stay away from white women. But I'm not just any white woman, and I'm nothing like that Jenny. I love him. He's my husband." Her eyes were sparkling with emotion as she looked at Mimi. "By Comanche law, anyway."

"Go find your man, Glynna. Talk to him. Tell him that you love him and that you want to be with him—no matter what."

"You're right," Glynna admitted, her spirits soaring as she finally realized what she had to do. "There's no way I can even think of leaving Texas until I've talked to Hunt and told him how I feel."

"I promise you, you'll never be sorry."

"You know me so well."

"I'm your mother." Mimi said it out loud and felt good about it.

"Yes, you are," Glynna replied, tears filling her eyes. "And I'm glad."

They embraced tenderly. There would be no more sorrow. There would be only joy in the future they would have together, making up for all the time they'd lost.

"Now, about Hunt," Mimi said. "What are you going to do about him?"

"I'm going to get dressed and go find him."

"Good girl. Let me know how it goes."

"I will, Mother."

Mimi hugged her again, then left her to get dressed. She felt at peace as she went back downstairs.

*   *   *

Charles was up, having breakfast with Tom. He started to confide in him the details of what had happened with Edmund. Tom stopped him, though, telling him that Hunt had filled him in on some of it, but that it was really none of his business. Charles appreciated his discretion. Tom was truly a gentleman. When Mimi came into the room, they both greeted her warmly.

"You're up early," Charles said.

"I wanted to have a talk with Glynna this morning."

"How is she?"

"She's fine," she said with confidence.

"Good. Do you want to join us for breakfast?" Tom invited.

"I'd love to," Mimi said.

A few minutes later Glynna entered the room.

"Has anyone seen Hunt this morning?" she asked as she found Charles, Mimi and Tom eating breakfast.

Tom answered, "He rode out last night."

Glynna suddenly looked crestfallen. "Do you know when he'll be back?"

"I don't imagine he'll be gone too long. Why don't you sit down and have a bite with us? Hunt may show up by the time we're through eating."

Paul came up from the bunkhouse just then to eat with them, and they enjoyed a companionable meal. When they'd finished, Tom rose to see about ranch business, and Glynna followed him outside to speak with him.

"Tom, I need to talk with you."

"What is it?"

"Well, I need to find Hunt. It's important that I talk to him as soon as possible."

"Is something wrong?" She sounded so intense that he was worried.

"No, something's right. I love Hunt, and I need to find him now, today, so I can tell him."

Tom grinned broadly. "I thought there was something special between the two of you."

"There is. I don't know if he's spoken to you about any of what happened while we were in the village, but we were married in the Comanche way. I consider him my husband, and if he thinks he can get rid of me this easily, he's sadly mistaken."

"I always did like a woman who knew her own mind." He was delighted that Glynna loved Hunt. His son deserved some happiness in life, and she was the woman to give it to him. She was spirited and stubborn enough to match him equally. She was perfect for him.

"Will you help me find him?"

"You feel like going for a ride? I can show you where he goes when he's got something troubling him."

"I'll go anywhere, but are you up to it?"

"For something as important as this, I'll make it. It's not too far. It'll do me good if we take it slow."

"Thank you, Tom."

"No, thank you, Glynna, for loving my boy."

She hugged him and returned to the house to tell the others their plans. Tom went to get their horses ready.

"Tom is going to take me to find Hunt."

"Good," Mimi said, glad that things were working out.

"So you do love him?" Charles asked. Mimi had been telling him and Paul about their earlier conversation.

"Yes, Papa, very much."

Charles went to give her a kiss on the cheek. "Then don't let him get away from you."

"That's why I'm going."

"Does Tom know for sure where he's gone?" Mimi asked.

"Tom said he often rides out in the countryside when he wants to be alone."

"Well, come with me for a moment. After our last adventure in the countryside, I don't want to take any chances. You aren't going anywhere without some protection."

Mimi led Glynna into her room and went through her things until she found what she was looking for.

"Here," she said, handing her the derringer. "Be careful. It's loaded. Do you know how to use it?"

"Hunt gave me a shooting lesson while we were together."

"Then you know what to do with this."

"Yes, and thank you. I'll feel better knowing I have it with me."

"We don't want to take any chances with your safety ever again."

"Glynna!"

Tom's call interrupted them, and Glynna hurried outside.

Paul followed with Mimi and Charles, and Glynna turned to wave to them as she rode out at Tom's side.

"Was that a gun I saw you carrying when you came out of the house?" Tom asked, having seen her put something that looked like a derringer in her pocket before she'd mounted her horse.

"After all the trouble I had the last time I went out riding, it seemed like a good idea to have a gun, just in case."

"You aren't planning on using that on my boy, are you?" he asked, smiling wryly. "Hunt can be pretty stubborn at times, but I don't think shooting him would help you any."

Glynna laughed out loud at his comments. "Two days ago I might have been tempted, but not today. Don't worry; Hunt is safe with me. I'll protect him."

"That's good to know." Tom believed that she was a strong enough woman to do just that, if the need ever arose.

They rode for about an hour before they came to the crest of a low-rising hill. Below them was a rocky stream bed.

"There's Hunt's horse down there," Tom told her, pointing out the place where Hunt had tied up his mount. "You go on down to him. You don't need me to take you any farther."

"Thank you, Tom." Her words were heartfelt.

"You're welcome. Good luck with him."

"I hope I don't need it."

She put her heels to her horse's sides and made her way to the place where Hunt had camped for the night. Tom watched until she'd reined in; then he rode on, hoping everything would turn out all right.

* * *

The three riders reined in before the house, and Maria came out to meet them. She eyed them cautiously, for they were strangers to her.

"Can I help you?"

"Is this the McAllister spread?"

"Yes."

"We're looking for Hunt McAllister. We're old friends of his, and we'd like to see him again."

"Señor Hunt is not here right now, but Señor Tom was just going to find him. He rode out that way," she said, pointing out the trail Tom had taken. "If you hurry, you can catch him and ride with him."

"Thank you, ma'am."

Maria nodded, wondering for a moment who they were, then shrugged and returned to her housework. Señor Tom would handle it.

John, Chuck and Will rode away from the house smiling. Things were going right for a change. They'd kept watch over the ranch for a few hours before riding in, looking for Hunt, but had seen no sign of him. When the old man had come outside, though, they'd recognized him and had known they were at the right place. Now all they had to do was find Hunt. The thought drove them onward.

Glynna dismounted and tethered her horse near Hunt's. She wasn't sure where he was, but knew he had to be close by somewhere. She considered calling out to him, but thought it would be better to surprise him.

Trailing along the edge of the stream, Glynna walked for about a half mile before she caught sight of him. He was standing ahead of her on the bank of the stream, watching her approach. He looked so handsome that her heart ached. This was the man she loved. This man was her husband.

Glynna wanted to run to Hunt, to throw herself into his arms and never let him go. She could see no welcoming warmth in his gaze, though, and so she held herself back. If anything, Hunt's expression was wary and cautious.

"Glynna? How did you get here?" Hunt asked as she drew near.

"I asked your father to bring me to you, because I needed to talk with you."

"About what?"

She smiled, hearing the defensiveness in his tone. "About how much I love you, Hunt McAllister."

Hunt stared at her, struggling for control. When he'd first seen her coming toward him, he'd thought he was dreaming. All night she'd haunted his thoughts, and all he wanted was to have her with him. He'd told himself logically that it wouldn't work, that she should go back home and forget him. But his heart had overruled his mind. He'd finally realized how empty his life would be without her, and then he'd looked up and she was there, walking toward him, looking more beautiful than ever.

"You know this is crazy, don't you?" he asked.

"I feel a little crazy, yes." She smiled slightly.

"Glynna, do you understand how hard this is going to be?"

"I understand how hard it will be for me to forget you. I understand how hard it will be for me even to think of having a life without you. You're my husband, Hunt. I want to spent the rest of my life with you. I love you."

Her words stripped away the last of his weakened defenses. He could deny himself no longer. He loved her. A life without her would be only bearable. A life with her would be ecstasy.

"Glynna . . ."

He took a step toward her, and it was all the invitation she needed. She flew into his arms, and Hunt crushed her to him, his mouth finding hers in a kiss of sweet promise.

"It won't be easy," he said between kisses.

"I love you. Nothing matters but that."

Hunt held her away from him, framing her face with his hands, gazing down into her eyes. "And I love you, Glynna. You mean everything to me."

"Oh, Hunt." His name was a whisper upon her lips. It was the first time he'd ever told her he loved her. The moment was perfect. She looped her arms around his neck and drew him down to her. "Kiss me, Hunt—please."

Her lips sought his in an exchange that told him without further words just how much he meant to her. They clung together, kiss following rapturous kiss.

"Glynna, will you marry me?"

She smiled up at him, her eyes aglow. "But we're already married, aren't we?"

"I thought you might want to have another ceremony, so your family could attend," he told her with a sensual smile.

"Yes, Hunt, I'll marry you," she answered, rising

up on her toes to kiss him again. "And you'll never be sorry."

"I know."

He wrapped her in his arms and held her to his heart. Glynna was thrilled. She had never known such happiness. Hunt loved her! They were going to be married!

"Well, well, well," a deep voice said loudly from behind them. "What do we have here?"

Hunt jerked away from Glynna to find himself facing his worst nightmare.

Glynna had had her eyes closed, and she gasped in shock at being interrupted. She spun around nervously to find three men on horseback looming over them, their guns drawn and aimed at Hunt.

"Who are these men?" Glynna whispered to Hunt.

"Jenny Ross's brothers."

She paled at the news.

"Looks like ol' Hunt here never learned his lesson, don't it, boys?" John Ross said venomously as he glared down at the two of them.

"It sure does, John. He's still going after white women, and I thought we done broke him of that," Chuck said.

"What are we gonna do about it?" Will asked, eager to have some fun with Hunt.

"What do you want?" Hunt demanded tersely.

"What do you think we want?" John countered. "You raped our sister, and—"

"You know that's a lie," he said without flinching.

"The hell it is!" Chuck said with a snarl. "You attacked our baby sister!"

"Didn't you ever listen to what she said happened

that afternoon?" Hunt faced them without fear. "Where is Jenny? What happened to her?"

"It's a little late for you to be worrying about Jenny," John said angrily. The little slut had run away from home shortly after the incident with Hunt, and they'd never heard from her again, but the breed didn't need to know that. "Right now, we want to finish what we started that day. Throw your gun down, McAllister. We're gonna string you up."

"This is just between us, John. Let Glynna here go. This has nothing to do with her."

"Hell, no, we ain't letting her go."

"If she's that much of a whore that she wants to mess with a half-breed, then she can pay the price," Chuck said, his gaze upon her. He stared at her for a minute; then he suddenly smiled widely. "Damn, John, you know who we got here?"

"Who?" The oldest brother looked his way.

"This here girl is the woman from the stage robbery a few weeks ago. She's the one who had all them artist's supplies in that fancy wood box." He was laughing. "I bet you didn't think you'd see us again, did you, honey?"

"It is you!" Glynna exclaimed, suddenly understanding why something about them seemed familiar to her. Now she recognized them fully. "You're the Wilson gang!"

"That's right, sugar," John told her, his gaze narrowing dangerously. Now that she'd recognized them, they couldn't let her live. "And I'll just bet you're the one who helped the sheriff in Dry Creek with those drawings for the wanted posters, aren't you?"

"I was glad to help him," Glynna declared, hating these men with a passion. She had thought them horrible when they'd almost killed Hank during the robbery, but after learning that they were the ones who'd tried to murder Hunt, she despised them with all her might.

John grinned at her. It was the most frightening look she had ever seen, but she did not show her fear. Instead, she gave a defiant lift of her chin as she glared back at him.

John ignored her and looked back at Hunt. "I thought I told you to drop your gun, breed!"

He deliberately fired a shot at Hunt's feet.

Somehow Glynna did not scream, but her fear turned to deadly determination. Her mother had given her the derringer, and she was going to use it. She would not stand by and watch Hunt be murdered, and she didn't doubt for a moment that these men were capable of shooting him down in cold blood. She slipped her hand into her skirt pocket ever so slowly.

"Why don't you just shoot him and get it over with, John?" Chuck said. "Then we can have some fun with the woman."

"Hell, why don't we just tie him up and let him watch us doing her?" Will asked, almost foaming at the mouth in anticipation of what was to come.

John chuckled at the two of them. "I like the way you two think."

"Forget all that, John," Hunt demanded, wanting to distract them from their thoughts of Glynna. "Let's fight—just you and me. Like men."

"You ain't a man! You're a breed, McAllister!" John

turned on him, his trigger finger itching for action. "Now drop the gun!"

Glynna knew it was now or never. She watched as Hunt slowly reached for his sidearm. The moment his hand was on the butt of the gun, she went for the derringer. Her movement was fast and sure as she pulled the small weapon from her pocket and fired at John, hitting him in the shoulder. His gun flew from his grip as he almost lost his seat. Complete chaos erupted.

"Kill them!" John screamed at his brothers.

Hunt was a fast draw, and he fired off two rounds at Chuck and Will. Their horses bolted. Chuck and Will tried to return his fire, but they were fighting their mounts and missed. Hunt fired at them both again, and the two outlaws fell to the ground dead. John was scrambling toward his gun, but Glynna ran to pick it up. She stood over him and pointed the deadly weapon straight at him.

"Don't move or I'll finish what I started!" Glynna promised, tempted to end his miserable life right then and there. "Hunt McAllister's more of a man than you'll ever be!"

John looked up at her and knew he was looking death in the eye.

"Here—let me have the gun," Hunt said, coming up behind her after checking to make sure the others wouldn't be causing them any more trouble.

Glynna handed it over. Then she looked up at Hunt, and started to tremble as the realization of what had just happened sank in.

"Oh, God, are you all right?" she asked, her voice unsteady.

"I'm fine, thanks to you." He gave her a quick, hard kiss that left her breathless. He had never seen such courage in a woman before. Glynna had been magnificent—a far cry from Jenny. Glynna had fought for him. Glynna had saved his life!

Hunt quickly tied John's hands behind him. He didn't trust the man—even though he was wounded—not to try something if he got the chance. Hunt wasn't going to give him the chance.

"What are we going to do?" Glynna asked when he'd finished restraining John and came to where she was standing a short distance away.

"We're going to take him in and turn him over to the sheriff," he told her. "I think the sheriff might have a few questions to ask him about the robberies and Eli Wilson's whereabouts."

"It will be good to know they're not going to rob or hurt anyone ever again."

"And then . . ." Hunt paused to look down at her. All the love he felt for her was shining in his eyes.

She looked at him expectantly, not sure what he was going to say next.

"And then we're going to get married."

"Today?"

"I can't think of a better time."

Tears filled her eyes as she gazed up at him. "If anything had happened to you, I wouldn't have wanted to live."

"I think I know just the clergyman to perform the ceremony. I don't think we'll have any trouble convincing him to marry us today, do you?"

"I hope not."

"I love you, Glynna, and I intend to spend the rest

of my life proving to you just how much."

Hunt took her in his arms, but didn't kiss her. He closed his eyes and gloried in the wonderful gift he'd been given in Glynna. He had never known love could be so sweet.

Glynna stood in Hunt's embrace, her heart pounding in a frantic rhythm. The thought that she had almost lost him terrified her to the depths of her soul, but as she held him close, reveling in his nearness and his strength, a peace unlike anything she'd ever known before came over her. She drew a deep breath and leaned back to gaze up at him. He looked strong and untamed, as wild as the land called Texas, and she knew she would love him forever.

Chapter Twenty

The candles were burning in the church, casting everything in a golden glow. Hunt and Glynna stood before Paul as he recited the wedding vows for them.

"I now pronounce you man and wife. You may kiss your bride," Paul intoned as he smiled at them.

Glynna turned to Hunt, and he swept her into a warm embrace before kissing her.

"Everyone, let me introduce to you Mr. and Mrs. Hunt McAllister," Paul announced.

Glynna and Hunt looked back at their family and friends. How they'd managed to put their wedding together in less than half a day they didn't know, but they were thrilled. Originally they'd thought they would have to be married at the Rocking M, but Mimi had insisted she was strong enough now to make the trip into town. So they had returned to Dry Creek. Paul had made the arrangements for the wed-

Bobbi Smith

ding after they'd turned John Ross over to the sheriff, along with the bodies of his two brothers.

Hunt led Glynna down the aisle to the back of the church, and everyone gathered round to congratulate them.

"Oh, sweetheart, I am so happy that things worked out for you," Mimi told Glynna, hugging her tightly. "I'm just sorry we didn't have time for a more formal wedding. I did so want to see you coming down the aisle in a white satin wedding gown."

"It doesn't matter what I'm wearing. All that matters is that I love Hunt and he loves me," she told her mother.

Mimi gazed at her daughter and saw that she was positively glowing with happiness. "You're absolutely right, darling. May you live happily ever after."

"Thank you, Mother," Glynna said, pressing a soft kiss to her cheek.

Charles came to her then, having already congratulated Hunt. "I'm glad you're happy, darling."

"Thank you, Papa. I love him very much. I hope you're not too upset about my decision to live on the Rocking M with Hunt and Tom."

"No, honey, a woman's place is with her husband, but I tell you, it's going to be awfully lonely back in the city with both you and Mimi gone."

"Why don't you move to Texas, too?" she asked, wanting him near.

"If there's some way I can arrange it, I'll do it. If not, I'll just have to come visit you every chance I get." He hugged her close, fighting back the tears that were threatening. "I'm going to miss you, sweetheart."

"I'll miss you, too, Papa."

Paul came to speak to Glynna and Hunt then. "I was talking to Charles and Mimi, and we decided you two needed some privacy for your wedding night. Here," he said, pressing a key into Hunt's hand. "It's the key to my house. It's all yours. We've all taken rooms at the hotel for the night."

"Thank you," Glynna told him, touched by his kind gesture.

Paul looked at her and smiled tenderly. "It seems I just found you and now I've lost you again."

"You'll never lose me. You're my father."

Their gazes met in loving understanding, and Paul kissed her on the cheek.

"I hope Mimi is half as beautiful as you are on our wedding day."

"Oh, she'll be the prettiest bride ever," Glynna promised him.

"Tomorrow I'm going to send a wire to the minister who saved my life all those years ago and ask him if he'll come to Dry Creek and marry us." Paul slipped an arm around Mimi's waist as he drew her to his side. "The sooner he gets here, the better."

"I agree," Mimi said, looking up at him adoringly.

Tom came to stand with Hunt. "You've got yourself one wonderful woman there, boy."

"I know," he answered with a grin.

"You see to it that you take care of that little girl, now."

"I will."

"I think maybe it's time we built another house out at our place. What do you say? Wes and Gib and me can start on it tomorrow."

"Thanks," Hunt said, truly touched by his father's generosity and caring.

"No, thank you, son." Tom hugged him and then went to kiss Glynna.

After Maria, Wes and Gib had wished them happiness, Glynna and Hunt made their getaway to Paul's house for their wedding night. They were thrilled at the prospect of having the privacy they so desperately desired.

As they reached the front walk of the small one-bedroom house, Hunt swept his bride up in his arms and carried her inside. He kissed her hungrily before setting her back on her feet. He locked the door behind them, and then, once they were sure the curtains were closed, he took Glynna in his arms again.

"I love you, Mrs. McAllister."

"I like the sound of that," she said with a purr, lifting her lips to his for a passionate exchange. "Mrs. McAllister."

After a heated embrace, they moved apart to explore the house for a moment. They didn't know when Paul had found the time to do it, but he'd arranged small bouquets of wildflowers throughout the house, and they perfumed the air with a heavenly scent.

"That was so sweet of him," Glynna said, touched by his thoughtfulness.

Hunt came up behind her and slipped his arms around her to bring her back against his chest. They stood that way, treasuring the sense of closeness and the joy of knowing they would never be separated again.

"You know, we've been married for several weeks

now, and we've never made love in a bed yet, my husband," Glynna said teasingly. "Do you think we could remedy that tonight?"

"I'd love to try," he said in a growl.

Hunt turned her to him, his mouth seeking hers. As he continued to kiss her, he lifted her in his arms once more and carried her into the bedroom. He laid her on the bed and followed her down, stretching out beside her.

Glynna gave a low moan of delight at the softness of the bed. "Beds . . . what a wonderful idea."

Hunt didn't waste time talking. He moved over her, his mouth taking hers again and again as the desire to claim her for his own grew strong and hot within him. When he started to work at freeing her from her gown, Glynna was quick to help him. The frustration of the small buttons made him impatient, but she only gave a throaty chuckle and stood up to undress for him. With great care, she slowly undid each offending button.

Hunt lay on the bed watching Glynna, his gaze hungry upon her. When finally she'd freed the last button and slipped the gown from her shoulders, he was there beside her, helping her to strip the dress completely away, along with the rest of her undergarments.

Glynna reached for Hunt then, wanting him to shed his clothes, too. It took him only a moment to undress. She went to him then, thrilling at the feel of his hard body pressed against her. He was all muscle and heat, and she couldn't get close enough to him.

Hunt took her hand and led her to their marriage

bed. Entranced by the beauty of their love, they came together on the welcoming softness, man and wife, bound together in God's eyes for all eternity. Their union was perfect and fulfilling.

All through the long, dark hours of the night, Hunt sought to please his bride. He gave her not only his physical love; he gave her his heart as well.

Glynna came to her husband in delighted rapture. He was her life and her love. She didn't know how she'd ever existed without him.

The future stretched before them in endless splendor. They would love and be loved.

Epilogue

New York City
Eighteen months later

New York society was all abuzz with excitement. At long last, the night of Western artist Glynna McAllister's exclusive showing at the Wentworth Gallery had arrived. Ever since it had been learned that she was returning to the city for a new exhibit of her work, the anticipation had been growing. All who were art lovers were eager to attend. Invitations were much sought after.

Glynna McAllister's works of the Wild West were known for their realism and beauty. Over the last few years her renown had grown. She'd been concentrating more and more on portraits, and her *Portraits of the Comanche* selections had been especially successful. They had sold out quickly, and the demand for more was growing.

Rumor had it that tonight the artist would unveil her most magnificent, most inspired work ever. It was mysteriously called only *Glynna's Masterpiece*, but everyone who was anyone in the art world could hardly wait to see it. A crowd was expected to attend.

The Wentworth Gallery had closed its doors at four that afternoon to prepare for the celebration that night. When it opened again at eight, a crowd was waiting to be admitted.

"This is so exciting! I just adore her paintings," one sophisticate said as she entered the gallery. "I can't wait to see what she's done new and different this time. Mrs. McAllister is so daring with her painting."

Those around her voiced their agreement as they followed her inside.

Within the gallery, Mimi, Charles and Paul all stood off to the side watching the crowd spill into the building.

"I always knew this would happen," Mimi said, looking over at her husband and her brother. "Glynna has worked so hard, and now, tonight, her dreams are going to come true. She has her own exhibition at the Wentworth, and everyone who's anyone in town has turned out."

"It is impressive," Charles agreed as he recognized a famous banker and two railroad tycoons among the crowd.

"I hope Glynna enjoys every minute of the evening. She's earned it," Paul put in, knowing how hard Glynna had been working on her new paintings.

"It's going to be a thrill to see everyone's reaction to her *Masterpiece*," Mimi said.

Across the room, Glynna stood with Jason Wentworth, the owner of the gallery, sipping a glass of champagne.

"What a wonderful evening," she said to the tall, distinguished, silver-haired man.

"It is indeed, when we have an artist of your caliber with us," he complimented her, lifting his glass to her.

"This has been my dream since I was a young girl."

"I'm glad Wentworth Gallery has had a part in making one of your dreams come true. Talent such as yours is rare. It's our pleasure to celebrate it with you—and with your adoring public. The demand for your paintings has been unheard of. Your popularity continues to grow. All I heard all week was how thrilled everyone was about your returning to the city. Have you enjoyed living in Texas?"

"I love it."

"It's a far cry from New York, isn't it?"

Glynna laughed. "You'll have to come to Texas one day, Mr. Wentworth. It's a whole different world from what you're used to here."

"I'm sure it is. I can tell by your paintings. They were always good, but lately they've been positively magnificent."

She smiled up at him appreciatively. His opinion as an art critic was highly valued, and she was thrilled that he enjoyed her work so much.

"Have you planned a time for the unveiling?" she asked him.

"Nine o'clock. Is that good?"

"That's perfect. I'll be ready."

Glynna moved off to mingle with those in attendance. She remained quiet, listening to the comments being made and reveling in the knowledge that people really did like her paintings.

Tom stood with Hunt in a quiet spot in the gallery, watching the crowds move through the exhibit.

"I never had any idea it would be like this," he told his son, thoroughly impressed with the turnout for the show.

Hunt's gaze was warm upon his wife as she circulated through the gallery, greeting guests and talking about her work. She was the picture of New York elegance and sophistication this evening in her fashionable, deep green, off-the-shoulder gown and sleek hairstyle, which emphasized the classic beauty of her features. Yet he knew that deep within her heart, she was the same woman who could shoot a gun and ride astride without hesitation. And he loved her.

"I'm not too comfortable all duded up this way," Tom remarked, feeling a little awkward in the suit and tie he was wearing.

The trip from Texas had taken its toll on him, but he wouldn't have missed this night for the world. He'd been Glynna's biggest fan ever since she'd given him the painting of the Rocking M with his own portrait in it. He knew she was the most talented artist he'd ever seen.

"I know what you mean, but it's only for one night," Hunt agreed. He, too, had been less than excited about giving up their usual gear for the required elegant dress. He hadn't been disappointed with Glynna's reaction to seeing him so dressed, though. He'd promptly had to get undressed to make love to her, just before it had been time to leave for the showing.

Glynna must have sensed his gaze upon her, and she looked his way. As their eyes met across the room, Hunt could see high color staining her cheeks, and he was certain she was remembering their quick, passionate mating only hours before. He gave her a knowing grin as she turned away to speak with another fan of her work.

"Is that your husband over there?" one elderly lady asked her, having caught the exchange between them. "We'd heard you'd gotten married."

"Yes, that's Hunt," she told her.

"He's so handsome. Where did you find such a good-looking young man?"

"Right in the middle of Texas," she answered, smiling, wondering if the woman would believe the true story of their first encounter.

"I'm a widow. Perhaps I should travel there and take a look around," she told her companions.

"I'm going with you if you go, Agatha," another gray-haired lady said.

"Ladies and gentlemen," Jason Wentworth announced. "It's time for the moment we've all been waiting for. Mrs. McAllister, if you'll join me, please . . ."

Glynna swept forward to where he stood next to the easel that held her covered painting. It was the centerpiece of the evening's display, and she was eager to see everyone's reaction when it was unveiled for the first time.

"Good evening, everyone, and thank you so much

for coming tonight," Glynna began. "I am delighted that you enjoy my work, and I am thrilled to unveil for you what I believe is my finest creation ever. I've entitled this one *Glynna's Masterpiece*. I hope you like it as much as I do."

A current of excitement ran through the gathering as Jason Wentworth carefully drew away the cover, and the painting was revealed for all to see. There on the canvas was Hunt's image in perfect likeness. He looked handsome, strong and mesmerizing, and in his arms he held a baby cradled against him. It was a glorious portrait that captured both the fierce male protectiveness in his expression as he gazed down at the child he would protect with his life, as well as the perfect innocence of their baby daughter.

"It's wonderful!"

Excitement spread through the crowd as people pressed forward to get a better look at it.

Glynna glanced across the room to where Maria had just appeared with nine-month-old Victoria. She gave the child to Hunt. Glynna motioned for him to come forward, and he went to her, carrying their daughter in his arms.

"My husband and daughter are my true inspirations, and they're here tonight to celebrate with us, too."

All eyes turned to follow Hunt's progress as he went to her side with the baby. A round of applause went up. The exhibit was a tremendous success.

Mimi, Charles, Paul and Tom looked on and were thrilled by Glynna's triumph.

Hunt bent to give his wife a gentle kiss. "Congratulations, my dear. I'd say you're a success."

"Glynna's Masterpiece"

"It's all because of you," she returned, giving him a serene look as she took their daughter from him. She had never known life could be so wonderful. She had Hunt and Victoria. "I couldn't have done it without you. You two are my inspiration. You've made all my dreams come true."

And they lived happily ever after.

THE LADY'S HAND
BOBBI SMITH
Author of *Lady Deception*

Cool-headed and ravishingly beautiful, Brandy O'Neal knows how to hold her own with the riverboat gamblers on *The Pride of New Orleans*. But she meets her match in Rafe Morgan when she bets everything she has on three queens and discovers that the wealthy plantation owner has a far from gentlemanly notion of how she shall make good on her wager.

Disillusioned with romance, Rafe wants a child of his own to care for, without the complications of a woman to break his heart. Now a full house has given him just the opportunity he is looking for—he will force the lovely cardsharp to marry him and give him a child before he sets her free. But a firecracker-hot wedding night and a glimpse into Brandy's tender heart soon make Rafe realize he's luckier than he ever imagined when he wins the lady's hand.

_4116-2 $5.99 US/$6.99 CAN

Dorchester Publishing Co., Inc.
P.O. Box 6640
Wayne, PA 19087-8640

Please add $1.75 for shipping and handling for the first book and $.50 for each book thereafter. NY, NYC, and PA residents, please add appropriate sales tax. No cash, stamps, or C.O.D.s. All orders shipped within 6 weeks via postal service book rate. Canadian orders require $2.00 extra postage and must be paid in U.S. dollars through a U.S. banking facility.

Name_____
Address_____
City_____State_____Zip_____
I have enclosed $_____ in payment for the checked book(s).
Payment <u>must</u> accompany all orders. ☐ Please send a free catalog.

BOBBI SMITH

THE LADY & THE TEXAN

"A fine storyteller!"—*Romantic Times*

A firebrand since the day she was born, Amanda Taylor always stands up for what she believes in. She won't let any man control her—especially a man like gunslinger Jack Logan. Even though Jack knows Amanda is trouble, her defiant spirit only spurs his hunger for her. He discovers that keeping the dark-haired tigress at bay is a lot harder than outsmarting the outlaws after his hide—and surrendering to her sweet fury is a heck of a lot riskier.

___4319-X $5.99 US/$6.99 CAN

MADELINE BAKER

The West—it has been Loralee's dream for as long as she could remember, and Indians are the most fascinating part of the wildly beautiful frontier she imagines. But when Loralee arrives at Fort Apache as the new schoolmarm, she has some hard realities to learn...and a harsh taskmaster to teach her. Shad Zuniga is fiercely proud, aloof, a renegade Apache who wants no part of the white man's world, not even its women. Yet Loralee is driven to seek him out, compelled to join him in a forbidden union, forced to become an outcast for one slim chance at love forevermore.

___4267-3 $5.99 US/$6.99 CAN

MADELINE BAKER

Author of Over 10 Million Books in Print!

Shattered by grief at her fiancé's death, lovely Katy Marie Alvarez decides to enter a convent. But fate has other plans. En route to her destination, the coach in which Katy is traveling is attacked by Indians and Katy, the lone survivor, is taken captive. Thus she becomes the slave of the handsome, arrogant Cheyenne warrior known as Iron Wing. A desperate desire transforms hate into love, until they are both ablaze with an erotic flame which neither time nor treachery can quench.

_4227-4   **$5.99 US/$6.99 CAN**

A WANTED MAN.
AN INNOCENT WOMAN.
A WANTON LOVE!

Renegade Heart
Madeline Baker

When beautiful Rachel Halloran took Logan Tyree into her home, he was unconscious. A renegade Indian with a bullet wound in his side and a price on his head, he needed her help. But to Rachel he was nothing but trouble, a man whose dark sensuality made her long for forbidden pleasures; to her father he was the answer to a prayer, a gunslinger whose legendary skill could rid the ranch of a powerful enemy.

But Logan Tyree would answer to no man—and to no woman. If John Halloran wanted his services, he would have to pay dearly for them. And if Rachel wanted his loving, she would have to give up her innocence, her reputation, her very heart and soul.

_4085-9 $5.99 US/$6.99 CAN

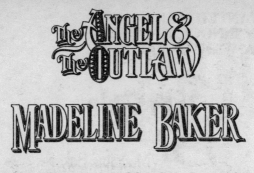

The ANGEL & The OUTLAW

MADELINE BAKER

Bestselling Author Of *Lakota Renegade*

An outlaw, a horse thief, a man killer, J.T. Cutter isn't surprised when he is strung up for his crimes. What amazes him is the heavenly being who grants him one year to change his wicked ways. Yet when he returns to his old life, he hopes to cram a whole lot of hell-raising into those twelve months no matter what the future holds.

But even as J.T. heads back down the trail to damnation, a sharp-tongued beauty is making other plans for him. With the body of a temptress and the heart of a saint, Brandy is the only woman who can save J.T. And no matter what it takes, she'll prove to him that the road to redemption can lead to rapturous bliss.

_3931-1 $5.99 US/$7.99 CAN

RECKLESS LOVE

MADELINE BAKER

"Madeline Baker's Indian romances should not be missed!"
—*Romantic Times*

Joshua Berdeen is the cavalry soldier who has traveled the country in search of lovely Hannah Kincaid. Josh offers her a life of ease in New York City and all the finer things.

Two Hawks Flying is the Cheyenne warrior who has branded Hannah's body with his searing desire. Outlawed by the civilized world, he can offer her only the burning ecstasy of his love. But she wants no soft words of courtship when his hard lips take her to the edge of rapture...and beyond.

_3869-2 $5.99 US/$7.99 CAN

By the Author of More Than 10 Million Books in Print!

Madeline Baker

Headstrong Elizabeth Johnson is a woman who knows her own mind. Not for her an arranged marriage with a fancy lawyer from the East. Defying her parents, she set her sights on the handsome young sheriff of Twin Rivers. But when Dusty's virile half-brother rides into town, Beth takes one look into the stormy black eyes of the Apache warrior and understands that this time she must follow her heart. But with her father forbidding him to call, Dusty engaged to another, and her erstwhile fiance due to arrive from the East, she wonders just how many weddings it will take before they can all live happily ever after....

_4069-7 $5.99 US/$6.99 CAN

MIDNIGHT FIRE

MADELINE BAKER

**"Lovers of Indian Romance have a special place on
their bookshelves for Madeline Baker!"**
—Romantic Times

A half-breed who has no use for a frightened girl fleeing an
unwanted wedding, Morgan thinks he wants only the money
Carolyn Chandler offers him to guide her across the plains,
but halfway between Galveston and Ogallala, where the
burning prairie meets the endless night sky, he makes her
his woman. There in the vast wilderness, Morgan swears
to change his life path, to fulfill the challenge of his vision
quest—anything to keep Carolyn's love.

_4056-5 $5.99 US/$6.99 CAN

Dorchester Publishing Co., Inc.
P.O. Box 6640
Wayne, PA 19087-8640

Please add $1.75 for shipping and handling for the first book and
$.50 for each book thereafter. NY, NYC, and PA residents,
please add appropriate sales tax. No cash, stamps, or C.O.D.s. All
orders shipped within 6 weeks via postal service book rate.
Canadian orders require $2.00 extra postage and must be paid in
U.S. dollars through a U.S. banking facility.

Name_____
Address_____
City_____ State_____ Zip_____
I have enclosed $_____ in payment for the checked book(s).
Payment <u>must</u> accompany all orders. ❏ Please send a free catalog.